The Amish Murder Mystery Series Bookset: Volumes 1-3

MARY B. BARBEE

MYSTIC VALLEY PRESS

This is a work of fiction. All of the characters, organizations, and events portrayed in this novel are either products of the author's imagination or are used fictitiously.

Editing Team: Molly Misko, Jenny Raith, and Laura Fry

Cover Design: Zahra Hassan

www.marybbarbee.com

Thick as Thieves

The Amish Lantern Mystery Series, Volume 1

Chapter One

Mercy and truth are the Lord's ways, his witness to all who seek Him.

Zechariah 7:9

"Sister, I don't think you've been listening to anything I've been saying," Beth said, slapping her hand on the flour-covered table. Tiny flecks of flour jumped into the air briefly as her hand landed on the aged mahogany surface.

Anna gritted her teeth, fighting frustration. Her identical twin sister, Elizabeth, could be so annoying sometimes. It annoyed Anna when Beth fixated on a particular topic for way too long. Anna knew that she should be patient with her – Beth could not help it sometimes due to her autism disorder – but it could sometimes be a challenge.

When they were children, Anna had even shorter patience with her sister. Their mother was notorious for taking Beth's side in every disagreement no matter what the situation. One year, the sisters had received identical dolls for their birthday. About a week later, Beth had accidentally dropped hers in the dirt and made a small stain on the part of the fabric that would have been the faceless doll's cheek. No matter what her mother did, she could not remove the stain. Beth was terribly upset - she struggled even at a young age to make sure everything was "just right." One morning, Beth claimed that Anna's doll was hers, and that the stained doll was actually Anna's. Looking to her mother to step in, Anna was completely hurt when her mother asked her to "just let Beth have the doll and play with this one instead."

Anna had no choice but to obey her mother, but it was many months - and maybe years - before her prayers were answered and she was able to forgive Beth and her mother for taking away something she had cared for and loved dearly.

As the twins grew into young teenagers, the sisters' relationship shifted. At this age, the twins' mother explained to Anna everything that made Beth different and special, and it all finally made sense. Shedding light on Beth's autism allowed Anna to open her heart and embrace Beth for who she really was and the struggles that she lived with. She learned how to be patient with her sister, and the twins' bond became stronger than ever before.

"I am listening to you, Beth. You don't have to get upset," Anna said in a quiet voice. Beth smiled gratefully. Beth was talking about her last child who had gone on his Rumspringa recently. She was terribly worried for him and felt that Jonah may be too young and immature to be sent out in the world alone. Anna didn't think so. Everyone in the family had done everything they could to prepare Jonah for the journey to come. Anna was confident that Beth was in panic mode without good reason.

"Do you think he'll return? I keep having these recurring dreams. I dream about what happened to Mrs. Philips' daughter. What if the same thing happens to Jonah? What if he chooses to stay there?" Beth asked, the dough she had been working on lay forgotten on the table.

Anna's chair scraped hard on the wood floor as she pushed it back to stand. Her lower back ached immensely as she rose. The twins were in their late fifties. And while Anna absolutely loved some parts about growing older, she was less enamored by the toll it seemed to be taking on her body. Sometimes when she looked in the mirror, she couldn't recognize the person that stared back at her. Wrinkle lines were starting to appear on her forehead and between her eyes, her skin creasing like a gently crumpled piece of paper.

The skin on her hands was starting to look thin, and she swore she was starting to see a few age spots surface here and there. Anna's husband was dedicated and said he thought she looked more and more beautiful each day, but she knew that it wasn't true and also knew that as an Amish woman, she was not supposed to care about her looks. Vanity was strongly discouraged in the community, so she kept these thoughts to herself, experiencing feelings of shame when they ran through her mind. More than her looks, though, one thing that she couldn't deny was that her physical energy was zapped a little more every day. But she would make an effort to remind herself that her emotional and spiritual energy felt more and more replenished with each rise of the morning sun. With age comes wisdom.

"Beth, this feels oddly familiar. Can we talk about how many times you've been through this before with each of your children? You always worry about them, and they always end up being safe and enjoying their Rumspringa. Jonah's not going to be any different. He's going to enjoy his Rumspringa and return to the community safely. Stop worrying," Anna said, walking over to where her sister was seated.

"That is very true. Thank you for reminding me of that, Anna." Beth and Anna met eyes. Anna wasn't sure Beth felt much better, but she knew that the conversation would end there... for now. Anna leaned over with a reassuring hug. Beth's beautiful hair was tucked neatly into her prayer kapp. Anna was always so impressed with how nicely put together Beth always looked. Her own hair took so much effort to keep looking neat and tidy under her kapp throughout the day, but Beth rarely showed a strand of out of place - looking the same from morning to evening with what appeared to be very little effort.

"And if ever something goes wrong while Jonah is away, you should know that I'll always be here for you. Now, let's get to work. Sunrise is approaching and we should be ready before it gets here," she said. Beth smiled thankfully and set her focus back on her forlorn dough.

With dawn approaching, the twins had a lot of work to do. For the past fifteen years, they had been managing a booth at the local farmers market each weekend, selling their now famous pastries and bread. Anna and Beth inherited their mother's love for baking. All the recipes their mother passed on to them were cherished and still included in their menu. People traveled from neighboring counties, and even states, to purchase their baked goods. Especially their breads, which were expertly baked using the sumptuous fresh butter produced on their shared farm. Tourists often asked how they could order more of their goods online to avoid a lengthy trip, but although Anna and Beth's community did have access to computers in the town's library, the sisters had no interest in taking the business in that direction.

Outside the window, Anna could see the chirping birds flying around in the surrounding trees. Their town was so peaceful and serene. That was one of the many things Anna loved about it. Their community was strong and tight knit, not unlike most Amish communities, and Anna was proud to call Little Valley home. However, their peaceful world had shattered with the recent break-ins and robberies taking place inside their sweet community. Last week, the Johns' home was raided. Their plants, tools, and even some of their animals were carted away while they were attending service.

The robberies terrified Anna. Back when she was a little girl, this would never have happened. She could not think of one individual whom she personally knew that was morally deviant enough to steal from his neighbors. Oh, how times had changed. Her life had changed, and now she lived with worry in anticipation of the day they would also be robbed. Would the robbers know that she had quite a sizable amount of money, earned from their business, stashed away underneath her bed? Would it all just disappear one day? How would she cope?

She shook her head, trying to clear her thoughts. Dwelling on the "what if's" was a waste of time - something she often told her children when they were younger and faced child-like worries of their own. The community was still safe. She had every faith that the English sheriff living in their town would solve the case of the robberies soon. However confident she was in his policing ability, Anna, just like most Amish residents in the town, still disliked the sheriff. Derek McCall. He was so uncouth, rude, and quite unlike the other Englishers living in Little Valley. The rumor among the community was that it was the sheriff who was partly responsible for the illegal gambling that was happening among the English in their beautiful county. If he wasn't responsible for starting the trend, he certainly didn't seem to be taking any real actions to stop it. Anna sighed heavily. She decided to refocus and shift her concentration back to the ball of dough sitting on the counter in front of her.

Dawn was fast approaching. Sunrise would soon flood light into the small room. The sisters were busy working in Beth's modest kitchen. Anna's house shared the farm and sat right next to her sister's. Anna was grateful that their husbands' relationships were also close, like brothers themselves, and that they understood the importance of the sisters' bond agreeing not to move them apart.

They heard the shuffling feet of Noah, Beth's husband, entering the kitchen. Anna pushed around the prayer kapp on her head until it was properly adjusted. She tightened it harder just as Noah's figure appeared.

"Good morning," Anna said, mixing the batter. Noah's kind eyes were sleepy and only partly open as he shuffled past Anna to grab a cup of coffee. His response was a nod and a half attempt at a smile. He had never been a morning person, but he had become accustomed to the clamoring noise of the women in the kitchen waking him up.

Age was creeping in and changing Noah, too. Beth could still remember the first time they met. He was a skinny man with beautiful light hair and amber-flecked eyes that twinkled delightfully even when he was sad. He had perpetually tanned skin, a beardless face, and a young lean figure. Noah was under his uncle's tutelage at the time, learning carpentry.

Still quite a handsome man, through the years Noah's face spoke of the hard work he performed each day. His hands had become callused and his shoulders broad. He filled out the shirt he wore, his arm muscles jutted out distinctly. The length of his well-tended beard – a sign of the length of their marriage – flowed gracefully down from his face. Beth was so grateful that he was still so healthy and agile, even past the age of sixty. She could count on one hand how many men of his age in the community were as strong as Noah was. As a matter of fact, the men all greatly relied on him and his mentorship when it came to community work – like the current restructuring going on at Simon's house.

Coffee cup in hand, Noah finally spoke to greet the sisters. "Good morning, ladies. You sure make a lot of noise every morning. Every day, I think I'm going to get used to it, but I never do." After a short pause, Noah quietly cleared his throat. "Ah, this smells good today. Added extra cinnamon?" he asked in beautiful Deitsch, the ancient German dialect often used among the Amish in North America. Noah wasn't as fluent in English as the women were. He spoke in the German dialect more than he spoke in English. Gulping the last of his coffee, Noah inhaled deeply. He walked over to Beth, straightening his suspenders, and kissed her forehead lovingly.

"You know it, Noah," Anna said delightfully. Noah's interest in their bakery excited her. She wished her husband would be half as interested in their work as Noah was, but she also realized that she had few other complaints about the man she married. He was pretty close to perfect in her eyes. The twins were lucky to have married such wonderfully devoted and kind men.

"Are you almost finished with the work at Simon's?" Anna asked. Her husband, Eli occasionally joined the men after his work on his farm. He often returned late at night, completely tired but full of praise for the carpenters' craft.

"I don't know how they do it. I have never been comfortable with heights, and their work is so beautifully done with such attention to detail," Eli would rave over a homecooked dinner. Anna would follow it with kisses on the calluses on his hand.

"I am sure that they are equally full of awe for successful farmers like yourself. You do work they'll never understand and provide so much for your family and community," she would reply to him. She was in awe of all the men in her family. The physical strength they exerted each day marveled her. Her husband's strength and dedication were especially admirable. He had single handedly built his agricultural business from scratch. When they were first married, her father-in-law had run the business into the ground. Eli folded his sleeves and set to work reviving the whole operation. Now, they were one of the most successful farms in the county. The corn produced on their farm was distributed and sold to customers miles away. Even well into the ripe age of sixty-five, Eli led her oldest son, Malachi, to begin to establish another stream of income with their farm's tobacco production.

With their children grown and all on their own now, the sisters' homes felt eerily empty. Anna yearned for simpler times when their houses were filled with rambunctious, playful children. Those days, Anna and Beth rotated childcare. The sisters did everything together as children, so it was no surprise that they were able to build their families together. When one of them fell sick or just needed a break, the other took over the running of their households. Meals were often shared. Clothes and schoolbooks were passed down. The children were close, hardly being able to tell the difference between a sibling and a cousin.

"No, not quite." Noah's voice pulled Anna out of her reverie. "It's going to take another few weeks. The entire roof needs to be changed. And that reminds me, please tell Moses not to forget what I asked him to bring for us. We need more tools, and he could help out," She nodded.

Anna's son-in-law, Moses, sold Amish-made tools in his successful store downtown. Some men in the community had been complaining a lot about his lack of participation in the ongoing project. She understood Moses' reluctant contribution. His business had grown beyond his imagination, and he was still struggling to find and hire a capable person to help in his shop. Sarah, his wife and Anna's oldest daughter, was pregnant with their third child. Moses made a conscious effort to divide his time between the store and home, but in the end, there was barely any time left for extra activities like community work.

"I'll be going down to their house as soon as we are done here. I'll make sure to remind him," Anna replied. Noah nodded, picked one of the baked cookies, and devoured it in one bite as he walked out of the kitchen.

The women continued their work in silence, counting and packing the baked goods they had made, taking inventory for their next day at the farmers' market.

Chapter Two

S ummer was ripening around town, and the smells of autumn lingered in the air. A large ball of yolky sun hung high in the deep blue skies, its slanted golden rays of light covering the town. Brown, red and yellow leaves fell off tree branches, carpeting the ground and making crunching sounds with footsteps.

Jude Tymon leaned on the wall next to the window outside of the small sheriff's office located off Highway 43. He was sipping a cup of coffee and enjoying the light gust of wind that drifted through the town. Moments like these were some of his favorite things about Little Valley.

The town was so cozy and beautiful. He liked the people and their culture. Although they didn't exactly embrace the presence of law enforcement in their town, that didn't stop them from treating the lawmen with a welcoming respect. Jude loved the overall sense of peace and quiet that hung over the town, too. There was rarely a crime, and that suited him just fine. Everyone lived and abided by the rules of their holy books and the Old Order Amish beliefs. Their pious lives made his job easier. He could sleep easy at night knowing that he would never be summoned out of bed.

It was a polar opposite experience to the big city jobs he had handled before moving to Little Valley.

Arriving in Little Valley just a little less than a year ago, Jude had grown a fondness for the solitude, but he was growing impatient with his status as deputy. He felt he had more experience and knowledge than he received credit for, and it was becoming a challenge to continue to act like the title he was given was good enough. He was born for greater things and he was getting antsy. For starters, he wanted a nicer home and to at least become lieutenant.

Jude tipped his coffee mug back and took his last sip before stepping back into the office and returning to his small desk. The sheriff's office was previously a small house, with the former front living room serving as the main office. There were just two desks, sitting on opposite walls. Sheriff Derek McCall's desk was about twice the size of Jude's desk, both simple and made of hardwood. Just past the front office was a tiny kitchen with space big enough for a sink, a rarely used oven and range, a compact refrigerator and freezer unit, and a total of four cabinets. The cabinets contained only one small copper pot, some sugar packets for coffee, a few tea bags and a multipack of ramen noodles.

A large heavy-duty door next to the refrigerator led to the room that held the unit's one cell. The makeshift jail was previously the house's bedroom, but it had been fashioned to work as the only holding cell, with an installed rolling steel door that had remained unused, at least since Jude had started. Inside the cell was a metal bunk bed with two uncovered mattresses that looked like they were maybe a hundred years old. To the right when you entered what was referred to as the "jail room" was a large broom closet, holding the few cleaning supplies that went mostly unused. It was easy to see that this was a luxurious walk-in closet, considering the size, used previously for hanging clothes and storing shoes when the house was a home.

Jude's mind turned to his colleague and the town's sheriff of just under ten years, Derek McCall. His desk had sat empty for the past few days, and Jude was mentally preparing for the arrival of the bigshot detective, Sean Stewart, from Nashville. He was set to show up at any time.

Thinking through the questions that the detective might ask him about Derek, Jude couldn't help but feel a little uncomfortable. Even though they were the only lawmen in town, they weren't exactly close. They worked well together, executing their plans and duties seamlessly but other than that, Derek avoided contact with Jude. Derek had always been a recluse; keeping to himself most of the time. The few things Jude knew about him were not exactly something Derek would want just anyone to know.

Jude knew that Derek suffered from gambling and drinking addictions. He was the type of addict that could still function from day to day, but his life was spiraling out of control. Jude offered to help in conversation a few times, but Derek wasn't the kind of man who would accept help, especially from people he thought were lesser than him. His pride kept him a prisoner to himself.

Jude and Derek had been working on solving the robbery case before he disappeared. Jude sank back into his hard wooden chair and flipped through the robbery report. He was due to submit that to the detective, too.

The sound of the old sports car could be heard coming from at least half a mile down the highway. Jude stood up, robbery report in hand, and quickly decided to change seats. Detective Stewart swung the door open and entered, instantly noticing Deputy Tymon sitting comfortably in the cushioned office chair behind the larger desk in the room.

"Deputy? Detective Sean Stewart from Nashville PD. I assume you're expecting me," the detective reached out to shake Jude's hand.

"Welcome to Little Valley," Jude responded, hand outreached. Jude was surprised to see that the detective stood at least one and a half inches shorter than him, on a good day. He slowly let out the breath that he had been holding since he heard the car door slam. 'Let the games begin," he thought.

Chapter Three

The buggy pulled to a stop near the carefully tended rose bushes. Amos jumped down from the buggy and hurried around the corner to Anna's side. He pulled the door open and helped her out. Anna thanked him and gave him a warm hug. Amos was Beth's second son and her favorite nephew. The boy was capable of doing anything he set his mind to, and he was so dedicated to his family. It was admirable. Anna had always felt so close to him and thought they shared commonalities and a special bond.

"Do you want me to wait for you or do you think you are going to be here quite a while?" Amos asked politely. Anna was holding a basket filled with fruits for her grandchildren. The basket was slung across her left wrist.

"I think I'll probably be staying awhile, Amos. I will just have Sarah drop me off when I'm ready to go. Thank you so much for your help," she said, touching Amos's forehead tenderly. Amos nodded and hopped back into the buggy with a youthful exuberance that Anna noticed and immediately envied.

Two young women walked down the street swinging their shopping baskets and waved to Anna. Anna recognized them from the church. They were sisters who recently moved to the community. One of them was recently married to the Amish owner of a diner downtown. She brought along her younger sister. They seemed enthusiastic to get to know everyone in their new community. Their faces were sun-soaked and lit up even more with the warm smiles they gave Anna.

"Good morning, Anna," they greeted chirpily. Anna returned the greeting with a slow wave.

"What a fine morning, isn't it?" she said. The two women stopped near the rose bushes to chat with her. That was another thing Anna was noticing lately about growing older. Younger people tended to treat people of her age with a bridled carefulness that bored Anna. A few weeks ago at the market, she met a young seller who spoke with an intense slowness. Anna wondered if the girl thought Anna was hard of hearing. She was just in her late fifties, and her feelings were easily hurt when she was treated as if she were much older. It's true that lately Beth would have to reassure Anna more than before that she was imagining things and remind her that they certainly still had many years left ahead of them.

The most important thing to Anna was to live long enough to see her great-grandchildren. Already, her first grandchild had turned fifteen this year. The Lord's plan was always the best, but Anna had frequently tailored and presented her own plan to the Lord, hoping that he would adjust his plans to accommodate hers. She felt like the Lord had almost always listened to her pleas. Wasn't she still living so close to her twin sister? It was a lifelong prayer of hers to never be separated from her sister. As little girls, they made what seemed like silly promises never to leave each other, but as they grew, they realized those promises weren't so silly. Anna couldn't imagine living without Beth. Beth wasn't just her best friend - she was her other half. She wasn't sure she would be able to breathe without Beth in her life.

"It *is* a lovely morning," the new bride said. Her blue eyes sparkled under the morning sun.

"Off to the store, I see. Make sure to grab some of those fresh raspberries. They are just delicious. I bought some the other day, and they go beautifully with your cottage cheese," Anna suggested. The woman smiled at her gratefully.

"Thank you, Anna - I love this time of year! The weather is gorgeous, the raspberries are in full bloom...," the bride's sister responded. Anna excused herself and wished the women safe travel and then climbed the short flight of stairs leading to the front door of her oldest daughter's modest home. A long rope sagged with freshly washed children's clothes, tied from one end of a tree to the other in the side yard.

The house was quiet since her grandchildren were in school for the morning. The curtains were tied back so she assumed her daughter was home. She knocked twice before the door was pulled open.

"*Maem*, I didn't know you were coming today," Sarah said in that familiar sing-song voice of hers. Her pregnant belly practically protruded through the light beige cotton fabric of her skirt and matching apron. You could tell by the handprints and traces of smeared flour on the skirt that it was another hectic morning getting the children fed and out the door for school.

"Do I need to seek permission before showing up to my own daughter's house?" Anna asked rhetorically, stepping into the humid house. She glanced around. Moses and Sarah had certainly made something for themselves with the life they created. The house was nicely kept and had everything they needed. Anna was proud of her daughter. She had certainly learned from the best and was willing to put everything she learned about housekeeping into work. She ran her household without a flaw. Sarah was her least problematic daughter, the one she was secretly most proud of and definitely the closest to.

"No, *Maem*. I was just concerned for your safety. You should know that the community isn't safe. Not with the insane robberies going on right now," Sarah said. The living room floor sparkled. The walls were bare. Couches and settees were arranged circularly with a beautiful oak center table. A flower vase with fresh flowers sat prettily atop the table.

"And what will the robbers steal from an old lady like me? The fruits I brought for my grandchildren?" Anna asked sarcastically, pointing down at the basket of fruits she held. Sarah responded with a grin that quickly disappeared.

"Unfortunately, they don't just rob the younger folks these days. *Maem*, I'm serious," she said. Anna patted her daughter assuredly.

"I'm fine, Sarah. Besides, Amos drove me here," said Anna. Gratefully, Sarah dropped the topic.

"Where's your husband this morning?" Anna asked, knowing that the hardware shop didn't open for another couple hours. Sarah picked up the laundry basket that over-spilled with the clothes ready for folding.

"He's out in the back, working on the buggy," she replied. Two weeks ago, someone had stolen their buggy. When the police recovered it, it was in terrible condition. Knowing Moses, he would probably work tirelessly to make the repairs himself. Anna would have preferred that they just let the buggy go. It seemed tainted with the same ugly cloud that recently descended on their town. Plus, who knew what the thief used the buggy for? She had mentioned these concerns, but as usual, her daughter waved them aside.

"Oh, good. I was hoping to talk to him. Noah wanted to confirm that he would bring over the tools they need for the construction going on at Simon's," she said. Sarah brought over the basket to the living room and dropped it on the center table, next to the flower vase.

"*Maem*, would you like some tea?" Sarah asked, standing over the table, hands resting on top of her pregnant belly.

"No thank you, dear. Why don't you sit down now and rest a bit? Let me fold these clothes for you." she said. Sarah exhaled gratefully and sank into the chair next to her mother. She sincerely appreciated her mother's help, but she had also inherited her independent spirit. They worked on the clothes in companionable silence.

Anna sighed inaudibly, sinking back into another round of reverie. Life had changed so much. She could recall when Sarah was only a child running around the kitchen with her sisters, giggling. Her little girl had grown up. Sometimes, she missed that little girl, but other times, she didn't. She was very pleased with the mother and woman Sarah had become, but not just Sarah. She was proud of the work she had put into all her children, and she realized once again just how blessed she was to have such a beautiful healthy family.

"How's *Dat*?" Sarah asked, breaking the revered silence.

"He's wonderful. You know his old backaches have resumed. I keep telling him after all these years of planting, it is time to retire and eat from the fruits of your labor, but does he ever listen to me? No. Instead, he keeps farming and complaining to me about his backaches. Sometimes, that man," Anna said, but with fond reflection. After being married for thirty-four years, Eli was still largely unchanged. He was still the same man she fell in love with. He was stubborn, hardworking, loving, kind, and generally pleasant to others. Anna was grateful for that consistency. Most women complained about the change in their spouses after marriage, Anna was glad she couldn't relate to that. Over the years, she had come to know her husband the way she knew the back of her hand, and she loved him deeply.

"You know *Dat*. He'll never change. He loves farming. The business makes him happy and fulfilled. Maybe you should stop trying to get him to stop. Maintaining a physical lifestyle is actually good for his health," Sarah said. Anna stopped herself from rolling her eyes.

"Good for his health huh? How is it good for his health if he keeps complaining about his back? You children.... you always think you are wiser. I have been married to the man for thirty-four years now. I think I know him better than you do. He needs to stop working at some point, it's that simple," Anna insisted. She would never admit it, but she enjoyed these little banters with her daughter.

"Why tell me then? He complains to you, you complain to us. To be frank, you two deserve each other. You are like two peas in a pod. I don't know why I bother," Sarah mumbled in a low, respectful voice. Anna grinned, and reached out with a gentle touch on her daughter's shoulder.

This sort of play arguing was part of their relationship and reminded her of the times when her children were teenagers. Her sons had been more difficult than the daughters, however. Her first son even tried to leave the faith after his first *Rumspringa*. To this day, Anna has never been as worried as she was when that was happening. In the end, though, everything turned out just fine, and her children all lived together close by in the community inside Little Valley.

Moses pushed the front door open, and the energy in the room instantly changed. He was the kind of man with a commanding presence - an extrovert, through and through. Whenever he came into a room, he brought with him an ever-bursting surge of energy that forced everyone to throw glances in his direction. It was the first thing Anna noticed about him when they met. It terrified her at the time, but it was accompanied by his kind smile and unpretentious goodness. She knew from the first day they met that he would be a good man and take care of her daughter. To this day, he had never proved her wrong.

"*Maem*! Good to see you this fine morning!" Moses said, his voice was boisterous, deep, and quite masculine. His hands and clothes were smeared dirty or he would've hugged Anna.

"*Gute mariye*, Moses," Anna warmly responded, smiling broadly at him. He was easily her favorite son-in-law. Not that she didn't love the rest of her family, but it was hard to compete with Sarah and Moses when it came to secretly picking favorites.

"Did Amos bring you here?" Moses asked, already knowing the answer. Moses knew that Amos was practically Anna's personal driver. Anna nodded.

"How is he? And *Dat*? And Aunt Beth?" he continued asking. Anna replied to his questions enthusiastically, catching Moses up on the latest with everyone.

"Noah asked me to remind you about the tools you were supposed to bring for them," she said. Moses groaned loudly, slapping the center of his forehead as he remembered that he had promised to bring them by days ago.

"I am so sorry. I know it must seem as though I'm not interested in the work going on there, but I just don't have enough time to go around. With Sarah's pregnancy and the demands at work, I haven't had any time to join the men at the end of the day," he said, apologetically.

"Oh, I understand that, Moses. I just want the rest of the men to understand, too. I just don't want them to see you in a different light. I wish you could...I don't know...maybe you could stop by the project and drop off the tools and explain things. Just to show that you aren't entirely indifferent," Anna said. Moses respected Anna and knew she was right.

"You're absolutely right, *Maem*. I have so much to do, but I should also make the community a priority. I'll do as you said later today or this evening." he said.

He excused himself and went into the back of the house. Anna could hear the water turn on in the bathroom sink as he prepared to go to work.

"He is a good man," she said to Sarah, simply confirming what Sarah already knew.

"He is. I am very proud of him and everything he does. He has really built quite a business from the ground up," said Sarah.

"Yes, it is truly impressive how far he has come. But Sarah, don't you think that you should ask him to hire some help? Surely, he cannot possibly run that store by himself?" Anna said. Sarah stopped folding her clothes and turned her attention to Anna.

"Thank you, *Maem*, but he actually has done just that. Do you remember Thomas? The man who owns the coffee shop next door to the Moses' store...? He actually hired Thomas for part-time hours. They make a great team together, so far. So, don't worry about Moses - he knows what he is doing," Sarah said. Anna dusted invisible dust balls off the surface of the folded shirt she was holding.

"I'm glad to hear that..." she said, reminded yet again that Sarah was in good hands. Sarah reached out and patted her mother's hand lovingly.

"I love you, *Maem*. Would you and *Dat* like to join us for dinner tonight and see the children?" she asked. Anna bobbed her head happily, adjusting her position on the chair to allow blood to flow through her whitened, tensed up ankles. She was dying to hug and kiss her wonderful grandchildren - she just couldn't get enough of that. Her mind drifted off to what baked goods she would be bringing to dinner.

Chapter Four

Moses loved Little Valley. His family moved here when he was a boy, and he had always loved it. The quiet streets, plains, sprawling farms, and familial relationships amongst the residents settled his soul. Unlike some of his childhood friends who had moved out of the community, Moses had never dreamt of leaving. He honestly never even had a passing thought of looking for life somewhere else. The curiosity of wondering what his life would have been if he wasn't born Amish just didn't exist with him. He couldn't be more perfectly and gratefully content as an Amish citizen of Little Valley, Tennessee. This was his forever home, where he would stay and raise a family that he hoped would also never leave.

His buggy rolled down the street pulled by a strong chestnut Standardbred, a gift from Moses' great uncle. The family's loyal horse stood tall at five years old with well-muscled shoulders and powerful legs. Moses stopped briefly to greet the pedestrians on their way to work and to the shops downtown. The Amish women always stood out in the crowd amongst the English in spite of their plain dresses and prayer *kapps*.

Additionally, lovers in the streets could be pointed out swiftly. There was a certain skip to their steps. Some of them held each other's hands while others discreetly brushed against each other's bodies in a way that made Moses smile. He easily and fondly remembered when he was their age. How free and unstoppable he felt. When he met and fell in love with Sarah, his entire world shifted. He became a completely different person - a better person. He couldn't imagine his life without his wife. She was his sunshine, burning ever so brightly and shedding light on his path on their journey together.

"Ah, to be young again," Moses muttered to himself, switching his thoughts again to remembering how carefree life was then. Growing up in a large household, his parents instilled in him a deep love and appreciation for family, nature, and community. His father – who was a very resourceful craftsman – never missed a single day of community work. He took Moses and his brothers to show them the importance of a work ethic firsthand. Moses sighed inaudibly. He tried to live strictly in his father's footsteps but lately, he could feel himself slipping.

Nothing had prepared him for the demands of adulthood, marriage, and fatherhood. His wife and children were a blessing, he knew this, but sometimes regardless of all he had to be grateful for, he longed for freedom and to be away from the tugging demands that could sometimes create such a pit in his stomach. He was merely in his late thirties but most days, he already felt like he was an old man. These feelings were enforced when the older men whom he knew well often stopped by his store on their daily walks. They would stop to chat with him.

Moses ultimately enjoyed those chats with the elder men. They kept him warm and less lonely, but there was a nibbling fear that lodged itself in his chest most often during the rides to and from the shop. During these times, he was still and would get caught up in his head. That's when these chats served as reminders of how different his life had become. Since he lost his childhood friend, Matthew, Moses was hesitant to nurture friendships with other men near his own age. He held onto the hurt Matthew caused him like an ant clinging to sugar.

"Good morning, Moses," someone called out, quickly pulling him out of his thoughts. Moses saw Jacob Lapp's widow waving frantically to him. He pulled his buggy to a stop carefully near the curb she was standing on.

"Good morning, Martha. Headed out to do some shopping this fine morning?" he greeted her. The broad brim of his hat blocked his view slightly, so he pushed it to the side just a smudge. Martha's smile was so genuine and heart-warming. She was an older woman in the neighborhood, and Moses looked out for her.

"Oh no, Moses. My grandson, Hezekiah, do you remember him? Well, he's fallen sick. Whenever he isn't feeling well, he always asks for his *Grossmammi*. I am just waiting for my son-in-law to pick me up," Martha's vivid, bright voice responded.

"Well then, Martha, you don't need me to drop you off at your daughter's now do you?" Moses asked pleasantly. Although he was late to work, he wouldn't hesitate to take Martha where she needed to go. His parents did not raise an unkind, unhelpful man. They taught him better than that.

"No, no, thank you for offering to help. How is your family?" Martha asked. Moses answered her questions politely. When she finally waved him goodbye, he picked up the speed just a bit and returned his focus to getting to the shop on time.

The sun was sitting high in the sky, a large ball of yellow rising majestically on its way to the other side of the world. Moses was already late to work. Early Autumn brought with it a lucid beauty to life in the community. Flowers were still in bloom, their colorful tendrils unfolding towards the sun as though beckoning for the splash of light that would liven them up. With the leaves just starting to turn colors, Autumn served as a great symbol for change - whether you were looking for it or not.

His buggy closed the widened distance until he soon stopped near the front door of the shop. He hopped out of the buggy and closed its door securely. Moses' store was situated between Thomas' coffee shop and Mr. Hatfield's flower shop. Looking over to Thomas' shop, he saw that it was closed again. Where could he be? This should be the prime time for a coffee shop to be open and buzzing with customers. Moses' feelings of recent concerns for Thomas started to grow. Not only was the closed sign hanging inside the door of Coffee World, but Thomas had also not shown up for work at the hardware shop in a few days.

More than just worry, Moses was starting to regret hiring Thomas. A few months ago, he had approached Moses and had pleaded to him for a part-time job. He opened up about how his coffee shop was collapsing and he explained that he needed a supplemental income to save the shop and make ends meet. Moses had suspected that he had money problems. Thomas had never proven to be a level-headed man as long as Moses had known him, so it wasn't a surprise that his business was struggling. He clearly had terrible business acumen, and knowing that, Moses had his reservations about taking him under his wing. But he wanted to help support Thomas' dreams. At first, everything was perfectly fine, and things were going well. Thomas seemed eager to learn and work. But just one month later, things took a turn. Thomas rarely showed up to work and the few times he did, he seemed disoriented and uninterested. Moses had decided to give him one more chance before firing him and was prepared to have that conversation with him today. But he needed Thomas to understand that Moses was a good man, not an idiot. He would not allow anyone to take advantage of his goodness.

"Good morning, Mr. Hatfield," he called across to his neighbor. Mr. Hatfield was watering some tulips displayed beautifully on the window ledge in front of the store. His apron was soiled and so were his fingers. A pair of cutters dangled from the work belt he had tied around his waist.

"Good morning, Moses. What a fine day it is huh?" he said inattentively. His mind was focused on the flowers. Anna once said that there were only two things Mr. Hatfield cared about in the world: his wife and his flowers. And Moses was inclined to agree with that. Hatfield's entire life revolved around his flower fields and shop and he had a large picture of his wife holding an elegantly arranged bouquet of flowers hung on the wall directly behind the counter. Mr. Hatfield's face would light up whenever Mrs. Hatfield came to visit, or when anyone asked about the photograph. The couple kept to themselves, and Mr. Hatfield especially was a man of few words. No one knew much about the couple or even where they had moved from exactly. He was an Englisher who showed up to town one day for a visit, fell in love with the area, and never left.

Moses tied up the horse and walked towards his shop. As he was fiddling with the keys to unlock the front door, a black Ford Mustang with a loud muffler dramatically pulled to a stop behind him drawing attention and interested stares from nearby pedestrians. Moses was annoyed.

A man that Moses did not recognize jumped out of the car and slammed the door shut. He was wearing a cowboy hat and boots with jeans and a plaid button-down shirt. He wasn't dressed in the badges and stars-inscribed uniform of the state troopers. The Stetson hat angled from his face. Moses saw his roughened face and aquiline nose and immediately felt the annoyance turn to a sense of dread.

"Howdy," he called out to Moses. Moses reluctantly returned his greeting. "I'm with the police force out in Nashville."

"How may I help you?" he made sure to ask with a kind tone. The man's eyes looked Moses over inquisitively. Moses wondered what he was doing in their town. They didn't need another police officer, especially one from

Nashville. The town had Derek and Jude to handle any necessary business. Encouraged by the two to be on a first name basis, the sheriff and deputy were respected enough by the community, but there was still a bit of distrust felt when they came around.

"How ya doin? Listen, I don't mean to be any bother but I'm looking for Sheriff Derek McCall. I understand no one has seen him for a few days, and I'm here to help with the search. Do you reckon you could point me in his direction?" the detective asked rowdily. His voice was too high, accented, and distracting. Moses had to really struggle to discern some of the words that came out of his mouth.

Derek was missing? Moses hadn't noticed or heard anything about that. He certainly didn't see Derek every day, nor was he particularly interested in having a close friendship with the man. Honestly, he thought the sheriff and his deputy should have been making more progress toward solving the theft cases that were recently popping up in Little Valley. Since the robberies started a few weeks ago, no one had yet been able to solve the case and apprehend the culprits.

"The Sheriff is missing? I wasn't aware. I mean, he would sometimes be seen driving around town in the mornings and maybe wave to anyone who cared to notice - but now that you mention it, I haven't seen him in a few days. That's all I know about his life and routine. We aren't exactly friends or anything so I wouldn't know what else to tell you." Moses said.

The detective spat out a thick glob of saliva onto the ground just to the left of his silver-tipped boots. His eyes never left Moses' face. Small beads of sweat started forming on the base of Moses' neck and forehead as he worked hard to keep a calm composure. The man's gaze was too piercing for his liking. Why was he staring at him like that? Surely, he didn't think Moses had anything to do with the sheriff's disappearance?

"Ain't that a shame? You two live in the same town and both of you have business here, yet you never even bothered to get to know him. I'm starting to get the impression you don't like Sheriff McCall - nice try hiding it, though," the man said, carefully watching for a reaction.

Moses was stunned. This wasn't the first time he was met with disdain because of the Amish lifestyle. He didn't dislike the sheriff. Like he explained, he didn't even know the man. What was this man trying to do?

"I don't dislike him," Moses defended himself. The man in the hat struck an assertive pose. His right leg was thrust forth with hands on his hips. His eyes narrowed to an uncomfortable slit. *But I definitely don't like you,* thought Moses. How could someone be so rude? Part of the distrust was from those moments in the past when Sheriff McCall seemed to show a certain sort of prejudice towards the Amish. The rest of the Englishers in town were usually very kind and accommodating, but the rude ones threw Moses off balance. There were a handful like Derek. Samuel, who ran the bar in town, was also this way, and maybe even more so. It didn't help Derek's case that he let Samuel get away with a lot of things that perhaps outside police officers wouldn't let happen.

There was no fighting allowed in Moses' world, and this feeling of defenselessness that Moses was experiencing was familiar but not exactly comfortable.

"Well, I definitely don't have the time or energy to argue with you. And I'm sure you have better things to do, making more hammers to sell to tourists or something... I guess I'll be sticking around until I get to the bottom of this. You make sure to let me know if you hear anything," he said. Moses nodded his head quickly. He was eager for the man to leave - this was starting to feel like an interrogation, and he needed to get to work.

"You have a good day now," he said, with a quick flick of his hat – a cowboy's goodbye. Moses watched him get into his car and drive off with the same reckless abandon. Moses turned and entered his shop, reaching to the left to switch on the overhead fluorescent lights. Typically, the buzzing sound of the lights had a comforting affect over Moses, but not today. Not after that unsettling encounter.

Taking a deep breath, the smell of tools filtered into his nostrils. He worked hard to push all of that unnecessary drama out of his mind and turn his day around. Humming to himself, he walked around the store opening the windows and carefully positioning the tools on the beautifully crafted display tables strategically placed around the small room.

"*Gute mariye*, Moses," Thomas' voice came from behind him. Moses turned to face the man. He looked so ashen. His hair was matted. Moses always felt that one could describe Thomas as a very average looking man. He was neither short nor tall. The nose on his face was small and straight. He had tawny brows and a weak jaw and low cheekbones.

Moses liked Thomas' green eyes, at least. They seemed so honest and all-embracing. The concept that your eyes are the windows to your soul seemed to apply to Thomas. On the day he came into the store to beg Moses for a job, Moses asked Thomas directly if he was broke. Thomas tried to avoid the question, but his eyes gave the answer that his lips didn't speak.

"You've been gone for a few days now, Thomas. I am very displeased. When you asked for this job, you said that you would do your best. This certainly isn't your best," Moses said, the impatience coming out loud and clear in his voice. He hadn't meant to scold him but as he spoke the words, he knew that it sounded that way. The air between them filled with tension, and things quickly became awkward. Thomas may be his employee, but he was not a child. He was in his late thirties, like Moses. There was no need to scold him.

"I wish I had a good reason for my absence, but I don't. I'm sure you don't want to hear that, nor do you want fabricated excuses. I'm terribly sorry, Moses. I recognize that you are helping me, and I don't mean to take advantage of your kindness," Thomas said, humbly. His sincere apologies melted the irritation inside Moses. His voice softened.

"But where were you? Is everything okay? Are *you* okay?" he asked. Thomas' coffee shop had sat next to Moses' hardware store for a few years, but they weren't close friends. They hadn't spent much time getting to know each other outside of the occasional nod at a service or a barn raising before Thomas approached Moses for part-time work. But Moses felt like he knew that Thomas was a decent man. He had seen Thomas and his group of friends gathered in the diner on several occasions. It made him long for a close friendship. His childhood friend, Matthew, had chosen the life of an Englisher after their shared time during *Rumspringa*, and Moses missed him terribly. But Matthew and Moses had, unfortunately, both developed crushes on Sarah. She had fallen in love with Moses, and Matthew couldn't bear to be witness to their happy life together. Moses wished things could have been different. It seemed such an unfair tragedy to have to choose between the two most important people in his life, and although he was happily married, he still longed for the bond he shared with his best friend.

In the diner, high-spirited discussions from Thomas' table of friends would float over to Moses, sorely reminding him of the fun he once had with Matthew. Most days, he stopped himself from walking over to their table to ask to join them. He would always talk himself out of it by telling himself that if Thomas wanted him there, then he would be invited.

"It's embarrassing, but sometimes, I just sink into depression. It has been a real struggle. You know...with everything that's happened... my business and all. It's often hard to just get out of bed and face the day. I know it's no excuse...." He paused, his jaws quivering visibly.

"No, I'm sorry for prying. I wish I could help out more," Moses dived in, wanting to relieve Thomas of having to put his feelings into words, and ultimately to shift gears in the conversation. There was work to do, and this morning seemed to be dragging on, full of unwanted distractions.

"Thank you, Moses. You've proven to be a good friend to me. I will never forget this," he said, setting a light hand on Moses' shoulder for a moment. Moses saw the tears misting his eyes, and again, he was overcome with an urgency to change the subject.

"Ok, well, now that you're here, let's get to work. Will you please go to the tool shed out back and grab the box of four- and eight-pound shop hammers that I set aside? Noah wants me to bring them to Simon's tonight. You've joined the work going on there before, right?" he said hurriedly, the words gushing out of him like water from a spicket. He was trying to fill the space between them with words and stop the tears that were threatening to flow from Thomas' eyes.

Thomas gathered his composure in record time. "Ah, yes. Bishop Packer called at my place to ensure I did that," he responded. Moses had forgotten how close Thomas and the Bishop were. The Bishop was Thomas' uncle. And strangely, Thomas never called him uncle. Everyone in town called the Bishop by his title, including his closest family members.

"Well, I haven't shown in a while and Noah's giving me grief about it. My father-in-law's in the same boat, but he's not as forthcoming as Noah is. Anyway, if you would grab that box of tools and place it behind the counter, I will be sure to take it with me when I head out this evening." Moses said. Thomas nodded and grabbed the keys dangling from the nail on the wall.

Moses worked on in silence for a few minutes, setting up the cash register. His silence was interrupted by Thomas' screams. Momentarily, he stood there stunned, trying to figure out the direction and source of the shrill scream.

Thomas flew in, his face was white as a sheet. "It's *baremlich*, Moses... out there..." Thomas struggled to get those few words out between gasping for air. Moses rushed out of the store, roughly pushing past Thomas with urgency as he stood holding on to the door frame with one hand, bent over clutching his stomach with the other. As Moses approached the open door of the toolshed, his senses were on high alert. Even before his eyes were able to adjust to the dim light in the toolshed, he knew by the stench that lingered in the air that the scene was not going to be good. Thomas was right. It was *baremlich*. At the sight of the body lying lifeless in the corner, Moses dropped to his knees, landing on the threshold of the shed he had built with his own hands, took his hat into his hands, and immediately began to pray.

"We have to do something, right?" Thomas said, moments later, quietly interrupting Moses' mumbling. Moses wiped his face with the palm of his hand, stood and straightened his suspenders. He replaced his hat on his head and found his composure.

"Dear *Gotte*, who could've done this?" he asked out loud as he led Thomas back to the shop to call for help.

Moses didn't need to be a wise man to realize that he was in trouble. The dead body was found locked up in his tool shed. He was certainly in trouble...

Chapter Five

Beth's youngest grandchildren ran around her with hyper energy. She was in the kitchen, making a cup of tea for their guests. Anna sat with the older girls in the living room, consoling the sobbing girl. Beth strained her ears to hear what they were saying. Anna's voice, as always, was low and soothing. The girl's voice was loud and tearful, so emotionally ridden that it was hard to decipher what she was saying.

Since she could recall, the twins had always been considered the wise women of the community. Women who needed advice, a shoulder to cry on, or someone to confide in often came to them. As a result, the twins knew quite a few secret things about most of their neighbors. Beth couldn't exactly recall what it was that originally made the residents so trusting towards them. Was it something passed down from their mother? Or the fact that they were born into the King family? Beth and Anna's parents spoke their surname with pride and honor and taught their children the importance of living their lives as leaders to stay true to their God-given name.

Whatever it was that positioned Anna and Beth in this light among the community, they felt privileged. Welcome guests came often, no announcement ever necessary, seeking advice and opening up about their darkest worries. Sometimes, Beth felt like an endless well absorbing and soaking in droplets of everyone's secrets. She wondered if she would ever feel full, but she was confident it wouldn't be anytime soon. Both of the sisters loved the interpersonal connections and were so grateful to have been assigned a life mission of problem solving and helping good people.

"Be careful, Esther!" Beth said to her granddaughter sternly, but with a sprinkle of warmth. Esther was a spitfire at three years old, with fine golden hair that looked like feathers and beautiful blue eyes that would melt any grandmother's heart. The little girl was precariously making her way up the tall stool to reach the kitchen table. Beth swooped in and grabbed her around the waist with one arm just as she lost her footing.

"But *Mammi*, I want to see what you are doing," Esther whined. Beth set her safely down on the counter next to her. Her mind was fixated on trying to figure out what the girl was telling Anna, but she kept a close eye on Esther at the same time. Finishing up the tea, she arranged the cups and teapot on a flower-patterned tray, making sure that each cup was in exactly the same position with their handles facing out and stacked on each saucer perfectly. Beth wouldn't be satisfied unless each little detail was perfectly in line. Once in order, she placed Esther back on the floor and carried the tray out to the living room where the guests were waiting.

"Tea's ready," Beth called out as she went. The distraught young lady wiped the tears that ran down her face with the white handkerchief Anna graciously gave her. She struggled to subside the sobbing. Her name was Mary Yoder. She couldn't be more than twenty years old. Beth and her sister had attended her mother's funeral last spring. Mary had been very close with her mother, and now that her parents were gone, she was at a loss. Her brothers were overwhelmed with consoling her and were trying to marry her off.

"I don't want to marry Joseph. I've always wanted to marry Luke. He's the one I'm in love with. If I can't marry him, then I don't want to marry anyone else." Mary said with a quiet conviction, her full lips were set in a strong pout. "What can I do to make them understand?" Worry carved faded lines onto the smooth skin of her forehead. She fidgeted anxiously with the handkerchief, folding it and unfolding it over and over again.

Mary reminded Beth of her second daughter, Judith. Judith was also stubborn and determined like Mary. Oh, how she gave Beth so much trouble when it came time to settle down with her husband. Now, she was married and living in another town with her husband. She was pretty sure that Judith had found happiness at last, but thinking now, Beth realized the last time she had heard from Judith was a few weeks ago. She made a mental note to pay a visit to her soon.

"Why are your brothers refusing to allow you to court Luke?" Anna asked. Mary's palms were clenched into fists, gripping the white handkerchief firmly.

"They say he is unfit to take care of me. But he can - I know he can! Luke is the hardest working man I've ever met. He is just having a little bad luck with his father's farm right now. He works on it, but the land never brings forth any harvest. I've suggested that maybe the land is cursed but he wouldn't hear of it," she lowered her voice to add that last part.

Beth restrained from outwardly rolling her eyes at the thought of a cursed land. Interestingly enough, Eli's farms, too, had once been thought to be infertile. At least they were until Eli took over the business from his father and turned everything around. Beth thought so highly of her sister's husband. She adored both of the men in their lives and said a quick prayer of gratitude with the passing thoughts. Anna's voice interrupted her thoughts. Beth sipped her tea and struggled to pay attention.

"If he is not blessed in farming, maybe he could try a different craft?" Anna asked. Mary hesitated a minute before replying.

"I've tried to get him to give up, but Luke's just not going to abandon his father's land. It was passed on to him after his father died. He feels responsible towards it," she said. Anna nodded as she was processing the information.

"Then, maybe he could consider hiring someone with more experience or reach out to an elder for more mentorship? It seems to me that Luke may be missing some key knowledge," Beth chimed in without an invitation.

Anna smiled approvingly at her and added, "There is certainly no shame in asking for help." Beth returned Anna's warm smile. Once again, the twins were on the same page with one quick glance.

"Oh, I'll mention that to him! Do you think he'll listen to me and take advice?" Mary cried. Mary was crippled with doubt as she wasn't truly sure if Luke held feelings as strongly for her as she felt about him. The whole situation was so stressful, and she was not prepared for navigating courting and relationships without her mother by her side.

Beth took a cup of hot tea and gently handed it to Mary.

"Here, take a sip," she encouraged her, using the motherly tone she used on her children and grandchildren. Mary listened and steam curled out of the cup as she took her first sip. The delicious tea seemed to immediately bring her comfort.

"There. Do you feel better?" Beth asked. Mary nodded enthusiastically; a small smile appeared on her face.

"Everyone always says our tea could make a widow feel better the night of her husband's death," Anna said with a sliver of pride. Beth agreed with her. When they were finished bragging about their tea, Anna took Mary's hand in hers. The girl's hands felt so smooth, youthful and untainted by cruel time.

"Dear Mary, it's important that you understand that when a man loves you, he has to show that he does. You should never guess if he shares feelings for you by not only his words, but also his actions. Love is definitely not always easy and smooth, and it can be confusing because sometimes it feels like the best thing in the world. There will be a few bumps on the way. Those bumps are set there by *Gotte* to test our love and faith in each other. You have the faith in this relationship. You are willing to do whatever it takes to make it work. But it is important to make sure that he also has the faith and desire to make you happy, protect you, and make you feel loved. If he does not feel that way, then you must open your eyes and your heart to someone else. Maybe that is all your brothers are asking of you." Beth spoke slowly and with much compassion.

Mary's eyes misted again as new tears began to form. They just hung on the surface of her eyes, neither spilling over nor disappearing back. Anna had a worried look on her face as she watched Mary's reaction. Beth was concerned, too. Had she sparked fear and doubt inside her? The truth, sometimes, can be bitter and hard to swallow, but she had hoped that she had delivered it with enough kindness.

"*Ach du lieva...* Mary, are you okay?" Beth asked hesitantly.

"You don't think Luke loves me?" she summoned the courage to ask. Beth and Anna exchanged glances before Anna reached out to retrieve the teacup and gently hold Mary's free hand.

Anna leaned in to answer Mary's question. "We cannot know that answer, my dear, but if you have to ask, maybe some more work is needed to find the truth. Mary, we are not asking that you should forget about your feelings for Luke and do what your brothers say and marry Joseph. We are asking that you think carefully. Test your faith in Luke. See if his love is as all-encompassing as it should be. Think with your head and not just your heart and see...."

Anna was interrupted by the sudden loud noise of the front door bursting open with such force that it hit the wall directly behind it. Sarah stood on the threshold looking disheveled with her hands around her pregnant belly. Her prayer *kapp* was loose on her head with stringlets of her brunette hair peeking out around her face and by her neck. Anna jumped up, nearly knocking over the tray of teacups and rushed towards her.

"*Ach du lieva*, Sarah! What's going on? Are you okay?" she asked, frantic from worry and leading Sarah to a nearby rocking chair to sit. Sarah became overwhelmed with tears and sobbing, catching her breath at the same time. Beth rushed to the kitchen to get a tall glass of water, while at the same time, asking her older granddaughters to gather the children outside to play.

Anna bent over Sarah and gave her a warm hug, mumbling prayers softly while removing Sarah's shoes. She was summoning so much patience, but she wanted desperately to know what in the world was happening that had her oldest daughter in such turmoil.

Beth appeared with a glass of water. Sarah gulped the entire drink without stopping, gasping for air another time as she handed the empty glass back to Beth. Anna knelt before Sarah, waiting.

Sarah took one look at Anna, and the words rushed out of her mouth.

"It's Moses. He's been taken." she said breathlessly. Shock fell on the house, and the twins once again communicated everything on their minds with one single glance. *This cannot be good.*

Chapter Six

"Well, well, well, we meet again," Detective Stewart said slowly and theatrically. A short cigarette dangled from his lips. Up close, Moses saw the strong outlines of his face. He had a defined jawline and sharp cheekbones. Stubble decorated the lower half of his face, attempting to hide its better features. His teeth were yellow and not straight. He reeked of smoke and leather.

Moses assumed that he was a man who liked to work alone when he sent Jude out of the room for the interrogation. Moses favored Jude a bit more than he cared for Derek McCall, the dead sheriff. He had witnessed Derek being outright rude to his fellow Amish brothers and sisters, but at least he could think of a few instances where Jude acted kindly to the community. The more he thought about it, he was starting to think that there may be quite a few people who wouldn't care if Sheriff McCall were dead. Not that he would ever say that to this scowling man before him.

"Well, I'm glad you kept to your promise and reached out to me when you found him," he smirked, lighting the cigarette. Smoke danced in front of his face. He inhaled a short puff as if it were a cigar and blew it out, the smoke hitting Moses directly in his face. Moses coughed, annoyed, knowing that the smoke would cling to his beard.

"Not a smoker, I take it?" the detective asked knowingly, with a slight shrug of the shoulder. Moses glared at him.

"No, I don't smoke or drink," Moses said with a set jaw. The detective fell back on his chair, with an overly dramatic surprise expression.

"Well then, what *are* your vices? I mean, how do you relax after a long day of killing someone?" he asked. Moses clenched his fist under the table. Fear and anger surged inside him. What was this guy trying to do? Did he seriously think he killed Derek?

"You don't have to worry about that because I have never killed anything in my life," Moses responded with a condescending tone. The detective laughed mockingly.

"You sure about that, Moses? Because the evidence is not looking good for you. Derek McCall, the county sheriff, was found dead as a doornail in *your* locked toolshed, brutally murdered with *your* hammer. I've got forensics running a DNA test on the fingerprints all over the hammer, and I am pretty confident the results will not work out well for you. This isn't a hard case to crack," he said confidently.

"It is my shed, and I made that hammer. Of course, my fingerprints may be at the scene and on the hammer, but I am telling you, Detective, I did not kill the sheriff. Please, you have to believe me. I am a family man. I have never even been involved in a fist fight" he said. The detective took a deep long drag on his cigarette and blew the smoke into the air.

"Why don't you tell me where you were last night and everything that happened up until you found poor Derek's body lying dead in your tool shed?" he asked after a few minutes of silence that felt like forever. Moses took a deep breath, making an effort to clear his head, trying to figure out what to say to clear his name.

"Alright. Last night, I arrived home from work at my normal time, around 5 pm, ate dinner, relaxed at home, spent time with my children and my wife, and went to bed. This morning, I woke, ate breakfast, visited briefly with my wife and mother-in-law, and I left home late for work because I was working on my buggy. My wife's pregnant and needed the second buggy to go shopping.

On my way to work, I saw Mrs. Martha on the curb, waiting for her son-in-law to pick her up. We spoke a little about her grandson not feeling well, and then I went on my way straight to my store. After that pleasant conversation with you, I had a conversation with my new part-time helper at the store, Thomas. I sent him to the toolshed to find some tools I had set aside for a project in my community. He screamed when he got there. I ran outside to see what was happening, and then Thomas and I ran inside to call you guys for help," Moses told the story as he recalled it.

The detective was silent for a minute.

"Hmm...still...something seems off. I think that...." The detective stopped talking. Moses heard the same sounds he did. His wife, her mother, and her aunt were outside banging on the door of the sheriff's office and asking for the detective.

"They here for you?" the detective asked Moses. He nodded. The detective grunted loudly.

"I hate this part of my job. Dealing with the hysterical family is always such a pain in the neck, especially the Amish. You folks sure know how to stick together, don't you? God forbid one of you is ever accused of a crime," the detective's sarcasm was not lost on Moses.

The detective paused, staring unflinchingly at Moses who tried his best not to look guilty. The man was trying to fish out something from him, and Moses was determined not to give it to him. He was not a criminal, and he would not be accused of a crime he didn't commit. Even as a boy, Moses struggled with killing insects - the phrase 'he couldn't hurt a fly' could quite literally be applied to him. How could anyone think he possibly killed someone? Let alone an officer of the law. Moses was a law-abiding man, just like his father.

Most importantly, this tragedy meant one thing: the town he loved and the community that resided there were not safe. There was a killer out there and the detective was in here, harassing Moses and wasting valuable time.

"Well then, I'm sure Jude will fill them in and let them know you probably won't be home for dinner," the detective said, matter-of-factly. Moses' heart began to race. He was very afraid and couldn't understand why this was happening to him. He flinched as he could hear the conversations happening outside of the small room he was confined in with this terrible man.

"Where is he? Where have you taken him? My husband is not a killer. The real killer is still out there! He should be the one you are interrogating...not my husband. I've known Moses for almost twenty-five years. He is *not* a killer," Sarah erupted, full of fire. Moses could imagine her almost grabbing the deputy's collar.

Jude responded, "Lady, lady, lady, please calm down. We're just doing our job. We have a lot of evidence against your husband, I'm sorry to tell you. A dead man's body was found in your husband's toolshed. The murder weapon was also found - and we're running a DNA test on the prints. Please go home and take care of yourself and your children. You're going to have to let us do our job. Please," the deputy said, sounding only a bit more comforting than the man Moses had been talking to for the last couple hours.

The air felt stale in the tiny room that was once a large closet but quickly turned into a pseudo interrogation room, only fitting a small square table and two chairs.

"Sir, what is your name?" Moses asked, trying very hard to not sound confrontational.

"Stewart. Name's Detective Stewart," he said, also sitting in silence, joining in listening to the interaction with Moses' family but watching Moses' reaction to all of it.

"Please, can I talk to my wife, Detective Stewart? My wife is pregnant and I'm sure it would be of comfort to see that I am okay and that all of this is just a mistake."

"Absolutely not gonna happen, Moses. We're not finished here, and if you don't tell me what you know, then you might get to fill your family in over one short phone call," the detective looked Moses dead in the face. He reached for the unopened bottle of water sitting on the table to the right of Moses and pushed it in his direction as to confirm that the two would be sitting there a while longer. Detective Stewart lit another cigarette, and Moses squeezed his hands into tight fists underneath the small square table. How could they put him- and his family- through this?

"Jude, I think someone's trying to frame my son-in-law. He didn't do this. Moses would never harm a soul. He doesn't have the heart to murder someone. And if it was him, why would he just leave the body lying in his tool shed for Thomas to find him? How could he possibly kill that man?" Anna was pleading to be heard.

"You let the right authorities worry about that, Ma'am. Why don't you go home and rest? We'll be speaking with all of you shortly, to corroborate his story. So, you're gonna need to save the stories for then. Detective Stewart is in town for the purpose of this investigation, and as your friend, I am telling you that it's best for you to go home. You don't want to make things worse for Moses, and we'll be in touch as soon as we know something more," Jude said, hoping that he was getting somewhere with the women. He recognized that the community and the local townsfolk had a lot of respect for these women and their family, and he didn't want to rock the boat any more than Moses' arrest already had.

Anna and Sarah were not satisfied with Jude's suggestion, but Beth interjected, "We should go and let these men do their jobs, then." She placed her arms around both ladies and gently escorted them out the door. She was hopeful that Moses would set the record straight and tell the detectives what they needed to know. She said a quick quiet prayer that the detectives would find the killer, and Moses would be home by dinner.

"Now, let's get down to business. Did you know that the sheriff was investigating the recent spike in robberies in this town?" the detective asked, turning the tone down a bit in an effort to make Moses trip up in the details.

Moses was working very hard to stay calm. The last thing he wanted was to appear to be an angry man that could lose his temper when provoked. He figured that the more he cooperated with this man, the sooner he could get home.

"I had heard about the robberies, and I just assumed he was investigating them," he replied. The detective had no notepad nor pen, and Moses wondered how this guy would take notes on important details if he even had any to share. He was simply busy sucking on cigarette after cigarette and staring at him.

"So, tell me about the robberies - or about what you *heard* about the robberies then," he asked. Moses was too shook to respond. Was it his imagination that now this guy was blaming him for the robberies, too? How would he even have time for this life of crime that he was being accused of? He didn't know how much longer he was going to be able to take this absurd questioning and accusations. He was a hard-working honest man, a good father and family man... and whoever did this was running free right now.

Realizing yet again that Detective Stewart was just sitting across the table, watching and analyzing every single movement and reaction to each question, Moses took a deep breath and pulled himself together.

"I'm not really sure when the robberies started but I think Mr. Fisher's widow was the first victim. You see she wasn't exactly born Amish. She...er...met Mr. Fisher during his *Rumspringa* and fell in love with him. As part of her old life, she refused to let go of her jewels. We didn't know that at the time until she was robbed of them. We didn't take it seriously because you know....it was just jewels. But the robberies spread. Farms were robbed. Animals were stolen. Valuables. It was horrible," he said. Stewart's eyes were steadfast on him.

"You know it's interesting that you mentioned the jewels," he said, rising. He walked over to the counter and brought out a brown envelope. He jiggled the envelope. Moses heard the sound of something bouncing around inside the paper walls. Detective Stewart walked back to the table and carelessly tossed the contents of the envelope onto the table. Something round, small, and glistening rattled on the table.

"Do you recognize this?" the detective asked. Moses shook his head.

"What is that?" he asked, naively. The detective picked it up, raised it to the light. It caught some of the sun rays and cast off reflecting bright light.

"That's an expensive diamond, right there. You've never seen a diamond before?" he asked again. Moses shook his head, silent. He had no use for expensive jewels - or any jewels for that matter. True to the Amish culture, he and Sarah had never even exchanged wedding rings, for rings were not allowed in their shared beliefs.

"That's certainly interesting because we found it in your tool shed," the detective said. Moses' eyes widened. What was going on? Who was trying to set him up? This couldn't be happening. His breathing suddenly intensified. He grabbed his chest. Was he having a panic attack? His health had always been solid, but at that moment, an intense pain hit him right in the center of his body as if he had been thrown off a horse and hit the ground hard. The room started to spin, a darkness seemed to be slowly creeping in, and he struggled to catch his breath.

"You okay there, fella?" the detective asked, he stood up and bent over Moses. Moses nodded, still gripping his chest tightly. A few deep breaths and he was starting to pull himself out of the spell he found himself under.

"Good. Alright, we are done for the day. I'm gonna take you back to the holding cell so you can get some rest and see if maybe you can remember anything else you might need to tell me. We'll pick back up tomorrow...oh, and you can have that phone call I promised," he said, knowing full well that Moses had no one to call since there were no phones in the Amish community.

Moses gripped the table ends firmly. His breath was still returning to normalcy. Unfortunately, his fear wasn't decreasing. All evidence pointed towards him as the suspect. Now he wasn't just a murder suspect; he was also the robbery suspect.

"In the meantime, I'm going to go have a long chat with the lovely Mrs. Fisher and see if she can confirm this as one of her jewels. You know, Moses, it might do you some good to admit to the crimes right now and plead for a lenient sentence," The detective said. He was standing near the door, holding its knob.

"I didn't do it," Moses said with a firmer voice. The detective shrugged.

"Well, then, have it your way," he said. He opened the door and motioned for Moses to stand and walk with him.

The doors of the single cell in the Little Valley police station slammed loudly. Silence soon descended in the room and began to punish Moses. He was left alone with his thoughts and fears. The fear was overwhelming. As he closed his eyes and lay on the cot, his pillow began to collect his silent tears. He was worried about his pregnant wife and his children. What would the community say about him? Momentarily, he was glad his parents were gone. This would kill his poor mother.

He rested his arm across his eyes, bent at the elbow and feeling heavy, soaking up some of the tears before they could run down his cheeks. His whole life looked very different at that moment. 'What am I going to do?' thought Moses, his heart temporarily replacing his fear with sadness.

Moses rolled over, dropped to his knees for the second time that day, and began to pray silently as the tears fell one by one onto the gray concrete floor.

Chapter Seven

Jude was surprised when Detective Stewart asked him to join him for the visit to Mr. Fisher's widow's home. The older detective intimidated him a lot and reminded him too much of what it was like working in LA. His bulky figure, thick accent and the condescending way he spoke were all part of the reasons Jude detested working with him. Stewart was a man who was used to getting things done his own way. He was a typical know-it-all, close-minded, and would never accept that someone else's work was better than his. Jude wasn't quite sure why the Nashville PD chose to send him out to investigate Derek's disappearance instead of someone more reasonable, especially considering the community.

The ride to the widow's house was silent and tense. It was an old house, recently repainted white, that stood apart from the rest of the town due to its elegance. The grass around the house was trimmed and neat. Brown-eyed susans and orange mums were blooming beautifully in the flowerbeds that sat under the large picture window next to the front porch.

"Well, here we are!" Stewart said, reaching for his cowboy hat that sat in the seat behind Jude. His thick Southern accent instantly made Jude cringe and roll his eyes. On the way to the front door, Jude walked carefully behind Stewart, allowing him to take the lead. Watching the cowboy hat in front of him, he was reminded of a dry joke Derek had made about cowboys. Jude couldn't recall the punchline, but it was definitely not something he would share with Stewart. This guy had no sense of humor - even for bad jokes - and he wasn't trying to give him any more reasons to not like him. 'Derek was an idiot anyway,' Jude thought, closing the door on that memory.

"I sure hope Mr. Fisher's widow is home. It sure looks dark in there," Detective Stewart continued saying. Jude mumbled a few inaudible words. He was ready for the long day to be over. Thinking back of the day's events, Stewart's arrival, discovering Derek's body, having to arrange for a coroner, and then with Moses' arrest and the family's visit, Jude desperately wanted to be sitting on his couch with a shot of whiskey in hand, calling it a day.

The detective banged on the door loudly, interrupting Jude's thoughts. Jude stepped away from the door. Nothing moved inside. The detective wiped the dust off a spot on the window and peered into the house.

"It's so dark in there. I'm not sure she's home," he stated, without turning to look at Jude.

"I saw her this morning heading out of the grocery store. I am almost a hundred percent sure that she would be home right now. Mr. Fisher's widow, Nancy, only ventures out in the mornings unless it's important," Jude responded. The detective turned to look at him. Curiosity furrowed the brows on his forehead.

"And how, boy, might you be so sure of that?" he asked, his eyes twinkled with mischief implying that Jude might have a personal relationship with the old woman past friendship. Jude was disgusted that he would even suggest it and refrained from reaching out and punching him in the mouth.

"Nancy is a kind woman. Sometimes, I stop by to check on her and see how she's doing. Without a child or close relatives to care for her, she could get lonely or might need something," Jude replied, obstinately.

"Well, aren't you the Good Samaritan," The detective said dismissively and returned to banging on the door. He took about half a second to relish in the fact that he had gotten a rise out of Jude. The deputy drove the detective crazy with his goody-two-shoes demeanor all the time. He couldn't stand fellow men of the law that were pushovers and people pleasers - nor did he feel like he could trust them one hundred percent.

Just as the two men were about to leave, there was a shuffling sound from the other side of the door. The door was pulled open slowly. Nancy's sleepy face peered out. Her hair was blowing out of the prayer *kapp* she had hurriedly slapped on her head. Stewart could see that time had bleached her hair white, and the hair around her temples was thinning.

"Who's there?" she asked, seemingly confused and a bit disoriented. Her face was puffy with sleep, and her eyes were slightly red. Detective Stewart cleared his throat. She looked at him and instinctively tightened her grip on the door, pushing it closed about an inch. Unfamiliarity registering on her face as she looked him up and down in one quick glance, taking in his plaid shirt, blue jeans and cowboy getup.

Jude noticed the confusion right away and stepped up. Nancy smiled at Jude.

"Good morning, Nancy. I am terribly sorry to interrupt your afternoon nap, but we do need to talk to you. Do you mind if we come in?" Jude said. All inhibitions gone, Nancy threw the door wide open.

"I hope everything is alright. These are troubling times in Little Valley," she said. The house was shrouded in deep darkness. Nancy shuffled to the windows and pushed the drapes wide open. Light flooded the living room. Pity instantaneously filled Jude's heart. Her house was covered in thick layers of dust. A once white silk magnolia flower in a glass vase, now dingy in color, sat on the coffee table sending a fine powder into the air around it as Mrs. Fisher's dress brushed up against it.

"Please sit down," she said. The plastic used to protect the couches from wear crackled loudly as the men sat down.

"Would you like anything? Water, tea, or coffee?" Nancy asked. Detective Stewart lifted his hand as if to wave the suggestion away.

"No, Mrs. Fisher. We are perfectly fine. This is not a social call. We will be out of your hair as soon as you answer our questions. Please sit down," the detective said. Nancy glanced suspiciously at Jude for reassurance. Jude gestured to the chair. She sat down hesitantly.

"Mrs. Fisher, I'm detective Stewart. I'm sure you must have heard that the county's sheriff, Derek McCall, was found dead today. I know that news travels fast out here," he started. Nancy's face crumpled in fear.

"Oh, yes, it was all everyone talked about in the store. In a small town like this, such news is big and terrifying. I've lived in this town for almost ten years now and I've never seen anything like this before. I never really liked Sheriff McCall but to think that someone could kill him so gruesomely and that the murderer is living amongst us is terrifying. I mean, who could he kill next? Me?" Nancy's nervousness was evident in her chatter. Jude could sense Stewart's impatience simmering inside him. The man lacked people skills. He was almost like Derek. Odd that he had never put that together before.

"Right, Mrs. Fisher, but we are actually here in connection with your stolen jewels. I understand that you were among the first victims when the robberies started. Could you tell me everything you remember from the incident?" Detective Stewart said.

Nancy cleared her throat. She took a moment to reflect. Her voice was brighter when she started speaking. Jude noticed the dark age spots on her hands. Freckles scattered across her cheeks. Wrinkles left deepened lines all over her face. He was amazed at how quickly she had aged just since her husband had passed away. He was instantly reminded of how his grandmother looked just months after they found his grandfather dead in his favorite big comfortable chair. Jude shook off the memories and returned his focus to the business at hand.

"Well, first, I am glad that the robbers didn't come at night or when I was around in the house. I would have died from a heart attack. They came while I was away, at the grocery store. When I got back from the store, I saw that the kitchen window was open. Someone had pried it open. Their shoes left dirty footprints on my house floors.

I was so terrified. I wished my sweet husband was still with me. If he were around, they wouldn't have dared robbed me.

I didn't need someone to tell me what had been stolen from me. I hoped they wouldn't find it, but they did. My entire jewelry box was empty. Everything inside it was gone. It felt like such a violation at the time, but eventually I was glad that burden had been lifted from me. I wasn't supposed to own those jewels, but I could never fully let go of them because they were handed down from so many generations on my mother's side of the family," Nancy said. She wrung her fingers nervously.

"What jewels did you have in the box?" Stewart asked directly.

"I had cut diamonds. The diamonds weren't set into rings or necklaces, which I always thought was strange... to just possess diamonds that you can't wear and show off to your friends. They were beautiful to look at, though. Shiny and just breathtakingly beautiful. Stephen, my husband, saw no harm in keeping them - in spite of his beliefs - because I couldn't wear them."

"So, you didn't see the robbers? Not even a glimpse?" Stewart asked. His voice was strained with the teensiest bit of disappointment.

"Nope. Not a glimpse. They were long gone by the time I got back. Detective, I do think they must have studied my routine for weeks. A few days before the robbery happened, I had this nagging feeling that I was being watched. It was really unsettling. Sometimes, I thought I could see a light from a parked car - or maybe it was a buggy lantern - in the far distance. It wasn't close enough to my house to tell for sure, or to get any details. You may think that this is the silly words of a deranged old woman, but I can assure you it isn't. I firmly believe the robbers cased the place to figure out when the house would be empty," she said. Jude swallowed back a smile from the widow's use of the slang phrase and made a note in his pad while Detective Stewart appeared disinterested.

"Is there anything else you can tell us about the figures or faces of the people watching you?" Jude asked tenderly. The detective shot him a deathly glare that said: *I'm in charge here. I ask the questions.* Jude lowered his face apologetically, and he instantly hated himself for that reaction.

"Oh no. Well, for one thing, buggies aren't exactly unique. Most people in town own one and they all look the same. Including dear Moses. By the way, I do not believe that Moses killed that man. There's no way. Moses doesn't have it in him," Nancy said. The detective didn't respond to that. Instead, he reached into his pockets and pulled out the envelope with the diamond. He showed it to Nancy who gasped with recognition.

"Do you think this might be one of your diamonds?" The detective asked. Nancy bobbed her head excitedly. The detective dropped it into her outreached hand, and she touched the beautiful cut stone gingerly.

"I think it must be one from my collection. It looks to be exactly the same size and beauty. Oh, it looks so familiar. I guess I didn't realize how much I truly did appreciate them. My mother gave them to me - did I tell you that? Oh, how I miss her so much. She never really forgave me for walking away from her and the Catholic church and embracing an Amish life. She was so disappointed when I told her that Stephen and I were moving so far away from her.

My mother never really understood why I fell in love with Stephen or why I was so willing to forsake everything for him. The truth is that

Stephen never demanded me to follow him. I wanted a change, and I wanted a new life with him. Oh, my dear mother - it had nothing to do with her, but she so regretted passing this heirloom to me ...and things were just never the same between us after that.... But I cherished it. It was the last thing she gave me. I wish I could have...." Nancy paused. The disapproving and impatient look that Detective Stewart shot her way made her stop mid-sentence. She glanced at Jude and his kind eyes encouraged her to speak again, but she now was ready for them to leave so she could return to her routine. It was almost time to start cooking dinner.

"I think it is one of my jewels - one of the ones stolen. Were you able to find the others? I had five, you know," she said.

"We found this one by itself in Moses' tool shed this morning. We are still trying to piece together the evidence and the details but as far as we can tell, Moses killed the sheriff and it had something to do with the robberies. So please, if there is anything you can remember to tell us, it would be greatly appreciated," Detective Stewart stood to leave. He adjusted his hat and Jude realized with disdain that he never removed it upon entering the house.

"I'm sorry, detective, but that's all I know. I've told you everything. Please can I keep this? It's the only thing I have left of my mother," she said. The detective shook his head, reaching out to retrieve it quickly from Nancy's closing fist.

"No, I'm afraid it's part of circumstantial evidence at the moment. We cannot let you have it just yet," he said, shoving his hand back into his pocket to retrieve the now crumpled envelope. He dropped the jewel back into the envelope and shoved it back into the pockets of his jeans, much to Nancy's dismay.

"Oh, please do be careful with it then. I've always taken such wonderful care whenever I am touching them. It may look and feel like a hard stone, but my mother always warned me that a diamond can break," said Nancy, looking the detective straight in the face and bracing herself for a not-so-nice response.

Instead, Detective Stewart thrust out his hand to invite Nancy for a handshake. She chose not to return the formality and instead turned toward the door to show the men out.

Caring less, Detective Stewart walked out of the house, his boots loud on the wood floors. "Thank you for your time, Mrs. Fisher. If you do remember any other detail you might have missed, please do not hesitate to come over to the sheriff's office. Anything useful to the case will be appreciated," he said.

Jude thanked Nancy personally after the detective had strode out.

"He's a mean one, that man. I don't trust him at all. Be careful around him," Nancy whispered to him, her nose pointed at the detective's direction. Jude chuckled.

"Thank you, Nancy," he said. Outside, the detective had already made it to the car, ready to get on with his day.

"What a waste of time. But I find it interesting that the same type of buggy Moses rode was spying on that old lady. She's not going to make a very strong witness though. Her story was all over the place and it's hard to believe details from such an old woman anyway. It's not going to hold up in the court. The defense will have it thrown out in seconds," he said angrily.

The Mustang rolled away from Nancy's house, and Jude looked back one last time. Nancy was standing by the window, watching them. Jude wondered if she would remember anything else.

Chapter Eight

Anna paced around the room angrily. She was lost in thought and wringing her hands. Sarah was sitting forward in the corner on an upholstered chair, crying quietly, her hands laying limp in her lap. The house was finally quiet. The family members and friends who had all come to offer their love and support were gone. The community was so wonderful about responding within hours with gifts of comfort. Lovingly made homemade bread, soups and baked goods filled the kitchen.

After sending Sarah's children off to stay with their cousins for some time, it was just Beth, Anna and Sarah left. Sarah was exhausted. She sat back on the chair, still crying, and blew her nose into a handkerchief.

Anna could not believe what had transpired over the last 8 hours. What started out as a normal beautiful day turned into a nightmare. Her precious daughter was in pain. Her beloved son-in-law was currently locked away. It seemed like the sky had fallen on her perfect life, breaking it into fragmented pieces.

"We have to do something. Moses didn't do this. I know it. I know my husband. *Maem*, you know you used to say that you know *Dat* better than anyone else? Well, I know Moses better than anybody," Sarah said tearfully. This was the first time she had spoken in hours, and in spite of the tears, her voice was filled with a mix of conviction and desperation.

Beth rushed and knelt by her side. "We know, sweetie, but what can we do? Sarah, you need to rest. You've been crying all day. Look, you are so exhausted. Your face is swollen. Think of your babies. They need their mother to be rested and strong," Beth said, gently placing her arm around Sarah, wishing she could protect her from all of this.

"How can you expect me to rest?! Everything is not alright. My life has been completely turned upside down!" Sarah said hysterically. She turned to Anna, "You know Moses, *Maem*! You've always said that he is your favorite son-in-law. You know that he couldn't have done this!" Anna sat down beside her daughter. She held both her hands between hers as she had always done when she was a little girl. She wanted nothing more than to fix this for her.

"Sarah, your aunt Beth speaks good truth. Believe me, I know that Moses didn't do this. I do believe he would never hurt anyone, and as long as I am alive, I will never stop fighting for him and for you. Let me think - I will figure out some way to help Moses. Now, you go lay down and rest. It's been a very long day, and it's important that you get some rest for the sake of your baby, do you hear me?" Anna said, kissing Sarah's forehead.

Sarah nodded her head. Beth helped her stand up. She wobbled towards her bedroom. Beth supported her with a strong arm around her waist as she walked.

Anna sat on the couch; her head was running in circles. There was so much to think about and do. How could she possibly help her daughter? If Moses' name was not cleared soon, it would drastically affect everything they had spent their entire lifetime building.

Beth returned to the living room. She found Anna on the couch, deep in thought. It didn't take her twin bond to see the worry on Anna's face, and

Beth was feeling it too.

"Ok, Sarah is resting. She is tucked in bed, she drifted off fast asleep almost right away, and the children are comfortable and fine to stay at Cousin Rachel's house," Beth said. Anna thanked her sister, relieved that she could now switch focus to figuring out how to get Moses out of this mess.

"It's just for one night though. What will happen when she wakes up tomorrow and Moses is still in jail, accused of murder? And the day after? Beth, we need to do something," Anna said. She stood up from the couch, again pacing up and down the room. Their husbands were fending for themselves at home. They were also trying to find out what they could about Moses' case earlier that day, but no one knew anything new.

The detective from Nashville was not a nice man. He wouldn't offer any help or comfort despite all the efforts from the men in the community, including the bishop. He insisted that Moses would remain in custody until he appeared in court for the initial hearing within the next 48 hours - or maybe even not until early next week considering the weekend.

No one was sure when her son-in-law's name would be cleared, and it was becoming excruciatingly clear that life would not remain the same for them regardless. Already, Moses' reputation had been tarnished. It was rumored that some people in the community actually did believe that he killed the sheriff. Anna was heartbroken when she got wind of the snide comments made about her family.

"What can we do, Anna? You heard what the men said. They said that we can't do anything more," Beth said. Anna abruptly stopped pacing. She met eyes with Beth, with the familiar stubborn determined look that Beth recognized immediately. Beth knew what that look meant, and she braced herself for what Anna was about to suggest.

"Yes, we can. We can speak to Jude. We can convince him to continue digging into the investigation. We can tell him that Moses could never hurt anyone. We can do our own investigation if we have to," Anna said. Her voice was becoming very hostile and loud. Beth felt excitement start to brew inside her, but she also knew that she should probably be the voice of reason.

"Anna, I get that you are upset about what happened, but I think we could get in a lot of trouble if we start poking our nose into the case. I don't want to step into danger, nor do I want to make things worse for Moses. Perhaps we need to get some rest and sleep on it. Tomorrow, we can think about this with clearer minds," Beth said. Anna was frustrated and she was simply not going to be talked out of this. She saw no other solution but to try to fix things themselves, and time was of the essence. Plus, she could never sleep with her mind just turning like it was.

Beth saw that she wasn't' getting anywhere, so she continued, "The evidence against Moses is overwhelming. You heard the detective yourself. As far as their law is concerned, he killed the sheriff."

Anna hurried to sit beside her. "You and I both know that Moses is being framed. We have to find out who is framing him. Perhaps it will lead us to the real killer. Please, Beth, you know I wouldn't ask you to help me with this if it wasn't so important. It's our family name that's on the line. We will forever be hitched to Moses. If this case against him sticks, it will affect us all. Please, Beth, say you'll help me," Anna begged.

Beth had never been able to say no to her sister. Not even as a child and certainly not as an adult. After a short moment of hesitation, she nodded her head and reached out to hold Anna's hand.

"If it'll make you feel better. We can try. But I'm warning you, I don't have a lot of faith that this will work," Beth said.

Anna hugged her. "Worry ends where faith begins, little sister," Anna whispered into her hair. She pulled back, and holding hands, the identical twins sat face to face, looking deep into each other's eyes. "We can do this," they uttered quietly, in unison.

Chapter Nine

T he farmers market buzzed with activity. The sisters had been up so late devising their plan for their investigation that they almost skipped out on their booth that day. Anna and Beth had worked so hard on preparing their baked goods, and Beth insisted they continue with their business. It was the perfect way to clear their minds from all the heavy thinking for a few hours. Beth reminded Anna of one of their favorite Amish proverbs, *'Greet the dawn with enthusiasm and you may expect satisfaction at sunset.'* This could be very fitting for the day that lie ahead.

Tourists flooded the farmers market, many of them looking to purchase Amish made products. Anna watched them frantically and couldn't help but wonder if one of them was the killer. Little Valley had always been safe for its residents. The Amish and the English residents knew better than to resort to violence. Nonviolence runs in the blood of Amish residents so clearly, Anna believed that the killer must be an outsider. What if the sheriff had gotten into a brawl with someone? What if the fight had resulted in his death? As hard as she tried, she wasn't able to keep the questions in her mind at bay.

The women were still searching for some clarity on exactly how to get started on their planned investigation. The men had tried to speak to Moses the day before, but the detective wouldn't let them. If only they could talk to Moses and ask him questions, maybe he would know what to tell them.

Anna and Beth had paid a visit to the tool shed in the middle of the night, hoping to be able to inconspicuously look around inside. They were convinced that they would find something in that shed that would exonerate Moses. But they found that the detective had locked it and wrapped police tape around it, further sealing the door. There was no way to get in without breaking the lock - and the tape. The sisters agreed that it wouldn't look good for Moses if they were caught trying to break in, or for themselves if they left fingerprints behind.

While Beth worked tirelessly, Anna continued to watch the shoppers. Suddenly, she had an uncomfortable feeling followed by a terrible realization. She realized she had grown quite distrustful of her fellow townsmen, just in the last 24 hours. The killer was still amongst them, possibly roaming around in plain sight right now. He could be any of these people, have a smile on his face, shaking the hands of the very people he might kill next. The thought sent a shiver down her spine. She was living in the same town as a killer. Little Valley was the precious town and the place she called home, but it now seemed tainted with dark evil.

"Good luck today, Mrs. Williamsburg," Anna heard someone speak behind her. Anna turned around to see Thomas. Anna smiled at him. He was mistaken. Beth was Mrs. Williamsburg, not Anna. Even though they had lived in the town all their lives, the community still couldn't tell the difference between her and Beth at times.

"Oh, thank you, Thomas," Beth said. Sarah had told her about Moses' kindness towards the man. When his coffee shop was starting to struggle, Moses took him in, gave him a part-time job to supplement his income, and was helping him get back on his feet. Thomas had always been thankful for the job.

Suddenly, Beth remembered that Thomas was the one who found the sheriff's body. Maybe Thomas knew something that could help her and Anna with their investigative efforts. She would be lying if she said that she worried a tiny bit that Moses might not have been the man he portrayed to the community and family, and she desperately wanted to get to the bottom of all of this to protect her sister and niece.

Beth summoned up the courage to ask, "Thomas, can I ask you a question? I know that you worked closely with Moses and that you were there yesterday when... you know... everything happened. We are just so upset about everything and really want to do something. Maybe you can help... maybe there is something that we don't know. Did you notice anything odd about Moses yesterday or the way he has been acting lately?"

Thomas' cheeks became flushed. His eyes started to shift. It was clear he wished he hadn't started a conversation in the first place.

"Mrs. Williamsburg, I'm so sorry about everything that is happening. I'm afraid I don't know anything more than I told the cops already. I really didn't notice anything odd with Moses. There was a little bit of tension between him and me before I headed out to the tool shed because... well, I wasn't really a dedicated employee. I barely showed up to work, and it annoyed Moses... I mean, with good reason. I get it. Moses has always been kind to me, though. He understood that I was struggling with some... stuff... some things happening in my life. Moses offered to help, even when I didn't deserve it. He's a good man. So, do I think he did this? No, I don't," he said.

Beth was overwhelmed. It was uncommon to start such a brash conversation with a man. Paranoia kicked in, and Beth felt like everyone was watching their interaction. She lowered her eyes.

Thomas' response also made Beth feel ashamed of her doubts about Moses. Of course, Moses was a good man. He couldn't have murdered the sheriff.

As if Anna felt Beth's emotions, she called out just in time, "Beth! I need you over here!" Beth muttered thanks to Thomas for the conversation, although he had already turned his back and was walking briskly away, and she hurried back to her sister.

Beth took one glimpse back and watched Thomas disappear among the crowd. Something was not adding up. She could feel it in her soul. Restless, she began to take inventory and count the pastries that remained on the table that sat at the front of the booth. She and Anna needed to wrap things up and be on their way. They were losing time.

Chapter Ten

Anna held onto Beth's hand tightly. Beth was squirming. She was struggling to calm her nerves. She was worried that her community might think it was wrong for the women to be seen in the company of men, unaccompanied. Especially a man who was not their relative. But Anna was determined to do what it took to free her son-in-law. She pulled Beth forward until they reached Jude's table. Thankfully, he was sitting in a corner booth, near the back of the diner, somewhat hidden from the full view of the other tables. The sisters squeezed themselves into the free space in the booth across from the deputy.

The diner was owned by an Englisher named Jessica. Jessica was a pretty woman in her mid-thirties, with short red-hair and a friendly smile. Anna and Beth had visited the diner on occasion with their families, and she was always welcoming and kind. Jessica would often return the business by purchasing their famous baked goods on the weekends, and sometimes you would find their cookies and muffins beautifully displayed on the counter under a glass dome. Today was one of those days since Jessica had been shopping at the farmers market earlier that morning. When the ladies entered the diner, Jessica was in the back, most likely busy preparing food for dinner or washing dishes from lunch.

"Well, hello, again you two," Jude greeted cheerfully. He was one of the few in town that could quickly tell the twins apart, but he never let on that he could.

Anna smiled at him, and responded "Good afternoon, Deputy Tyman." Beth's eyes were cast down, her hands gripping her thighs in an effort to keep them still.

"We've been through this... please, call me Jude," the deputy responded, finishing the last bite of his club sandwich and wiping his mouth with the paper napkin that was previously placed politely on his lap.

Beth's eyes darted around the diner, as though searching for anyone that would identify them, but Anna's gaze met Jude's confidently.

"Hi, Jude. We are sorry to interrupt your lunch, but we would love a minute of your time if you don't mind," Anna started. Dipping a french fry in ketchup, Jude chewed and swallowed, then he deliberately folded his napkin, wiped the corners of his mouth, and dropped it on the table. The delayed response did not go unnoticed.

"We wanted to talk to you about Moses," Anna continued. Jude's face clouded.

"You know that I am not at liberty to discuss the case with you ...or anyone for that matter," Jude whispered, his tone was conspiratorial. It made Anna automatically lower her own voice.

"I know you can't, but I think you know that Moses is innocent. You know that the evidence against him is fabricated. Please, we need your help. We just want to prove his innocence. Surely there is something that can be done... surely you can help us," Anna persisted. Jude shook his head.

"The detective is so focused on nailing Moses with this. I agree that I don't think he killed Sheriff McCall. But what can I do?" Jude said. Anna leaned forward, her eyes were narrowed and intense.

"You can tell me anything that can help me prove his innocence. Please, anything. What do you know? Why is the detective so set on charging him if he didn't do it? Is it because he is from the Amish community? And why would anyone want the sheriff dead?" she pummeled the deputy with questions, still at tone just above a whisper. Jude hesitated. He shook his head again.

He leaned forward toward the sisters, elbows resting on the table and fingers interlaced. "Well, all I can tell you is that.... Detective McCall was in the middle of solving the robbery cases going on in this town. You know how rough around the edges the sheriff was. And he was very private about the work he was doing - he hardly shared it with me, which was also odd since we always worked on everything together. My suspicion is that he was very close to solving the case, so the robbers murdered him. We found incriminating stolen objects in Moses' tool shed. I mean, apart from the body, we also found incriminating objects there. That suggests that Moses was behind the robberies and he killed the sheriff because he got too close," Jude said.

Beth gasped loudly, slapping her hands across her mouth. Anna grabbed her hand again without taking her eyes off of the deputy sitting across from her. "But Moses isn't a robber. He would never do that," Anna said.

Jude shook his head sadly and sat back. "I know... but it's very hard to prove that in court when there is so much evidence pointing to him. Unless you can prove that Moses isn't the killer and thief, he is gonna be charged with both crimes. And believe me," Jude continued, "you do not want this mess to spiral into a trial. They're usually messy and may go against the tenets of your faith. I'm so sorry, ladies, but that is all I know. I wish I could help you but there isn't anything I can do," Jude said, rising from his seat and reaching for his wallet. He dropped two ten-dollar bills on the table.

"I wish I had better news, I really do. Take care of yourselves," Jude said as he turned to leave.

Anna thanked him for his time, wished him the same, and watched him walk away.

Jessica walked up to their table bearing a kettle and some coffee mugs.

"You two look like you could use some of my homemade hot chocolate. It's so good to see you here! How are you holding up? I heard the terrible news and I have been thinking about y'all. I hope you're doing okay." Jessica said, thoughtfully. She flashed them a warm smile. She had pale milky skin, rosy cheeks, and long lashes that seemed to curl upwards- thick with mascara. Her eyes were a beautiful deep green, and they had the prettiest shape to them.

"Thank you, Jessica," Beth said, accepting her own mug. Jessica slipped into the space that Jude had just vacated from and poured the fragrant hot chocolate for the sisters.

"I was so sorry to hear about your son-in-law. Moses is a kind man. He would never hurt someone. Besides, Derek was a horrible man. I'm sorry to say this but most people didn't like him at all. He crossed a lot of people. Just the other day, he was in here nearly fighting with Samuel Graber. Apparently, they had a bet of some sort or something, and Sammy won but Derek refused to pay up. It went from zero to sixty super fast. I had to ask them to leave... and basically take it outside. I swear they were acting like children," Jessica spoke, getting frustrated just remembering it.

The twins had their full attention on her, sitting forward and listening for every little detail in her story. Anna was thrilled with the new information. Suddenly, she had a potential lead. Ideas were starting to form in her mind. Jessica was right. Derek had not been a good person. For most people in town, he was a despicable man. She was reminded that several people had reason to harm him. All she had to do was figure out the people that wanted to harm him and start eliminating people, one by one.

"Please tell me more about this fight with Mr. Graber," Anna said. She knew about Samuel - he was an Englisher who was well-known around town for his drinking and gambling. He even opened up a gambling house in town, much to her community's dismay. At first, the men of Little Valley didn't think it would grow to much, but as more Amish men were shunned from their community after becoming gamblers, that changed. The men of the community became anxious to end the business. Samuel was very uncooperative. He boasted that he had lived in Little Valley for a very long time and had the right to conduct business as much as everyone else. Anna couldn't remember where things had ended with that...

"Oh, you know how short-tempered those two men were. I think Derek owed a couple hundred bucks and wasn't willing to pay up. He actually tried to use his position as the sheriff to intimidate Samuel, but it didn't work. They literally threw hands... erm, I mean, they fought on the street right outside the diner. It was late, so thankfully there weren't many people dining here, but they all gathered at the doors and windows to watch and listen to them brawl outside. Now, ladies, I wouldn't be at all surprised if Samuel knows a thing or two about what happened to Derek. I can't believe that they think it was Moses," Jessica said, shaking her head.

Anna squeezed Beth's hand under the table, trying to hide her excitement. This felt like it could be something significant. But she couldn't help but wonder why the detective hadn't pursued Samuel?

"Thank you, Jessica. You have no idea how much this means to us," she said, rising. She touched Jessica's hand lightly, noticing for the first time that she had a small heart tattooed on her right ring finger, just above the middle knuckle. "And thank you for the delicious hot chocolate, too," Beth chimed in, her nerves settled since Jude had left.

"My pleasure, ladies. Anything I can do to help, please let me know. And don't be strangers! I love visiting with you!" she said, once again showing her perfectly straight white teeth. Anna made promises of returning as she and Beth headed out of the diner.

The twins didn't have to utter a word or even make eye contact to know exactly where their next stop would be. Beth's emotions were torn between dread and excitement.

Chapter Eleven

M oses heard the jangle of the jail keys and the heavy footprints of feet approaching. His stomach tightened into twisted knots. The sound of the old heavy door terrified Moses. He definitely appreciated the idea of the doors opening, but whenever the door banged, Moses feared that it would be a sound he would be forced to hear the rest of his life. He was due to appear in court for his initial hearing on Monday, and his fear intensified with each passing hour.

A young, uniformed officer he didn't know appeared, swinging the keys as he approached the door leading to the jail room. Moses had heard his voice earlier that day as he was greeted by the detective. Detective Stewart had shown the young officer around while Moses was lying on the bottom bunk, eyes closed in rest, so this was the first time Moses was actually seeing the kid's pimply face.

"Howdy," said the kid with an accent as thick as molasses. The young officer was assigned as temporary help to watch over Moses during the weekend. It was a cushy job - he basically got to sit in the office with his feet propped up and look at his phone. Moses hardly even made a noise. The officer was told that Moses was arrested for murder, and he would admit that even he was shocked to hear it.

Moses was grateful for the solitude, but the quiet forced him to think about his own life. He wondered what would happen to his family if he was found guilty of murder. Sarah was still very pregnant and fragile. How would she survive without him? How would his children survive without him? The community would probably take care of them, but it would not be the same. And the community would forever have the stigma of once living with a murderer in their midst. Shame – unbridled, pure and fiery – descended on Moses as he thought about it, even though he was completely innocent.

"You're awake. You have a visitor - approved by the detective," he said. Moses rose from the cot he had been sitting on and stretched. Without responding and eyes cast down, Moses waited for the door to slide open. Untended, Moses' clothes were starting to look dingy and dirty.

The officer handcuffed Moses. He ran through a few quick instructions - laying out consequences for disobeying any rules - and asked Moses if he understood. When Moses nodded, he took his arm to lead him to the front office where he had set up two chairs facing each other a few feet apart.

Sarah sat in one of the chairs, waiting for him. She was sitting straight, with her hands resting on her rotund stomach. Moses' heart ached painfully at the sight of his wife in such an environment. The beige dress she wore flowed downwards and covered the ground near it. Her *kapp* was secured tightly on her head. Moses took a deep breath before sitting across from her.

Sarah wanted to jump up and hug him and never let go, but she was instructed that they would not be allowed to touch... just talk... and only for a few minutes. The detective prided himself on allowing Moses to meet Sarah outside of the cell... after all, he could have insisted that Sarah see Moses sitting behind the bars instead, but Sarah's father, Eli, was able to convince the detective otherwise with a few folded bills pressed into his hand.

"Are you okay? Are they treating you right? Do you need anything?" Sarah asked, with a throat full of choked tears. She was saddened at seeing Moses like this. The strong, confident and joyful man she married looked older and lacking spirit or hope. She remembered the day he proposed to her. Most girls would have been absolutely thrilled by the prospect of marrying the love of her life. Not Sarah. She started panicking. She asked questions about how they would survive. Moses took her in his arms, rubbing her back and reassuring her that they would make a perfect couple and that everything would be alright. Her heart ached to have that man back home with her right now.

Moses suddenly became aware of what Sarah may be seeing and tried to fake some confidence and optimism for her sake. He was the man of the house after all and there was a need for him to be strong for his family. But Moses also knew that he had never been successful at pretending with Sarah. She saw right through him. She had seen right through him when the business struggled a few years ago – before the tourists started flooding into their town. He had tried to withhold the truth and reassure her that business was thriving, but there was no fooling her. Much to Moses' relief, though, Sarah didn't judge him for struggling as a businessman. Instead, she rolled up her sleeves and helped him formulate plans to save their business. That is when Moses realized that it is true what they say, 'behind every successful man is a strong woman.' Sarah was the strong woman that he planned to spend the rest of his life with, provide for her, and love her dearly. This was not going to get in the way of that plan. Surely the truth would be exposed, and Moses would be set free.

"I am fine, Sarah. *Gotte* is with me. I have no doubt that this big mistake will be behind us in just a matter of time," Moses said, convincingly.

Sarah blinked away her tears. "That's why I'm here. I mean, of course, I needed to see you - I miss you so much. I've never even spent one night away from you since we married. ...I need to talk to you. I know you didn't do this. But I have to ask you... do you know who killed Derek and left him in your tool shed? Do you have any ideas?" she asked, her warm chestnut eyes were pleading for answers.

The officer cleared his throat, and Moses wasn't sure if it was on purpose. Moses looked over and saw that the young man was again lost in his phone. Moses wasn't sure if he was listening or if it even mattered. He knew that Sarah needed to hear something, and he was searching for the right answer.

Moses looked back at Sarah and met her gaze. "I'm so sorry, Sarah, but I just don't know. The sheriff and I weren't exactly the best of friends but there wasn't any bad blood between us either. I have thought about a million times, but I have no idea who could have killed him in such a brutal way. I don't even know how or why they used my shed to do this fateful deed," Moses replied.

Sarah listened, disappointed. She yearned to just reach out and hold her husband's hand.

"Do you think we should hire a lawyer?" Sarah asked, not knowing the first thing about the legal process.

"I will be assigned a state defense attorney. I think I will meet him on Monday at my initial hearing in Lewisburg. Let's just wait and see what happens next. Let's just have faith that this will be over soon, the killer will be found, and my name will be cleared."

"Whatever you say, I will agree with, dear. You are my husband. I love you deeply. I will organize a prayer group right away and send up prayers for your release. And I'll assure the children that you will be back home with us soon. Thomas has offered to run the store for you while you are away" Sarah said, her voice breaking in the last words. She couldn't hold the tears back any longer. She reached into her pockets to pull out a handkerchief just as the officer said loudly, "Ok, time's up."

Moses, searching for something inspirational to say before he was taken back to his temporary home, managed to utter Sarah's name as she was leaving. She stopped and turned around. Moses said, "Remember...no winter lasts forever." She replied, "...and no spring skips its turn."

They exchanged smiles through their tears as hope was once again restored.

Chapter Twelve

A cooling wind pushed in through the window, ruffling the dirty curtains. The room that doubled as a bar reeked of alcohol, smoke and body odor. Beth and Anna held their dresses tight just below the waist in an effort to keep any particle from this filth on the floor from clinging to them.

"*Ach du lieva*, the stench!" Beth muttered. Anna squeezed her hand reassuringly. Her eyes were focused and narrowed in on Samuel. She was there to determine if Samuel killed Derek. 'He definitely could have killed him,' Anna thought to herself, as she took in the scene in front of her.

Samuel was a large man, unkempt and rough looking. The button-down plaid shirt he wore looked worn thin, dirty and too small for his shape. He sat at a worn-out poker table with two English women, scantily dressed, makeup smeared, and three half-drunk obnoxious men. Playing cards were laid out in front of each player and in the center of the table among plastic poker chips. One man and one woman each held a few cards in their hands.

Anna pushed her fear aside and said a quiet quick prayer to summon courage to approach the table. When did her beloved Little Valley become the den of such a frivolous, disgusting collective? It was no wonder the men of the community were clamoring for the business to be shut down. This place was disgusting.

"Samuel?" Anna asked, when she approached the table. The man looked up from the cards he was holding. Samuel squinted his eyes as if he were trying to see them better. He did not know these ladies, but he knew they didn't belong there.

"I'm sorry ladies but this house is off-limits to lady folks like you. I don't want the drama of having to explain to the rest of your kinfolk how you lost all your money," Samuel mumbled. Did he really think she would even for a second want to play one of these games? Or was he trying to insult them? Anna wasn't sure, but she didn't care. Either way, she had a mission to accomplish.

"We're not here for a game or to gamble," Beth said, with disgust. Samuel chuckled.

"Good because you wouldn't have gotten any. Do your husbands know where you are right now?" Samuel continued. "I'm folding," he said, as he lay his cards down in front of him. The woman with the cards left in her hand let out a loud bellow, stood up roughly, sending her chair backwards, and proceeded to lay forward on the table. Her cards were forgotten, and her arms surrounded the pile of chips as she proceeded to drag them toward her.

Samuel swiveled on his chair to face the women and stood. He was much taller than Anna had remembered. Of course, she had only seen him in passing on the streets and at the market, but standing right in front of him now, she suddenly felt very small.

Wanting to get right to the point, Anna said, "We are actually here to talk to you about Sheriff McCall," Anna said.

Samuel's face showed no emotion, as he looked down at her, waiting for her to go on.

"We know that you fought with him days before he disappeared..." Anna continued.

Samuel's demeanor changed and he walked past the sisters, towards the bar. "Ah, so I see why you're here. I should've known. One of your kind was accused of Derek's murder and you're trying to pin it on me now. Since when did the two of you become detectives? You'd better be careful; this could be a pretty dangerous game you're playing."

Beth began to wring her hands. She couldn't bear to even look at Samuel. She was fighting the urge to grab Anna's arm and run out the door. Samuel was right - they were way in over their heads. What were they thinking?

Anna, on the other hand, sounded unphased and continued as if Samuel didn't scare her at all. "We've spoken to several other people that were present during the fight. You threatened to kill Derek if he didn't pay back what he owed. Now, what exactly do you think the police will do with that kind of information?" Anna asked. Samuel stepped forward with a voracious force that made Anna back away.

"You really think the police will believe a mere threat spoken out of anger over the mountain of evidence they have against the guy who owns the hardware store? You must be delusional. Yes, I fought with Derek a few days before he disappeared. Yes, it was all a coincidence. No, I did not kill him," Samuel said angrily.

Like Beth, Anna wanted to run, but this was the only way to clear Moses' name. "So, then I guess you won't mind telling me where you were on the night of the murder?" she asked.

Samuel shrugged. "I'll tell you what," Samuel leaned in close to Anna's face. She hid her overwhelming feeling of disgust when the smell of alcohol and smoke hit her like a ton of bricks. "I'll tell you where I was that night when you show me your badge," Samuel finished with a look of amusement.

Anna felt her hopes slipping. She bounced back on the soles of her feet. It was time to go.

Her mind was racing. Maybe Samuel was too drunk and distracted in life to carry out such precise killing and the framing of Moses in such a particular manner. Besides, killing the detective and framing Moses seemed intertwined. Even if Samuel had a reason to kill Derek, what was his reason for framing Moses? And how could he possibly get into the toolshed? Nothing made sense. Anna was becoming increasingly frustrated.

Samuel was still staring at her, so Anna dared to ask one more question, "Well, is there anything that you can tell us about the sheriff that could help clear my son-in-law's name?" she asked desperately, hoping for some hint of sympathy from this horrible man.

Samuel stepped back and sat down on a bar stool. He shook his head. "All I can say is that man was not as clean as everyone thinks he was. He was as shady as they come. I don't know details exactly, but I know shade when I see it. The guy would come in here and gamble without paying up what he lost. He was such a jerk, and I'm glad he is dead and out of my way," Samuel said.

Anna looked around the room. "How many people did he owe money?" she asked. Suddenly all the men looked suspicious. She wondered if there was anyone amongst them right now who could harm the sheriff.

"A lot of them... and no, before you ask, no one in here killed that man... no matter how furious we were with him. What do you think this is? A congregation of murderers?" Samuel said, fire flashing across his eyes.

Anna had heard and seen enough, and Beth was already halfway to the door. "Oh no, of course not. Thank you so much for your time, Samuel," she said.

Samuel waved them off as if he were swatting at an annoying housefly. He turned back to the bar and motioned for the bartender to pour him a drink.

Beth was holding the door open for Anna as she approached. She couldn't wait for the two of them to get away from this place and try to decipher what all of this new information meant to their investigation.

Chapter Thirteen

J ude's house was certainly not his dream house, but it would have to
work for now. Its small size often made him feel claustrophobic - he
never understood how he could get the word "cozy" to apply to his home.

The storm door banged in response to a loud knock. He sighed,
dropped the book he had been reading, and stood, feeling sore muscles as
he moved. Pulling it open, he was shocked to see the old twins from the
Amish community on his doorstep. Why wouldn't these women let him
rest? He was just the county's deputy and didn't have the clearance to
discuss the case with them.

"Dear Lord, what are you doing here? It's almost dusk," he said, peering
above their heads at the darkening sky. Jude recognized Anna as the one
who seemed to do most of the talking. He liked how active she still was
despite her age. Not that the other twin, Beth, wasn't active enough but
she lacked the confidence her sister had and often avoided eye contact. Her
eyes were shifted down toward her chest as her sister spoke. It was little tells
like this that proved to be the easiest way to distinguish which twin was
which.

"Please let us in, Jude," Anna said, remembering that he asked them to call him Jude earlier that day at the diner. "We want to talk to you about a potential angle to the case that we feel could exonerate Moses."

Jude sighed and pulled the door open. The women filed in. They stamped their feet hard on the welcome mat, releasing the sand, stones, and browned grass that was stuck underneath their shoes. Jude pointed them to the couch. They sat down carefully and close to each other.

"Do you need anything?" he asked. They shook their heads and thanked him for the offer.

Jude fell into the chair and crossed his legs. "So, what did you want to talk to me about?" he asked.

The ladies exchanged glances before Anna decided to speak for them, again.

"You are probably tired of hearing this from us, but we are one hundred percent sure that Moses didn't kill that man. So, we started asking around town, trying to find out who did. Did you know that Derek was not actually a very popular sheriff... meaning, a lot of people really didn't like him," she said inquisitively.

"You shouldn't do that. You need to leave this case for the police to figure out. You could be in way over your heads," Jude said. 'These women are out playing detective when they have probably never even witnessed a hint of violence or law-breaking in their entire lives,' Jude thought, shaking his head.

"My son-in-law is in jail right now. We don't even know if the judge will be lenient enough to grant bail. So yes, we are taking matters into our own hands. It's not like we have a choice," Anna snapped ...and paused. When Jude didn't respond, she continued.

"We found out that Derek wasn't exactly liked in this town. So many people had so many reasons to hurt him. What if one of them did? Look at Samuel Graber for instance.... he fought with Derek and...." She paused when Jude gestured to her. He knew about the fight. Samuel and Derek were never close. It was not a surprise that the fight happened.

"A fight doesn't prove anything, Ma'am. It doesn't hold up in court next to circumstantial evidence," he said.

Anna's face fell. "All we are asking for is your help. We need help. There must be something you can tell us. Since you are not allowed to investigate this case, maybe we can. We need to do something to save Moses," Beth pleaded, before turning to look back at Anna.

Jude exhaled noisily. "Alright, alright... Stewart is going to kill me... but we found a piece of paper with an address on it. We haven't checked it out because Stewart doesn't think it's worth his time... and he is just set on charging Moses anyway... but that address feels strangely familiar. Have you ever heard of 1507 Peace Lane?" he asked.

The twins stared at each other, confused but excited.

"I don't know what the address has to do with anything, but it could be worth looking into," He said hurriedly. "I would never forgive myself if something happened though, so promise me that you'll leave right away and head straight to the sheriff's office if you find anything at all that might be dangerous."

The girls thanked him for his help and bounded out of Jude's house with spirited energy. He smiled as he watched their reactions. It crossed his mind that the old women may be experiencing more excitement than they've ever had in their life. Why deny them that? He picked up his book, pushing the guilty conscience that plagued him to the back of his mind.

Chapter Fourteen

Thomas struggled with the heavy secret that threatened to burst out of him. He would never forget the sight of the bloodied body he found in the tool shed. Since then, he had not been able to sleep well at night. When the police asked questions, Thomas hoped they couldn't see through the lies. He wanted to tell them that the keys to the shed had been stolen from him the previous day when he went into Samuel's bar for a drink and a game, but he was ashamed of the truth coming out. He couldn't bear revealing that he was one of the Amish men who patronized Samuel Graber's unholy joint. Neither could he reveal that gambling was part of the reason his business was nearly destroyed.

Pity for Moses filled him, almost paralyzing him. Moses saw through him. When Thomas asked for help, Moses refused until he knew the cause of his money troubles. Thomas eventually opened up about his gambling problems, but Moses had already suspected and needed Thomas' confirmation as a sign of trust. And now, Thomas carried so much guilt for Moses' arrest.

He was grateful that Moses didn't reveal his secret to the entire community. He kept quiet about the issue and tried to help Thomas the best way he could, but now, he was sure that everything would come into the light. And how could Thomas blame Moses if it did? Moses had always been there for him and as far as he knew, his secrets still remained quiet.

A few nights before Derek was found, Thomas lost the set of keys that included his house key. On that set was also the extra key to the shop and tool shed that Moses graciously entrusted to him. Thomas spent the drunken night searching around for it. When he couldn't find it in Samuel's bar, he headed to the shop. He thought perhaps he must have left it absentmindedly somewhere around the shop.

That night, he saw some figures in the dark - two men - arguing at the corner located just a block down from the store. Although he had heard two voices, only one of the figures came into view, and it was Derek.

"Hey, Derek!" Thomas called out drunkenly. Derek seemed agitated that night. He glanced around near the bushes anxiously. Thomas neared him and reached out for a friendly handshake greeting. Derek ignored it.

"Man, are you wasted..." Derek said, with disgust. Thomas and Derek were buddies at Samuel's bar. They were drinking buddies, really. He knew that Derek drank a lot, too, so Thomas was taken aback with the rude greeting. On what moral ground could Derek stand to judge Thomas? It wasn't surprising that the bishop had recently chastised Thomas for his reckless behavior, but he didn't need to be scolded by Derek, too. Derek's drinking was just as bad, if not worse than his, Thomas thought sulkily.

"What are you doing out here so late at night?" Derek asked. Thomas stumbled around, nearly tripping. Derek reached out to catch him before he fell.

"I could ask you the same thing..." Thomas said defensively. Derek steadied him on his feet.

"I am on night patrol. Jude's out sick.," he replied.

Thomas raised his eyebrows slightly. "Is that so? Well, I'm just looking for my keys. I must have dropped them somewhere" he said, trying to pull it together after realizing if Derek was on the job, he could potentially book him for being intoxicated.

"Did you check your pockets?" Derek paused, waiting for Thomas' response.

"Of course, I did," Thomas slurred.

"Well, it's dark out here and everything is closed, so you're not going to find them tonight. It's too late. Let's get you home," he said. Derek led him to his car. It was the second time Thomas had ever ridden in a car. The first time was during his *Rumspringa*. Thomas wondered if he would even remember this ride tomorrow.

Once at Thomas' home, Derek picked the lock until the door opened. He pulled Thomas into the room and pushed him onto his couch. Derek took off, banging the door shut, and Thomas proceeded to pass out.

Thomas slept through the next day and on the second day when he returned, he found Derek's body in the tool shed.

Even in the haze of his mind, he could sense that something had been up with Derek that night. Who had he been arguing with? He heard voices but only saw Derek because he stormed out of the bushes. Or perhaps, he was hallucinating and remembering things that didn't really happen.

Thomas didn't tell the police about that night because he was embarrassed and wasn't even one hundred percent sure of what he saw and remembered. The only thing he knew for sure was that he was very drunk that night. His mind could have fabricated everything else.

So, why did he feel so guilty? And how could he explain the body found in the locked tool shed?

Thomas had decided it was time to talk to Moses and tell him what he knew. As he sat in the sheriff's office, waiting to visit Moses, he pushed back the fear that accompanied opening up to him about that night. Moses would be disappointed in him for not speaking up sooner.

Jude led Thomas through the kitchen into the room with the cell. There was a chair sitting on this side of the bars. Moses was standing on the other side. His beard was disheveled. His eyes were bloodshot. His body was feeling sore from the cot and lack of activity, and Moses looked tired and defeated.

"Good *Gotte*, you look so worn out, Moses. ...But still better than me on my bad days," Thomas said, trying to lighten the mood. Moses smiled slightly, in more of an effort to help make Thomas feel more comfortable. It didn't go unnoticed. Thomas wouldn't have expected Moses to act any differently. He was probably the most selfless man Thomas knew.

"How are you doing, Thomas? Are things turning around for you?" Moses asked. Thomas nearly teared up. Even though Moses was in more trouble than Thomas, he still took the time to show Thomas that he cared about him very much.

"Yes, thank you for asking. Things are better," Thomas replied. Moses nodded, seemingly glad to hear that.

"I'm proud of you. How's business? Sarah said you offered to hold down the shop? That is much appreciated" Moses said, his eyes already fixed on the book Thomas was holding. Thomas' hands held the book strongly.

"Things are fine, indeed, Moses. But I didn't come here to talk about business as much as I did to see how you are doing. So, tell me, how are you really doing?" he asked.

Moses shrugged. "I'm here. How do you think I'm doing?" Moses asked sarcastically. Thomas sensed a lacing of bitterness in his words... or was that the guilt again? Thomas felt helpless. He knew how he could help but... 'oh, Lord, forgive my cowardice,' he thought.

"I know that you are innocent, and the Lord will vindicate you soon enough. Please, don't lose faith, Moses. You have so many people praying for you," Thomas said. He hated how much he sounded like his mother. When his father was dying from a terminal disease, his mother never wavered in her faith. Whenever he felt his faith waning, she would call him back to the fold. Her words were so full of confidence and assurance that Thomas believed his father would get better. When he didn't, Thomas was so angry with her and at the weightlessness of her comforting words. Right now, he wanted to share them with Moses but thought of their futileness.

"Thank you, Thomas," Moses said, not knowing what else to say.

Thomas flipped open the hardware shop's ledger book he had brought to show Moses. Since Moses' incarceration, he had retrieved an extra set of keys from Sarah and began managing the business. He was comfortable running the shop, and he was actually enjoying it quite a bit. Thomas was excited to review the books with Moses and show him how well he was doing. It was a relief that Thomas was able to manage the store, but Moses longed to return to his previous life, one in which he hugged his wife and children before heading off to work.

He trusted Thomas to manage the shop's finances and cover his household's expenses while things were being sorted out, and the books solidified that things were indeed in order.

Jude arrived to let Thomas know that his visiting time was up. Thomas stood and shook Moses' hand through the bars. Moses thanked him emphatically for filling in for him. Thomas thanked Moses for believing in him enough to handle it. Stepping up to Moses' responsibility required a certain level of sobriety, and Thomas was willing to step into those shoes. He liked wearing them. With no reason to drink again, he channeled all his energy into the business.

Chapter Fifteen

Beth walked around the trailer, looking for an opening. Anna was on the lookout. The address Jude gave them turned out to be a flower field. The flowers were blooming brightly, uncurling toward the sun to absorb the energy and life it gave them. At first, the twins had been confused. They wondered if the address had been wrong. But as they ventured into the depths of the flowers, they discovered an overgrown gravel path that led to a shrub-covered backyard. A gently flowing river cascaded against rocks nearby, making a loud splashing sound that comforted the soul.

The girls were convinced the trailer had been empty - and deserted - for many months, if not years, but the door was tightly locked and secured. Beth picked up a rock and hammered on the lock. The loud noise was stressful even though there certainly couldn't be anyone within earshot.

"Don't do that, Beth. We don't want anyone to know that we were here, and I don't need you to hurt yourself" Anna chided her sister. Beth didn't love that Anna tended to scold her like a child sometimes, but now wasn't the time or place to get into that. She made a mental note to discuss it another time and tossed the rock aside.

"Let's try the windows...oh look, this window is open. Beth, help me push," Anna squealed excitedly. Together, they pushed the window until it opened. Anna climbed in, with Beth's help from below. She landed with a noisy thud on the floor. She groaned quietly in pain. After rising carefully from the ground and stretching out her body, she manually opened the door from inside, letting Beth in.

The trailer was almost empty. There was a bed in a corner and some papers scattered across the table. There was no electricity - nothing happened when the light switch next to the door was flipped. Sunlight streamed in through the sheer curtains, casting an odd glow and enough daylight to see by. 'It would have been a different story if we had come to explore this place last night,' Beth was thinking. It had taken a light argument and a lot of convincing for Anna to wait until the morning, but it simply was not smart to go searching around for clues to a murder at an unfamiliar property after dark.

"Look at this," Anna cried out, interrupting Beth's thoughts. Paper clippings from newspapers were attached to the wall.

"Dear Lord! Derek was involved in a drug bust in New York. This newspaper shows his picture as Robert Williams, not Derek McCall. It says that he was involved with taking down some drug lords...it looks like his undercover work led to the arrest of some pretty scary people." she said in wonderment.

This could be it. The answer they had been waiting for. Derek had changed his name and was hiding in Little Valley. What if some career criminals from New York had found him?

"Are you sure about that?" Beth asked. Anna nodded, flipping through the papers. She grabbed the papers and stuffed them into the bag they came with. Derek was hiding and all she could think of was approaching the detective with this information. This was much bigger than them, but there could be a whole shift in the angle of the case. Moses could be exonerated.

Suddenly, Beth clapped her hands across Anna's lips.

Beth put one finger up to her mouth. Anna held her breath. She was realizing two terrifying things just at that moment.

First, she realized how much danger she and her sister could be in, standing in the living room of what could be the headquarters used to hunt down Derek.

And second, Beth had heard someone approaching the trailer. The footsteps were getting louder and louder on the gravel path that led through the front yard.

Anna quickly and quietly reached over and turned the lock on the front door. "Quick, we need to get out the way we came," she whispered to Beth. The twins squeezed themselves through the window, one at a time, hitting the ground just as the key was turning in the doorknob of the front door.

Anna could feel the wind whip past her face as she ran through the field of flowers towards the cover of the woods, holding tightly to her sister's hand. As she ran, she only wished for one thing: that she had gotten a clear view of the person who had a key to that trailer...

Chapter Sixteen

Anna paced up and down the room impatiently. She clutched the papers close to her chest. Beth sat on the chair, trying to catch her breath.

"You should sit down, Anna. You're going to give yourself a heart attack. I'm not ready to live without you just yet," Beth said, hoping to lighten the mood a bit. Anna waved her hand in the air, content to pace around.

They had sent Amos to ask Detective Stewart to come see them right away. The sisters were very nervous about going into town and feeling very much in danger. Stewart was due to arrive any minute and Anna was a basket of nerves. She had never been so afraid in her entire life.

The ends of their dresses still had leaves clinging to them and were damp from wading through the river as they ran from the trailer. They didn't bother with changing or cleaning up. Their minds were too distracted, and they didn't want to leave each other's sight for one second.

A question kept ringing in Anna's mind. Who had they escaped? He had the key to the trailer, so he was certainly the person who owned the trailer, right?

She wished that she had gotten a good look at the man. Remembering now, Anna was so scared. They might not be alive if they hadn't heard the footsteps when they did, or what if the killer had been in the trailer when they arrived? What if he had seen them leaving? What if he followed them back to their homes? The questions were dancing around out of control in her head, and Anna was regretting ever getting involved.

There was a knock at the door and Amos hollered out, "*Maem*, Aunt Anna?" The sisters bounded toward the door and yanked it open.

"I heard you ladies wanted to see me? This better be worth my time" Stewart said, as he stood on the other side of the threshold, clearly annoyed with having to come out to their home. He sounded very short and impatient.

"And let me tell you, ladies, again, I am not in control of what happens to Moses. He is going to court tomorrow, and the judge will decide bail, not me," Stewart said, cutting off Anna who was about to speak.

"Detective, please come in! I think we found something. Look at this," Anna said loudly, frantically motioning him to enter. Once everyone was inside, Beth shut and locked the door. Anna showed the papers to Stewart. He read through patiently. Anna bounced around before him, waiting to hear his thoughts.

"I'm very familiar with this case - it was a very popular one. It happened a few years ago. This guy, Robert Williams, was one of the good guys working undercover and it was a drug bust gone wrong. One of the big drug lords was killed in a shoot-out, but so many others got away. Sergeant Williams had to flee New York because his life was in danger from the rest of the gang members," he said, pausing to observe the ladies' faces. Anna was surprised that he didn't get it.

"Do you realize that Robert Williams is Derek McCall?" Anna asked, bewildered. "What if his past caught up with him? What if he was killed as revenge for what happened to the drug lord?" the torrent of questions exploded from Anna. Stewart laughed.

"I think it's sweet what you are trying to do for your son-in-law but it's time to give it up. Where did you even get these clippings?" he asked, his eyes narrowing with seriousness. Anna shrank back, taking the clippings from him.

She didn't want to lie, so she began to cry instead. It wasn't much of an effort, however. Anna was emotionally exhausted with this guy. Why wouldn't he believe that this scenario was likely? Could he be in on it, too?

Wanting to end the whole scene, Detective Stewart lowered his voice and said, "You should give this up. Even if the drug lords killed Derek, why would they go through all the trouble of hiding the body where it would eventually be discovered? That's not their MO, and it doesn't explain the robberies and the stolen goods found at the crime scene," Stewart said, confidently. Anna's last drop of energy was zapped. She felt tired and hopeless. What else would she do? Beth sidled up next to her, wrapping her arm around her shoulders.

"Thank you for your time," Beth said to the detective. Amos walked the detective out as Beth helped Anna get settled on the couch before heading to the kitchen to start a pot of tea.

Chapter Seventeen

T homas decided it was time to come clean to the detective. The sheriff's office was so stuffy, the air felt as old as the house itself, and a musty smell hung in the air. He had made it to the office, but he sat there, struggling with where to start.

Detective Stewart and Jude were sitting on chairs opposite Thomas in the main office area. Stewart's eyes wandered around and he fidgeted with a loose thread on the hem of his shirt. He was clearly bored and so tired of going back and forth with everyone in this case. Jude, on the other hand, was kind and interested in what Thomas had to say.

Focusing on Jude, Thomas cleared his throat, ready to begin.

"Sometime today, Thomas," Stewart said, irritated.

"Okay...as you already know, I found Sheriff McCall's body. It's kind of shocking to see such a terrifying sight. And I haven't been able to get it out of my head," Thomas began.

Stewart rolled his eyes. "This is law enforcement, not your psychologist. If that's what you need help with, go see a therapist. You said you had some information to share with us and that is what we are all gathered here to hear, so get on with it," Stewart said, unsympathetically.

Thomas could not stand this man. Did he learn nothing from Derek's death? Derek was a jerk who couldn't bother to be kind to anyone. Everyone seemed shocked at his death, but they were more shocked at the thought of murder happening in Little Valley. No one truly cared about his demise, and that's because when he was alive, Derek didn't care about anyone. Stewart had better watch his back, acting like McCall, or he might end up regretting it.

"Stewart, clearly Thomas is traumatized. You have to let him go at his own pace," Jude said thoughtfully. Thomas gave Jude a grateful glance. Stewart sat up straight and set his eyes firmly on Thomas. The steely coldness of his eyes was so intense that it almost made Thomas stutter.

"I want to tell you what I saw on the night that I think may have been the night Derek was murdered," Thomas began. The words flowed out of his mouth. Jude's brows furrowed with concentration. He made a big show of writing down words on his pad while Stewart just leaned back and listened pensively. When Thomas was done, Stewart remained quiet for a while.

"I just want to know why everyone in this godforsaken town is trying to convince me that all the evidence we have against Moses means nothing. I've never seen this kind of solidarity in all my years of being in the service. The man killed someone with a hammer and left evidence all over the place for us to find, but no one wants to believe it. So, what, you are all trying to tell me is that Moses is a saint?" Stewart exploded. His voice billowed.

"No, that's not what I mean to say. He is not a saint, but he isn't a murderer either," Thomas protested. Stewart kicked back his chair.

"Sir, please, can we just calm down and check out what he said? There may be an element of truth there," Jude reasoned with him. Stewart was reluctant.

"How many elements of truth are we going to keep searching for? First, those old ladies keep hounding me to check this and that out. And now, Thomas. It's a waste of my time. They all have conflicts of interest. The old ladies are related to Moses while Thomas is apparently a close friend and trusted to run his shop. I have no interest in wasting any more time. This is just getting ridiculous," Stewart said, exasperated.

"This time, it may be different. Thomas, did you hear the voice or see who McCall was arguing with?" Jude asked. Thomas shook his head.

"Again, as I said, I couldn't hear anything they said. And Derek dashed out of the bushes. It was too dark to make out the figure," Thomas said.

Jude nodded and wrote down something on his page. Stewart stared at them as if he couldn't believe it. What kind of a small-town operation was this? Stewart just really wanted to get back to Nashville, far away from these simple folk.

Thomas couldn't believe it either. He couldn't believe that Stewart was such a lousy detective, especially coming from Nashville. He was really trying to do the right thing here, and Stewart wasn't even willing to listen to him, let alone take him seriously.

"I can't believe this. This is madness. The words of a drunken man will not hold any water in court. Please, stop wasting your time," he said, snatching the note from Jude.

Thomas began to protest, but Stewart interrupted him right away.

"I don't want to hear it. Please. You were drunk on the night in question. You couldn't have possibly seen clearly. So, what you are trying to tell me is that Derek stole your key and returned to the tool shed where he was murdered? Or someone else found your key, knew it went to the tool shed, and lured Derek there to kill him and frame your friend. It doesn't make any sense, and honestly, maybe it sheds a suspicious light on you instead. How about that? You can't remember what happened, but you remember running into Derek, and you had the key all along... maybe

YOU are the one who killed him in your drunken state and left him there to be found," Stewart raged.

Thomas shook his head, panicking. "No, that's not what happened. I know what I'm saying. I didn't kill Derek. I couldn't do that to anyone." Thomas said. Stewart chuckled.

"Yeah, right, and you saw a figure in the dark through your beer goggles, right?" he asked.

Thomas stood up abruptly. He would not stand for this any longer. The Lord knows he tried to help. If this was the way it was destined to be, then so be it. He would not sit and listen to someone berate him or turn his words around and especially not accuse him of the murder!

"If that innocent man is sent to prison, it will be on your head," he said to Stewart before leaving the office. As he left, he heard Jude's calm voice chastising Stewart.

No matter what, something seemed even more out of whack than before he confessed. The detective seemed exceptionally desperate to nail Moses. Thomas wandered out of the station headed toward his borrowed horse and buggy. His straw hat was pulled over his head to protect him from the blazing sun. He muttered a short prayer for Moses. Thomas was deflated. He had really thought his confession would help Moses. Clearly, he was wrong.

Chapter Eighteen

It was Monday afternoon and the early morning hearing resulted in Moses remaining incarcerated without bail. Anna had become even more depressed than Sarah. Beth was at a loss. She tended to her sister and her niece simultaneously. Sarah and the children had moved into her parents' house since Moses' arrest. Sarah said their house seemed suddenly too big and scary to live in. Beth slept over at Anna's, most of the time, taking care of whatever - or whoever - needed it. She hated seeing her sister like this. Anna spent all her time in bed, staring at the ceiling and doing nothing. Not even the chatter of her grandchildren was enough to raise her spirits. The children would try to play with her, but when she didn't respond, they would just go find something else to do, leaving her in the soupy river of sadness she seemed to be drowning in.

But Beth refused to give up on her sister and knew she would get through this. She cooked food, brushed her sister's hair, fed her, and sat by her bed reading the holy book and praying to herself. If Anna recognized everything Beth did, she didn't show it. Neither did Beth expect any thanks in return. If the situation was reversed, Anna would do exactly the same thing for Beth.

Leaving the house in the care of their cousin Rachel, Beth bounded up the stairs that led to the small library set up in town by the Englisher, Mr. Wilson. Beth could not shake the information that the sisters had found, and her curiosity would not be satisfied until she checked out this one last detail - and she held onto the hope that the Little Valley library would have the answer she needed to quiet her mind.

Mr. Wilson greeted Beth at the front door, calling her Anna. Beth responded to the name, amused by the fact that no one in the town could still tell the twins apart. Perhaps because she was chatty today, Mr. Wilson had assumed that she was Anna. Beth didn't mind the anonymity that being an identical twin gave her sometimes. It could be comforting as if there were a cloak of invisibility thrown over her. Anna was often seen as the face and mouthpiece of their relationship, and Beth loved being in the background.

"How may I help you today?" Mr. Wilson asked. He was a sweet man who was about their age and Beth had always had suspicions that he had an innocent crush on Anna. His wife died a few years ago. His interest in Anna was exposed years ago when they were much younger, but he was an Englisher and Anna fell in love with Eli. Beth liked the fact that he respected Anna's decision when she turned him down. But since his wife's death, Mr. Wilson refused to remarry, and Beth often wondered if Anna was single, if he would again pursue a relationship with her.

"I'm looking for information regarding a specific incident in New York regarding a cop and drug lords," she said, handing the clipping she had managed to sneak out with. Mr. Wilson took the newspaper and read it carefully.

"This way, please," he said. He chatted merrily all the way to where the microfiche readers are found. Adjusting his glasses, he scrolled through pages and pages of newspapers, while Beth looked over his shoulder. She waited patiently until he found what she asked for. He stood up, relinquishing the seat to Beth.

"Please don't hesitate to call me if you need anything," Mr. Wilson said before heading back to his desk. There was a boyish smile on his face, like a high school teenager in love. Beth chuckled to herself.

"I'll be sure to do that. Thank you, Mr. Wilson" she said. Beth settled down to work. She flipped through the pages of the newspaper, reading and studying and jotting down notes on a pad. The research was going slowly. She was about to give up when she saw a picture that made her gasp. It was the picture of a young boy clinging to his mother outside a courthouse.

Leaning forward, she raced to the front desk where Mr. Wilson was sitting. She showed him the newspaper frantically, unable to articulate her words.

"Do you...see that? Do you see what I'm seeing?" Beth asked the questions spiraled out of her mouth without pause. Mr. Wilson stared at her, confused.

"Quick, I need you to help me confirm this. Do you have a way to get this boy's information?" she asked, desperately. Mr. Wilson nodded.

"Yes, I do - let me print it for you," he said, leading the way towards the front, "and if it's okay with you, I think I would probably just like to stay out of it."

Beth assured him she would keep his involvement (although practically nonexistent) private. She couldn't wait to get back to tell Anna that she had just solved the case. Moses was going to be freed!

Chapter Nineteen

Beth dashed into the house with girlish energy that reverberated around the room. She ran right to Anna's room and leaped onto the bed next to her. Anna groaned and turned away from her.

"I figured it out! I figured it out!" she said, brimming with excitement. Anna pulled the cover over her head. Beth pulled it away.

"Seriously, Anna, I went to the library and I solved the case! Moses is going to be freed!" Beth could hardly stay calm.

Anna met her sister's gaze. "What did you figure out?" she asked, pushing away the papers that were being thrust into her face.

"Everything!" she said. Anna sat up, tired, but eager to listen to her sister's story.

"So, remember those news clippings we found in the.... No, come on, let's get to the sheriff's office. They need to hear this directly," Beth stopped. Her excitement was too all over the place and she didn't want to tell the story twice.

She hopped around spiritedly, helping Anna get dressed. Anna was frustrated with the display of emotion, but she also knew and trusted that her sister really did have something worth the ride to the sheriff's office. Anna knew that there was no point in asking her questions because she would never reply to them.

Anna put on her dress, *kapp*, and slippers. They dashed out of the house.

Beth opened the door to their buggy and the sisters jumped in. She handed Anna the papers and Anna glimpsed at the picture of a young boy holding onto his mother.

Before Anna could ask any more questions, Beth began to drive the buggy. She picked up speed and drove recklessly. Anna was thrown side to side, hanging on for dear life.

Anna cried out to her. "You are going to get us killed!" she said. Beth was focused, power flowing from her arms. Where had she found the strength to drive like that? Anna was marveled Beth still knew how to handle the buggy. They hadn't driven a buggy since they were teenagers. Their father taught them how to drive but as soon as they got married, they didn't need to drive anymore.

They turned towards the outskirts of town where the sheriff's office was located. The road was empty with tall grass looming on both sides. Anna heard the low hum of the car first. It seemed like it was hidden somewhere near the bushes. She turned to look out on her right side. Beth's scream made her turn back. A black car made a quick swerve from nowhere, hitting their buggy. They were thrown around as Beth lost control of the buggy. The horse neighed loudly, running wildly. The cart broke off at the link that connected it to the horse. Anna didn't stop screaming until their cart turned on its side and narrowly avoided hitting a nearby tree trunk. In shock and a bit disoriented, she couldn't clearly see the face of the figure approaching them.

She blinked. Her sight was blurry. She tried to stay awake for as long as she could, but her mind shut down, pulling her into a dreamless sleep as she slipped into unconsciousness.

Chapter Twenty

When she woke up, Anna found her arms and legs tied, lying on a cold hard floor. Her body ached all over. Her sister laid beside her, also tied up, but completely passed out. Blood trickled down the side of her face. Anna moved carefully, shifting her weight slowly, trying to reach her.

"Beth!" she called softly. Beth didn't move. Anna prayed she was still alive. Her head ached with pain. The lower part of her body was on fire. She tried to remember what happened. She closed her eyes and all she could recall was a car swerving into the road from nowhere, knocking their buggy off the road, the horse racing away. She remembered a blurry figure approaching them.

Darkness covered the room except for a small bulb of light that dangled from the ceiling in the center of the room. Anna strained her eyes, looking for details. The place looked like maybe it was an abandoned house. The floor was bare and wooden with dark stains. A clear white plastic bag was spread on the floor just beneath each of the sisters. The windows were boarded shut. Fear spread through Anna's body. She wasn't sure how they were going to get out of this and return home to their families.

"Beth, wake up! Oh my God!" Anna cried. The door opened. Anna's mouth fell open as she saw who entered the room.

"You!" Anna mouthed.

He smiled and a chill ran down Anna's spine. "I warned you to drop the case. I told you that you were only going to get into trouble if you continued pursuing it," he said.

Thoughts began to swirl inside Anna's head. The paper clippings...the trailer...the intruder...the young boy in the picture outside the courtyard... Beth's excitement... Suddenly, everything fell into place. She understood Beth's eagerness to get to the sheriff's office. She had found out about Jude and wanted to report him to the right authorities. But how did he find out? There were a lot of questions she wanted to ask.

"You deliberately told us about the trailer, didn't you?" Anna asked. Jude leaned close to the light, his face had changed from the sweet, kind man Anna trusted to a dangerous, unrecognizable monster.

"Yes. I was supposed to take care of the two of you there but then you waited until the next morning and I didn't get there in time.... I saw you run off but, in the daytime I worried someone might hear," Jude said. He walked to the table and chair set up and grabbed a seat.

Anna was so paralyzed with shock. In a thousand years, she would have never guessed Jude was capable of killing Derek, let alone planning her and Beth's murders, too!

"You ran us off the road. You killed Derek! You...You did all of this. You knew my sister had found out about you. How did you know that?" the questions poured out of Anna's mouth. She was so confused. So many things were happening at once, her head ached, and it was so difficult to keep up. There were a lot of suspects on her list, but Jude had never been one of them. How did he manage to deceive the entire town?

"The two of you weren't satisfied and just wouldn't let it go," he said, slowly loading bullets into his gun. A ray of light shone from a crack in the boarded-up window and landed on the barrel of the gun. Anna shuddered. Pain shot from her right knee. Her hands and feet were tightly bound. She couldn't see any way to escape from here. She was running out of hope.

"Why? Why did you frame my son-in-law?" Anna continued asking. Jude didn't look up to reply to her. She couldn't tell what he was preoccupied with.

After a pause, Jude replied, "He was simply an unfortunate casualty. I miscalculated his usefulness though. I thought he might just accept his fate when the town turned on him, but this godforsaken town.... the unity in this town and in your family...your relentlessness in trying to prove his innocence...all of that was about to foil my plan, and I could not let that happen," Jude spoke with an intense disgust that seemed to emanate from somewhere deep inside him. His hate made Anna quake with fear.

"Your plan?" Anna asked. If she was to die, she might as well understand the full story. Jude turned to her, waving the gun in the air.

"This is not a movie, Anna. You are not going to ask me a bunch of questions, for me to just explain the whole plot. I am not going to tell you why I did everything I did," Jude said. Anna didn't need him to. Fueled by the fearlessness that came from accepting her fate, she spoke up.

"You don't need to anyway because I already figured it all out. So, let me tell you. Derek was a cop in New York, right? He was pursuing a case about a notorious drug lord in New York. He infiltrated the drug lord's network by acting as one of them. He worked undercover and used the information he gathered to take the drug lord down. The drug lord was arrested and sent to prison, but they weren't able to detain everyone, so Derek found himself in danger. He changed his name and fled to a small town to keep himself safe. Am I right?" Anna paused.

Jude's full attention was on her. His left eyebrow was arched upwards as if he was enjoying the show. When he didn't respond, Anna continued.

"Shortly after the trial, the drug lord killed himself in jail," she said. Jude raised a finger, interrupting her.

"No, he was killed in jail," he said.

"Of course. But there's a tiny problem that no one anticipated. The drug lord had a young son. A young son who was as callous and evil as his father had been. After his father's empire was taken down, the young son disappeared. Like his father, he never forgets. And he certainly doesn't forgive. After a few years, he reappears with his own changed identity. He joined the force. No one knew who he was. His father had become a closed case, another man forgotten by the system. This infuriates the son who wanted to carry on the legacy of his father. But in order to do that, he had to first eliminate the people who had taken his father down. There was only one way to do that – by becoming one of them. The son was dedicated and worked his way into the position he needed. He is a patient man, this boy. Just like his father, he plots and waits in the shadows patiently like a predator targeting a prey," Anna paused.

Jude's smile was becoming wider. He was definitely enjoying Anna's storytelling. The gun was laid on the table, and all his attention was on the woman.

"He strategically got what he wanted, a position working closely with the man who took down his father. He built his trust, devised a plot to include a few robberies in the local small town, and just when the man least expected it, the son struck, taking him down.

That son is you, isn't it? We are here right now because my sister found out the truth about you, didn't she?" Anna finished her story.

Jude clapped theatrically.

"You are good. I underestimated you two. I did not believe you would ever figure it out. I mean...you were going after scumbags like Samuel and never thought to look where you least expected to find the predator," he said. Anna bobbed her head.

"You can kill us. I don't care but please, let my son-in-law go. His family needs him. We are older. We've lived our lives, but my son-in-law is a good man, and his family needs him. Please," Anna begged.

Jude seemed to look through her. "You have no idea how much I suffered to get to this moment. I never would have thought that scumbag would hide out in a town such as yours. A perfect, peaceful world to live out the rest of his miserable life. But a snake will always be a snake no matter how many times he sheds his skin. The police thought he was feeding them information about my father's empire when the truth was that he was also feeding our rivals with information, too, causing even more deaths. He was always a thief. He hated this town. He felt trapped and was planning to leave. Problem was that he didn't have enough money to leave. So, when I suggested we should start robbing here, he quickly jumped onto it. The old fool - he began to trust me more and more as we started stealing together," Jude chuckled. "I guess you could say we were thick as thieves," Jude smirked. A satisfied expression passed across his face.

"Until he died, he actually thought I was trying to cheat him out of the treasures. Little did he know I had no use for the stolen treasures. My treasure was to seek revenge for my father. He would never rest until his betrayer was killed. That was the family code. Anyway, the night it happened, we were looking for a place to store our stolen treasures. We had run out of options. That was when Thomas came along, drunk and staggering. Derek grabbed the keys from him when he took him home. The tool shed was the perfect place to hide the goods until we found a better option, but once we were both there, I had the brilliant idea. I could finally carry out my revenge and be free as well. All these years of planning, and it turned out to be spur of the moment.

What I didn't anticipate was.... you," Jude said, his voice dipped into a low growl as he added the last part. Anna shivered. From the corner of her eyes, she could see Beth moving slightly. Anna prayed to the Lord for help. She hoped someone would come to their aid. Anna had no strength to fight.

"I see your sister is waking up. Maybe we should just get to it, then," Jude said as he approached her, holding the gun. Anna squirmed, shaking dramatically. She started yelling but Jude stuffed a wet cloth into her mouth. A burning sensation spread from her mouth to the rest of her body, making her drowsy. Her head fell to the side. Her eyes closed.

Chapter Twenty-One

Levi and Ruby raced all the way to the station. Ruby's *kapp* had loosened on her hair but she didn't notice. Levi's face was sweaty. They panted heavily. The sheriff's office was quiet and empty. Levi wasn't sure anyone was there, so he started hollering out for help. Usually, Levi would be scared of what would happen when news of his love affair with Ruby, the Bishop's daughter, got out in the community but today, he didn't care. He had lives to save. They were still pretty shaken by the sight they had seen. To keep their affair secret, they always strayed far from the rest of the community to the quiet areas where no one dared venture to. Or so they thought until they witnessed the kidnapping of the old twins.

"Hello!" Levi called out, beating his hands on the front desk table. Ruby bounced around, shaking tremendously. Levi wanted to reach out and touch the base of her neck and reassure her that everything was going to be alright. The detective wandered out of the jail room. His face showed his annoyance with the noise.

"What now?" he bellowed. His booming voice resonated around the room. Levi burst out in a torrent of words, explaining what they saw. The detective's face showed various arrays of emotions as he listened to the teenagers talk. With great timing, the young police officer sauntered into the sheriff's office, showing up to manage the office again and monitor the office's one inmate.

The detective was frantic. He jumped on the phone and called the state police, quickly explaining that he needed backup.

Turning back to Levi and Ruby, he said, "I need you both to go back home and make sure you stay in your homes until I call for you. Do you understand me?" They bobbed their heads and raced off.

The detective grabbed his gun and gave the officer quick orders to stay put until he returned.

"Lock the office and don't open that door for anyone but me. Got it?" the detective barked. The young police officer nodded yes with fear in his eyes.

Chapter Twenty-Two

Detective Stewart blamed himself for not seeing the signs. He should have noted the way Jude seemed unnaturally interested in the case and figuring out all the tiny details. Stewart should have known that Jude was just trying to cover his tracks. He was too calm and collected when they found the body, too, and he had been clearly vying to fill McCall's position after things settled back down.

"If those two old ladies had just kept to their own business, though, I would've figured it out soon enough - and they wouldn't be in danger right now," he thought, exasperated.

The car drove roughly to the spot where Ruby and Levi saw them enter. The building was ancient and almost collapsing. It was the perfect den. No one would ever suspect to look for him here. Backup arrived and stopped a distance away. Stewart motioned that he was going to approach the building. The men fell into formation behind him. Stewart tiptoed close to the building. The windows were all boarded up and there was no sound to be heard. Stewart entered stealthily through the back door. The house was quiet. Stewart turned towards the large room on the left and saw Jude positioning the sisters' bodies on the plastic, dragging them to the center of each piece. He had a good mind to shoot him from this range, but he stopped himself. Jude had set his gun down, and Stewart knew the law.

"Put your hands in the air, Deputy!" Stewart commanded, approaching the living room with his gun pointed directly at Jude's face. Jude's hands went up. The look of shock on Jude's face was very satisfying, as Stewart met his gaze.

"Oh, you are going to be spending a very long time in prison!" Stewart uttered to Jude through gritted teeth as one of the uniformed officers proceeded to snap handcuffs onto the cooperating criminal. Stewart was angry that Jude had fooled him, too. Jude smiled unapologetically at the detective as he was led away.

Stewart rushed to the women and untied them. The women were weak, but they were still alive. He had arrived in time. As he waited for the ambulance, his mind ran through all the times these old women tried to get him to do his job. If he had listened to them.... Jude would have been arrested sooner and Moses would be home with his family by now.

He swore to make sure that Jude spent the rest of his life behind bars and to make sure that Little Valley got the law enforcement it deserves.

"Jude.... It's Jude..." the twin lying directly next to him muttered. Stewart bent low to listen to what she was saying. He smiled at her kindly.

"Yes, I know. He's been arrested. You did it, Ma'am. You did it," he said....

Secrets in Little Valley

The Amish Lantern Mystery Series, Volume 2

Chapter One

For nothing is hidden that will not become evident, nor anything secret
that will not be known and come to light.

Luke 8:17

"I'm so excited," Beth squealed as she reached across the table and squeezed Anna's arm. Anna stopped writing for a moment to look at her twin sister. Anna chuckled, her lips spreading into a wide grin. Ever since they were little, Beth would get so excited about planning a party. Although the actual social gathering would always cause her anxiety as the event approached, it was all the little details that she really enjoyed planning.

Beth struggled as a high-functioning autistic for many years. Whenever needed, her twin sister, Anna would slide right into care-taking mode. Anna watched for signs that Beth was feeling anxious in crowds and pulled her away for a few minutes. She pointed out to Beth when she had become overly obsessed about something, and she had grown to understand that some of Beth's habits were just part of their lives together.

"Yes, these are definitely exciting times. We have so much to thank Gotte for, after all this community has been through." Anna tried not to think much about how just a few weeks before, her son-in-law had been arrested for a crime he hadn't committed, and how terrifying all of it had been for the entire family. She was so grateful for his freedom and the powerful bond that Moses and her daughter, Sarah, shared - it had surely helped them through the hard times.

Moses was such a good man. Even though he had only been free for a day, he spent hours in his barn carving the most beautiful cherry wood cane for Anna. Since the accident, Anna couldn't walk without help, and Moses's wonderful gift allowed her the independence she craved.

A knock at the door from the other room interrupted Anna's thoughts, and she took note that Beth quickly jumped up to see who was there. My, how she has changed, thought Anna. Beth suffered from autism and would typically be the last to answer the door, but things were different now. She seemed more confident, more brave, since the traumatic events from a few weeks ago. Even though Anna suffered physically, Beth recovered quickly and naturally fell into caretaker mode for her twin sister.

Anna felt a pit in her stomach as she recalled the fear she felt that day. Desperately trying to clear Moses' name, the sisters had found themselves face-to-face with a killer. Thankfully, their efforts had helped solve the murder, and the killer was arrested, but the entire experience shook the community to the core. Little Valley was recovering and Beth and Anna hoped that the celebration would bring some focus back to the happiness and comfort that Little Valley had once offered their loved ones.

Anna's oldest daughter, Sarah, walked into the kitchen, her pregnant belly entering at least 12 inches ahead of her. "Daughter! What a lovely surprise! How are you feeling? Come sit down," Anna said. Sarah graciously took a seat in the chair next to her mother, leaning back slowly to allow room for the precious baby she was carrying. Her hands instinctively caressed her stomach.

Beth brought a small upholstered footstool from the living room, propping Sarah's feet on the stool while removing her slippers. She placed a handmade quilt around her shoulders to keep her warm. The temperature had dropped with the threat of winter starting, and the house held a chill that the small wood stove couldn't seem to keep at bay that day. Normally, the twins would have the house warmed from the hours of baking in the ovens, but they had decided their stock of baked goods was sufficient for the upcoming farmers' market scheduled for the weekend ahead. During the colder months, they typically sold less, and they especially welcomed the break this year.

"I'm exhausted. I've been having a few cramps off and on this morning, and the smallest things just take so much energy. How are you, Maem?" Sarah touched Anna's damaged knee gently.

"Oh, I'm fine! The English doctor says I will be ready to get back to my morning walks with Eli in just a couple weeks," Anna winked at Sarah.

"No, she won't, Sarah," said Beth firmly. "She will do no such thing. The doctor says her knee is healing nicely, but I think we'll be playing it safe for a while, especially with the cold season. You know how our bones can start to hurt at this age."

Anna waved her hand in the air as if Beth was overreacting.

"On the contrary! I'll be turning 60 years old before I know it, so I've got to keep my heart pumping," Anna said. She knew Beth meant well, but Anna didn't like being told what she could not do - and she also knew that Beth was fully aware of that.

Beth rolled her eyes and turned away to tend to the tray of teacups and cookies she was organizing for the three ladies to enjoy.

"You have three years to go, still, Maem, and you could use the rest," Sarah said, with a serious look directed at her mother.

"Denki, Sarah, but you don't need to worry about me," Anna said, looking over at her daughter. She adored Sarah and was so proud of the woman she had become. "Tell me about your cramps. Do you think you will have the baby today?" She reached over and touched Sarah's protruding belly with care, feeling for movement.

"The doctor says the baby could arrive anytime, but the first two babies were both so late in arriving. I think we still have a couple more weeks to wait," Sarah said.

Beth laid the tray down on the table next to Anna and in front of Sarah. "Well, we just need to make sure you're going to be feeling well in time for the celebration! I wouldn't mind holding my niece while you and Moses relax and enjoy all that we have prepared for you."

"Did you two hear about Matthew, Moses's best friend from childhood? He has requested to return to the community. If you remember, he did not return after his Rumspringa. He has been living in the nearby town of Springston, but he came to visit after hearing about Moses' arrest. I think he must have realized that he had made a mistake leaving the community. He has requested forgiveness from the bishop and the elders." Sarah spoke, the words stumbling out of her mouth between brief breaks here and there as if she were feeling a bit out of breath.

"That's glorious news!" Beth exclaimed. "I had hoped and prayed for so many years that he would return. If the elders approve, then we will have reason to celebrate both Moses and Matthew's return home! Gotte is gut!"

"Yes, that is so wonderful," Anna agreed, "and speaking of the party, I'm so excited to tell you all about the delicious food we have on the menu. Let's start with the dessert, my favorite, of course." Anna smiled at Beth. "We are baking three of your grandmother's famous cherry cobblers. And at least 3 batches of the sugar cookies. We'll need to borrow your glass cookie jars, if you don't mind. Our cookie jars are all reserved and used for transporting the goods to the market on the weekends." Getting lost in the list in front of her, Anna didn't notice right away that Sarah's breathing had become heavier.

"Maem," Sarah said as a whisper before taking another deep breath, "I think... I'm having the baby." Her face was flushed, her eyes filled with a unique mix of excitement and pain.

"Ach du lieva!" Beth cried out, jumping up to run by Sarah's side.

"Beth, dabber schpring and tell Eli to get the buggy ready! We're having a baby!!"

Chapter Two

W^{*here is she?*} Levi asked himself, pacing up and down the riverbed. To reduce his anxiety, he sat down next to the stream. His reflection floated along the surface of the water, slightly warped by the gentle current. Levi Mast had just turned fifteen. He still had what his mother would call 'baby fat' on his oval, boyish face. His eyes were bright and his nose was perfectly straight. It was getting easier and easier to see his father's face in his image each day that Levi grew older. He was finally growing a bit taller, and he hoped that he would be as tall as his father when he reached the other side of puberty. Levi rubbed his arms, tanned from the long hours of working outside under the sun on his family farm, and looked around, searching for a sign of Ruby.

His concern for her absence increased. Levi called out Ruby's name. Sometimes they would play games where one or the other would hide, but he was sure she wouldn't have carried on for this long. *Maybe she is confused about where or when we were supposed to meet,* he thought to himself, although he knew that was unlikely since they always met at their secret spot around the same time every other afternoon. Between the stream and the tall trees, Levi had formed a heart shape with a collection of rocks he had found and brought to their favorite spot. Ruby had thought this gesture was so romantic. Levi remembered her beautiful smile and the excitement he felt when she jumped into his arms the first time she noticed the rock pattern he had created.

He was usually the one that was late, and this day was no different. Some days it was difficult for Levi to get away with all the work that he had on his plate. He helped his father on the family farm and in the small corner store that his father built to sell their farm's bounty of produce. On busy days, as soon as he could get away, Levi would run like lightning to find Ruby sitting patiently next to the "heart rocks." But today, she wasn't there to greet Levi, and he had a strange feeling about it.

He shook his head as he pushed the feelings away. Maybe he was just feeling guilty for being late again - especially since Ruby never gave him a hard time about it. She was always so positive and light-hearted. She was such a joy to be around and when he was away from her, he counted the minutes until they could be together again. Levi knew they were young, but he could not imagine life without her.

Ruby also loved this special spot and their time together, almost as much as Levi did. She was younger than Levi - only 18 months younger, at thirteen years old, but she wanted to take things slow and avoided talking about the future too much. She knew she wanted to explore the world outside of Little Valley just as her older sister had, but Levi was set on staying home. He wasn't even sure if he was interested in experiencing Rumspringa. Ruby wanted to explore, and she longed for the day when Rumspringa would finally be in front of her. Her sister had decided not to return to the community for baptism after Rumspringa, and her parents were heartbroken to learn of her decision. Ruby wasn't sure she would follow in her sister's footprints exactly, but she was eager to find out why Esther had chosen the path she did.

All the same, Ruby thought it was exciting to meet Levi in private. Only her closest friend, Grace, knew about their secret meetings. She told Grace all of her secrets, and she fully trusted that Grace wouldn't tell anyone else. The two of them had been best friends and neighbors all of their lives, and they had built a bond that was unbreakable.

The young lovers knew that their secret love affair, as innocent as it was, would bring so much shame to their families if revealed -especially since Ruby's father was the bishop in the community. They were far too young to be dating. Regardless, Ruby didn't care. And neither did Levi. They couldn't stay away from each other, and they were willing to risk it all just for those fleeting moments in their secret space by the stream in the woods.

Levi decided that he would give Ruby a few more minutes before heading home. Maybe it wasn't as late as he thought it was, or maybe *she* was the one that was running late this time. Ignoring his sixth sense nagging him, he allowed his thoughts to wander back to when he first met Ruby. Levi had a tough time trusting girls and falling in love since his first experience. Two years before, when he was twelve, Colette, the beautiful blonde girl who lived next door broke his heart. The experience hardened him and made him wary to even look at another girl for a while. He knew he had plenty of time for love and romantic relationships later in his life. But, he met Ruby at a wedding celebration held in the community, and anyone could immediately see that she was by far the most beautiful girl in the community. When he asked about her, his older brother quickly let him know that she was the bishop's daughter and shouldn't be approached. His friends all talked about befriending her but none mustered the courage to actually do so. Levi was intrigued.

One day, as if it were fate, Ruby hand delivered a message from the bishop to his father's farm when his parents were at the market and he was alone. He was struck by how beautiful and articulate she was. The two young teens spent the next hour - almost two - chatting, laughing, and flirting with each other. It felt so comfortable and natural. It surprised him when it came time for her to leave, and he felt the urge to not let her go. She told him later that she felt the same. After that day, Levi couldn't stop thinking about Ruby. He would find excuses to sneak around the church or any other place he suspected Ruby might be.

Soon after, he ran into her in the town and walked her home. And then that soon became more and more common. Ruby feared their appearance in town might become suspicious, and loving the excitement of it all, she suggested they meet in the woods by the stream. And it was history from there.

Dusk was settling, and the sun was playing hide and seek between the tall peaks of the trees. Levi guessed he must've been waiting for an hour or more now, and he was stricken with worry. He had to leave and head home, but he was conflicted. He didn't want to go without seeing Ruby, but he told himself that the only explanation was that something important must've come up.

With a sigh, Levi decided he would have to wait until their next meeting to find out. He headed home with his head hanging low.

Chapter Three

It was another beautiful day in Little Valley. The sky was a brilliant color blue, and the trees were almost bare. The air was still, leaves lay scattered on the ground- their once vibrant colors turned dingy. The temperatures were dropping, and if these weren't all clear signs that autumn was turning into winter, the decrease in the tourist boom served as a solid reminder instead.

Mark Streen sat on the front porch outside the sheriff's office, drinking his first cup of steaming black instant coffee. He was new to the position of Mainstay County Sheriff, recently appointed by the County Commission to take the seat until the next election, and he welcomed the peace and quiet on the outskirts of Little Valley, where the sheriff's office sat.

Derek McCall had been serving as Sheriff for almost a decade before him, and since they had falsely accused a local Amish shop owner of McCall's murder, Mark knew that he had a big job ahead of him when it came to making amends with the community. He was up for the challenge. As a Christian himself, he admired the Amish and their disciplined lifestyles, so when he was approached with the opportunity to protect and serve Little Valley, he immediately started a plan in motion. His plan not only included helping these folks rebuild the trust in lawmen over the next 10 months, but he was hoping to establish a relationship that would then lead to an election win, when the time came. He had always wanted to live out in this area, and he felt blessed to have received the call.

Sheriff Streen was set to interview an officer that morning for the deputy role, and he was looking forward to it. The candidate was a young man, but eager to relocate, as well. He had served temporarily in this office recently, covering weekend shifts, and he was also looking for a long-term position, working closely with the community.

After what these people have been through, I can't imagine much more could happen, thought Mark, as he finished the last sip of coffee. He rose to his feet, and with perfect timing, the expected young man pulled up to the station in an older white Toyota pickup truck. Seeing the Sheriff standing outside, he didn't waste time. Dressed in full uniform, the junior officer jumped out of the driver's side of the truck, and hurried to the porch, energetically hopping up the steps. He couldn't be a day older than eighteen, Mark thought. The young man was thin and lanky, with traces of acne on his cheeks and dirty blond hair, styled in a crew-cut with a little too much hair gel. He stretched out his arm, a wide smile across his face.

"Good morning! You must be Sheriff Streen. It's a pleasure to meet you. The name's Chase Brown." The Sheriff shook his hand and returned the greeting. They exchanged niceties: the sheriff asking how Chase's trip went, Chase asking how the sheriff's day was going. Holding the door open, Mark invited Chase to have a seat in the front office.

"Ah, it's good to be back," Chase said. "It really feels homey in here.. and out there, too," Chase pointed out the window, referring to the town.

The sheriff's office was an old small house refurbished about twenty years ago. What used to be the living room was the front office, holding two desks - one twice as big as the other, but each with older vinyl covered office chairs. The wheels on the chairs felt as if they were tired and didn't wish to roll on the hardwood floorboards, and they grunted when the chair moved even the tiniest bit. In the corner of the front office were two additional upholstered "visitor chairs." The cushions on the chairs, once white floral patterns but now gray, did not extend to the backs of the chairs and there were no armrests, but it made little sense to replace the chairs over the years since visiting the Sheriff's Office was so rare.

The former kitchen remained in use as the small kitchen for the Sheriff's Office, but instead of canned foods, flour, and pasta, the cabinets were filled with coffee grounds, artificial sweetener and ramen noodles. There was a steel door in the kitchen that looked out of place, leading to the area where the home's single bedroom had been refashioned into a single holding cell. It sat empty of prisoners and only contained an old bunk bed with uncovered mattresses that had yellowed over the years. A small stained sink and toilet were also crammed in the small space.

Standing in the front office, you could easily see back to the empty cell since the steel door was propped open. Chase glanced back there briefly and said offhandedly, "...first time seeing that empty."

"I can't imagine it has had many occupants," the Sheriff responded. "Let's have a seat. I just have a few questions for you. I won't keep you long."

Chase nodded, took a seat, checked to make sure he had turned off his cell phone, and met Mark's gaze. He knew eye contact was important in an interview and he really wanted to make a good impression. "Well, first of all, let me say, thank you for the opportunity to interview. I'm glad to be here, and I am very interested in working with you."

Mark thought that sounded a little rehearsed, but he made a mental note that Chase was making a decent effort. "Good, so, how long have you been working with the police department? And why do you want to transition to a deputy role?" Mark knew there wouldn't be much action in Little Valley and wanted to make sure that this young man wasn't expecting that.

"Well, to be honest, I only just started on the police force out east. I'm looking for a place to start my career, a position where I can learn. I want to work in a community setting where I can get to know the town and the people in the town. I want them to see me and feel safe. And I want to find a place to make my home. I don't have any family - both my parents passed away when I was young, and I floated around the foster care system in the Nashville area for all my upbringing. I want stability and when I was assigned temp duty here a few weekends ago, I got to meet some citizens of Little Valley. And I don't know, it just felt right." Chase paused. He realized that he had been talking a lot and he searched the Sheriff's face to see if he had become disinterested.

The Sheriff liked everything he was hearing, but he wanted to keep a poker face in front of Chase. "What do you think you bring to this position and what are your expectations? I want to make sure we're on the same page."

Without hesitation, Chase responded, "I am willing to learn whatever you'll teach me, sir," he made a point to call Sheriff Streen the respectful name to give the impression that he would stay in line. "I want you to trust me to have your back, and lean on me for help when, and if you need it. I think you and I could make a great team, to be blunt. I am easy to work with. I'm eager. I know my place and I'm good at following direction..." Chase stopped talking abruptly. He knew that this had taken a weird turn. It almost sounded like he was begging for the job - which he probably would, if asked - but he also didn't want to taint the good impression he had started with just a few minutes earlier. "I'm just driven, sir. I want the job and I believe I'm the right one for it."

Sheriff Streen held up his hand and lowered his head slightly as if to politely silence young Chase. He could tell that the young man really wanted the job, and he liked the idea of having someone completely green in the position. Mark found working with younger mentees refreshing. He had never worked with someone quite this young, but there is nothing worse than having to work day in and day out with someone who thinks they know better than you and constantly tries to challenge you. He looked forward to having someone he could teach and mold. "When can you start?" Mark stood and stretched out his hand as a sign of an official offer.

Chase couldn't hide his excitement. He jumped up, almost knocking over the visitor chair, and responded, "Seriously? I got the job?"

"Well, as long as you're ok with the pay and..." Mark paused briefly and looked around, "and the boredom, then, yes, you've got the job."

"I'll take it," Chase smiled from ear to ear. Everything was falling into place just as he had hoped.

Chapter Four

Anna leaned on her cane and watched Eli and Noah as they moved the large mahogany table towards the wall of windows in Beth's living room. "Please make sure it's centered," she directed. Anna wasn't able to help with the heavy lifting, but she was happy to serve as the director of the event instead. Beth buzzed around like a busy bee behind the men, moving the chairs into a large uneven circle on the outskirts of the living areas.

Little Valley was blessed with perfect temperatures for the day of the homecoming celebration. "It's like *Gotte* turned up the heat so we could enjoy the wonderful fresh air," Beth joked earlier. The day before, it felt almost like mid-winter, but on this day, no wool coats would be necessary. A cape would be comfortable enough.

Beth began placing the white cotton embroidered tablecloth on the table. "I love when we have reasons to use *Maem*'s beautiful tablecloth," she said. Her face was beaming with excitement.

"Yes, it is certainly beautiful," Anna agreed.

The front door was partially propped open, and Mr. Hatfield entered. "Excuse me, Mrs. Miller," Mr. Hatfield said politely, "I noticed the door was open."

"Ah, come in please.. you have perfect timing!" Anna greeted him. "How are you, Mr. Hatfield?"

Mr. Hatfield owned the flower shop next to Moses' hardware store, and when he got wind that the community was celebrating Moses' return home, he offered to provide the flower arrangements. The sisters only had plans to collect wildflowers, but graciously accepted Mr. Hatfield's gift.

"Fine, fine, thank you," said Mr. Hatfield, avoiding eye contact. He seemed a little on edge, nervous and uncomfortable, but the sisters knew that was normal demeanor for him.

"And how is your wife?" asked Anna. Mr. Hatfield's wife, Samantha Hatfield, kept to herself and had hardly ever spoken to either of the sisters despite the twins' effort to greet her upon meeting at the farmers' market or around town. The sisters were sure that Samantha did not have any friends here in Little Valley. They had only seen her alone or with Mr. Hatfield. She would always walk a step or two ahead of him when they were together.

"She is well, thank you. She sends her congratulations to Moses for his release and return home. We both knew that Moses was innocent of killing Sheriff McCall, and we are happy that the truth came to light. How is Moses? Is he here yet?"

"Ah, I'm afraid not yet, but he should be here soon if you'd like to wait with Eli and Noah outside," Anna replied. "Moses and his family are adjusting well to his return, thank you for the kind thoughts. Sarah, Moses' wife, just had her third baby, you know. She is such a good baby. Everyone is happy and well."

"That is good to hear," Mr. Hatfield said. "A new baby must be very exciting. Mrs. Hatfield and I were never able..." He stopped in mid-sentence and shifted his eyes to the table in front of the window. He cleared his throat and took a step towards the table. "Shall I set these flowers here?" he asked. Without waiting for a response, he set the carefully arranged flowers down in the center of the table. The beautiful mix of white, blue and yellow shades looked perfect against the elegant tablecloth.

"Oh! They look so beautiful!," Beth exclaimed, holding her hands in front of her as if in prayer.

"Thank you so much, Mr. Hatfield," the sisters said in unison. It wasn't uncommon for the twins to finish each other's sentences or to say the same thing at the same time, and most of the time they didn't even realize it happened.

Mr. Hatfield nodded, "You're welcome. Good day, now. I should get back to the shop. Please tell Moses I said hello and to stop by the next time he is at the store."

"I'll pass the word along," Anna said as he turned toward the door to leave. "Have a wonderful weekend," she called out.

Before returning her attention to setting up the party, Anna said a silent prayer for Mr. Hatfield and his wife to find happiness. She had a sinking feeling that joy was missing from their lives, and she prayed for positive change.

Beth meticulously arranged the sisters' beautiful baked goods on the table, lining the dishes up so they created a symmetrical pattern. Beth's autism took over when she was working on anything that required attention to detail, but the results were flawless. Anna attributed Beth's perfectionism to create refined and delicious cookies and bread to their success in business. The careful details on each pie, cobbler, loaf of bread, and cookie made it nearly impossible for anyone to pass their booth at the farmers' market without stopping to look at what was laid out on the table.

Next to the baked goods laid teacups, a pot of hot coffee, glasses, and a pitcher of water. Just as Beth laid out the small set of dessert plates made of china, the guests started to arrive. The large living room and dining room areas began to feel a bit smaller, as the community gathered. The men entered to grab a quick drink and a bite to eat and then headed outside to the large porch while the room filled with the women's chatter.

The women of the community cooed over Sarah's new baby, Rosemary. Anna checked in on Mary, a young woman who had come to her a few weeks before distraught over feelings she had for a man that she wasn't sure loved her back. "How are you, Mary?" asked Anna, warmly.

"I'm doing so good, Mrs. Miller, thank you so much for asking!" Mary responded, with a teacup in hand. "Luke is busy preparing his farm for the winter, but with Eli's mentoring, he is optimistic that Spring will bring healthy crops." Mary paused and lowered her voice to a whisper, "And, I think he might propose soon, too!" She smiled an impish grin.

"That's wonderful!" Anna responded, sincerely happy for Mary. Beth and Anna's younger sister, Susan soon interrupted their conversation.

"Anna, you have to tell me the secret to making your bread so fluffy. I know that you and I both use *Maem's* recipe, but I cannot make it rise like this no matter what I try!"

Beth overheard the conversation and quickly stepped in to be included. "Little sister, that is our best-selling product at the market. Are you sure you are using the right amount of salt?"

Anna spoke up speaking to both sisters, "Susan has the exact same recipe. It has to be the size of your pan, Susan. That really can make such a big difference."

The conversations among the women continued, while outside, the men discussed their plans for preparing their land and animals for the winter. Remarks about the odd weather were exchanged, and the discussion turned to business.

"How has business been, Cousin Moses?" asked Amos Troyer. Amos was Sarah's cousin, Beth's second oldest son. The circle of men turned their attention to Moses.

"Decent. Business is decent, with tourism settling down and all," Moses responded. There was still a sense of tension around Moses, for some of the community had fallen into the belief during his arrest that he was indeed guilty of killing Sheriff McCall. With his release and the discovery of the killer, there was a sense of embarrassment that remained in the air, like a gray cloud just before a thunderstorm. But Moses was a forgiving man, and he did not hold any grudges against anyone in the community. He was so grateful to be back home with his family and just in time for Rosemary's birth.

Eli was impressed with Moses' resilience, but he was conscious that it might still be tough to talk about it. Wanting to change the subject, he interjected, "I'll tell you what, just in the past few months, the tourism has really boomed, eh? I guess you all have heard about the bed-and-breakfast that is being built in town. And has anyone seen that drifter around? Where did he even come from? He gives me the creeps."

"I saw him walking out near your place, Bishop Packer... just yesterday," said Christopher Yoder. Christopher was a thin, young unmarried man with a strong jawline and thick glasses that made his eyes seem small. "Did you interact with him?" Everyone's attention turned to the bishop who had been exceptionally quiet since he arrived.

It seemed as if Bishop Packer wasn't feeling well. He had indeed been trying to find a good time to exit the party early, but no one else knew how distracted he was. He and his wife, Margaret, had wanted to show their support for Moses, but they were secretly distraught because their daughter Ruby had not come home the night before.

"No, I didn't see anyone out of the ordinary," he responded, but he fought to keep his emotions hidden. For the first time, he wondered if

Ruby could be in trouble. He had just assumed that Ruby was up to no good like her older sister, Esther, since their disagreement over breakfast. The bishop had assumed that she was staying away to punish him or make a point, and that she would return after she cooled off. But now he couldn't ignore the sick feeling that was forming in his stomach. Bishop Packer quickly excused himself and went inside to collect his wife.

Chapter Five

"Gimme another shot, Archer." Samuel Graber's words came out as a slur as he slid his empty shot glass down the bar towards the young bartender. Archer Melgren caught the glass swiftly and set it in the sink. He grabbed a clean shot glass and the nearby bottle of Jim Beam, pouring it expertly as if it was all one single action. Against the regulations, Archer never even closed the bottle when Samuel was sitting at the bar. Some nights he couldn't even keep up with the bar owner's refill requests and considering Samuel had a short temper - *and* Archer really needed the job - it could be a pretty stressful situation. Tonight Samuel seemed determined to drink the bar completely out of liquor. Archer may be young, but it was easy to sense something was bothering his boss.

"Wanna talk about it?" asked Archer. He was reluctant to open up the conversation, but it was practically expected of the bartender to lend an ear. Not only did he want to keep his job and give a good impression, but talking out problems with the customers just seemed like part of the job. And he was often told he was a good listener. There was no denying that some citizens of Little Valley saved a pretty penny by showing up to the pub for much needed "therapy." No appointment needed, of course.

Samuel grunted. "I'm mad as hell," he said as he slammed the empty shot glass down on the shiny cherry wood bar top. "That damned new sheriff in town is threatening to shut down the gaming in here. He says it's causin' problems in town. We all know that it's only causin' problems in that God-fearing community down the road. I make good money off those games and the games bring in the crowds. We're gonna end up in over our heads if he shuts down the tables."

As if on cue, a loud roar rose in the air from the rowdy group of regulars huddled in the corner of the dimly lit room. It was dusk, and the crowd that Samuel referred to hadn't yet arrived. There were three men and two women - all very familiar faces to Archer - that had decided to spend their late Saturday afternoon together at the Little Valley pub. One of the men stood, dealing another round of cards, as the other players chattered incessantly about who *really* won the previous game, and who was going to win the next one. The games seemed pretty innocent to Archer- except for the occasional fights that resulted from too many drinks and too many losses.

Since he had started tending the bar about a year ago, he had seen a few Amish fellows wander in the bar sheepishly, usually very late at night, to try their hand at the game. They stood out like sore thumbs with their plain clothing and mannerisms. They never ordered drinks, and they were always more polite than the rest of the patrons. Samuel would always give them a hard time relentlessly during their visit, but he would never turn away a player with cash. Archer knew Samuel saw the Amish as easy targets in the game. Samuel had commented recently that he could afford the new car he wanted if he could just get more Amish to come play.

So, Archer was not fully surprised at the news that Samuel shared, but he still dared to play devil's advocate and defend the nice guys. "Did the sheriff say specifically that it's the Amish community that is the problem? I can't actually imagine he could shut it all down just because they asked for it."

Samuel looked at Archer with cold eyes and a clenched jaw. Archer took a step back and wished he could suck all the words he just uttered right back into his mouth. Archer berated himself silently and tried to regain his composure. *What was I thinking?!?* He stuttered, "I mean, you're probably right. I just..."

Samuel interrupted him with a loud slap on the bar that got everyone's attention. "What are you trying to say, boy? Are you on their side or mine?" Samuel's eyebrows furrowed over his eyes like dark thunderclouds and Archer could see spittle resting on his bottom lip. "Don't you work for me?" he asked the rhetorical question and then, his voice returning to his normal slur and tone, asked, "maybe you'd rather go work for those freaks? I'm sure they'd be happy to have you."

"That's not what I meant, Samuel, you're misunderstanding me," Archer said, trying to hide the disgust he felt for his boss. He felt his shoulders creep up to his ears and took a deep breath. "I was just trying to see if there might be another reason, so I could help you figure it out."

"That *is* the reason, kid" Samuel responded, spit flying in the air as he spoke the words. He swallowed the last bit of his beer, tipping the bottle back. Archer placed another shot in front of him with no coaxing this time. "The sheriff is trying to say that we're breaking county laws *and* he's accusing me of using the games to pad my own pockets. But I know he's just trying to get on *their* good side. After what happened when those idiots arrested that hardware shop owner, he thinks he can make it alright and get back in their favor. It's stupid and it's ridiculous. And I'm gonna fight it, I tell ya."

Archer, relieved to see that Samuel was slipping back into a more annoyed and less hostile mood, paused before saying, "You're probably right. Maybe I can talk to the sheriff and see if there's a license we're missing or something like that?"

"You must think I'm a fool," Samuel responded, jutting out his chin and rising to his feet. "I don't need some kid to save my bar. I'll deal with the sheriff and I'll deal with the Amish, too. It's time they learned a lesson about who owns this town. You just worry about serving drinks. And don't make me regret tellin' ya either." He turned and walked toward the obnoxious group of players at the old tattered poker table in the corner of the room.

"Nice talking to you," muttered Archer when Samuel was out of earshot. He shook his head as he gathered the empty beer bottle and shot glass and placed them in the sink. He grabbed the dingy rag out of the tub of bleach water, wrung it out, and proceeded to wipe down the bar. He tried to push any worries to the back of his mind, chalking up the experience as just another pointless conversation with just another drunk. But Samuel's threats replayed over and over again in his mind.

Chapter Six

T he room was dark except for a small crack of dim light that shone from underneath the door on the adjoining wall. There was the faint sound of water dripping slowly, but no other noise could be heard. Ruby did not know where she was, but she knew she was in trouble. She remembered waiting for Levi in the woods. He was late again. When she had heard a noise, she thought Levi was playing their usual game, hiding in the trees. But then... tears trickled down her cheeks as she remembered how someone else had jumped out and grabbed her. The man had covered her mouth with a cloth. Everything went dark, and she couldn't remember anything else.

How long have I been here? Ruby thought. Without any windows, it was impossible to decipher what time of day it was. She had been taken from her and Levi's spot in the woods in the late afternoon just a couple hours before dinnertime. Surely her parents would be concerned when she didn't arrive for dinner, unless... Ruby shook her head, remembering how she had recently not come home for dinner. It was just last week. She and her father had argued over the house rules, again, and she had decided to teach him a lesson and hide at Grace's house for a few hours. She really just wanted to see if her father would even worry about her, or if he would prefer it if she weren't there. In the end, it was Ruby that snuck in the house after dark, stealing some bread and a couple cookies from the kitchen before slipping into bed. As far as she was concerned, her point was made. Her father worried about what other members of the community would think more than he cared for her feelings. Ruby was convinced that her older sister, Esther, had felt the same way. The next morning Ruby's father greeted her for breakfast, and they never spoke about the missed meal again. Oh, how Ruby regretted that now. Would he even know she was in serious trouble?

She blinked her eyes, trying desperately to accustom her eyes to the darkness. Trying not to panic, she decided to try to sit up and see if she could stand. She thought she saw what must be a door leading out of this horrible place. As she lowered her feet to the ground, she quickly realized she was barefoot. The floor was hard cold concrete, and she felt a cold band of metal around her right ankle. Reaching down, she realized she was chained to the bed. She gasped. Any attempt to remain calm was immediately forgotten.

She opened her mouth to call out for help, but her throat was dry - and it hurt terribly to swallow, much less to scream. Her mind was racing. She knew she had seen the man before, but she couldn't place where, or figure out who he was. She couldn't even see his face clearly in her mind. Her head was so foggy, she couldn't think.

Ruby swallowed again, and she raised her hands to rub the front of her neck instinctively. She was so thirsty, her tongue felt swollen, and her throat felt like it was on fire. *I need to get home*, Ruby thought, wringing her hands. Ruby was diagnosed with epilepsy when she was only five years old, and she feared she was going to need her medicine soon. She hated that she lived in fear of having a seizure day in and day out, but as she grew older, she had come to understand the importance of taking her medicine every day. As long as she took care of herself, there was less of a chance of her falling into an epileptic seizure.

Frantic, she began to feel around in the dark. The bed she was sitting on had an elaborate metal frame with a curved design on the headboard. Ruby ran her hands along the curves, and touched the cold hard wall behind the bed, feeling the lines and textures of a brick wall.

There was a small round wooden table sitting next to the bed. As she explored it with her fingers in the dark, she found only a plastic bottle sitting in the center. She thought it felt like the shape and the pliable plastic of a water bottle you might find at the general store, and she hoped she was right. She could hear the pop of the seal on the cap as she turned it. She lifted it to her mouth and drew comfort as the room temperature water soothed her throat. After a few swallows, she had some relief, but she soon realized she should probably be more conservative and save some water for later. After all, she had no idea where she was, if she would get more water, or if she was left to die.

She took a deep breath and tried to gather herself. Ruby closed the water bottle and set it back on the table. She laid back down and closed her eyes, steadying her rapid breathing. The mattress was actually very comfortable, more comfortable than her bed at home. Although her own bed was cozy enough, Ruby had never slept in such a soft bed as this. The sheets and heavy comforter smelled brand new. The new smell reminded her of the pastel pink sheets her *Maem* had given her for her birthday a couple years ago. She loved the way the new sheets smelled when she first opened the packaging. Wanting to preserve the scent, she had begged her *Maem* not to launder them.

Shaking her head, she sat up again, refusing to allow herself to feel comfortable. She needed to think. Her eyes had adjusted to the darkness a bit, and she could discern the shape of what looked like a cluttered workbench against the back corner of the room. There was a large utility sink just next to that, and what she had thought was a door, definitely was one. That appeared to be all there was in the room besides the bed and the small table next to her.

She could feel that she was wearing a long cotton gown. She believed it must be a nightgown, similar to the one she wore to bed each night. Her blonde hair was down and fell around her shoulders. She shuddered at the thought of someone else changing her clothes. Where were the shoes and clothes she was wearing when she was taken? Where was her *kapp*? Ruby was terrified.

She called out, "Hello?! Can anyone hear me? Please, I need help!" Her throat was feeling better from the water. She called out for help a few more times, but her voice seemed to evaporate in the damp heavy air. There was no response. No sound at all.

What am I going to do? Her heart raced. Realizing she was out of options, she decided she had better lay back down. She needed to stay calm and put together a plan. Ruby laid her head on the soft pillow and pulled the down feather cover up close to her face. Her eyelids felt heavy, so she gave in and closed her eyes. She began praying silently and drifted off to sleep.

What seemed to Ruby like only a minute later, she woke to the sound of a key unlocking the door. She began to tremble as a figure entered the room. A stream of light shone directly in Ruby's face instantly blinding her. She put her hands up as if to shield the light from her eyes and tried to see who was standing in front of her.

"How are you doing?" the male voice asked with a neutral tone.

Ruby didn't respond. She was overcome with fear. *This can't be real,* she thought.

"Listen, I know this is probably scary for you," he said again, in a matter-of-fact tone, "but you won't be down here for long."

The light continued to shine in Ruby's face. She lowered her hand and cast her eyes to the floor. Tears fell down her cheeks. Her body shook, and she wrung her hands, remaining silent.

The man shifted his weight to his left foot and said, "Well, like I said, this is only temporary. I just thought I'd check on you. I actually didn't expect you to be awake."

"What do you want from me? What are you going to do with me?" Ruby asked, her voice quiet and shaky, and her eyes still downcast.

"That's not actually up to me," he responded. Seeming suddenly frustrated, he quickly reached over and set down an extra bottle of water on the table next to her and briskly turned and left the room, locking the door behind him.

"Wait!" Ruby called out, "Wait! Please, come back! Please, you have to help me!!"

She heard another heavy door shut - maybe a few yards away - and then she found herself again sitting in silence and cloaked in darkness. Overcome with emotion, Ruby threw herself down on the pillows and sobbed loudly. *How could I have been so stupid to meet with Levi in the woods? Why couldn't I have been a better daughter and obeyed my parents? I wish so badly that I was with my mother right now, and even Dat.* As frustrating as her father could be, she would give anything to be sitting next to him, safe and sound at home.

Ruby's head was pounding, and she felt so tired. She could barely keep her eyes open, and her stomach grumbled from hunger. She wished more than ever that she had not left the breakfast table without eating that morning.

As tears streamed down her face, she closed her hands together in prayers of forgiveness and begged *Gotte* to save her. Once again, she drifted off to sleep.

Chapter Seven

Relaxing after the celebration, Noah and Eli were spending the afternoon taking advantage of the unusually warm temperatures, preparing their gardens for the upcoming colder months. Anna and Beth were sitting in Anna's living room, fabric laid across their laps. The sisters were busy sewing their latest quilting project. They were working on a traditional shadow box quilt with dark winter blues, greens and shades of gray, and were about a third of the way into the project. The hope was to finish the quilt before the holiday to give as a gift to Moses' childhood friend, Matthew. Matthew had left the faith during his *Rumspringa*, but was recently forgiven and permitted to return to the community after fifteen long years. He was a very close friend of Moses, and Moses had missed him terribly while he was away. All the men in the community were pleased that Matthew was back, and he was set to work with the others preparing the different community farms for the approaching winter. Matthew was a single man with an attractive, clean-shaven face, and there were more than a couple single women who wished he would look their way.

"The party was wonderful, wasn't it, Sister?" asked Beth, although she already knew Anna's answer.

"*Ja*, it was a blessing indeed," answered Anna without losing pace. Her threaded needle moved like steady waves in an ocean. The twins had sewed dozens of quilts in their lifetime together, and enjoyed the entire process from beginning to end. "Isn't baby Rosemary just as sweet as she can be? She is such a delightful baby."

"*Ach jah*, she is so fantastic! I am so grateful to see Sarah and Moses and their little family happy again" Beth said. Then, as if she just remembered something, she asked, "Have you heard anything about the new sheriff? I've only just heard he hired the young officer that worked on the weekends while Moses was..." She hesitated to even say the word, and she didn't have to - Anna knew what she meant.

"We should bring them some bread as a welcome gift," Anna responded.

Beth nodded in agreement. "*Ja, gute* idea, *schwester*."

Just then, there was a loud knock on Anna's heavy wooden front door. Anna was still relying on a cane to get around easily, so Beth quickly lifted her side of the quilt off her lap and set it down on the couch, careful to not let it touch the floor. She rose from her seat and called out, "coming!" as she proceeded toward the door.

Opening the door, Anna could hear Beth say, "Oh, *gute mariye*, Bishop Packer! Please come in. *Wie bischt?*"

Bishop Joseph Packer entered the living room with his head bare, straw hat in hand. He was a distinguished older gentleman with a long beautiful beard showing his many years of marriage and dedication to his kind wife, Margaret. Anna knew by the lack of color in his face and his worried expression that something was not right.

"*Hallo*, ladies," the bishop said as he nodded at each of them. "Thank you for your hospitality, but I'm afraid I am here for an urgent favor to ask of you."

"*Wilkumme*, Bishop, how can we help?" Anna asked. She had forgotten all about the quilt that laid in her lap. Briskly placing her needle in the pincushion, she set the quilt aside and was on her feet within seconds, her weight leaning on her cane.

"Well, I'm afraid my Ruby may be in some trouble. She hasn't come home, and her *maem* and I are worried. At first, we thought she might be *rutsching* around, but when she wasn't in bed this morning, well..." The bishop paused, his eyes downcast at the floor.

Anna and Beth exchanged glances.

When it was clear that the bishop wasn't going to continue, Anna hobbled a few steps closer and touched the bishop's arm. "Please remember, Bishop Packer, that difficulty is a miracle in its first stage. Everything will be okay - it is *Gotte*'s will. Please, how can we help?" Anna wasn't quite sure what would follow that question. A few months ago, her immediate thoughts would've been that the twins might be asked to help console the bishop's wife, but it crossed her mind that this favor may be bigger than that considering their recent involvement with the investigation into the former county sheriff's murder. The sisters had always been referred to as the "wise women" in the community - would they be asked to help find Ruby?

The sisters knew Ruby, of course. She was the bishop's youngest daughter and possibly the prettiest young teenage girl in the community. She had striking blonde hair and piercing eyes that matched a clear blue sky. The sisters had just recently seen her when they dropped off baked goods to the Packers's home as a thank you gift. She and her friend, Levi Kimes, had been an integral part of saving their lives just a few weeks ago.

Anna straightened up a little without realizing it. She was ready to help in any way necessary. She again looked at Beth who was looking to Anna for a sign that they were on the same wavelength - and with one glance; the sisters knew they were indeed thinking the exact same thing.

Relieved that the sisters didn't ask any questions about how he could've waited so long to investigate, the bishop proceeded, "I know that you two were helpful in communicating with the law on Moses' behalf, and I was wondering if you would join Margaret and myself..."

Beth interrupted the bishop's sentence, "Say no more, Bishop Joseph. We are happy to help in any way that we can."

Anna nodded emphatically.

"*Denki, denki.* Margaret is waiting outside in the buggy now," the bishop said, not wanting to waste any more time than he already had. He had been nervous about approaching the sisters for such a favor and had made sure to ask permission from their husbands, Eli and Noah, beforehand. Eli and Noah had assured the bishop that the women would be excited and more than willing to help. Both husbands trusted and believed that Ruby was fine, and that this would certainly not be as dangerous as the last experience.

The two women grabbed their coats and headed out the door behind the bishop. Beth had returned to driving a buggy just recently and actually looked for an excuse to drive one as often as she could. There weren't many women in the community that drove - mostly men would drive the women where they needed to go, but Beth enjoyed the feeling of independence and freedom it gave her, and her husband trusted her with driving without him.

Beth and Anna told the bishop and his wife they would meet them at the Sheriff's Office shortly and climbed into Beth's buggy.

"Please be careful and take it slow," Anna said.

Beth rolled her eyes. "You always say that, *Schwester*. I'm always careful."

Anna looked at her sister with an all-knowing look and repeated herself, "Just be careful."

With driving lines in hand, Beth cued the horse with a clicking sound. As the horse started to trot, Anna's right hand grabbed onto the side of the buggy, her left hand clutched her cane.

The sisters pulled up to the station a few moments after the Packers had arrived. Their horse was tied to the post, but they had not ascended the steps to the porch just yet. They stood together waiting for Anna and Beth and a sense of relief washed over their faces when the sisters were in sight.

After securing their horse and exchanging reassuring words with Margaret Packer, the sisters led the way into the Sheriff's Office.

Sheriff Mark Streen rose to his feet as soon as the four Amish citizens entered through the front door. There were three middle-aged women and a gentleman with a long beard and full head of curly brown hair under a straw wide-brimmed hat. The women wore similar plain dresses with aprons. Their hair was pinned neatly underneath their securely fastened *kapps*. Two of the women were identical twins, allowing Sheriff Streen to quickly make the connection that he was meeting the infamous Anna and Beth for the first time. The sheriff was pleasantly surprised to see them and welcomed all of them with a warm smile.

"Hi, folks! Thank you for coming by! I'm the new sheriff in town. Name's Mark Streen. Normally you would get to meet Deputy Chase Brown, too, but he's running a little late this morning." He stretched out his hand to Bishop Packer and Joseph shook his hand, removing his hat with his left hand.

"Welcome to Little Valley, Sheriff. It's good to meet you." The bishop responded.

Anna wanted to interrupt the pleasantries and get right to business, but she worried it would seem disrespectful towards the bishop, so she remained quiet and patient.

The bishop continued, "My name is Joseph Packer. I'm the bishop of the Amish community here in town, and this is my wife, Margaret. These are good friends of ours, Anna Miller and Beth Troyer." He paused briefly before continuing. The sheriff nodded politely at each of the ladies as Bishop Packer introduced them. "We're here today because our daughter, Ruby, is missing. She's thirteen years old, and, well, she didn't come home last night."

"Please have a seat," said the sheriff, quickly collecting the two desk chairs and two visitor chairs and forming a semicircle in front of his desk. He was convinced this office had never seen so many visitors at once, and realizing there were not enough chairs, he promptly leaned on the desk in front of the group and pulled a small black notepad out of his front chest pocket.

"Ok, let's start from the beginning. Your daughter, Ruby, is missing - when was the last time you saw her, sir?" Sheriff Streen asked politely.

"I saw her last at breakfast yesterday morning." He stopped and glanced at Margaret. She grabbed his hand and gave him an encouraging nod. "To be honest, Sheriff, Ruby and I haven't been getting along very well lately, and she stormed off during breakfast yesterday during a slight disagreement we were having." He looked at the twins seated next to him, afraid of what they were thinking of him with that last bit of information. He wanted badly to be a good father, and he struggled with disciplining his daughters. His first daughter, Esther, had challenged him and accused him of being too strict - and then she had brought him so much shame when she did not return from her *Rumspringa*. And now Ruby was following in her footsteps, repeating the same hurtful actions as her sister. Joseph did not know how he could do things any differently. He was frustrated and had turned to *Gotte* so many times and was still waiting for clarity.

As if he were reading his thoughts, the sheriff responded, "Raising teenagers can be tough, for sure, Bishop Packer - is it okay that I call you that, sir?"

"Yes, that is fine. Thank you," the bishop responded, his voice quiet.

Turning to Margaret, Sheriff Streen asked, "Ma'am, did you see Ruby after breakfast at all?"

Margaret responded without meeting Mark's eyes, her chin quivering as she fought back tears, "No, sir, I am afraid I did not. Ruby has run off like this before. She goes to her friend Grace Schwartz's house. When she does this, I know she is safe and just needs to cool off. I expected her to come home in the middle of the night like she has before, but she wasn't in her room this morning and her bed was still neatly made. I ran to Grace's house myself, but Grace and Mrs. Schwartz said they had not seen her since yesterday afternoon. That is when..." Margaret's voice drifted off and she began to cry, holding a white linen handkerchief to her face. Beth, sitting next to her, reached over and put her arm around her shoulders.

After a quick grateful look at Beth, Joseph continued where Margaret left off. "It's also important to mention, Sheriff, that Ruby is epileptic. She was diagnosed with the seizure disorder just after her fifth birthday. She hasn't had a seizure in several years, but she takes medication every morning, and she doesn't have it with her, as far as I know," he explained. Margaret sobbed quietly and raised her face to look at the sheriff, her wet eyes pleading for an answer.

The Sheriff looked at the notes he had scribbled, taking a quick breath. An epileptic thirteen-year-old girl not returning home for the night was pretty serious, and he knew he couldn't waste any time. He was in a tough spot. This community had been through a lot, and this could either be an opportunity to build more trust among the good people. But if handled poorly, things could rapidly turn the opposite direction.

"Do you have any suspects in mind, Bishop? This can be a hard question, but do you know anyone who would want to hurt Ruby?"

The bishop shook his head emphatically. "We don't personally know anyone that would want to hurt us or our daughter, Sheriff, but someone in our community - a young man named Christopher Yoder - mentioned that he saw a homeless fellow walking on the road near our home the night she didn't come home. We are very concerned that she might be in danger."

"Ah, ok - I'll make sure to meet up with Mr. Yoder and get more details about who and what he saw then," the sheriff responded.

The sheriff stopped writing and looked up. He met Joseph Packer's eyes and with a firm tone, he said, "Bishop, I want to move quickly to get your daughter home safe. I'm going to file a missing persons report and put out what we call an Amber Alert, but first, I'm going to need a photo of Ruby and a description of what she was wearing the last time anyone saw her."

Joseph's heart sank down into his stomach. The Amish community did not take photos, so he could not imagine how he could provide that. And the plain clothing that Ruby was wearing yesterday could match dozens of girls her age in the community - he wasn't sure that would be much help either.

For the first time, Bishop Packer forgot all of his prideful worries of what people would think of his personal relationship with his daughters, and came face to face with the worst fear of every parent. He looked over at his wife. Margaret's face was turned down, her hands were in her lap and her eyes were closed. Joseph knew she was praying for Ruby's safe return.

Beth reached out and squeezed Anna's hand. They didn't have to say a word or even look at each other to communicate. They both knew they were headed to the Schwartz family farm.

Chapter Eight

C hase was already running late for work. He worried that it might look like he wasn't taking his new job seriously, so he decided to stop at the coffee shop in town to grab a couple of "fancy coffees" for himself and for the Sheriff as a sort of peace offering. He knew he should work harder to make a good impression on the Sheriff, since he had been awarded the deputy position just days before, but it was one of those mornings where everything was going wrong for him. He was hoping to use the excuse of stopping to get coffee in a crowded coffee shop as the reason he was late. He didn't want to lose this job, especially not this soon.

When he pulled up to Coffee World, he fondly remembered how he had first seen Ruby here a few weeks ago. It was a weekend, and he was on lunch break. He had wandered into the only local coffee shop when she immediately caught his eye. She was the most beautiful thing he had ever seen. She was standing in the corner with a girlfriend, waiting on her order to be prepared. When she looked his way, their eyes met, and he held her gaze feeling as if a moment had stopped in time. She smiled at him and her face lit up like an angel. He could see the shine in her brilliant blue eyes from across the room. Her golden blonde hair was pinned neatly into her Amish *kapp*, a style he found very attractive. She was wearing a plain beige Amish dress and apron, but there was nothing else plain about her. She was the most breathtaking girl Chase had ever laid eyes upon, and he was convinced that his world changed instantly.

Chase was standing in the short line to order his coffee when he heard the barista call out the name Ruby. The gorgeous girl reached over to grab her drink, smiled at the barista and thanked her. Chase thought, *even her name is perfect!* Ruby and her friend began walking toward the door. Chase thought she was headed his way, and his stomach filled with butterflies. He felt his face turn red and instinctively, he looked down at the floor.

When he lifted his eyes just a second later, he caught the sight of Ruby and her friend leaving the shop. She had walked right past him. *I'm so stupid!* Chase blamed himself for missing out on the opportunity to speak to someone so incredibly special. He rushed out of the coffee shop, the bell on the door ringing softly as he pushed it open. He was determined to catch up to her and say something - anything. But when he reached the street, there was no sign of her anywhere. He spent the next hour walking around the town's shops and the farmers' market in search of the girl before returning to work.

He was sullen and couldn't get her out of his mind. He even dreamed about Ruby that night when he slept. He was convinced that it was not a mistake that she was set in his path, and he wondered how difficult it would be to convince her to fall in love with him even though he was not of the Amish faith. *We will figure it out together*, he thought.

As if it were destiny, the two crossed paths again the next day. This time, Ruby and a young man, another friend of hers, had come to the station frantic to report that they were witness to a crime. Ruby was terribly shaken, and the boy she was with looked at her longingly as if he wanted to wrap his arms around her to comfort her. Fighting to keep his composure, as well as his career, Chase fought the urge to swoop in and hold her and tell her everything would be alright. He knew it wasn't the right time to do that just yet.

Chase noticed that she kept her distance from her friend, and he wondered if she were trying to show Chase that she wasn't interested in the kid romantically. Before Chase could step in and start a conversation with Ruby, the detective sent her and her friend away and ordered Chase to snap out of it and call for backup.

As much as Chase wanted to run after Ruby again, he knew the timing wasn't right. He didn't want their next meeting to be one associated with witnessing something horrible, so he vowed that he would one day see Ruby again, in a better situation. He made the phone call while he watched her and the boy walk away from the station. He thought he might have seen the boy grab Ruby's hand just as they turned the corner out of sight, but he couldn't be sure.

A few weeks later, when Chase heard that there was an opening for a deputy in the county, at the same exact station, he knew the stars were aligning once again. He couldn't have been happier when he found that he had been selected for the new deputy position. He believed everything in life was all about timing, and it had finally become time to make the next move.

Chase smiled as he jumped out of his car and entered the coffee shop.

Chapter Nine

It was a Thursday morning, and Moses was busy taking inventory of the different tools in his shop. He took pride in organizing the tools in his shop based on how they should be stored in one's tool box. He recommended that his customers have at least two layers in their toolbox, with the tools that are most often used stored in the top layer. Top layer tools would typically include tools such as a claw hammer, a set of pliers, a flathead screwdriver, a Phillips head screwdriver, an adjustable wrench, and a tape measure. And he had these items displayed in the front of the store since they were his most popular items.

He paused a moment to take a deep breath. He loved being back in his shop. He had come so close to losing it all when he was falsely arrested and, for a brief time, he worried that he would never have this moment again. He loved the way the shop smelled. It was a unique mix of wood and metal. Sarah had commented once, though, on how she didn't care for the way the shop smelled. She made a special candle for him to burn in the shop to replace the scent with "something the customers will like more," as she described it, but the wick remained intact months later. She hardly ever visited the store since the kids were born, but he kept the lighter near the candle just in case she were to ever drop by for a surprise visit. He would be quick about lighting the candle to show his appreciation for the well-meaning gift.

Just as he was returning his focus back to inventory, Moses' attention was turned to the front of the shop as his oldest friend entered wearing the friendly smile that Moses had missed for years.

"Good morning, Moses!" Matthew said, in a melodic voice. "Or should I say *gute mariye*?" He winked and his smile broadened. Matthew was on cloud nine since the bishop and the elders of the community had forgiven him and welcomed him back into the community. He lived in the English world for over a decade, and he missed his dearest friend, Moses. Moses had missed Matthew just as much, and was thrilled to hear he was returning.

"Still getting used to speaking *Dietsch*, eh, Matt?" Moses teased him. "*Wie bischt, bruda*?" Moses asked, reaching out to slap his arm in a friendly manner.

"*Wunderbar*," said Matthew, his accent just as good as the day he left for Rumspringa.

"What brings you to town?" asked Moses, setting his clipboard and pencil down on the counter and turning his full attention to Matthew.

"I was actually sent to purchase a couple new handsaws from you for the Weaver barn project. Seems we have a few more young men training with us this coming weekend, so we could use a couple more tools to put in their hands."

"Ah, *ja*. I will grab those then. Tell me, how are things since you've been back? Anything new happening? Since Rosemary was born, I feel like my life is fuller than ever. I'm missing spending time with friends and hearing the latest news. I haven't had time to help with the community building or anything. I know everyone must think of me as an outcast." Moses ran a hand through his thick hair. He made a mental note to ask Sarah to give him a trim this weekend.

"Things are good. I am staying busy helping whoever needs help around the community. It is an investment in rebuilding relationships with people that had long forgotten me and proving my worth again. I am blessed that I can take some time to do that and live comfortably on my savings for now." Moses felt as if he wasn't quite sure what Matthew had been doing for work in the English world. He wanted to set aside some time to rebuild his relationship with his old friend some time soon.

Matthew continued without missing a beat, "I will say, though, that the elders approached me with something to think about.. I wanted to get your advice, if you have a moment." Matthew trusted Moses more than anyone, and since he was a businessman in Little Valley, he would be the best one to consult on this matter.

Moses was curious. "*Oll recht*," said Moses, nodding.

Matthew explained to Moses how several people in their community had become concerned about the bed-and-breakfast that was being built. It was an Englisher that was building the sort of hotel, which would typically be no worry except that he was fashioning it to look and feel like an Amish home. He was mimicking their farmhouses and serving food that he was labeling as "Amish cuisine." The community wasn't too sure what to think of the fake Amish tourist trap.

On top of that, the Englisher had approached a few of the women at the farmers' market that sold their handmade goods, haggling to buy their crafted items below cost so that he could then turn around and sell them in his establishment. He was promising things that couldn't be trusted - like long term profits. The Englisher didn't seem to want to take no for an answer, and continued to badger the women and to try to sabotage their sales at the market over the past few weeks.

The elders were asking Matthew to step in as a mediator since he had so much experience as an Englisher himself. "My concern, *bruda*, is what if I can't make this guy see the light? What if he doesn't listen to me?"

Moses stroked his beard in thought. "This *Englischer* sounds *deerich*, indeed, and I wonder if he might be dangerous. I worry for your safety, but I also understand the concerns of the community. Since this doesn't really sound like something we could take to the law, though, I see why they are asking you to step in. No matter what, though, mind your step. It sounds like he may be the type with a quick temper. Remember, no matter what he says to you, it is better to give others a piece of your heart than a piece of your mind."

Matthew responded, "Of course, *bruda*. I will be mindful. I will speak with him as two men with the same end goals, and remind him that there is enough tourism to go around for all of us. I am still just so shocked at how busy Little Valley has become since I was last here. The tourists bring with them a good energy, though, and they ultimately bring benefits to all of us. The world is a big place, there's enough room for everyone, even in Little Valley." Matthew smiled.

"*Ja*, it's true. I have faith that we can find a way to get along with the new owner, as well. If he doesn't listen, the next step I would recommend is consulting my mother-in-law and aunt, the twins. They seem to have a way with problem solving and may have more insight. Keep me posted and let me know if I can help with anything, Matt." Moses replied, returning a warm smile beneath his beard.

"I will. *Denki*, Moses. Now, let's get to what I owe you for the tools, and I'll let you get back to counting." Moses wrapped the saws, and with a tip of his hat, Matthew left the shop. He was already on his way to see about meeting with the owner of the bed-and-breakfast.

Chapter Ten

Joseph's face went white when he saw the Sheriff's car stop in front of his house. It had been three days since he had last seen Ruby's face, a carbon copy of his wife's when she was young. It had been three full days since he had last heard her youthful voice and her innocent childlike giggle. His hand shook as he reached for the doorknob and opened the front door. Without a word exchanged, he gestured for Sheriff Streen to enter his quiet home.

He called softly for Margaret to join them in the living room. She rushed in, wiping her hands on her white apron. Her hands had not stopped working since Ruby had vanished. Margaret was not the type of person who could sit still and just wait. Many women from the community had stopped by to offer help and support, but Margaret insisted she needed time to be alone, to work and to pray. Aside from Ruby walking in that front door, these tasks were the only things that could bring her comfort.

The Sheriff removed his cowboy hat, but he remained standing until the older couple took a seat on their couch in front of him. The two sat on the edge of their seats, both literally and figuratively. No words were spoken.

The Sheriff thought the parents looked as if they may have aged a bit over the past few days since they first approached him for help to find their teenage daughter. His heart was filled with dread.

Joseph and Margaret sat holding hands. They were afraid to ask the question, but it didn't need to be spoken. It was clear why Sheriff Streen had come to visit.

The Sheriff sat in the large high-backed upholstered chair, situated caddy-cornered to the couch. He also leaned forward, sitting on the edge of his seat, his elbows resting on his knees and his hat dangling by his thumb and index finger. He lifted his face to see Margaret and Joseph pleading with their eyes for the Sheriff to deliver good news.

He cleared his throat before speaking. "Bishop. Mrs. Packer. It pains me to tell you why I'm here today. I'm so sorry, but I do not have good news about your daughter, Ruby." he paused for just a moment, allowing the parents to hold on to each other a little tighter and brace themselves for the words he needed to say next. "Ruby's body was found this morning. I'm afraid she is no longer with us. I am so sorry. I know she was very special, and I want you to know that we will find who is responsible."

A heartbroken scream came bursting out of Margaret's small, fragile body. The sound of her sobs replaced the thick silence that had previously hung in the air of the small room. She collapsed in Joseph's arms, her body shaking, exhausted and grief-stricken. Joseph cried silently, his tears falling onto Margaret's shoulder as they embraced one another. Joseph held his wife close, as if he wanted her to know he would never let her go. Strands of her hair fell out of her *kapp* and around her face, as if her tears were not enough to express her extreme sadness.

The Sheriff cast his eyes back down to the floor out of respect. He continued to sit quietly, sharing the solemn moment with the Packers for a while longer. He had never carried this sort of burden in all the years that he was on the police force, and he was running strictly on instinct, waiting silently for them to make the next move. He figured the bereaved parents would either ask him to leave or ask for more information, but he was going to let them dictate which of those actions he took and comply in the best way that he could.

When Joseph could speak again, he uttered one word just barely above a whisper, "Where?" He wasn't prepared to ask for any more details just yet - not in front of his wife. He wanted to see his daughter, and he knew his wife would want that, too. He would have more questions, but not until after he saw that Margaret, and Ruby, were taken care of.

"She was found in the woods just about a mile away, Bishop." The Sheriff spoke softly and carefully, hoping to lessen the heartache. "Tall trees and beautiful wildflowers surrounded her. She laid peacefully next to a small stream until Levi Kimes found her. I understand he was a close friend of Ruby's."

The bishop nodded. His tears suddenly stopped falling as if there were none left and a numbness seemed to take over his entire body. Still holding onto Margaret, his mind began spinning. *She was in town? Surrounded by flowers? Left in the woods to die?* Nothing was making any sense.

Among many, the bishop's emotions were those of shock, regret and guilt. *This can't be real,* he thought.

Margaret lifted her head and looked directly at the Sheriff. Her eyes were red and swollen, her face was tear-stained and her expression was one of confusion, sadness, and fear all together in one. Her expression at that moment would leave an impression on Sheriff Streen's memory for a lifetime. Her mouth opened as if she wanted to speak, but there was no sound. Joseph interjected and asked the question that both parents wanted to know: "When can we see her?"

Chapter Eleven

W ord spreads fast among Little Valley, especially something so paralyzing as this. The sisters took charge of planning the arrangements.

"Grace's father has offered to make the coffin," said Anna. "And Moses will make the gravestone."

"How can you just jump right into planning the ceremony, *schwester*, as if this wasn't a murder? We have to help find the killer! He could still be among us!" Beth exclaimed, pulling on her sister's arm to get her attention.

"*Ja*, Beth, I know. But, need I remind you that we are not detectives? What do you think? Just because we got involved with freeing Moses does not mean that we are trained police officers, now does it? My knee isn't even all the way healed from our last excursion, and to be honest with you, I'm worried about the fact that there have been such terrible crimes. And in such a short time. I'm starting to wonder if Little Valley is where we should stay." Anna's words poured out like water out of a broken faucet.

"What are you saying, Anna? Do you want to leave Little Valley? How could you say that? All of our family is here! We have lived here all of our lives and have many years left." Beth shook her head in disbelief.

Anna held Beth's hand and responded with a persuasive tone, "Beth, just think. Over the past few months, our lives have been impacted by robberies and murder. And it's not just that. Little Valley is changing. Tourism is growing, and it's not all good. We have someone in town that is building a bed-and-breakfast that mimics our lifestyle for profit, and we have drifters now!"

Beth interrupted, "We have heard of only one drifter, Anna."

Anna continued persistently, "but what if he did this to Ruby? We can't be sure that we are still safe here."

Beth took a deep breath and reached up to gently turn Anna's face back to hers. "That is why we have to get involved, Anna. We can investigate and find out what happened to poor Ruby and set our minds at ease. If it's the drifter, he will be arrested and the new sheriff will put new laws into effect to keep any other danger out of Little Valley."

Anna looked long and hard at Beth before shaking her head slowly. "You are naive, *schwester*." She paused. Anna didn't want to rule out moving away. She had privately been discussing it with Eli. She knew how Beth panicked when she was faced with change, and then there were their children. Beth was right about leaving their family behind, but Anna hoped they would all be on board. And she needed Beth to help research possible areas to relocate that were safer but close enough to easily return to visit if they wanted.

"I am going to remind you, Anna, of our mother's favorite proverb: Regrets over yesterday and the fear of tomorrow are twin thieves that rob us of the moment." Beth said as if that was the end to the conversation.

Anna rolled her eyes, "Sister, I think you're taking that too literally," she continued, "but I promise that I will put these thoughts on the shelf for now - at least until after Ruby's funeral service. Promise me, Beth, that this will be our secret until we decide together what is best."

Beth hated secrets, but she promised her sister that she wouldn't tell anyone. She vowed to herself that she would try very hard to change her sister's mind about Little Valley. It was their home, and Beth wanted to stay there forever.

Beth and Anna had just turned their attention back to Ruby's celebration of life when Noah walked in with Sheriff Streen in tow.

"Beth and Anna, look who I found in the front." Sheriff Streen's cowboy hat was in hand and he nodded at the sisters, his face unable to hide the stress and worry that he carried.

"*Hallo*, Sheriff," Anna and Beth said in unison.

"What can we do for you?" Anna took the lead.

Noah responded before the sheriff had a chance to mutter a word, "He is here to ask you two a few questions about Ruby's disappearance, and, you know..."

The sheriff nodded. "If you two have a minute," he asked, politely.

The twins nodded in agreement. Anna could feel Beth's excitement stirring. Noah bid farewell and headed out the kitchen backdoor, anxious to get back to work.

"Can I offer you some tea?" Anna asked the sheriff. "The kettle is still warm."

"No, thank you, ma'am," the sheriff looked as if he was distracted, fidgeting with his hat and his eyes shifting. "I won't be long. I just thought I should come by to check on you, first of all. Since you were with the Packers at my office the other day, I am assuming y'all knew Ruby pretty well. How are you doing?"

"*Gotte* is there to give us strength for every hill we have to climb. We believe that Ruby was called to a living hope of salvation with *Gotte*. We were just planning her celebration of life." Beth responded as Anna nodded in agreement.

The sheriff wasn't sure if he should be surprised by their lack of grief showing or if that was just 'the Amish way,' for everyone except those closest to the victim, of course. He nodded and waited for a brief moment before continuing.

"Good, good," he said, hoping that agreement was the right response and wanting to get to business. "I won't deny that the reason I'm here is because the two of you have quite the reputation among the local law folk for your recent involvement in a murder case. It wasn't even that long ago, was it?

Anna noticed Beth's knee started moving slightly in a steady rhythm. She knew Beth was about to burst with anticipation, and she herself started to feel a sense of unease. She knew they were lucky to walk away safely from the last adventure and she had no interest in risking her and her sister's lives again. She wasn't sure why, but a kidnapping and a murder of someone in their own community felt much more dangerous than finding an Englisher dead in Moses' toolshed behind his shop. She also knew that she cared deeply for the bishop and Margaret, and she couldn't imagine what it must be like to not know who did this to their daughter.

The sheriff continued speaking during Anna's train of thought. "I am hoping that you two might be able to shed some light on the case." The sheriff noticed the sisters looking at each other. Neither responded, so he continued, "anything you can contribute at all..."

Snapping out of her swirling thoughts, Anna tightened her *kapp*, stood up leaning on her cane, and said, "Sheriff, we will help you find who did this."

The sheriff looked confused. "Um, wait. That's not..." he stuttered.

Beth was on her feet, too, and with a louder voice than the sheriff and Anna expected, she chimed in, "Yes, thank you, Sheriff, for reaching out to us. We will see what we can find out and help get to the bottom of this."

The sheriff was flabbergasted and not sure if he should encourage this or not. On the one hand, he couldn't expect these older women to make much of a dent in the investigation, but on the other hand, he had hit a brick wall with the drifter being cleared with a solid alibi and lack of motive.

Beth reached out her hand with an invite for a handshake from the sheriff. Anna chuckled at her sister as she ushered Sheriff Streen out the door.

Finally gathering himself, the sheriff stopped on the porch just outside the front door and said, "Wait. I need you to know that I didn't actually come here to enlist you two as my deputies. I only wanted to ask if you knew anything. I have Deputy Brown for help. I do *not* want you to get hurt - I hope you are hearing that loud and clear. I don't mind you asking questions from the locals since so many people know and trust you around here, but don't go investigating and doing detective work without my knowing about it. Do you promise?"

Anna was actually relieved to hear the sheriff say those words, but Beth had already turned into the house to collect her coat. All thoughts of planning the funeral service were replaced by finding Ruby's killer.

To Beth, that also meant there would be an end to secrets and a guaranteed lifetime of happiness in Little Valley for her and her family.

Chapter Twelve

Levi's parents were worried about him. They knew that he and Ruby Packer were friends, and that finding her body in the woods was devastating. But they weren't sure if or when he would return to the normal happy kid that they had raised.

Levi went through the motions each minute of every day, but he was overcome with guilt. He couldn't stop picturing Ruby's face, once flawless and full of joy, and then, still, pale, and lifeless. His heart ached like he had never experienced before, and at times he would have trouble breathing. There were no tears to bring relief. There was no sleep for escape. Their secret died with Ruby - and he planned to keep it with him forever, like a locked chest of treasure.

The sheriff appeared in the large open doorway of the barn. Levi tried to keep his breathing steady and his face emotionless. He watched as the sheriff and his father had a conversation, but the tone was too low to make out what they were saying. Both men turned to look at Levi and time slowed down, as if suspended. Levi's father gestured for him and somehow

Levi felt his body start to move, slowly, one careful step at a time, his gaze never leaving his father's face.

His father said something about Levi needing to go with the sheriff to the office to answer questions, and all Levi could do was nod. His voice had stopped working - Levi struggled to mumble even the smallest word. He wanted to grab hold of his *dat* and tell him everything. He wanted to cry out for help and let the truth roll off his tongue, but something was keeping him from doing any of that.

For the first time in his life, Levi sat in an English car - the sheriff's car - and he wasn't sure he would even remember it at all. He turned to look out the back window. He saw his father briskly jumping into the family's buggy, securing his hat and roughly whipping the driving lines, motioning the strong horse to move quickly. His mother stood on the threshold of the house, she had her apron crinkled in her hands as if it were a handkerchief. Levi regretted the cloud of concern that hovered over her face. He knew he was the cause of all of this, and he wished more than anything that he could just turn back time.

They arrived at the sheriff's office in what felt like record time to Levi. Sheriff Streen stepped out of the car and opened Levi's door for him, gesturing him to exit the car and come inside. Levi followed along as if he were a tamed horse.

Walking into the front office, Levi's head hung low. Deputy Chase Brown was sitting straight in the antique desk chair behind the smaller desk. His face was directed at Levi, his expression was a mixture of contempt, anger, and disgust - but to his disappointment, Levi didn't even notice he was in the room. Chase noticed Levi's glazed look and wondered if he even knew where he was at.

Sheriff Streen had noticed Levi's face, as well. He needed to ask Levi some important questions considering he was Ruby's friend and he was the one who found her dead, but he was afraid that the kid might need counseling instead. In an attempt to put Levi at ease, he led him into the kitchen area and shut the heavy door leading to the jail cell. He showed Levi where the bathroom was located and he offered him a bottle of water. Levi seemed to barely comprehend the question and shook his head no before looking back towards the ground.

The sheriff wished Levi's father would arrive so they could get on with the questions, and he was starting to regret asking him to come into the office at all. He was hoping that it would have the opposite effect on him and lead to some clues, but he was starting to wonder if Levi was even capable of answering questions at all in the state he was in. And, he didn't want to traumatize the kid anymore than he clearly already had been.

Levi's father finally walked through the front door of the Sheriff's Office just as Levi sat in one of the visitor chairs placed directly in front of the sheriff's desk.

"Ok, thank you for coming out this way, Mr. Mast. I'm not sure Levi is feeling too well, so I'll try to make this quick." The sheriff picked up a pen and set his reading glasses on his nose. "I just need to ask your son what he remembers about the day that he found Ruby in the woods."

Mr. Mast looked at Levi who stared straight ahead with a blank stare, mouth slightly open. "Can you tell the sheriff what you remember, son?" he asked, after putting his arm around his son's shoulders. He could tell Levi was scared and he wished he could erase all of this.

"I don't know..." Levi's voice was quiet and trailed off as if lost in the wind.

After a pause, the sheriff then asked another question, "Can you tell me what you were doing out there that day, Levi? It was early in the morning, wasn't it?"

Levi sucked in air and closed his mouth tight. He shook his head and looked at his father. Mr. Mast felt a tug at his heart. He pictured Levi as a young five-year-old boy. He instantly remembered the day when Levi had climbed the ladder to the roof of the barn. Once on top of the roof, he became so scared of falling that he couldn't find the courage to step back down the ladder. Levi's father had to climb up the ladder and help him find his footing on every step of the way down. And he was willing to help him find his footing again now, faced with the memories of finding someone - a friend of his even - dead on the ground in the woods. He didn't know why he was out there, either, and had wanted to ask Levi that question himself, but he trusted there must have been a good reason.

Mr. Mast turned his attention back to the sheriff. "My apologies, sir, but I think I need to take my son home. I can reach out once he is feeling better or if he remembers anything that might be helpful."

The sheriff had no reason to keep Levi - he wasn't a suspect, and he was a minor - so, he nodded in agreement. He rose to his feet, reached out to shake Mr. Mast's hand, apologized for taking his time and thanked him again for coming out. He watched as the father and son pair left the office and walked to the window to watch as they climbed into their buggy, heading back to their home.

He let out a sigh. He was at a dead end. He was secretly hoping the twin sisters would find something - maybe the boy would feel more comfortable talking to them.

As the sheriff went to take his seat, Deputy Brown spoke up for the first time since Levi had set foot in the office and said, "If you ask me, that boy is as guilty as a bear with his paw in a beehive."

Chapter Thirteen

T he twin sisters entered the diner and chose seats at the counter. The diner was empty - lunch was still a few hours away. Anna and Beth wanted to chat with Jessica McLean, the owner, and see if she had heard anything out of the ordinary from the Englishers about Ruby's disappearance and murder. With their booth at the farmers market scheduled for the next day and Ruby's funeral on Sunday, and now their investigation underway, their lives had become very busy. They spent the morning baking their mother's favorite apple butter cakelets, preparing the caramel sauce separately. Plus, at the request of Anna's daughter, Sarah, they had also made a couple batches of the butterscotch cinnamon rolls that they had perfected together over the years, setting aside some for the sale. The sisters also wanted to drop some off as a thank you gift for Mr. Hatfield for the beautiful flowers he brought for Moses' party. And they had made just enough to bring to Jessica to add to her case of baked goods that she offered her customers.

After all the baked goods were packed up and the kitchen was clean again, the sisters were off on their mission to get to the bottom of who was behind the latest crime.

Anna and Beth could hear the clatter of porcelain plates and pots and pans behind the swinging doors leading to the kitchen area of the diner. Jessica was busy cleaning up from breakfast and preparing for the lunch crowd. The doors pushed open and Jessica appeared in front of the twins. Her face lit up with a warm smile when she saw the two middle-aged women sitting at the counter. She was holding a wet dingy rag and a bottle of cleaner and her wavy red hair flowed down her back, the sides tied back away from her face. A few curly strands of hair had fallen near her temples complimenting her fair skin and blue eyes. Light freckles looked as if they were sprinkled like fairy dust on the bridge of her nose and fullness of her cheeks. She was a very attractive woman, young and sweet. Although the twins had visited with Jessica on several occasions, Anna realized now that she really didn't know much about her personal life. She made a mental note to make an effort to get to know her better after things settled down. She was reminded of her conversation with Beth the day before about considering moving out of Little Valley and she pushed away the sadness that followed her thoughts.

"Oh my gosh, hi ladies! I am so glad to see you! How long were you sitting here? I'm so sorry to keep you waiting!" Jessica spoke quickly, her voice friendly and excited. Before waiting for Anna and Beth to respond, she spotted the white box and exclaimed, "Oh! Please tell me that is some of your delicious baked goods that you have brought for me!" She set the cleaning supplies down and stood with one hand on her hip.

Beth was the first to answer. She felt comfortable around her, which said a lot about Jessica since Beth often felt uneasy around people, especially those outside of the community. "We made butterscotch cinnamon rolls. We just know you'll love them. We finally perfected the recipe and they sell out pretty quickly at the market when we have them on the table."

Jessica closed her eyes briefly and brought her hand to her stomach as if she was imagining just how delicious the rolls tasted, "Oh, wow, I can't wait to try those! I'm not even sure I'm going to share them with my customers - I may just keep them all to myself!" She chuckled. And then, as if remembering her manners, she said, "Thank you both so much. That is very sweet that you thought of me. What can I get for you? Are you hungry for brunch? Tea? Coffee?"

Anna responded with a wave of the hand, "Oh, I'm not hungry. I'll just take a cup of coffee if you have some already freshly made. No sugar or cream, please." She looked to Beth.

"I'll take the same, please, Jessica," Beth said. There were only a very few things that the sisters ever did differently - so few that they could be counted on one hand. They had the same favorite food: chicken and dressing. Blackberries were their favorite fruit, and they both favored the color light blue. The twins cooked and baked the exact same way - so much so that their own husbands couldn't tell their breads apart - and the same applied to their sewing and cleaning. There was a slight difference in how they pinned their hair, what books they chose at the library, and Beth liked to drive a buggy where Anna preferred to ride, but that was about it.

Jessica poured hot coffee into three separate mugs and invited the women to join her in the large corner booth. "This is actually perfect timing for a break," she said, settling in across from Anna and Beth. "I think I could probably guess why the two of you are here today, although it's always great to see you."

Anna spoke, "Thank you - we feel the same, but, yes, we should probably get straight to the point so you can get ready for your lunch customers. Forgive me if I am being too direct, but have you heard or seen anything strange - you know, about sweet little Ruby Packer's vanishing and death? I'm afraid the sheriff doesn't have much of a lead, and our whole community is just in shock.. and scared."

"If we can help solve the murder then we're sure to set a lot of minds at ease," Beth interjected. "The Packers, as you can imagine, are just so shocked that someone would want to hurt their youngest daughter."

Jessica nodded, "Oh, I cannot imagine what they must be going through. It is just terrible." She paused for a moment to take a sip of the hot coffee. "I've been thinking about it," she said, leaning in towards the sisters. She lowered her voice instinctively despite the empty room. "I'm not sure if y'all know that the new deputy was rejected by Ruby right before she went missing."

The sisters shook their heads, "No, what do you mean?" Anna asked, her curiosity peaked.

Jessica continued, her words flowing out quickly as if she was going to burst if she didn't tell someone. "Well, there were a few people sitting at the counter, so I know I'm not the only one who saw it, and honestly, I kinda feel bad for the guy. But, yeah, Ruby was here with her best girlfriend - I think her name is Grace. Those two are such sweet girls, well..." She caught herself speaking in the present tense and decided not to correct herself. "They were sitting here sharing a piece of cake near the end of the busy lunch hour last weekend. The deputy had walked in and walked right up to them, like he came in specifically to see them - not to eat. He didn't look around for a place to sit or anything. He stuck out his hand for a handshake - to Ruby, understand. He was pretty much ignoring Grace. And he introduced himself. I think he said his name was Jason, but I'm not sure. Then he said that he was the new deputy. Ruby looked a little confused, probably wondering why this guy, a few years older than her, was bent on talking to her exactly. She definitely looked like this was the first time she was seeing this guy." Jessica took another sip before continuing. The sisters were hanging on her every word, nodding quietly here and there.

"So, anyway, he said he had seen her at the coffee shop before and he wanted to tell her that he thought she was the most beautiful girl he had ever seen. Just like that! He said it just like that!" Jessica exclaimed, shaking her head as if she still just couldn't believe it. "I was thinking, is this guy flirting with Ruby? He had at least three or four years on her. I mean, yeah, she's strikingly pretty, but she's so young!"

"Well, Ruby turned all shades of pink and looked even more uncomfortable, I'll tell ya. I don't even think she responded to that - and I'm not sure he really needed a response to it, now that I think about it. He continued on and said he wanted to take her out on a date. Just like that. He didn't *ask* her out on a date, understand me. He said the words, 'I wanna take you on a date.' Well, that's when Ruby looked over at me. I had made my way over to her by now, sensing that she might need some backup. And I asked her if everything was alright. Instead of answering me, she looked up at the deputy and responded simply, 'No thank you. I am not dating yet.' and that was that. That girl was so confident. I was proud of her." Jessica stopped talking, waiting for a reaction from the women sitting across from her.

Beth was intrigued, "Well, what happened next? How did the young man react when Ruby told him that?"

Jessica shrugged, "I'm not really clear where it went from there. At that exact moment, Samuel Graber came in making a scene, and I was pulled away to deal with that again. But, when I turned back, they had all left. There was a tip on the counter with the empty plate. I can only assume that the boy took the hint and bowed out - and that Ruby and Grace left for home. That was the last time I saw her. I'm so sad about that. I really liked her." Jessica's voice had slowed, and her eyes misted over. "It just breaks my heart that someone did something so terrible to her."

Beth and Anna nodded in agreement. "Yes, it's true, but in our faith, we believe that creation and destruction are the two ends of the same moment.

Ruby has found salvation with the Lord, and although she will be missed, we trust that *Gotte* has a perfect plan," Anna explained.

Beth picked up right where Anna left off and said, "Jessica, you said that Samuel came in making a ruckus. What was that about?"

Jessica rolled her eyes. "It's always something with Samuel," she said. "He was pretty angry. I guess he had just found out that the sheriff shut down gaming in his bar, for good." She hesitated and then with her eyebrows pushed together, she looked back and forth slowly from sister to sister and said, "It wouldn't be right for me to not mention that Samuel has been going around outwardly threatening your community. I mean, y'all probably already know that, but in case you don't, please be careful, he is a volatile person, and it sounds like he blames y'all's community for the whole gaming shutdown and he intends to make someone pay for it."

Anna looked surprised, "What do you mean? What does he intend to do?"

Jessica relaxed her shoulders and leaned back in the seat, "I'm not sure he'll do anything, to be honest. I personally think he's all talk. He really used to be a nice guy. It's just that his drinking has gotten so much worse, and I think he is gettin' caught up with the wrong crowd. I seen him hanging out with that new Englisher, Hank somebody. You know, he's the one that is building that bed-and-breakfast on the west side of town. Those two seem like they're in cahoots about something, huddling together in this here booth, talking with hushed tones. I think they're up to no good, but they're mostly pretty harmless like two young boys acting like fools."

"I see," said Anna. "Well, I'll be sure to pass the word to the community, if not just for safety. Thank you for letting us know."

"Yes, thank you for everything, Jessica," said Beth, "but we should probably run. We have to meet with Mrs. Packer and finalize Sunday's funeral arrangements."

"Oh, please let me know if I can do anything at all to help," Jessica said, cleaning supplies in hand again.

"You've been a wonderful help today," Anna assured her. Jessica was relieved to hear it. She often wondered if she said too much and worried that she gave the wrong information or impression of something, but she would admit that it felt good to tell someone all of this. She also wondered why the new sheriff hadn't come to ask her anything yet. She looked forward to getting to know him better. She hoped he was a better guy than the previous sheriff in Little Valley.

The twins thanked Jessica again and headed on their way. Once they sat in the buggy, Beth picked up the driving lines, but paused and looked at Anna. "We just got so much information, *schwester*. It almost looks like we could have two, possibly three potential suspects! The deputy, that terrible man, Samuel - and Hank Davis, too."

Anna nodded, "*Ja*, I know. I was thinking the same thing, *schwester*. One thing is for sure, there are a lot of secrets in Little Valley. But, I am confident that we are much closer to the truth than we were this morning."

Beth agreed. "Let's head to see Mrs. Packer. We are later than expected," she said just before she signaled for the horse to trot forward.

Inside the diner, Jessica snuck her first taste of the delicious butterscotch cinnamon rolls. *There's no way I'm sharing these*, she said to herself, as she placed the plain bakery box behind the counter to take home with her after closing.

Chapter Fourteen

Margaret Packer stood in her kitchen, one hand caught in midair holding a half peeled hard-boiled egg. Her other hand was resting on the counter. Her eyes were fixed on the empty rope swing in the backyard. The swing hung from a branch in an old oak tree, and she watched it as it swayed softly in the gentle breeze. *Ruby is with Gotte now*, she recited in her mind again. The whole thing seemed so hard to believe, and she found comfort in saying those 5 words to herself throughout the day. She set the egg down and turned to take a sip from the hot steaming cup of meadow tea sitting on the table behind her.

She glanced out the front window, checking to see if Anna and Beth had arrived yet. Joseph had left about an hour before to visit Jacob Schwartz. Grace Schwartz was Ruby's best friend and her father, Jacob, had built the coffin for Ruby's funeral tomorrow. He and Joseph planned to transport the coffin into town to the funeral home so that they could have everything ready for tonight's viewing and tomorrow's ceremony. Anna and Beth were going to visit with Margaret and make sure all the other accommodations for the event were in place. Margaret was preparing a light lunch for the women to share.

There was no sign of Anna and Beth's buggy yet, so Margaret turned back to finish preparing the egg salad. Just as she was finishing setting the table, she spotted their buggy. It surprised her to see Beth as the driver, but she had heard that she had taken to driving her and her sister everywhere. She opened the front door and welcomed each of the women with a hug.

"*Denki* for coming," said Margaret as she gestured to take their coats.

"Of course, Margaret. *Wie bischt?*" Anna asked with compassion in her eyes. Margaret appreciated the effort but had already grown tired of the special treatment she was receiving. She never expected for parenting to be such a challenge and full of heartache. First, her daughter Esther had broken her heart by choosing to leave the faith and now, someone had taken her beautiful Ruby away. Margaret had chosen her name based on the scriptures, specifically Proverb 3:15, "She is more precious than rubies; nothing you desire can compare with her." *Ruby was indeed precious,* Margaret fought back tears as she grappled with her grief. *Ruby is with Gotte now.*

Clearing her throat, Margaret avoided Anna's question and invited the girls to sit down and eat with her. "Would either of you like meadow tea with your lunch? I have made my mother's famous egg salad and we have bread and butter to share."

Beth responded, "Oh, you shouldn't have, but that sounds delicious! I love your mother's egg salad recipe - it's the one with green olives and pimento, right? Your recipe has inspired mine for many years. It's my husband, Noah's, favorite."

"*Ja,* it is delicious, Margaret, and I would say that Beth's is pretty close," Anna said lightheartedly as the women took their seat. "I'll just have water, I think, though. *Denki.*"

"Me too, Margaret. Water is fine for me, as well." Beth chimed in. "We just had coffee at the diner with Jessica. We went to ask..." Anna kicked Beth under the table, and Beth stuttered, "I mean, we went to bring her some of our baked goods. For her customers, I mean." Beth recovered, realizing that she almost put her foot in her mouth telling Margaret the real reason for their visit with Jessica.

"Ah, how is business for Jessica, then? I haven't seen her in a while, it seems." Margaret asked, filling the three glasses in front of her with water from the steel pitcher.

"She seems well. She sends offerings of help if you need anything at all," Anna spoke carefully, still unsure if Margaret was ready to discuss Ruby and wanting to be respectful.

"That's very kind. Joseph and I have been showered with kindness the past couple days." Margaret responded, her words trailing off as she pushed the dish of egg salad toward the women.

The women helped themselves and since the door to the conversation had been opened, Anna continued, "Do you need any help, Margaret? Anything at all? I mean, Beth and I are helping to organize tomorrow's ceremony, but is there anything else we can do for you?"

Margaret sat staring at the cup of tea placed next to her glass of water, her plate was empty. She needed to talk to someone about what she found in Ruby's room, and she trusted Beth and Anna. "Yes," she finally spoke. "I do need something. I need to share a secret that I am holding, and I know I can trust the two of you to know what to do with it." She looked up and her eyes met Anna's. If one's eyes are the window to their soul, Anna thought, then she was sure that Margaret's soul was troubled, overwhelmed, and most importantly, she was lost. She reached out to take her hand into hers.

"Certainly we can help," Anna said with strength in her voice. "First, let us pray together." Beth closed the circle by holding Anna's and Margaret's free hands, and the women bowed their heads. "O Lord, we thank you for this nourishing food we are about to eat as well as for the family that we sit in company with. Almighty *Gotte* and Heavenly Father, you who know and recognize everyone's heart, we ask you to help and guide us to make the right decisions during this time of distress. Teach us to act according to your will, for you are our God." Beth recited the prayer quietly.

After a brief pause, the women said "Amen" in unison.

"*Denki*, Beth, that was beautiful," Margaret said, taking a sip of her tea. "I had a late breakfast, so I think I'll just munch on a piece of bread, but please enjoy." She motioned to the women to begin eating despite her empty plate.

After compliments for the tasty lunch were given and received, Anna speaks up, "What is this secret you are carrying on your shoulders, Margaret? We want to help in any way we can."

Margaret straightened up in her seat, reminded that she had mentioned it a moment before. "Oh yes," she said. "Let me go grab it and I'll be right back." She left the room quickly and returned just seconds later with a school notebook in hand. She placed the notebook in front of the sisters. "I found Ruby's diary last night."

Beth let out a short gasp. "*Ach du lieva,*" she muttered.

Margaret's hand laid on top of the diary. She continued, "You must understand that I haven't shared this with Joseph yet. There are some things in here that may hurt him deeply, and I want to avoid that."

"Ruby is a good girl, but she is very confused about why her older sister left the faith. She misses Esther - the two girls were close - and she blames her father for most of it." Anna noticed how Margaret spoke of Ruby in the present tense, and for a moment, she wondered if Margaret could heal from this. Her life would look very different now, and Anna couldn't imagine what that must feel like.

"But, there is something near the end - in the more recent entries - that is really shocking. I guess Ruby and Levi Mast were sort of secretly dating. Ruby mentions a few times that Levi had more serious feelings than she did, and they were meeting in secret. She wrote that no one else knew about it except for Grace - Grace Schwartz, her best friend. I know what you're thinking - it's embarrassing and a big part of why I haven't told anyone yet, especially Joseph. Ruby was only thirteen." Margaret caught herself from using present tense that time before continuing, "She shouldn't have been breaking the rules."

She let out a heavy sigh, removed her hand from the diary and slumped back in her chair, feeling a mixture of emotions, but relieved to have finally shared what she had found. It had been so hard to keep this secret from Joseph even for this short of time. But, he loved Ruby so much and he would be shocked to know of her breaking the rules of their faith like this.

Beth wanted to grab the book and devour it like a lion who hasn't eaten in weeks, but more importantly, she wanted to be respectful. "May we read it?" Beth asked gingerly.

"*Ja,* you may." Margaret nodded, thanking her for asking.

The sisters pushed their lunches aside and opened the notebook carefully. Ruby's handwriting was straight and neat. She started each page with "Dear Diary" on the top left and the date on the top right. Margaret was right, there were quite a few pages concerning disagreements with her father, followed by detailed accounts of her encounters with Levi.

What Margaret didn't mention, however, was the several entries right alongside the recent entries of her escapades with Levi where Ruby mentioned that she felt as if she was being watched, or followed. Ruby couldn't seem to shake the uneasy feeling she got during these episodes, which happened mostly in the evenings or early mornings, she had recorded. Ruby also mentioned that her mother disregarded it, describing Ruby's fear as the result of Ruby's "overactive imagination." Ruby wrote that she desperately wanted her mother to believe her - that her fears felt very real.

Margaret sat patiently across the table from the sisters waiting for them to finish reading. As soon as the book closed, she spoke, "Well, do you think Levi could have..." she didn't want to say the words out loud, but she knew she had to... "hurt Ruby? Do you think he could have hurt her? I don't know him very well, and he is so young. But I don't know what to do."

The sisters were stunned. This diary may very well be an important piece of the puzzle.

Beth spoke, "We couldn't say for sure, Margaret. I think we are both shocked about Ruby and Levi's secret, but I can't imagine young Levi...."

"But, I do think it's important to tell the sheriff about this, Margaret. We can impress on the sheriff how important it is to keep the details secret for as long as we can, but if it could help find who did this, well, then, that is what is best for the community overall." Anna interjected. "Everyone knows that Ruby loved her father, Margaret, and he will forgive her words when they reach his ears."

Margaret nodded and then replied meekly, "If you think it could help the investigation..."

"With your permission then, we will hand over the diary with care to the sheriff. We have met him and he seems kind and respectful - he's not like Sheriff McCall. We can trust him." Anna responded, again, holding Margaret's hand in her own.

"Now, let's get busy setting up for tonight's viewing," Beth said, "..if you're ready, Margaret?"

"*Ja*, I am ready," Margaret said out loud, rising from her seat. In her mind, she recited those five words: *Ruby is with Gotte now.*

Chapter Fifteen

R uby's funeral was indeed a celebration of life, full of beautifully sung hymns and solemn prayer and silence. Amish communities from miles away traveled to attend and show the Packers comfort. Margaret and Joseph's oldest daughter, Esther, attended the funeral as well. She sat in the front, in a modest English black dress, hair pinned up with a black lace covering the top and back of her head. She held her mother's hand throughout the service and then hugged her tightly goodbye directly after the burial ceremony. She chose not to exchange words or hugs with her father, and it appeared as if he expected nothing else.

The community of Little Valley gathered together for a celebratory meal after the burial proceedings. Anna and Beth had prepared food for the masses and as with most gatherings in their community, the men tended to gather outside, in the barn or the yard. The women stayed inside and visited among each other, providing comfort to those closest to Ruby and telling beautiful stories about her life.

"Can I please have a moment to speak with you?" Grace tugged on Anna's arm, touching Beth's arm, as well. She couldn't remember if she had ever spoken directly to the older twin sisters before now, and she was a bit nervous. She had heard so much about how Mrs. Miller and Mrs. Troyer had freed Moses and she knew they were known as the wise women in the community. And it was for both of these reasons that she needed desperately to speak with them.

Anna and Beth looked at each other. They recognized the young girl right away as Jacob's daughter and Ruby's best friend, but Anna wondered if they should step away. Margaret was just a few steps away, seated on a comfortable chair, her own mother on one side and her cousin on the other. They were drinking tea and having quiet conversation. Anna decided they could step away for just a few moments, and Beth took no convincing to do so.

Grace felt a sense of relief when the two women agreed to join her outside to talk privately. She followed Anna and Beth out the side door and down the wooden porch steps. There were two sturdy benches there set next to each other, facing out to the open field. There were many sunsets that the Packer family had watched from these seats over the years, and Grace remembered sitting on them with Ruby a time or two, as well. The women sat next to each other and Grace sat on the other, turned toward them slightly.

Grace closed her eyes and took in a calming breath. Today was difficult for her, despite the faith that Ruby was with the Lord. She missed her best friend terribly and couldn't imagine a life without her in it. She blinked back tears and faced the sisters. She noticed how much they looked alike and definitely couldn't say which was which if she were asked.

"*Denki* for talking with me," she said, her voice trembling.

"Of course, Grace," Anna answered, waiting for Grace to continue.

"Ruby and I were best friends," she said quietly. She again tried to blink back tears, but one escaped and slowly trickled down her cheek. "We grew up together, and we told each other everything."

Beth leaned forward and touched her shoulder, "*Ja*, we know this is hard. Take your time. Let us know how we can help you."

Grace took another deep breath and exhaled slowly. "*Denki*. The thing is that Ruby told me something in confidence and I promised not to tell another soul. And I haven't. I haven't told anyone at all. But I think Ruby would want me to tell someone now that she's... gone." Grace looked down at the grass in front of her. She wasn't sure if this was the right thing to do, and she was scared. She didn't want Ruby's father to be angry with her, but she was conflicted. She knew they had not found who killed her best friend and Ruby's secrets might bring justice to that terrible person.

She looked back at the twins, her eyes wet and dull, and tried to speak but her nerves were causing her to struggle. Now that she had the women's attention, she wasn't sure where to begin. Just when she started to doubt her decision to say anything at all, Anna spoke.

"Grace, we know about Levi," she said in a kind voice that she hoped would bring comfort to the young girl.

Grace's face and neck flushed a slight tinge of red and her eyes widened. "You do?" she asked in surprise.

Beth answered, "*Ja*, we know they were in love and were meeting secretly."

"Well, I don't know if you could say they were in love exactly. Levi may have said they were, but Ruby wasn't sure. She was just, well, she liked Levi, but she told me she wasn't in love with him. They weren't *schmunzla* or anything like that. Ruby said they would just talk when they met in the woods. She thought he was very nice, and I think that she liked the attention he gave her mostly."

When Grace took a pause, Beth asked, "Did you say they met in the woods?"

Grace nodded, "*Ja*, they had a secret spot where they would meet. Ruby loved it there, but she would complain that Levi was usually late." Still turned toward the twins, her right foot hanging off the bench didn't quite touch the ground. Her leg slowly started to swing rhythmically like a metronome as she became more comfortable talking with the women.

The twins would have normally exchanged glances upon discovering that it may be that Ruby was found at her and Levi's secret spot, but they both noticed that Grace was feeling more relaxed and wanted her to continue.

Grace continued, "I'm surprised Levi told you about their secret. I'm not even sure that he knows that Ruby told me about it. I was thinking that his conscience feels pretty heavy about that now that she is gone. I mean, Bishop Packer and Mr. Mast would be furious, even now, if they found out."

Before the twins could have explained that it wasn't Levi that told them about the secret meetings, Grace continued, "But what I wanted to tell you - and the thing I don't know who to tell - is that Ruby was scared. The week before she died - or maybe it was two weeks, I'm not sure - Ruby kept feeling like someone was following her, or watching her. She couldn't pin it, but she was sure it was happening. One time, when she was walking from her father's barn to her house, she heard a sound - I think she said it sounded like a twig broke or something. She stopped and turned around, but it was almost dark so she couldn't see really well. She felt like someone was there. And really close. She said she ran to the door, but once she got there, she thought she heard the motor of a car close by. She told her *maem*, but her *maem* didn't believe her."

"Then another time, she was laying in bed about to drift off to sleep when she saw a small round light reflection shining on the wall next to the bed. She was facing the wall and she said that the light was on her bed and then moved to the wall, and she thought it was coming from her window. She turned around to see if someone was shining a light in her window and the light went away, like it was just turned off. She ran to her *maem* and *dat*'s room, but again, her *maem* said she was imagining things."

Grace stopped and said, "I don't mean to say anything disrespectful for Mrs. Packer. I told Ruby that she was a good *maem*, and to be honest, Ruby did have a good imagination."

The twins nodded, and Anna said, "*Ja*, Mrs. Packer loved Ruby very much. Did Ruby ever see anything more than that, Grace?"

"I'm not sure. I feel like she said that it happened more than that, but I can't remember exactly now. But, she was frightened, and now I'm frightened that she may have been right.. and if I don't tell this secret to someone, this person might hurt someone else," Grace's nerves and fear were starting to build inside her again. She fidgeted, struggling to sit still on the bench, and begged, "What should I do? Should I tell Mrs. Packer? Can you please help me tell her? I don't want to say the wrong thing, and I'm so nervous about that. And I'm scared." She covered her face with her hands as her tears returned.

Beth moved over to sit next to her and draped her arm around her shoulders. "Everything will be okay, Grace. I promise. We will talk to Mrs. Packer. Please don't worry. You did the right thing. *Denki* for telling us. We will need to tell the sheriff this information, though, so that he can do a thorough investigation. He might want to ask you some questions about it, but he is a very kind man and you can trust him."

Anna chimed in, "*Ja*, and we can be there to help support you, too, if you'd like."

Grace uncovered her face and leaned into Beth's embrace. "I would like that very much," she said, speaking barely above a whisper.

"Ok, then," said Beth, her voice at a higher pitch. "Let's go back in before everyone starts to wonder where we've gone," Beth chuckled and gave Grace one last squeeze.

Anna reached over and wiped Grace's face with her linen handkerchief and squeezed her hand. "Everything is going to be okay, Grace. It is *Gotte's* will."

Grace nodded. She felt such a sense of relief after speaking with the women. The women rose to go in, Anna leaning on her cane. Grace straightened her *kapp* and rubbed her palms down the sides of her dress. Entering the Packer's house through the side door, no one seemed to notice they were gone. Grace thanked Anna and Beth one more time and headed off to find her friends. Beth pulled Anna aside and whispered, "I wonder if we should have asked Grace about the deputy."

"I didn't have the heart to put her through anymore storytelling or questions. We can leave that up to the sheriff," Anna said firmly, looking at Beth with a stern look in her eye. She knew Beth wanted to solve the case without the sheriff, but Anna wasn't sure that was going to be smart, or even necessary.

Beth registered the look and knew exactly what Anna meant. She decided not to challenge it. This wasn't the time or place to discuss the details of how Ruby was killed. She was willing to put a pin in it. For now. But this conversation wasn't over.

Chapter Sixteen

"Yes, ma'am. Okay. No, I am listening, and I will follow up on it. Thank you for calling." Mark Streen replaced the old phone earpiece back into its cradle and sat back in his chair, a heavy sigh escaped his lips.

Deputy Chase Brown set his cellphone down on his desk in front of him and looked over at the sheriff. "Everything ok?" he asked.

"Yeah, it's fine. That was Shirley Hatfield. She and her husband own the flower shop in town. She said she overheard the drifter talking to himself outside her shop this morning saying that he killed Ruby Packer in the woods. I'll tell ya, everyone thinks they are a detective in this town. Everyone has a theory. But, you said that you saw that guy the night Ruby went missing - and you can't have a better alibi than the deputy himself. Plus, where would he even hide her? He simply couldn't mastermind something like that." Sheriff Streen ran his hands through his hair. The lack of sleep showed on his face.

Chase nodded. "Yeah, I'm with you. There's no way that guy killed Ruby. He was probably just muttering something to himself. Everyone is on edge, so the florist's wife must've just heard what she wanted to hear. We don't have any real leads, though. We have to be missing something. I think we might need to come to terms with it being some random murder by someone passing through town."

Mark looked over at Chase and shook his head. "I don't think so. Something in my gut tells me it's someone here in town. The autopsy report showed bruises around her ankle as if she was bound in some way - but not with rope. Maybe it was metal and she was chained to something somewhere, but she didn't look like she had spent any time in a dungeon or anything like that. She didn't have any drugs in her system. She died of an epileptic seizure. No signs of trauma. Nothing under her fingernails. The body left us no clues to go on except for that mark and bruise on her ankle. I'm stumped."

"We're missing something," said Chase.

"Yes, definitely. We can tell that she was well-cared for in custody. Whoever took her must have cared deeply for her, maybe even treasured her. I think I'm going to go visit Hank Davis today. There's something about that guy that I can't quite put my finger on. He seems to have some weird fascination with the Amish community, so I don't think it would hurt to check his alibi. Do you mind holding down the fort until I get back? I don't want to miss an important phone call with a lead." The sheriff stood and stretched his back, arms reaching toward the ceiling.

"Yep. I can do that. Let me know if you end up needing backup once you get to Davis' place. He definitely seems like trouble." Chase wished he could ride along with the sheriff. He wasn't optimistic that any new leads would be coming into the office, but he was still too green on the job to challenge anything his boss asked him to do.

The sheriff had one arm in his coat when he heard the sound of a horse's hooves on the pavement out in front of his office. Glancing out the window, he saw the twins securing their horse and buggy to the post. They were up the porch steps and through the door in a flash.

"Sheriff, I'm glad you're here. We have something to show you," the twins spoke. Their identical faces showed that they were there on business. Each grabbed a visitor chair from in front of the window and pulled them close to the sheriff's desk. Beth nodded to the deputy, acknowledging his presence, but neither of the sisters had come to speak to him. It was the sheriff they wanted to speak with and share what they had just learned.

"Hello, Mrs. Troyer and Mrs. Miller. How are you?" Sheriff Streen had removed his arm from his coat and sat back down, pencil in hand, hovering over a blank yellow pad of paper. He had hoped that what the sisters were bringing him today was better than anything else he had been hearing.

"If you don't mind, Sheriff, we're just going to get right to it and tell you why we're here," Anna said, the words rushing out of her mouth. "We visited Margaret Packer yesterday, and she gave us Ruby's diary."

Beth pulled the diary out of her quilted handbag. It was a small notebook, plain on the outside. She held it in her hands gingerly.

Anna continued, excited to share their findings and their suspicion, "Ruby was being followed. Her best friend, Grace Schwartz, confirmed that Ruby had been uneasy, feeling as if someone was watching her the last few days of her life. Ruby and Levi Mast had been meeting secretly in the woods, and we think whoever was following her, knew this and grabbed her while she was there." Anna took a deep breath.

"Levi was meeting her secretly in the woods? What do you mean by that?" Sheriff Streen asked, slightly raising an eyebrow. His hand was still on the writing pad.

Beth interjected, "Levi and Ruby were having a secret love affair, we found out. Grace confirmed it. They were meeting out in the woods near a stream and a field of wildflowers. It was very innocent, but it had to be in secret because Ruby was not given permission by her parents to date just yet."

"That's beside the point, though, Sheriff," Anna interrupted sternly. "The point is that Ruby was being followed. By a stranger. Her secret meetings with Levi just opened up the opportunity for the stranger to take her." Anna looked over at Beth and exchanged worried looks. This conversation was not going as planned and was taking a turn in the wrong direction. The Mast family was a respectable family in the community and they knew Levi to be a happy, kind young man. They didn't for one second think he had anything to do with Ruby's demise.

The sheriff reached out for the diary. "May I see the diary, please, ma'am?" he asked politely. Beth handed the notebook to him hesitantly. The room fell silent as he reviewed a few pages, starting at the back of the book with the more recent entries. "What else do you know about this innocent love affair? What exactly did Grace say about Ruby and Levi's relationship? Did anyone else know about their secret meetings?"

What have we done? thought Anna. Her mind was racing. Her instincts were telling her that Levi was not Ruby's killer, yet she may have just presented all the evidence needed to make him suspect number one in the eyes of the law. Until just now, she hadn't made the connection that Levi had never told anyone since Ruby's disappearance about their affair; that he had found Ruby's dead body in their secret meeting place; and then there were the comments made by Grace and by Ruby herself in her own diary that Levi was more invested in their relationship than Ruby was. *Ach du lieva*, Anna thought, she needed to fix this.

As if again reading her sister's thoughts, Beth responded to the sheriff's questions and said, "We only know what we've told you and what's in the diary, Sheriff. We believe the killer was watching Ruby and followed her out to the woods and grabbed her when Levi wasn't there." And then, as if she had almost forgotten, she said quickly, "And we also spoke with Jessica

McLean. She owns the diner in town, and she said that..." Beth stopped and looked over at Chase.

Chase met her eyes with a blank expression and said, "Please do go on, Mrs. Troyer. What did Jessica say?"

Beth felt the hair raise on her arms. She immediately looked back at the sheriff and grabbed Anna's hand. Was the deputy mocking her? Challenging her to tell the sheriff about how he had been rejected by Ruby? She wondered if Sheriff Streen even knew that story. She continued as if the deputy weren't in the room, and said, "Ms. McLean said that Samuel Graber and Hank Davis have been telling a few people that it's the community's fault that you shut down the games in his establishment. And they have threatened us with revenge."

The sheriff sighed and responded with a kind voice, "I'm so sorry to hear that, Mrs. Troyer and Mrs. Miller. I will definitely talk to both of them and ask them what they know about Ruby's disappearance. If they are behind this at all, I will get to the bottom of it." He paused for a moment and set the pen down on the pad carefully, next to the closed notebook. "Unfortunately, I am also going to have to talk to Levi again, as well." Seeing the look on the women's faces, he continued, "Please don't worry. I realize that Levi is young and I will be sure to include his parents and speak with respect when I am asking him about the affair. I can only assume that his own parents do not know about this either. And you may be right, Levi may have nothing to do with Ruby's death, but right now, he is the only suspect that we have considering the evidence."

"Oh, please, Sheriff, we are positive it wasn't Levi. He is a boy with morals, a hard worker, and he has such promise. Something like this could ruin his future and his family's reputation in the community if it were to get out. Please. If you are going to approach him, please do so discreetly. For the sake of his family." Anna paused and then looked over in the deputy's direction. She thought she caught a glimpse of a smirk on Chase's face that disappeared just before anyone else could see it. Meeting and holding her gaze with the deputy confidently, she spoke, "I'm afraid we may be uncovering a few more secrets in Little Valley before this is all said and done."

The sheriff was focused on his notepad, adding details to remember to ask Levi about. His left hand held the diary propped open on his desk to the last written page. He mumbled, "Oh, I think you may be right, ma'am. I think you may be right."

Chapter Seventeen

After seeing the sisters to their buggy and thanking them for coming in, Sheriff Mark Streen returned to the office to gather his things.

Deputy Chase was holding Ruby's diary, thumbing through the pages. He wasn't looking for clues. He was looking for any mention of his own encounters with the girl. So far, he had found nothing. He hadn't told anyone about his fascination with her, but he was more overcome with a sense of grave disappointment. He just knew there had to be a diary entry about the day the two of them met and how Ruby was smitten at first sight.

"Well, I don't mean to interrupt you," the sheriff said teasingly, "but I'm gonna head out to go talk to Levi. I'll talk to him and his dad on their farm this time and try to keep things low key like I promised Mrs. Miller and Mrs. Troyer."

Chase looked up. "I don't know why you don't just bring him on in. My bet is on that horse, for sure. Young or not, he's the one with the motive and the means."

"Yeah, but I'm not sure he is the mastermind we're looking for either. His youth is a problem. It brings up the same question - where would he have kept her? I'm hoping to get some answers, and I'm not ruling him out, but it just doesn't feel right either." Sheriff Streen set his cowboy hat on his head and before he left, he joked, "Don't get so caught up in that girl's diary that you don't hear the phone ring."

Chase chuckled and responded, "Yeah, good luck with the boy. Ask the right questions and the truth will probably come pouring out of that kid. You'll probably have the case closed by sundown."

The sheriff walked down the steps and sat in his patrol car. He took a deep breath as he started the ignition. *Surely, this boy couldn't have killed that poor girl,* he thought. One thing is for sure: he didn't want to believe it.

The five mile drive to the Mast's family farm felt like one of the longest drives of his life. His mind was running at top speed as he was remembering Ruby's notes in her diary about how Levi's feelings were stronger than hers. Besides the fact that they were meeting secretly, and that he had ironically found her body in their favorite meeting spot, it was that one sentence that he couldn't let go.

The sheriff pulled up to the Mast home. The large home was painted a light blue with gray shutters. The house was an Americana style with an open covered porch that wrapped around all sides. A lazy orange tabby cat was taking a nap on one of the cushioned seats on the porch in a ray of sunshine. A brown hound dog sporting a grayed snout raised his head from his lounging position just a few feet away from the porch. He let out a muffled bark that was more like a grumble as the sheriff's boots touched the driveway. The sheriff approached the front door and the excited barks of a smaller dog could be heard from inside, either warning the family or welcoming the guest - the sheriff couldn't quite tell. Either way, the barks were followed by the sight of Mrs. Mast standing in the doorway, holding the door open.

"Well, hello, Sheriff Streen. What brings you out this way?" She asked with a warm smile. Her voice hid any concern she was feeling, but her deep brown eyes couldn't help but tell the truth.

The sheriff remained at the bottom of the porch steps, removed his hat, and replied, "Hi, Mrs. Mast. My apologies for the unannounced visit, but I was wondering if Levi and Mr. Mast were around?"

"They should be in the barn, or just out behind it, Sheriff. There's lots of work preparing for the winter right now, so they've kept busy. You can go on back there, if you'd like. Can I bring you some iced tea or anything while you're here?" She asked, fighting to keep her voice from shaking. Levi had just started to eat again after a couple of days, and she noticed that he seemed a little more rested this morning. She was so worried that he wasn't yet ready to talk about what he saw on the day he found Ruby - and that it might send him a few steps back in his recovery.

"No thank you, ma'am. I won't be here long. Just checking in on things." Sheriff Streen had hoped the words would put her mind at ease. He felt compassion for her, knowing how emotionally distraught Levi was the last time he had seen him. He knew it must be hard for a parent to see their child suffer.

Becca nodded and watched as the sheriff made his way down the stone path toward the barn behind the house. She closed the door and returned to the kitchen. She said a prayer for *Gotte's* protection over Levi before she continued to peel potatoes.

The sheriff entered the barn. Both sliding doors at the front and at the back of the barn were pushed open creating a sort of corridor through the horse stables. The sheriff called out, "Nathan?" When no one answered right away, he continued through the barn and called out, "Levi? It's Sheriff Streen."

Nathan Mast poked his head out into the back opening and said, "Sheriff Streen. Hi, there. We're just back here. Come on back."

The sheriff exited the back door of the barn to find Levi and his father hard at work. They were both wearing rubber boots up to their knees and were elbows deep washing out the troughs used to store their animals' feed. Two pitchforks and three shovels of varying heights leaned against the back barn wall, sparkling clean. The ground was wet so the sheriff was careful where he stood. He reached out to shake hands with Nathan first, then Levi.

"Hi, fellas," said Sheriff Streen. "You two look like you've been working hard. Can you take a break for a few minutes to chat? I've got a few things I want to share with you." Streen tried as hard as he could to make the conversation sound lighthearted. He didn't want to go into this with a closed mind or come across intimidating in any way.

Levi looked at his dad with a worried look. His stomach turned and he grumbled something that the sheriff couldn't quite make out. Nathan gave Levi a cross look, as if it were a warning, then turned to the sheriff with a half smile. "Sure thing, Sheriff. Wanna just take a seat in the sun on those hay bales?" He gestured to a collection of four single bales that sat next to a tall pile stacked neatly.

"Perfect," said the sheriff, making his way over to the closest one and taking a seat. The father and son followed right behind him and sat across from him, next to each other.

"Levi, how are you feeling? The last time I saw you, well, you weren't feeling so good. I'm sorry about that whole thing. I was hoping that taking you down to the office might make you feel safe - but I don't think it had that impact on you at all." The sheriff noticed how Levi's shoulders were starting to relax and lower down below his ears a bit, so he had hoped he was building trust.

"Honestly, the reason I'm here is to find out more about Ruby. You see, the investigation into her death is still going strong and I'm asking everyone I can to share anything they know to see if I can get a clue. As a matter of fact, after this, I'm headed to the Schwartz home to talk to Grace since she was Ruby's best friend and all." The sheriff noticed Levi's shoulders get tight again. He began to fidget, moving around as if he couldn't sit still. The sheriff figured Levi knew that Grace knew about the secret meetings, and Levi's reaction confirmed that suspicion.

Nathan noticed the change in his son's demeanor, too. He reached out and put a hand on his shoulder, "Son, let's just tell the sheriff the good things you remember about Ruby. That's what he wants to hear. Tell the sheriff about your friendship and the things you two liked to talk about. What kind of things were her favorite things?"

"That's right, Levi. I have all I need to know about the day you found her. I'm just looking to get to know Ruby better, and I know the two of you were friends." The sheriff nodded and smiled a warm smile at the boy.

The expression on Levi's face was one of distress. He burst into tears and roughly wiped them away with the backs of his hands. "*Dat*, I have to tell you something," Levi said, sobbing. He pushed his dad's hand away and stood on his feet. "Ruby was more than a friend," he shouted. "She was going to be my wife! We loved each other. We were secretly meeting in the woods so we could spend time together. We were hiding everything because she wasn't supposed to be seein' anyone yet. The bishop was very strict about that. But we loved each other!" Levi cried as he uttered each word. The sheriff could see spit spray into the air from his lips as he spoke.

Levi continued, his hands down by his sides. He stomped his foot like a toddler and cried, "And now we can't ever be together! She's gone forever! My heart is broken and I couldn't tell anyone! I'll never love anyone more than I loved her!" He threw himself down onto the bale of hay as if it were a mattress, his face resting on his bent arm, his body heaving from the sobs.

Nathan sat there in complete shock, unable to speak for a moment. He looked at the sheriff, his eyes begging for answers, but the sheriff waited to respond or say anything.

"Son," Nathan said. Levi continued to sob, face down in the hay. Nathan reached out and touched his back. "Son, I'm sorry. I had no idea. Please, son, sit up. There is a lot more to talk about here." His voice was weak and trembling. He was putting the pieces together in his head slowly. This is why the sheriff is visiting again. Levi found Ruby's body in the woods - and that's where they had been meeting, secretly, behind everyone's back.

Nathan looked at the sheriff as Levi continued to weep. He had put the puzzle together. His boy was in trouble.

Chapter Eighteen

"Thank you for meeting with me today," Matthew Beiler said, his brow furrowed and his chin lifted. Matthew stood with Hank Davis in the front parlor of the farmhouse style bed-and-breakfast, finally face to face with the owner.

A quilt made with shades of red, white and purple hung on the wall next to the door leading to the dining area. There was a simple brick fireplace on one wall, a basket filled with cut pieces of wood was set on the hearth. A simple evergreen wreath hung on the bricks above the fireplace. There was a sofa with wood trim that bordered a woven fabric of neutral colors. A colorful braided rug lay on the hardwood floor floating in front of the sofa. A pair of beautifully crafted rocking chairs sat together in front of the picture window that ran from ceiling to floor.

Hank had postponed this meeting as long as he could - but now, he was ready to have the meeting and move on. He wasn't fond of the Amish and he was especially confused about what he knew about this guy, Matthew Beiler. Matthew dressed like them, but he didn't have a beard. Hank couldn't understand why anyone would want to come back to that lifestyle after living like normal people for a few years, and then on the flip side of that, he questioned why the community even allowed him to come back after that long. Regardless, he was annoyed that those people had sent Matthew as their spokesperson. He was no idiot - he knew it was because Matthew had experience outside of the community. He was far from impressed though. No one was even really sure what Matthew had done for a living before he returned.

One thing Hank knew for sure was that ever since he had decided to open a bed-and-breakfast in Little Valley, the Amish people had been up in arms about it. They were trying to stop him from making money off the tourism boom that the town had seen, and they were just plain ignorant to think that they could keep all the benefits of that to themselves. He had watched those people try to take down his friend's bar. Samuel Graber had to remove the gaming in his bar, and it didn't take a genius to see who was behind that. Hank would not let them impede his business growth, though. He had already started fighting back. He was pretty sure that was why this joke of a man stood in front of him now. *Game on*, he thought to himself. He stiffened his posture, his arms crossed in front of his chest.

"Nice place you have here," Matthew said, interrupting Hank's thoughts.

"Yeah?" Hank asked, raising an eyebrow. "What is the purpose of your visit today, Mr. Beiler? I don't have time to pretend like we're friends."

Matthew hesitated to answer but maintained eye contact. His tongue ran along the inside bottom of his lip and he drew in a breath. "Why can't we be friends, Mr. Davis?" Matthew asked but his eyes were not friendly.

Hank scoffed. "I tried to give y'all a chance to share in the big profits that this place is going to make, but y'all didn't want nothing to do with it. Maybe you should go back to your little Amish town and get caught up on the actual facts of why we're not gonna be friends, *Mr. Beiler*," Hank responded angrily, moving his neck and head back and forth as he emphasized Matthew's name.

Matthew refused to be provoked. "Well, then, there must be some kind of misunderstanding. One proverb we live by says *'Our duty is not to see through one another, but to see one another through.'* We don't want to share in your profits, but we do wish you well."

Hank put his hand under his chin, overacting as if he were deep in thought. "Hmmm... then I wonder why we're meeting." He crossed his arms again, and feeling annoyed, he said, "Please enlighten me. Why exactly are you wasting my time right now? And you can cut out the riddles."

Remaining calm, Matthew responded, "I want to bury the hatchet. Make amends. Start fresh." He reached out his hand for a handshake and said, "What d'ya say? Can we start over?"

Hank didn't shake his hand. "I'll tell you what, you go back home and tell your people that if they want to be friends," Hank lifted his hands and moved the first two fingers on each hand to imply that he was putting quotations around the word 'friends,' "then, they can agree to sell me their goods at cost so I can resale them in my storefront when I open. Ya know, we can consider it a friend discount." He winked at Matthew.

"I see," Matthew said, lowering his outstretched hand. "Well, the thing is that we're not really in the wholesale business, and to be honest, your customers would be our customers at the market. We provide for our families with the income we make on our goods and selling at your proposed friend discount takes away from that and in some cases might cost us in the end. It's just not good business, you understand."

Hank shrugged. He couldn't care less what worked for them. He doubted they knew much about business anyway. The Amish lifestyle fascinated the tourists, and his plan was to replicate that for his guests the best way he could to draw more visitors. "Well, I guess I could buy at a price just above cost. Still at a discount, though. But then, y'all are gonna have to raise your prices at the market so I still have the best price here in my storefront. I would sign that contract."

"Why would we do that, Mr. Davis? Again, that makes little sense for us. We would be happy to sell you items in bulk, at bulk pricing, and then you can price them however you like. But we will remain in control of our retail pricing." Matthew's patience was clearly waning.

"I'll think about it," Hank said as he reached out and slapped Matthew's arm, "and y'all should think about it, too. Y'all aren't used to competition out here in Little Valley, but it's here now - and this is only the beginning." Hank spoke with condescension, "Sometimes in business, we have to do things we don't want to do, just to stay alive. It can get pretty ruthless, I'll tell ya. There can be some hard lessons to learn, but maybe you've got a few more proverbs to help y'all through it."

"Okay, you think about it then," Matthew responded, ignoring Hank's attempt to ruffle his feathers. "I'm sure I'll be seeing you around town." He tipped his hat and headed toward the door.

"Yep. I'm sure we'll see each other again," Hank replied, following him. "I'll be opening the doors here in just a few weeks, so y'all still have a little bit of time to think about it. Maybe I'll come see you next time."

Matthew stopped a few steps outside the door, his foot on the edge of the welcome mat. He turned around and said, "Please do come visit sometime. I'd be happy to show you around." But the look on his face didn't convey the same message.

Just as Matthew untied his horse and mounted his buggy, the sheriff's vehicle arrived and parked in the small lot next to the bed-and-breakfast. Sheriff Streen parked in the parking space next to the one that had a sign with the image of a horse and buggy with the words, 'Amish Buggy Parking Only. Violators will have to walk.' Hank wondered if the sheriff thought it was funny. Since he had stuck that signpost in the ground, he had never seen anyone park there.

The sheriff tipped his hat to Matthew as he approached the porch, and Matthew returned the greeting before heading down the street.

"Howdy, Sheriff," Hank said. "What brings you here today? Running a permit check?"

"Why? You got gaming tables set up inside or something?" The sheriff responded, letting Hank know he caught that innuendo.

Hank gestured for the sheriff to enter the front door, leading to the parlor. "Wanna have a seat, Sheriff?" He asked, secretly hoping the answer was no.

"Actually, I wouldn't mind a tour of the place, Hank. I haven't seen the inside of your operation just yet," the sheriff said, removing his cowboy hat.

"Ah, well, you might just have to wait for the rest of the public. The rooms aren't all ready yet. I'll let you know, though. Heck, I'll even give ya a sneak peek a day or two before opening day, if you'd like." Hank paused briefly before continuing, "Is that why you stopped by? To see the unfinished rooms?"

"Well, I also just wanted to check in on you, Hank. See how things are going. I've been hearing a few rumors that you've been pretty unhappy with some of the recent happenings in Little Valley, and I thought maybe I could help you work that out." The sheriff looked Hank dead in the eye.

Although Hank didn't care for Sheriff Mark Streen, the last thing he wanted was trouble from the law. "I don't know anything about these rumors you're referring to, Sheriff. I've been pretty focused on getting my place restored and ready to open. I haven't been paying much attention to anything else that is happening around Little Valley, to be honest."

The sheriff nodded and asked casually, "Where are you living at, Hank, when you're not working?"

"I live here. I have a suite in the back of the house. Why?" Hank was starting to feel uneasy.

"Oh, I'm just curious. Maybe you could show me that room?" Hank felt the sheriff's eyes drilling through his own.

"Well, you're gonna have to have a better reason than curiosity to see my room, Sheriff. I mean, I'm curious how your car drives, but I'm not asking to take it on a test drive, am I? What's the meaning of this? Get to the point." Hank was ready for this conversation to end, but he had a feeling Sheriff Streen was just getting started.

"I got nothing to hide, Hank. It would be a strange request, but I would be happy to let you take my cruiser on a test drive if you asked nicely." The sheriff chuckled.

Hank straightened up and stepped closer to the sheriff, his shoulders back and his chest puffed. "I have no interest in driving your car, Sheriff. Get to the point and ask me what you came here to ask."

Without hesitation, the Sheriff said, "I'm sure you've heard about the Amish girl who was found dead in the woods across town. I was just wondering where you were last Sunday night, a week ago, Hank?"

Hank felt a knot forming in his stomach, but he fought for his face not to show it. "I'm pretty sure I was at Samuel Graber's bar until closing, and then I came home. Here. I came here and went right to sleep. Early the next morning, I met with some contractors to get started working on the landscaping out back. I would be more than happy to get you their contact info, if you need it."

The two men stood less than a foot apart, staring at each other for what felt to Hank like an eternity. Finally, the sheriff spoke, "Sure, I'll take their info and I'll just double check that timing with Samuel, as well. I intended to stop by and say hello to our friend anyway."

Hank reached into his back pocket and scrolled through his phone until he found the landscaping company's information. Sheriff Streen jotted the information down in a small notebook he kept in his front pocket. Hank saw that his hand was shaking slightly, and he hoped the sheriff didn't notice that, too. Hank closed his phone and said, "And say hello to *our friend*, Samuel, for me, will ya? I haven't seen him in a few days."

"Yep," said the sheriff, as he placed his cowboy hat back on his head. "Alright then, since I have to wait for the grand tour, I guess I'll just let myself out. Nice talking with you." The sheriff turned around, his hand on the inside of the door and said, "Oh, and before I forget. I'll need you to stay in town until I can confirm your story. And some advice: If you want to fit in here, maybe show some more respect to those who were here long before you moved in. You'll catch more flies with honey than with vinegar, you know."

Hank nodded. "Have a good day now, Sheriff." Hank muttered sarcastically. He shut the heavy front door and exhaled. *Last thing I want to do is fit in with those freaks*, he thought. He wiped the beads of sweat that rested on the back of his neck. He hated that he let the sheriff get under his skin like that.

Hank walked to the kitchen and pulled the refrigerator door open. He grabbed a cold beer and popped it open using the built-in bottle cap opener fastened to the side of the refrigerator-freezer unit. He took a big gulp and then headed back into the parlor to relax, locking the basement door as he passed it.

Chapter Nineteen

"Should we go see Moses after we drop off the cinnamon rolls to Mr. Hatfield?" Anna asked Beth. Beth was holding the reins in her hands, her eyes forward on the road in front of them.

"*Ja*, that sounds good to me. I haven't seen his shop in a long time. After that, I need to pick up a few things at the grocery, if we have time." Beth said. Beth couldn't stop thinking about Ruby and her disappearance. The sisters had not heard any news about an arrest yet, and Anna made Beth promise that for just one day, she would take a break and not speak of it. The sisters had questioned everyone that they could - except for Samuel and Hank Davis, but their husbands had pulled the plug on that, saying the two men were too dangerous. The sheriff had assured them he would follow up with them. Anna said it was time to let him and the deputy take the lead now.

Beth also wondered about Levi and his family. She had been saying extra prayers for them ever since the sisters brought the diary to the sheriff. The sheriff said he was going to go meet with Levi and Nathan Mast that day, but they had yet to hear anything at all about the conversation. She hoped

Levi was absolved from suspicion and that the sheriff had moved on to the next person on the list of suspects.

Beth pulled up to the tie in front of Moses' hardware shop and secured the horse there. She preferred to park there since he was family and the parking spot gave a little bit more grace to those like herself who weren't that skilled at parking. Anna handed the box of cinnamon rolls to Beth to hold while she carefully stepped out of the buggy. She reached back in to grab her cane.

"You'll be done with that cane in no time, *Schwester*," said Beth.

"*Ja*, I have my doctor's appointment next week, and I've been putting more and more weight on my leg without any pain. The cane is starting to feel like it's just in the way now." Anna said. They chuckled together.

"It's going to take more than that to hold my sister down, I'll tell you what," said Beth, smiling.

"Well, let's hope there aren't any more accidents worse than that in my future," said Anna, winking at Beth.

The two headed into the flower shop. They wanted to give Mr. Hatfield a box of cinnamon rolls to thank him for the beautiful flower arrangement he brought over on the day of Moses' celebration.

The women stopped to admire the displays of beautiful tulips, tiger lilies and roses just inside the door of the shop. They hadn't been in the shop more than a minute when they heard raised voices coming from the back office. Beth grabbed Anna's arm just as Anna opened her mouth to announce their presence and raised her finger to her lips.

"They're gonna find out, Henry, and I will not go to jail because of your stupid decisions," the female voice could be heard across the shop.

Beth and Anna looked at each other, wide-eyed and frozen. They knew they shouldn't be eavesdropping. Anna felt a pit in her stomach.

"Shirley, they're not going to find out. There is no way they'll even suspect us, and besides, we'll be gone in just a few days and I've arranged for all traces to be erased. It's not like we haven't done this before." It was Mr. Hatfield's voice. The sisters recognized the voice instantly.

Beth gasped and Anna clasped a hand over her sister's mouth.

"That's the problem, Henry. I'm getting too old to keep running away because of your mistakes. I really liked it in Decatur, and I was starting to like Little Valley, too. Don't do me any more favors. How about you stop bringing me presents that I didn't ask for? It wasn't even my birthday and what a ridiculous connection that her name was the same as my birthstone." Her tone was demeaning and cruel.

The sisters couldn't believe what they were hearing. Could they be talking about Ruby? Did Mr. Hatfield take Ruby, and why would he do that?

The sound of packing tape stretching and then being cut drifted out of the office. Beth thought it was the perfect time for the twins to escape without being noticed, but the sound of footsteps approaching soon followed.

Anna opened and re-shut the door hard. "Hello? Mr. Hatfield?" She called out, sounding cheery. Beth instantly knew to play along.

Mr. Hatfield entered the front of the shop just seconds later, his face flushed and his hair disheveled. A look of surprise crossed his face. He smiled at the women and greeted them with a tone louder than normal, "Hello, Mrs. Miller and Mrs. Troyer."

Anna continued to act as if the twins had just arrived and noticed nothing unusual. "Hi, there! Beth and I came by to drop off some of our famous butterscotch cinnamon rolls to show our appreciation for the lovely flower arrangement you brought by the house for Moses' celebration. That was so kind, and we really do appreciate it. The cinnamon rolls are from our whole family, including Moses and Sarah."

Mr. Hatfield composed himself and said, "Ah, yes, that's very nice. You didn't have to do that, but my wife loves sweets, so I am sure she will enjoy these." He took the box into his hands and set it on the counter. "Is there anything else I can do for you today?"

"No, thank you, Mr. Hatfield. We'll let you get back to business. We just wanted to stop by for a minute." Anna responded, calm as a cucumber.

Beth interjected, "Yes, we have to pick up a few things at the grocery while we're out. Please do tell Mrs. Hatfield that we said hello." There was no sound at all coming from the back office. Either Mrs. Hatfield was hiding in silence or she had slipped out a back door.

"Absolutely, I will tell her you stopped by. Have a good day and thank you again!" Mr. Hatfield smiled.

The twins turned to leave, waving goodbye and complimenting the flowers on the way out the door. As soon as the door shut behind them, the sisters hugged each other, shaken from what they had just witnessed.

Anna exclaimed in a loud whisper, "Dear *Gotte*, this can't be true!"

Beth nodded and squeezed Anna's hands, "I think we just got the clue we've been looking for, *Schwester*. But let's slow down. Are we sure we heard what we think we heard?" It was all so shocking. They knew that Mr. Hatfield was peculiar, but what if they misunderstood the conversation? Accusing someone of kidnapping and murder was not to be taken lightly. "Should we go to the library and see if we can find out anything before we tell the sheriff?"

Moses spotted the sisters on the sidewalk in front of his shop and came outside to greet them. "Well, *hallo, Maem* and Aunt Beth! *Wie discht?*" As soon as his feet hit the threshold of his store, he felt like he might be interrupting a heavy conversation. "Everything ok?" Moses asked. As he got closer he noticed the women looked as if they had just seen a ghost.

"*Ja*, Moses, we're fine," said Anna, looking back at Hatfield's flower shop. Turning back to Beth, she lowered her voice again and said, "I don't want to waste any time. We don't know if they know we heard them or not. They could be getting ready to leave town right now." She turned to her son-in-law, "Moses, can you drive me to the sheriff's office? It's an emergency." Without waiting for an answer, she said, "*Schwester*, you go ahead to the library in your buggy and then meet us at the sheriff's office. Please hurry."

Beth nodded and moved quickly. As she was climbing into her buggy, Anna took Moses's arm and led him into his shop. Moses was confused, but sensed the urgency, and he trusted his mother-in-law and aunt completely. Moses moved quickly to close his shop as Anna stood at the front door, wringing her hands and waiting.

Beth arrived at the town's small library within just a few minutes. She parked the buggy and tied the horse to the post out front, and bounded up the stairs to the front door of the library. She almost ran into Mr. Wilson who was leaving the library, keys in hand.

"Oh my goodness," said Mr. Wilson as he saw Beth. She was certainly on a mission. "I was just closing up," he said as Beth rushed past him and headed toward the back of the library.

"I'll just be a minute," Beth yelled out as she headed toward the microfiche readers.

Mr. Wilson was a kind man, about the same age as Beth and Anna. He had opened the town's library with the inheritance left to him by his family. He loved books - the way they smelled, the way they felt, the way they lined up on the shelves. He was an avid reader himself, and he enjoyed recommending books to anyone interested. Since his wife had passed a few years ago, he took comfort in his little library more so than ever before. He had a small farm of his own and he would share the extra fresh eggs and vegetables with folk who would come in to borrow a book.

Over the years of growing up in the same town, the sisters considered Greg Wilson and his late wife friends. Despite a crush Mr. Wilson had on Anna years before, he always struggled to tell the two sisters apart. When he would run into them, he would try to guess, but more often than not, he would guess wrong. So, he wondered which sister had just passed him in such a rush just now. It was uncommon to see one sister without the other, and he followed her to see if he could help find anything.

Walking up to Beth, he said, "Is that you, Anna? Or Beth? You know, I'm never sure."

Beth was distracted, but she answered, "It's Beth. Ok, this is going to sound strange, but I'm looking for newspaper articles, or anything you can find, about the disappearance and even murder of young children in Decatur happening about a year ago. It has to be an unsolved crime."

Greg took over Beth's spot at the reader, adjusted his glasses and began scrolling through pages of newspapers while Beth looked over his shoulder. They were traveling back much further than a year ago at this point and Beth was just about to give up when Greg stopped at an article with a photo of a man and woman with a young girl. The girl looked to be about twelve years old. She had beautiful features with long blonde hair, but she wasn't smiling.

"Wait. Is that Mr. and Mrs. Hatfield?" Greg asked, shocked. Beth nodded. She was speechless, busy reading the article. The headline read, 'Young girl disappears into thin air. Parents offer a reward.' The date on the article went back almost ten years.

Greg jumped up. "Let me grab it off the printer," he said, rushing to the front desk. Beth followed right behind him. He handed her the printed article and wished her luck. He had quickly packed up a few fresh eggs in a soft cloth bag while the page was printing. Once she had what she needed, Beth thanked him for his help and headed out the door. She needed to meet Anna and Moses at the sheriff's office as soon as possible. Greg waved goodbye to Beth, calling out, "Please be safe, Beth!"

About fifteen minutes later, Beth pulled up at the sheriff's office and hurried inside. Beth and Moses were sitting in the chairs in front of Sheriff Streen's desk. Both the sheriff and Deputy Chase were on the phone -

Sheriff Streen was using the landline and Deputy Brown was talking on his cellphone.

"Yes. Hatfield. Do you have any record of a couple living there named Shirley and Henry Hatfield?" Beth could hear a bit of excitement in the young deputy's voice.

And from the sheriff, Beth heard, "I'm looking for any female young teen murders in the area."

Beth squatted down between Moses and Anna's chairs and held out the printed article for them to see. The paper was slightly crumpled as Beth had shoved it into her handbag during the rush to get to the sheriff's office. Moses jumped up and offered Beth his seat.

"*Denki*, Moses," Beth said as she turned the chair to directly face Anna. Moses moved to hover between the two of them and Beth said, "I have it all right here, *Schwester*. It's hard to believe, but Mr. and Mrs. Hatfield are definitely not the people we thought they were."

The sheriff hung up the phone and Anna passed the paper over to him. "Sheriff, we have more evidence right here from the Decatur Daily paper. That's Mr. and Mrs. Hatfield right there."

Beth interrupted, "And that's their adopted daughter. The article says she went missing. That can't be a coincidence, right?"

The sheriff looked over at the deputy. He had just put down his cellphone. "Nothing yet, Sheriff, but they're gonna keep looking and call me back."

"Well, we better get out to the Hatfield's place and ask them some questions, Deputy. I'm gonna need you to go with me this time, so let's lock up." The sheriff then turned to the women and Moses, "Thank you so much for all of your help, but we've got to take it from here. Please go home and be safe. And let's just keep all of this a secret until we know more. If you hear anything else, let me know. I'll be around to let you know what I find out."

Beth, Anna and Moses gathered their things and exited the office. The three of them gathered in by their parked buggies for a short quiet prayer together before heading home. They prayed for safety for the sheriff and the deputy. They prayed for answers for the Packers and for the rest of the community. And they prayed for any necessary forgiveness for the Hatfields.

Chapter Twenty

The sheriff and the deputy pulled up at the Hatfield house, parking just off to the side of the mailbox. There were colorful flowers everywhere - some in pots on the porch, others were expertly landscaped, and even more cascading out of window boxes. The front door was painted a beautiful turquoise blue with a brass doorknob and matching knocker. The house itself was a light yellow with stark white shutters. From the outside, everything seemed perfect.

As the sheriff and deputy were stepping out of the cruiser, the deputy spotted a stream of smoke from the backyard and exclaimed, "Sheriff! There's a fire around back!"

The two ran on a brick path lined by trimmed hedges around the side of the house and laid eyes on Mr. Hatfield nursing a large bonfire in the center of his backyard. Laying on the ground next to the fire looked like a brand new twin mattress and a pile of bedding.

"Is he about to burn up the evidence?" muttered the sheriff, quietly. He motioned for the deputy to stay where he was at and watch the front of the house. He took a step out from the side of the house into Mr. Hatfield's view and called out, "Mr. Hatfield?"

Mr Hatfield looked up and instantly lost all color in his face. He didn't move, and he couldn't speak.

"Hi there, Mr. Hatfield," the sheriff spoke as he continued to approach Henry and the fire. He had one hand resting lightly on the butt of his gun that sat in his holster. "It's Sheriff Streen. I'm not sure we've met."

Mr. Hatfield remained motionless and silent. His shoulders were hunched over and his arms hung by his sides like limp noodles.

The sheriff continued. "I'm just here to ask a few questions, Mr. Hatfield. What d'ya say we go inside and chat?" As he stepped closer, he saw a tear fall down Mr. Hatfield's cheek and land on the top of his navy blue polo shirt, just above the pocket. "Are you okay, Mr. Hatfield? Let's go sit down."

Henry Hatfield just barely nodded his head and then turned slowly toward the house. The sheriff quickly pushed the mattress and the pink polka dot sheets and matching comforter away from the fire with his foot before following Mr. Hatfield into the back door of his home.

They walked through the kitchen and into the dining room. There were packed boxes lined up along the walls on either side of the windows. Through the large front window, the sheriff could see the deputy standing on the side porch. The living room furniture was wrapped in plastic, and from the dining room vantage point, the sheriff could see more boxes were pushed behind the sofa.

Mr. Hatfield sat down at the head of the table and rested his elbows on the table. His fingers were tightly interlaced and his hands were visibly shaking.

"Where's your wife, Mr. Hatfield?" the sheriff asked first.

Mr. Hatfield remained silent, staring ahead, tears now falling at a steady rate.

"Mr. Hatfield, do you want to tell me why you're upset right now?" the sheriff continued. He was pretty confident at this point that Mr. Hatfield was guilty, but he needed a confession.

"It's not what you think." Henry blurted out the words as if he had been holding his breath for too long. And with the words finally released, he began to sob. He held his face in his hands, his shoulders moving in rhythm with his quick breaths. "I know you think I killed Ruby Packer," he managed to utter, his voice trembling.

When the sheriff realized he wasn't going to say anything else, he said, "Did you kidnap Ruby Packer, Mr. Hatfield?"

Henry didn't answer, but he didn't need to. Right as he asked, Mrs. Hatfield came running into the room from the side hallway, screaming her husband's name. Sheriff Streen pulled his weapon and the deputy quickly entered through the front door, weapon in hand, as well.

Shirley Hatfield was a tall thin woman with a sharp long nose and thin lips. She wore her mousy brown hair in a short blunt haircut. Her voice was shrill as she screamed, "Henry! Don't you dare say anything! You didn't kill that girl! They can't prove anything!" She reached into her skirt pocket.

The sheriff yelled out, "Stop right there! Don't move! Both of you put your hands in the air!"

Henry looked up with a look of terror as he saw the sheriff's gun pointed at Shirley and the deputy's gun pointed at himself. He raised his arms into the air. "She has nothing to do with this," his voice pleaded to the sheriff but his eyes were panicked and focused on his wife. "Please, you don't understand."

At that moment, Shirley pulled a small .22 gun out of her pocket but before she could even point it forward, the sheriff fired a shot into her shoulder. Henry screamed out, "NO!" but it was a few seconds too late. Shirley screamed and fell backward. Her head fell perfectly positioned as if she were resting on the rolled up braided carpet that she had bought from the farmers' market just a month before. "You shot me!" Her voice sounded like the screech of an injured parakeet, small and harmless.

Henry jumped up sending his chair flying backwards, instinctively wanting to rush to her side, but the sheriff spoke loud and stern, "Sit. Down." The deputy had collected the .22 pistol with his handkerchief, his hands noticeably shaking, careful to not touch it and leave his own fingerprints on it anywhere.

"Deputy, call 911. Let them know we have two 10-15s. And we may need backup. We're taking these two in and I want to search the place and collect the evidence out back for DNA testing. Make sure that fire is put out, too." The sheriff said without taking his eyes off of Mr. Hatfield.

Mrs. Hatfield laid on the floor groaning and clinging to her arm, "I'm bleeding," she said with a high-pitched whine.

"Stay still," the sheriff said. "The ambulance is on its way." Shirley sat up, her face bright red. The sheriff instructed Deputy Brown to handcuff her one arm to the leg of the china cabinet next to her. The deputy fumbled but managed to secure Mrs. Hatfield. He stood up with weak knees and looked over at the sheriff. Sheriff Streen nodded at him in approval, and he headed out back to make his phone calls and extinguish the bonfire.

Once outside, Chase took a deep breath. He felt his heart racing. Now that he had stepped away, he was feeling overwhelmed with emotion and found himself working hard to fight back tears. As he approached the fire, he saw the pile of bedding. Everything still looked brand new. He would never again buy a new set of sheets without thinking about the ugliness of all of this. He couldn't imagine how scared poor beautiful Ruby must have felt while she was in captivity with these crazy people, and for the first time, he was doubting his decision to pursue the life of a deputy.

Was he cut out for this type of work? He tried desperately to stay focused as he started to make his phone calls.

Chapter Twenty-One

S heriff Streen sat across from Henry Hatfield at the Lawson police station. Lawson was the closest city in Mainstay County with a full size operation, so Mr. Hatfield had been taken there for custody and for his trial. Sheriff Streen had asked if he could spearhead the interrogation and try to get a confession from him. Although the police were pretty confident they could use DNA evidence from the bedding and the mattress that were collected from the Hatfield property to confirm that Ruby was held hostage there until she died - they still didn't have the full story.

After some rest and knowing what he was up against, Henry had agreed to talk to Sheriff Streen. Shirley Hatfield had been treated in the hospital and was also being held at the Lawson jail. She was staying quiet and was waiting to speak to her attorney.

"We weren't able to have children of our own. Shirley and I. But after years of trying and waiting, we were finally chosen to adopt a perfect little girl. She was a baby, just over one-year-old when they brought her to us. Her name was Iris, like the flower. We were living in Decatur then, and we were so happy. I just knew that we were going to be happy forever." Mr.

Hatfield paused and looked up at the sheriff. His eyes were dark and dull. "But that's not how life works."

The sheriff nodded, checking to make sure the recorder light was still shining red, indicating that the conversation was being recorded. Henry had agreed. He knew what he did was wrong. He just wanted to put it all behind him, do his time and live a different life. He hoped that cooperating with the police would allow for some leniency when it came to deciding his fate. Most importantly, he wanted everyone to know that he wasn't a killer. He never meant to hurt anyone.

"When Iris was almost twelve years old, we decided to get away and take a family camping trip. We rented an RV, and we took a cross-country trip out to the Pacific Northwest. The beaches were beautiful there. We had stayed a couple nights in a few different RV parks along the Oregon coast, but then I suggested to Shirley and Iris that we try to rough it one night. I had surprised them with a tent that I had packed away in one of the outer compartments of the camper rental. Iris was so excited. Her favorite book was about a family of three that went backpacking and camping. She had been telling me and Shirley all about how the family ate freeze-dried meals for dinner and oatmeal over a propane stove for breakfast. I wanted to do something like that for her, so we decided to park the RV and backpack out into the mountains and set up camp at a lake."

Henry stopped to take a sip of water from the water bottle that Mark had offered him. His stomach turned as he remembered leaving the same brand of bottled water on Ruby's bedside table in his basement just days earlier. He took a deep breath and continued, "Anyway, things went wrong, and something terrible happened to Iris. It was an accident, and we lost her. We were never the same after that, Shirley and me."

Sheriff Streen wanted to ask what happened, but knew it was best to let Henry continue telling his story. He was seeking closure on Ruby's case. It was clear that there was some history here, but he would happily leave that to the detectives.

Henry slumped forward in his chair. He leaned over, his hands clasped together in his lap and his upper arms pushing against the edge of the table. "We loved Iris more than anything. You have to believe that. But, we were scared that we were going to get blamed for her death. And it was already hard for us to lose her. So, we went home." He put his head in his hands. "We went home without her and reported her missing. We even offered a reward. No one ever found her, I don't think."

The sheriff was having a hard time keeping quiet. He drew in a slow breath and checked again to make sure the red light was still blinking on the recorder.

"So, that's how it all started," Henry continued. "Then, the next chapter begins with my marriage suffering. Shirley started to blame me for Iris's death, and she would say really mean things. I think she began to hate me, but I needed her. She was all I had left. So, I tried to fix things. That's all. But every time I tried, something would go wrong. Ruby was gonna be my last try, I promise."

Henry took another sip and fell quiet. The sheriff spoke, "Tell me about Ruby, Henry. Why did you pick her?"

Henry's mood seemed to change slightly as he sat up straighter. A small smile showed on his face as he began again. "The first time I saw Ruby was when I was watering the flowers outside my shop in Little Valley. Her face glowed like an angel and her eyes shone in the light. She looked so much like Iris - more than anyone else - and I think she was just a year older than Iris was. So, it seemed like we could pick up right where we left off."

Sheriff stifled the shiver he felt run down his spine.

Henry continued, staring past the sheriff as if he were talking to someone standing behind him. "I heard her girlfriend say her name, and I knew it was fate. You see, Shirley's birthday is in late July and her birthstone is the ruby. I know it wasn't her birthday, but I thought Shirley would still be so excited when she saw her and found out her name."

Henry's face changed. His eyebrows furrowed. "But, she wasn't excited. She's never happy. I worked so hard to give her Ruby. I studied her patterns without her knowing. I followed her a few times out to the woods. That boy she met was often late - she honestly deserved much better - but one day, he was late. And I was prepared. I finally had my chance. I grabbed her and took her home." Henry stopped and looked directly in the sheriff's eyes and said, "I didn't hurt her. I had bought a fancy new bed and a pretty new bed set so she could be comfortable."

The sheriff nodded. "What happened to her, Henry? What happened to Ruby?" He asked, working hard to keep a kind and trusting tone.

Henry looked away again. "It's always something, I swear. Like I said, Shirley wasn't happy. I think it's because Ruby was Amish, but I can't be sure. Anyway, we had an argument, and I swore I was gonna return her. But then, I came down to bring her dinner, and she said she wasn't feeling well. I thought it was a trick, but even if she was sick, how was I supposed to take her to the doctor?" Again, his eyes met the sheriff's, pleading for understanding. He continued, "Anyway, I came back upstairs and asked Shirley what we should do if Ruby was really sick. She said I 'made my bed, now deal with it.' The next morning, I brought Ruby breakfast, and she was dead." He took in a quick breath. "I guess she was telling the truth. Ruby told me she had epilepsy, but I didn't know that. I thought she was making it up. I was gonna let her go, I swear." He repeated those words again, but this time, his voice sounded childlike and his eyes were cast down at the table.

The sheriff clenched his hands into fists under the table. He felt like he probably had heard enough and didn't want to give this guy another minute of his time, but Henry continued. "She looked so beautiful and peaceful. I knew she loved the woods, so I just brought her back where I grabbed her and figured that the boyfriend might get blamed for it. I panicked."

The sheriff had heard enough. He needed a break. "I think that's all we need today, Henry," he said as he motioned for the door to be opened.

Henry stood up. "You gotta believe me that I didn't kill her, Sheriff. I was gonna let her go, I swear!" Henry begged for understanding as the police officer fastened handcuffs on Henry.

Sheriff Mark Streen was speechless. He opened his mouth but he couldn't think of anything to say. And maybe that was for the better. He remembered his mother telling him years ago that "some things are just better left unsaid" and he'd never found a more fitting time to apply that little phrase.

He placed his cowboy hat on his head and walked out of the room ahead of Henry. He wanted to get back to his new home in Little Valley and tell the Packers, and the twins, the deputy, and everyone else, that the case was officially solved. The bad guys were locked away, and the town was safe and sound again.

And he was going to do whatever he could to keep it that way.

Chapter Twenty-Two

"Could you please pass the butter, *Schwester*?" Anna said. Beth reached over and picked up the china butter dish and handed it to Sarah who handed it to Moses. Eli and Noah sat at the heads of the large rectangular table in Anna's open dining area. Anna sat to the right of her husband, Eli, while Beth sat to the right of her husband, Noah. Matthew shared the side of the table with Beth, and Sarah and Moses shared Anna's side of the table. Sarah's two young children were playing quietly in the living room. They had finished their dinner earlier and would join the adults for dessert.

Sarah's youngest child, Rosemary, had finally fallen asleep in her arms. Beth offered to take her to the bassinet. When Beth returned to the table, Sarah said, "We have so much to celebrate tonight, my *wunderbarr* family."

"*Ach ja*, indeed, we do, daughter," Anna responded. As she finished spreading butter on her roll, she reached for the roll on Eli's plate to do the same. The twins had cooked together to prepare their favorite chicken and dressing dinner. Sarah had boiled green beans from the freezer and seasoned them beautifully, and of course, the sisters added fresh homemade baked rolls to the night's menu. A glass pitcher of iced meadow tea with slices of frozen lemon floating on top served as the centerpiece to the dinner.

Beth chimed in, "We can all sleep so much better now that we have a *gut* sheriff and deputy team in Little Valley."

"That's true," said Sarah, "not to mention a couple pretty smart investigators in our own little community." She winked at Anna. Beth grinned and nodded.

"We can thank *Gotte* that our Anna and Beth are safe," Noah said, squeezing Beth's hand. "Maybe it's time to take a break from police work for a while," he said, setting his fork down and looking directly in Beth's face.

Anna exclaimed, "I second that!" Beth rolled her eyes, and laughter rose into the air above the table filling the room with warmth. "And we can thank *Gotte* that my cane... as beautiful as it is... is retired next to the fireplace now, and that my knee has fully healed."

"Amen" said Sarah, Beth and Eli in unison.

"And Matthew, you have some *gut* news to share, too, eh?" Moses asked, encouraging him to share.

All eyes were on Matthew when he said, "*Ja,* it's true. It's exciting, indeed. Just before the arrest, I had closed a deal with the Hatfields to purchase the flower shop. They had asked me to keep it a secret until after they had moved, which I thought was strange, but now I guess it all makes sense..."

"Congratulations, Matt!" Eli reached out and gave Matthew's arm a light pat. "That's *wunderbarr* news! You and Moses will be *nochbers*!"

"*Ja,* I am so excited for our *schtores* to be right next to each other. Sarah will have to make two lunches now every day," Moses nudged Sarah with a grin.

"*Ja,* no problem. I've got all the time in the world," said Sarah, laughing.

"What will you name your new *schtore*, Matthew?" Beth asked.

Matthew paused, "I'm not sure. I'm open to suggestions, if anyone has one. Beiler's Flowers doesn't sound too *gut*, I don't think. "

Anna and Beth looked at each other and said in unison, "The Secret Garden!"

Sarah and the men burst into laughter. "That's perfect!" Sarah exclaimed.

Anna and Beth smiled at one another from opposite corners of the table. Without speaking, they knew that moving away was no longer on the agenda. Little Valley was their home, and their family was too important to leave behind.

"The Secret Garden, it is," said Matthew, his face beamed.

Noah raised his glass into the air, and everyone followed suit. "*Gotte* is *gut*! A toast to health, happiness, and success!"

The family cheered, "For sure and certain!"

Saving Grace

The Amish Lantern Mystery Series, Volume 3

Chapter One

For by grace you have been saved through faith; and that not of yourselves,
it is the gift of God;

Ephesians 2:8

Rachel leaned against the counter, her arms folded across her chest. Her face turned a light pink. "Jacob, why do you act like this is nothing? It honestly feels like you're just taking your time. You know you have to go talk to the sheriff about what happened last night. Is there a reason why you're dragging your feet?"

Jacob sighed and set his fork down on his plate next to a half-eaten piece of toast and fried egg. He was exhausted, and his head was pounding. "*Ja,* Rachel. I have every intention of going and talking to Sheriff Streen this morning. What does it matter if I wait to finish my breakfast first? You act like the barn is still on fire."

Grace sat next to her father at the table, watching the interaction between her parents. The Schwartz family never argued. She was taught to exhibit patience and respect with each person, especially her family. She flipped her egg over and her stomach followed suit. Last night was terrible, and Grace worried that it may have caused long-term damage to more than just her father's workshop.

Glancing at Grace, Rachel looked back at her husband, her angry stare softening. She sat down at the table on the other side of Jacob across from her daughter and rested her hand on Jacob's arm. "What we went through last night was *baremlich*. Although it is heartbreaking to see all your beautiful work go up into flames, *liebchen*, we must thank *Gotte* for protecting us from the fire. I am so grateful for the running water that our community had installed, but I can't stop thinking, who would've wanted to harm us? We will all sleep much better when the *gut* sheriff finds the person behind all of this."

Jacob placed his hand over his wife's and looked up from his plate, his kind eyes meeting hers. "*Ja. Denki, my lieb*. I think I am still just a little shocked. And I'm worried, of course." He rose from his seat before a tear could escape his eye and turned toward the oak hat stand he had made when he was a teenage boy. The hat stand was the first piece of furniture brought into the house that the community had built for him and Rachel almost 15 years ago. The hat stand was made to look like a tree with thin branches, and Jacob could remember how his mind was filled with thoughts about the family he would have as he carved each detail in the hardwood. To him, the hat stand represented a family tree, full of love and happiness. He proudly placed his hat on a branch each evening when returning home for the night.

"I will go now. The two of you stay put until we find out more. Even though we had almost the whole community here last night, there may be clues in the yard or out by the shop."

Grace spoke quietly as Jacob adjusted his suspenders and fit his wool felt hat on his head. "*Dat*, please dress warm. I think it is going to be chilly today." She looked as if she had more to say, but she fell silent, her brow furrowed.

"*Ja, dochder*, you don't have to worry about your *dat*." He walked over and kissed his daughter on the forehead. "As a matter of fact, you don't have to worry about anything at all," Jacob said as he looked into his daughter's beautiful eyes. Every day she looked more and more like her mother, and he was very proud of the young lady she was becoming. Rachel and Jacob had decided to name their only daughter, Grace, as a way of expressing their thanks and gratitude to *Gotte*. Unlike many of the families in their community, Grace was an only child. Shortly after their marriage, Rachel and Jacob had received the sad news that Rachel faced health complications and would not be able to have a child of her own. However, the couple, and the community, prayed diligently, and by the grace of God, Grace was conceived and born healthy. She was their special miracle baby, and they loved her dearly.

Rachel rose and met Jacob at the door, reaching out to embrace him with a big hug before he walked out onto the porch. "Do you want me to join you?" Rachel asked. Jacob shook his head and turned to walk down the steps, but Rachel reached out and grabbed his arm. "Jacob, the community will build another shop."

"*Ja*, I know. Let's just take things one step at a time," Jacob said over his shoulder as he descended the porch steps and turned toward the back of the house to hitch his horse and buggy. He realized right away that he had indeed forgotten to wear his coat but he didn't want to turn back. He didn't know how much longer he was going to be able to keep his tears contained, and he didn't want his wife and daughter to see him break down. He didn't want them to have to worry about him on top of the fear that they were all feeling. He stuffed his hands into his pockets and tried to ignore the sick feeling that sat in his stomach like a heavy stone at the bottom of a lake.

Jacob needed to get in his buggy and take some time to himself to summon the strength to discuss what happened with the sheriff. Jacob was confident that he knew why it was his shop that was set on fire in the middle of the night. He was sure it was his fault, and he needed to ask *Gotte* for forgiveness first and foremost. Then, he would tell the sheriff. And then, he would tell Rachel.

Chapter Two

Beth pushed the lace curtains aside and opened the living room window. Small, curved wrinkles appeared in the corners of her smile as the fresh scent of early Spring drifted inside her cozy warm home. This was her favorite time of year, and as she leaned out to look, she was excited to see that the snowdrop bulbs she had planted in her front flower beds last Fall had just started to bloom. Their stark white petals hung down like drops of milk dripping off their stems. Beth inhaled a deep breath of fresh air, closed her eyes and said a quick prayer of gratitude for the beauty that surrounded her.

With Spring, specks of color were popping up all over Little Valley. The blue and yellow wildflowers were rising above the tall grass in the rolling fields on the outskirts of town. The flowering trees that lined the streets were blooming and casting brilliant shades of pink and purple that enticed townsfolk and tourists alike to take long walks, with or without an umbrella in hand.

Along with the light freshness that Spring brought to the air, there seemed to also be a sense of renewal and optimism shared among the

Amish community in Little Valley. The trials and tribulations that had hovered over the community the past few months were starting to feel like a thing of the past. And with growing popularity, business was booming all over town. The Amish-owned shops along with small craft booths hosted at the weekly Farmers' Market brought the community good fortune, for which everyone was grateful.

Beth and her twin sister Anna spent most of their time together, their houses sitting on the west side of the community on shared property so that they could remain close even after they married and raised families. But, this morning, Beth was spending extra time alone with her husband, Noah.

Noah, a carpenter by trade and an elder in the community, coordinated building projects for the community. Since he had returned from helping extinguish the fire at the Schwartz home in the early hours of the morning, he was distracted. Jacob Schwartz had converted his barn into a wood shop for creating and storing his beautifully handcrafted bed frames, dressers and hutches. The flames from the previous night destroyed everything. Beth knew Noah would go to great lengths to arrange for a very special barn-raising event for Jacob and his family.

"*Denki*, dear wife," Noah said as Beth placed a plate of freshly baked biscuits on the table next to Noah's favorite cheesy breakfast casserole. "This looks and smells delicious."

Beth nodded and sat down next to him, reaching for the serving spoon and piling his plate high. Steam rose above the plate, and she warned him it was still very hot as she set the porcelain plate back on the table in front of him. Noah reached for the coffeepot and poured his wife a cup of coffee, topping his off as well. The couple held hands and said the same prayer of thanks that they had muttered each and every day since they were married nearly forty years ago.

After a few bites, Beth started the conversation. She had been so eager to hear all the details of the night before, but she knew Noah was tired from only a few hours' sleep. She practiced great restraint to wait until now to finally dig for information. Living as a high-functioning autistic, Beth had learned a few tricks over the years to distract herself when she was feeling anxious. Saying prayers of gratitude and counting her blessings were most effective, and those were the tricks that had kept her focused this morning.

"I'm so glad no one was hurt last night," Beth said, hoping Noah would open up more about what happened.

"*Ja*, although Jacob's shop is completely burned to the ground, it is a blessing that his family and horse and buggy were all safe." Noah took another bite, "Mmmm, this is so delicious, Beth. I think it gets better and better every time you bake it." He smiled at her, his eyes glinting.

Beth rolled her eyes and smiled back. "You say that every time I cook this casserole, Noah. It is the exact same recipe every time. But *denki*. I'm glad you like it."

Wanting to turn the conversation back to the fire, Beth asked, "Do they have any idea how the fire started?"

"No, not that I know of, but before everyone left, there was talk that someone must have set the fire. With all of Jacob's furniture stored in there, and him being so careful with all of it, I honestly think there's no way it could've happened any other way." Noah shook his head. "But we've had such a nice quiet few months... I hope there is a simple explanation."

"Me, too," said Beth, but she had a familiar sinking feeling in her stomach. "Anna and I will definitely bake something for the Schwartz family and visit Rachel this afternoon. Let me know how we can help with planning a barn-raising, as well."

"Oh, I will definitely lean on you to help plan it. I am heading into town this morning to talk to Moses about ordering the wood and supplies that we will need. Once I have all of that in place, we will get the word out and plan the project. We don't want to waste any time. I'm sure Jacob has a lot of rebuilding that he will have to do to fill orders now that his entire back stock is gone." Noah set his fork down next to his empty plate and leaned back in his chair.

Beth stood to clear the table. Noah asked her, "What else do you have going on today?"

"Well, let's see. Anna and I are caught up with prep for this weekend's Farmers' Market, so there isn't any more baking needed for that. We can even dip into that supply to share with the Schwartz family, I'm thinking. I am meeting both Jonah and Abigail for lunch at the diner - I'm so excited to see them both!" Beth's oldest daughter, Abigail, was ten years older than her youngest son, Jonah. The two siblings always had such a tight bond when they were children, and Beth's heart was warmed watching their relationship evolve as they grew, and their lives changed. Visiting with the two of them together would surely be the highlight of Beth's day.

Returning to her mental list of tasks for that day, Beth continued, "Oh, and I need to get Abigail's old room ready for Eva since she is arriving soon." Beth was looking forward to hosting Eva, especially since she hadn't seen her since she was little. Marianna was Beth and Anna's favorite cousin when they were young girls, and Eva was Marianna's second daughter. Marianna had moved to be closer to her in-laws in Missouri, but she and the sisters exchanged letters often. Recently, Marianna had sent a letter to Beth and Anna asking if Eva could come stay with one of them. Eva was ambitious and wanted to learn a few advanced baking techniques and open a bakery in Little Valley. She had never been married, but she was independent and wanted to establish a business of her own. That sort of autonomy was becoming more and more prevalent among modern Amish communities, and Beth admired her courage.

Noah rarely questioned anything Beth wanted to do, and this was no exception. "A busy day then. That's *gut*. I wish I could join you for lunch, but please tell Abigail and Jonah hello for me. Let's plan to have Jonah over for a family dinner soon. Ever since he moved out on his own, I feel like I hardly see him outside of worship services. I still don't know why he was in such a rush and didn't stay home until he was more settled."

"Well, he wanted his independence, I guess," said Beth, leaning against the counter. "It's the same with Eva. Kids are different these days. They're more independent and anxious to grow up. The little bit of labor on the farms that he is doing with Eli and Nathan Mast is doing well for him for now, but you're right, he needs to commit to learning a trade because I believe he is terribly unhappy."

"I always wanted him to join me in the carpentry business," Noah said as he placed his hat on his head.

"Right. I know, dear." Beth paused. She knew it disappointed Noah that Jonah didn't want to follow in his father's footsteps. "There's still time for him to follow that path. Let's just keep praying for him to find his way."

"*Ja*, you're right. A great deal of what we see depends on what we're looking for. I should go. I will see you later, dear." Noah hugged his wife and headed out the back door.

Once the breakfast dishes were cleaned and returned to the cupboards, Beth walked into the bathroom to finish getting ready for the day. She brushed her teeth, removed the covering veil from the top of her head, and re-pinned her hair under a freshly cleaned prayer *kapp*. Back in the kitchen, she ran her hands down the front of her pastel pink dress and straightened her white apron before slipping on her shoes. She said one more quiet prayer of gratitude and closed the back door behind her as she stepped out onto the wraparound porch of her home.

Beth turned to see Anna walking briskly towards her, wearing an almost identical dress, *kapp* and shoes. "*Gute Mariye, Schwester!*" Anna called out to her sister.

"I was just headed your way, *Schwester*!" Beth said, returning the warm greeting.

"Oh *gut*. I wanted to check in on you and especially Noah. How is he? Is everyone okay out at the Schwartz's?" Anna's husband, Eli, was already out working the fields this morning, and she hadn't had a chance to connect with him about the fire.

"Come on in," Beth said. "There isn't much I can tell you just yet, but I have a feeling there's more to come."

Chapter Three

S heriff Mark Streen hung up his cowboy hat as he entered the office. The new hat stand was a gift from the Amish community only recently, and he already enjoyed the little touch it added to the room. The handcrafted detail that Jacob Schwartz took the time to add to each of his pieces was remarkable, and this gift was no different.

Today was an important day for the sheriff. His new deputy was due to report to his first day on the job in about an hour. Sheriff Streen had made a mistake in appointing his last deputy, but he was optimistic that he had made a better choice the second time around. Christopher Jones appeared to be an honest, likable family man with nearly a decade of experience under his belt. His extended family was located just about 45 miles east of Little Valley, and he and his wife were excited to move closer and to feel settled in such a beautiful small town. They had two small boys, not quite school age yet, and Christopher expressed that it was the perfect time to find a new place such as Little Valley to call home. Mark admired Christopher's family values. He hoped that one day he could also share his life with a wonderful wife and one or two children, but he had not crossed paths with the right person just yet.

Most importantly, Mark and Christopher's personalities had a strong natural synergy that Mark was confident would benefit their working relationship and most likely turn into a strong friendship, as well. They were both laid back in nature, easy to talk to and easy to trust. Mark felt that, much like himself, Christopher would approach the law and the people they served with respect. And he was glad to hear that Christopher also enjoyed spending his down time outdoors. In a perfect world, they would together be dedicated to catching criminals, and when things were slow and calm, they could focus on catching some fish.

The front office soon filled with the scent of coffee from the four-cup coffee maker in the nearby tiny kitchen. Previously a small house, the sheriff's office was renovated about twenty years before, fashioned with one simple holding cell that sat empty most of the time. The office was on the outskirts of town with a couple dozen acres of undeveloped land positioned all around it giving the impression of isolation, even though it was only a few miles down the highway to the Amish community in one direction and a few miles up the highway in the other direction to a few small subdivisions.

Just five minutes before the hour, Sheriff Streen watched Deputy Christopher Jones park on the gravel parking area in front of the office and step out of his car. He was a tall, slender man with a slight athleticism to his build. He also wore a cowboy hat and boots, but that wasn't uncommon among the townsfolk in these parts who weren't from the Amish community.

Before Christopher could reach for the door handle, Mark swung the front door open and reached out his hand. "Good morning! It's great to see you!"

Christopher responded with a firm handshake and a broad smile. "It's great to be here, Sheriff. Thanks again for this opportunity. I'm looking forward to working with you."

"I've been looking forward to this, as well, Deputy," the sheriff said. "Come on in. I'll give you the grand tour of the place." The conversation between the two men was comfortable and easy as the sheriff invited Christopher to hang his hat and then proceeded to show him around the kitchen, bathroom and cell. He pointed to the new deputy's desk which sat to the left of the front door. "I know it's a bit smaller than my desk, and honestly, the desks were here when I moved in. It doesn't make much sense to me for the desks to be different sizes, so I've reached out to Jacob Schwartz to build a couple matching ones for us. He is the fine gentleman who built that nice hat stand right there. He does beautiful work, as you can see, so I'm excited to see how the desks turn out."

Mark's voice trailed off as he was distracted by the sound of a horse and buggy approaching. He looked out the window and said, "Well, that's odd. That's Jacob right there."

Christopher said, "Oh good! I'm excited to meet him."

Mark opened the door as Jacob ascended the steps to the front porch of the office. "Jacob Schwartz! It's good to see you! Your ears must be burning. I was literally just telling the new deputy here about our new desks. Come on in and meet him."

"Good morning," said Jacob. Mark could tell right away that something was wrong. It was clear that Jacob wasn't there to talk about the new desks.

"Jacob Schwartz, meet Deputy Christopher Jones," Mark motioned towards Christopher who approached with hand outstretched.

"It's a pleasure to meet you, Mr. Schwartz," said Christopher.

"*Ja*, nice to meet you, Deputy," Jacob replied.

Mark wanted to jump right into business, so he invited Jacob to have a seat and then asked, "Jacob, what brings you here? Something tells me you're not here to take more measurements."

"No, I'm afraid I'm here to report a crime," Jacob responded, his hands clasped tightly in his lap. He looked at the sheriff, his eyes were red and Mark noted that he looked exhausted. He nodded and Jacob continued, "My wood shop, er, my barn, caught on fire in the middle of the night last night. At first, I wondered if it was something I did, if I was reckless or careless leaving a lantern lit or something, but I just couldn't think of how. The men in our community came together, and we were able to put the fire out, with the help of the county fire department, of course, but not before the whole thing burned down to the ground." He paused and rubbed the back of his neck. Mark thought Jacob might be fighting tears, but he couldn't be sure.

"I'm so sorry, Jacob. I know you must have been heartbroken to see all your work go up in flames like that. I hope no one was hurt?" Mark sat in the old chair behind his desk and motioned for Christopher to pull up a chair next to him. He picked up a large yellow pad of paper and pen and handed it to Christopher.

Jacob continued, "No, sir, thank *Gotte* no one was hurt. But, it is a terrible thing that happened. Like I said, I thought maybe it had been my fault - although I couldn't figure out how - and then I found this note tacked onto the front door of my home." He handed Mark the note.

Holding the note in his hand, Mark read the writing aloud, "'What is your saving grace now?' Hmmm... that's an odd thing to write, for sure. What do you make of it, Jacob?" It was detective work 101 to ask the victim of a crime how they interpreted a clue such as this, and he was happy to see Christopher lean forward in anticipation of the answer.

Jacob sighed. "To be honest, Sheriff, I'm not sure. You know that my only daughter is named Grace, so if the note is referring to her, I am terrified that it means she is in danger somehow. On the other hand, I was thinking that it could just be a reference to my faith. In my religion, the saving grace is a blessing from God that is granted to save a sinner." He dropped his chin toward his chest and looked down at his hands.

"Well, it certainly does sound like the fire wasn't an accident, and this is definitely a clue that can help lead us to the perpetrator," Mark said. After a quick breath, he asked the most important question, "Do you have any idea who would want to burn down your barn, Jacob?"

Jacob shifted in his chair a bit, his eyes still downcast. He answered reluctantly, "*Ja*, I do think I know who did this to me and my family." He paused and raised his face to look directly at Mark, his eyes becoming moist and turning gray as if he were about to reveal a terrible secret. "There is something no one in my community knows. It is something that I am terribly ashamed to admit. To even say out loud." A tear rolled down Jacob's cheek and landed on his crisp white shirt leaving a small dingy wet spot. He reached up and wiped away the tear stain on his face with his sleeve. "About six months ago or so, I ventured into the Little Valley Pub out of curiosity. I had overheard a few men in the community talk about how much fun they had there - even though it is against our rules. I couldn't stop thinking about it. I'm sure it was the devil's work that led me in the doors and sat me down at that gaming table. At the time, it felt exhilarating. I am so ashamed to tell you that, but it's the truth." Jacob shook his head, disappointed in himself, but he continued telling his story, "Well, at first, I was winning a lot of money, and I was having a lot of fun. So then the owner of the establishment, Sam Graber, invited me back, and I was flattered, in a weird way. I went back a few times. Secretly, you understand. And before I knew it, I was hooked. I felt like I had gotten the hang of the game, plus I had built trust with the owner so much so that he offered for me to play with money I didn't even have. The winnings could be even bigger that way. I don't even know why I cared about the money. In my community, we don't strive to be rich with material possessions. But, you see, it got messy and things got out of control."

Mark sighed and leaned back in his chair. His stomach turned somersaults. *I knew Samuel was up to no good!* he thought to himself. He had only recently shut down the gaming tables at Samuel Graber's bar on the instinct that the games were not being regulated legally, and it turns out his instincts were right. Letting players get in over their heads, playing with money they didn't have, was certainly far from legal... or ethical, for that matter. There was no place for that in Little Valley.

The sheriff snapped out of his thoughts as Jacob continued with his confession. "I ended up losing more money than I had. And I ended up owing Mr. Graber a lot of money." Jacob wiped away another tear. "I didn't have the money, and I couldn't figure out how to pay him back without revealing my secret to everyone." His breathing quickened, "That's when Samuel showed up at my house. Thank *Gotte* that my wife and daughter weren't home that day. He demanded the money, but I still didn't have it. He threatened to hurt me if I didn't pay him, and I promised I would find a way to pay it the next week."

Mark knew where this story was going, but he remained silent to let Jacob continue with his story uninterrupted.

"Then, I went to the bar with some of the balance owed, hoping to buy more time. I had to pull from my family's savings. Mr. Graber was sitting alone with Mr. Davis, the owner of the new bed-and-breakfast in town. Mr. Graber said that they had been talking, and he didn't want my money - which was a relief at first - but he wanted to call it even if I could convince the men in my community to sell him the extra lots of land we own. You see, when we first established our community here in Little Valley over twenty-five years ago, the community all pitched in together to buy extra lots of land. We wanted to make sure we had plenty of room to grow. And we have definitely grown and built on some of those lots over the years, but there is still quite a bit of space that is undeveloped. Mr. Graber said that he and Mr. Davis want to build some sort of park for recreational vehicles or something like that, and they want our land for that."

Jacob stopped and inhaled a long deep breath. "Sheriff, he just wouldn't take no for an answer. I left there with the money I brought, but with a much bigger problem. I tossed and turned for the next few nights. There was no easy way for me to convince the community to sell that property, especially when Mr. Davis had already been harassing us about lowering our prices at the market and in our stores. Everyone thinks he is trying to take control of the market and push us out of business and maybe even out of Little Valley."

The sheriff nodded. Christopher was taking notes quietly next to him, his eyes on the notepad.

"So, I summoned the courage to approach him again. It was just a few days ago. I tried to explain to him that our land would not be for sale, but that I had every intention of paying him back the money I owed him." Jacob wrung his hands and shifted in his seat again. "Mr. Graber became furious, and he told me I had exactly one week to find a way to sell him our land. Or I would regret it. He was very unreasonable, but I didn't think it would go this far. Now I don't know what to do. He won't let me pay him back, and the land is not mine to sell." Jacob's eyes widened as he leaned forward. "I'm not afraid to admit that I am scared, Sheriff. I'm scared for my family and for my community. I don't know how to stop him from hurting me and the ones I care about."

Mark wished he could make this right, but unfortunately, an anonymous note and no other clues did not warrant an arrest of Sam Graber. And the illegal gaming practices in which Jacob participated made things even murkier with the law.

"First of all, thank you for your honesty, Jacob. I can't advise you on the ethics of lying or how to approach this in your community, and unfortunately, considering the entire situation, I can't even honestly provide you with much protection. However," the sheriff said slowly, "I *can* promise to move swiftly with an investigation into the cause of the fire. The best-case scenario is we find a clue on the scene that leads us to arrest Sam Graber for arson. So, go home. Make sure no one even walks around that burned barn of yours. I need to call the fire department first, but we'll head that way right after I hang up the phone."

Jacob stood, thanked the two men, and headed swiftly out the door.

Mark picked up the phone and dialed the number to the Mainstay County Fire Department. "Hi, yes, this is Mark Streen, Mainstay County Sheriff. I'm calling to talk to the chief about a fire in Little Valley that occurred last night or early this morning."

As he sat on hold, waiting to speak to the fire chief, he looked over at Christopher. "If you want a cup of coffee, you'd better grab it now and drink it fast. It looks like it might be a pretty exciting first day on the job for you."

Chapter Four

The sheriff's car drove up slowly and parked in the gravel driveway just to the side of the Schwartz home. Sheriff Mark Streen and Deputy Christopher Jones stepped out on either side of the car and tipped their hats almost simultaneously to greet young Grace who was sitting on the porch swing. The swing was painted a deep red, a perfect contrast to the steel gray color of the Schwartz home.

"Is your father home, Grace?" Mark called out. He knew Grace from a previous case solved just months earlier, and he was impressed by her manners, intelligence and confidence, especially for a young teenage girl.

"Yes, sir. He's right around back. Feel free to walk on back there. He's expecting you." Grace answered before rising to her feet to head back inside.

"Thank you kindly, Grace," the sheriff responded with a smile and another quick touch to the brim of his hat. The two men took only a few steps around the side of the house before they had a full view of the charred remains of Jacob's workshop. Hanging in the air was a faint smell of smoke mixed with the pungent odor of wet burned wood. The men found Jacob behind his house, just as Grace directed. He was lying on his back on the ground, his head and shoulders hidden under his Amish buggy. The men could see a nearby small handmade stall, made just big enough to hold the one horse comfortably. It was cozy and practical, well built and sturdy. The horse inside the stall whinnied quietly and shook its head almost as if it wanted to communicate with Jacob that someone had approached.

"Hey there, Jacob," the sheriff called out. Jacob jerked as if the sheriff had startled him. It did not surprise Mark that he had been lost in his thoughts after all he had confessed in the sheriff's station that morning. Jacob dropped the wrench he had in his hand and scrambled to his feet, brushing the dirt off the backsides of his trousers.

"Sheriff. Deputy." Jacob greeted each of them with a quick handshake. "Thank you for coming out. I've tried to keep everyone away from the, uh, shop, like you asked. But, we had almost all the men in the community here last night, so I'll honestly be surprised if you'll find anything clue worthy."

"Right. It's a long shot, for sure, but we'll take a look, all the same." All three men stood facing the crime scene. There was a moment of silence before Mark spoke again. "No need for you to follow us, Jacob. Christopher and I will go check it out and let you know if we find anything."

Jacob nodded, and the sheriff and deputy headed towards where the barn once stood, stepping carefully, eyes focused on the ground in front of them. There were dozens of footprints in the wet mud left behind after the men had sprayed water to extinguish the fire. The many footprints could have been from the work boots of the community or the firefighters, some from smooth-soled boots similar to what Jacob wore that day, as well as a few different types of general sneakers. There was nothing distinctive, and most of them were footprints on top of footprints. Mark and Christopher agreed that, unfortunately, the prints wouldn't be of any help.

Not finding any clues at first glance in or around the charred ashes either, Christopher suggested they split up and look a few yards out in all directions on the dry land to see if they might find any signs of anyone who had approached the barn that evening. After a thorough search, the two men came up empty-handed. The only tire tracks they found were from the fire truck and tracks from buggy tires.

Mark had learned a good deal about the Amish community since he had arrived in town less than a year before, and he thought it was unlikely that any of them would be responsible for the fire. It disappointed him that the search turned out to be fruitless. The only evidence they had was the note Jacob had found tacked on his door. The question, "What is your saving grace now?" was confusing. After what the town had just recently been through a few months ago, Mark truly hoped that this note wasn't a threat for sweet Grace Schwartz. The best-case scenario was that it was a simple poke at the Amish faith, meant to scare Jacob enough to get results.

The sheriff and deputy returned to Jacob's backyard and found him leaning against his house sitting on a perfectly wrapped bale of hay. His eyes were closed. His hand rested on the top of the hat next to him. The gentle breeze blew a few strands of his hair in and out of his face ever so slightly. As the two men approached, Jacob opened his eyes and stood on his feet, quickly placing his hat back on his head.

Trying to hide his disappointment, Mark reached over to give Jacob's shoulder a firm pat and said, "Well, sir, we didn't find any clues or anything helpful out there, but we've still got the note. The deputy and I will take a harder look at that and we'll do some digging around town. We'll get to the bottom of it. You just stay safe and take care of your family. Let me know if you think of anything else, of course." The sheriff leaned in and with his voice lowered, he muttered, "And stay away from Sam Graber, Jacob. Even if you offered to give him what he asked for, it would never be enough. He would just try to take more. Promise me you'll stay away from him and keep your nose clean. If he did this, we'll find out and we'll book him."

Jacob nodded as his shoulders slumped forward. "Thank you, Sheriff. Thank you both for your time," he responded. It was evident to both Mark and Christopher that Jacob had hoped to sound strong and confident, but his voice was thick with worry.

Just as they turned to leave, Noah Troyer approached from the side of the house. "Good morning, folks," Noah said. He nodded to Jacob and patted him on the back and reached out with a welcoming handshake to Mark first, and then to Christopher. "Not sure we've met," he said to the deputy.

"Mr. Troyer, this is Christopher Jones, the new deputy of Mainstay County," Mark introduced him proudly.

"Pleasure, sir," Christopher greeted Noah with a warm smile and a firm handshake.

"Please, call me Noah. It's a pleasure to meet you, as well," Noah said. Turning to look back at Jacob, he said, "I guess we all know why you two are here. It's terrible what happened to Jacob's shop and all his beautiful furniture. I hope you were able to find something to help find out who did this to him."

"Unfortunately, we weren't able to uncover any more information, but we're going to do our best to find out who the culprit is, for sure," Mark said. "We want you all to know that we are here to protect you. Please don't hesitate to reach out if you need anything at all." Christopher nodded in agreement.

"Thank you, sir," said Noah. "Jacob is a good man, and we've already got plans in motion to help him rebuild."

"You've got a great community here, men. It's really incredible to see how much you care for one another," Mark responded. "Well, we've got a case to solve, so we'd better get busy. Have a good day, and like we said, Jacob, we'll be in touch with any news."

The sheriff and deputy returned to their car and slowly pulled out of the gravel driveway, headed back to the office. "It sure was great to meet Noah. He seems like a good guy," Christopher said.

Mark turned on his blinker to make a right turn onto the highway. "Oh yeah, just wait until you meet his wife and her twin sister. Those two are quite the pair, and something tells me you'll probably meet them sooner rather than later."

Chapter Five

"What a great idea to meet for lunch today, *Maem*!" Abigail was the spitting image of her mother. She had the same kind blue eyes, straight nose and welcoming smile that the twins shared. She sat across from Beth in the front window booth of Little Valley's diner. The view from the window included the local coffee shop, her son-in-law's hardware store, and Matthew Beiler's flower shop, all lined up in a neat row across Main Street.

"Your *dat* and I were just saying this morning how we don't get to see enough of you children. Everyone's lives seem so busy all the time," Beth said, lifting the silver pot of coffee to pour herself a cup. Steam rose into the air just below her face as she stirred one blue packet of sugar into her drink.

"Well, *Dat* does always say, 'Blessed are they who are too busy to worry in the daytime and too tired to worry at night," Abigail grinned.

Beth chuckled, "*Ja*, that is true. That is one of his favorite proverbs, for sure." Turning the conversation a bit more serious, she continued, "Unfortunately, he is living quite the opposite today. I guess you heard about the fire at Jacob Schwartz's home last night?"

"*Ja,* it is *baremlich.* Jeremiah joined the men to help, but he was of the last to hear and arrived just as the fire was extinguished. He said it burned the entire barn to the ground. There was nothing left." Abigail's husband, Jeremiah, worked as a leather smith, creating and selling custom horse saddles to his customers. Earlier that morning, Jeremiah described the heartbreaking scene to his wife, his own eyes brimming with tears as he imagined the heartbreak of Jacob seeing all his hard work burst into flames.

Abigail adjusted her posture to sit up straighter and continued, "I'm glad that my *bruder* isn't here yet, actually, because I wanted to talk to you about something in private."

Beth placed her coffee cup down on the table and met her daughter's eyes, with one brow raised slightly higher than the other. She felt a pit in her stomach again, and she immediately knew that it wasn't good news she was about to hear.

Abigail cleared her throat. "I'm just going to get right to the point." She took a deep breath and then the next words came rushing out as she exhaled, "Jeremiah and I are thinking about leaving Little Valley." She dropped her gaze down to the table and traced the line that the sunlight was casting on the dull surface with her finger. She didn't need to look at her *maem* to know that this news would upset her.

Beth gasped dramatically and placed her hand over her heart. "What?! No! You can't leave, *Dochder* - I won't let you!"

Abigail raised her eyes to meet her mother's. "*Maem.* You know I'm not a child. The bottom line is that Jeremiah and I are worried about all the crime in Little Valley. It doesn't feel safe here anymore. We love being close to you and *dat,* and the rest of the family, but we have to protect our children... your grandchildren." Abigail was referring to her beautiful twin boys and their younger sister, but she also wanted to have more children and Jeremiah was hesitant to continue growing their family in a town surrounded by danger. The recent murders had originated the thoughts of the move, but then last night's fire had pushed more urgency into her husband's voice when they discussed it further that morning.

Abigail reached out to hold Beth's hand. Her mother's skin felt paper thin and the age spots seemed more apparent today than before as she struggled with the thoughts of moving out of town. Glancing back up at her mother's face, she immediately saw the tears welling up behind the blinking eyelashes.

It was Beth's turn to clear her throat. She swallowed back the tears and responded, "This is your home, Abby. What would it be like for all of us if you and Jeremiah and the kids were not at the worship services? Where would you go? Jeremiah would have to start his business all over again." She paused and squeezed her daughter's hand before pleading, "Tell me you'll pray about it long before you make such a big decision."

"Of course, *Maem*, of course. Jeremiah is not the type to make rash decisions. We are only discussing the possibility now, and we are not telling anyone. As a matter of fact, he would probably be upset with me if he knew I told you. He wouldn't want you to worry. And neither do I." Abigail knew her mother well enough to expect her to run to her twin sister, Aunt Anna, and figure out a way to convince them to stay - and maybe that's why she'd told her. Abigail didn't want to leave, but she also knew that Jeremiah's arguments and concerns were valid.

Just at that moment, the two women were greeted by Abigail's favorite *bruder*, Jonah. "*Hallo! Wie bischt, Maem and Schwester?*" He leaned over and embraced Beth with a warm hug, changing her mood immediately, before sliding into the booth next to Abigail and throwing his arms around her neck.

"Where'd you come from, *bruder*?" said Abigail, teasingly.

"I know, I'm late," Jonah grinned. He quickly pushed back the blond curl that had fallen in his eyes. "I've had a busy workday already, and it's only now lunchtime."

Beth's face beamed. Jonah's presence had pushed her sadness to the back of her mind. "You look so *gute*, my *sohn*. I bet you are *hungerich*."

Abigail jumped in, "Jonah is always *hungerich, Maem*. Have you forgotten already?" The three laughed heartily. Abigail was so relieved to change the subject, and she was delighted to see her little brother again. Ever since they were young, the two had gotten along famously. When he was a toddler, Jonah always chose to sit in Abigail's lap. And as he grew a little older, Abigail helped Jonah with his studies and read to him at bedtime. It was hard to move out of the home when she was married, but she welcomed Uncle Jonah into her own children's lives, and they loved him just as much as she did.

Abigail was very proud of the young man Jonah was becoming, but since he had returned from *Rumspringa* and moved out of her mother's home, she rarely saw him. She felt as if there was so much to find out about his life, and she knew her mother felt the same way.

"*Ja*, let's eat!" Jonah said, rubbing his hands together.

Noticing that Jonah had arrived and giving them a few minutes to read the menu, Jessica, the owner of the diner, approached the table a few minutes later. She was wearing a beautiful broad smile and her eyes twinkled. "Are y'all ready to order?" She asked, her notepad and pencil in hand.

"I think so," Beth answered for all of them. "Go ahead, Abigail," she nudged.

As Abigail began to recite her order, the bell on the front door rang and Matthew Beiler entered. Jessica looked up as he came in, and their eyes met. Holding up a manicured finger, she politely interrupted, "Excuse me, one second, please."

Jessica called out, "Welcome to Heaven's Diner! Please have a seat, and I'll be right with you."

Matthew responded with a wave and the same big smile, his eyebrows raised ever so slightly. "Take your time, Ms. Jessica," he responded, as he took a seat.

Jessica reached up and flipped her hair back off her right shoulder, and Abigail couldn't help but notice that her cheeks had turned a light shade of pink. Abigail and Beth exchanged glances and grinned as they watched the scene unfold. It didn't take a wise woman to see that there was something a little extra happening in the exchange between those two.

Then, noticing Beth, Abigail and Jonah at the table, Matthew called out, "Ah, *gut daag*, Troyer Family!"

The three responded with warm welcomes and pleasantries.

Jessica paused to allow for conversation between the two tables. After a brief moment, she returned her focus to collecting their orders and cheerfully asked, "Ok, so where were we?"

Chapter Six

Abigail reached over and picked up the coffee pot on the table. Jessica had just refreshed it before heading off to prepare the table's lunch order. Jonah leaned forward to sniff the aroma of freshly brewed coffee beans as Abigail filled his cup. She topped off her mother's cup next, and then her own.

"So, little *bruder*, tell us how you've been," she prompted.

Jonah took a long sip and set his cup back down on the table, already half-empty. He relaxed against the back of the tall booth seat cushion. "I've been *gut*. I've been *gut*," he said. "There's a lot of work to be done between Uncle Eli's farm and Mr. Mast's farm. Those two are definitely keeping me busy."

Beth interjected, "Are you learning a lot?"

"*Ja*," Jonah answered flatly.

Beth pushed a little bit further. "Do you enjoy the work?"

"I guess so," Jonah said. "As much as you can enjoy work, I guess."

Beth sighed and responded, "Well, Jonah, you know that no dream comes true until..."

Jonah chimed in and they finished the sentence in unison. "...you wake up and go to work," they said.

Jonah shook his head. "I know, *Maem*, I know. You sound like *Dat.*"

Abigail sat quietly. She knew Jonah was going through a phase of wanting his independence. So many Amish boys learn their father's trade and grow up to follow in his footsteps, but for whatever reason, Jonah was resisting that path for himself.

"I don't want to be a carpenter, *Maem*. I know that I am letting you and *Dat* down, but I need to figure out my own way in life. I don't want it handed to me. And honestly, I'm not as talented at woodwork as *Dat* and Mr. Schwartz are. Nor do I enjoy it as much." Jonah sat up and leaned forward resting his elbows on the table. "I get bored easily with that stuff, *Maem,* making the same furniture all the time, using the same tools every day. It's not that I'm lazy. I want work that has more variety, I think."

Beth nodded, and both took a sip from their coffee cups at the same time.

Abigail asked Jonah, "Do you make good money working on the farms, Jonah?"

"It's not bad," Jonah said, "but since Eli and Mr. Mast are mostly teaching me and didn't necessarily need an extra hand on deck, I feel guilty that I am taking extra from their pockets."

Beth shook her head, "No, Jonah, that's not true. They are happy to have you helping them."

"It is true, *Maem*, but don't worry, I work hard to bring extra money into their businesses. I try to pay my keep, I guess you could say. I still would love to find something that provides a passion for me. I would love to find something of my own." Jonah clasped his hands together, his face turned up briefly "I pray for it every day, and I have faith that *Gotte* will give me what I am looking for in due time."

"*Ja, Gotte* is *gut*," Beth agreed. "Let your *dat* or I know if you need anything, *sohn*. We both support you in your journey and want you to be happy."

"Ok, *Maem, denki*, but I know *dat* is disappointed. He wants me to work with him, I know this." Jonah emptied his cup and leaned back again.

Beth cringed slightly and responded, "Jonah, come to dinner and have a talk with your father. Like you are talking to me and your sister here. He will understand, but you have to explain it to him. Maybe he can even help you find what you're looking for."

"My saving grace," Jonah muttered as Jessica appeared with their food on a rolling cart.

"We have the club sandwich and fries for the wonderful Mrs. Troyer," Jessica said, as she set Beth's plate on the table in front of her. "And we have the broccoli cheese soup and garden salad for you, Sweetie" she recited, setting down the bowl and plate on the table in front of Abigail. "And finally, we have the cheeseburger and fries for you, Young Man," Jessica said as she picked up the last plate off the cart and set it down in front of Jonah. "And we have ice water for everybody. You have napkins on the table there by the window, and ketchup right there, too. Is there anything else I can get y'all?"

Beth spoke, "This looks wonderful as always, Jessica. Thank you so much!"

"You're so welcome! Enjoy!" Jessica sang out as she walked back towards the kitchen. She glanced over at Matthew's table and called out, "Your lunch is almost ready, too, Matthew." He responded with a smile.

Beth said quietly, "*Händt nunna.*" Abigail and Jonah joined her by placing their hands in their laps, closing their eyes and bowing their heads in silent prayer. Just a minute later, Beth uttered "Amen," and Abigail and

Jonah responded "Amen" in unison, lifting their heads and reaching for their silverware.

Abigail changed the subject. "*Maem*, how is Aunt Anna? Is her knee fully healed?" Several months ago, Beth and Anna had gotten into a wreck in their buggy and Anna had to walk with a cane for some time afterwards.

Beth smiled and nodded, "*Ja*, she is back to taking her daily walks and moving around like it was never hurt. She sends her love to both of you today."

"Oh, *gut, gut*. Please send our love back to her." Abigail said between bites of lettuce.

"And I guess you both know that Eva is coming to stay with us for a little while?" Beth asked, holding her sandwich in one hand and a french fry in the other.

Jonah looked up from his meal, "Oh, she is? I didn't know. Is everything ok? Why is she coming to Little Valley?"

Beth swallowed her bite and explained how their cousin was visiting to learn baking skills from Beth and Anna. "She has dreams to open her own bakery one day. She makes the best fudge I've ever tasted, which is difficult to make... but she wants to learn specifically about baking breads and pies. I am looking forward to having her."

"I will have to come by and see her after she gets settled," said Abigail. "She and I always had so much fun when we were young girls, and I haven't seen her in ages!"

The conversation continued as Beth shared how well things were going at the Farmers' Market, Abigail shared the latest funny stories about her children, and Jonah learned about the fire at the Schwartz home. Rising out of the booth to head back to their busy lives, Abigail noticed Jessica sitting across from Matthew. A half-eaten piece of apple pie and a cup of coffee sat on the table in front of Matthew, and a glass of water in front of Jessica.

The two seemed very comfortable, like old friends, laughing and enjoying fun conversation.

Beth raised her hand and called out to Jessica as she, Abigail and Jonah headed for the door, "Thank you, Jessica, for lunch! We'll see you next time. Matthew, have a great day! We'll see you for dinner on Sunday at Anna's, I hope?"

Jessica scrambled to her feet, her cheeks turning pink again, and waved goodbye. "Thank you for coming in," she called out. She headed toward their table to grab the dirty dishes.

Matthew turned toward the door and responded, "*Gut daag! Gut* to see you all! And yes, I'll see you on Sunday, Mrs. Troyer!"

The diner door shut behind them. Abigail turned to Beth and said, "Are they...?" Beth shrugged her shoulders, her eyes wide and eyebrows raised. Jonah chuckled and shook his head, "Nothing gets by you two. Abby, you are becoming more and more like *Maem* every day." Abigail grinned, threw her arms around her mother's shoulders and exclaimed, "Well, that's a compliment!"

Chapter Seven

It was just past noon, and Hank Davis's stomach was growling. He knew he needed to get back on a better schedule, but it always felt like there was still so much to do to be ready for the Amish Inn grand opening. He jumped up the front porch steps, returning from a quick visit with Wyatt Nichols, the owner of the garage next door to Hank's bed-and-breakfast establishment. With a bribe in hand, Hank had been able to get Wyatt to agree to limit the use of the shop's air compressor to late morning or afternoon hours after the grand opening. When Hank scouted a place to set up a bed-and-breakfast, he didn't think about how loud the garage would be, and he suspected that the noise might become an issue with guests, especially in the early mornings.

The team meeting that Hank had scheduled was set to start in about ten minutes, so Hank headed to the kitchen to grab a quick snack. He passed Peggy Fremont in the living room. Neither said a word to the other. Peggy was busy dusting the antique furniture. Fifteen years in the cleaning business, Peggy was accustomed to being invisible to her house cleaning clients, especially to Hank. She was thin but fit, her mousy brown hair swept up into a high ponytail. Stray strands of hair framed her face. She was a single mother of two young girls and was grateful for the work. Not unlike the rest of the employees working for the Amish Inn, Peggy looked forward to the business that the grand opening would bring.

Hank entered the kitchen and found Ryan Green, her strong hand gripping a wooden spoon, stirring slowly in a big pot. She greeted Hank when he entered, "Hey there, Hank." Ryan was a tall woman with broad shoulders and thick blonde curly hair that would fall just past her shoulders if she didn't have it tied back in a low ponytail just below her chef's cap. She held herself in a way that meant she was not to be messed with. Her voice was firm and confident, her eyes piercing and intense. Even her name evoked masculinity and strength. Hank had never met a woman named Ryan, but her name didn't matter to him since she was meant to be hidden in the kitchen. So far, she seemed to be the right one for the cook's position at the Amish Inn.

Hank's stomach ached when the aroma of the beef stew hits his nostrils. "That smells incredible," Hank responded. "I'm starving. When will it be ready?"

"Oh good. It's ready now. I was thinking about sharing it at the meeting and see what everyone thinks. It's an Amish beef stew, you know. I found the recipe online." Ryan grabbed a ladle and filled a large soup mug with the thick brown stew from the pot.

"I would hope it would be Amish, seeing as that is what I hired you for," Hank snapped. He snatched the mug from her hand and grabbed a spoon from the silverware drawer.

Ryan rolled her eyes. "You have terrible manners, has anyone ever told you that?" She asked the rhetorical question with her hands on her hips.

"Hmmm. Mmmm," Hank responded with a mouth full of really hot beef stew. He opened his mouth and waved his hands in front of it, as if it would cool it down. He rapidly grabbed a drinking glass from the shelf, yanked open the refrigerator, and pulled out the gallon of milk. He poured a bit of milk into the glass and gulped it down, hoping to cool off his mouth. "Aaahhhh," he grunted as he exhaled.

"Serves you right," Ryan said. "Didn't you see me take it straight out of the pot?" She chuckled, and Hank was annoyed.

"This tastes like store-bought stew, not homemade stew. It needs more work. I expect you to serve our customers dinners that blow their minds. This stew isn't it." He set the mug down and grabbed a granola bar from the pantry. "The meeting is starting in a few minutes," he said, and he turned and left the room.

Back in the living room, Hazel Thompson, Logan Clark and Sebastian Lee had joined Peggy. Logan was the maintenance man, or handyman, as Hank referred to him, for the bed-and-breakfast and Sebastian took care of the landscaping and outside building maintenance. Logan was a skinny young kid in his early twenties with light hair styled in a crewcut. Sebastian was the complete opposite of Logan. Sebastian was a large, burly, older man with long dark hair tied back in a long braid. He wore a black bandana rolled up and tied around his head, covering most of his forehead.

Logan and Sebastian were standing in the back of the room chatting about the most recent baseball game, but their chatter ended once they realized Hank had entered the room.

Hazel was Hank's assistant. She was a petite middle-aged woman with small square glasses placed precariously on her turned-up nose. She was sitting in one of the large upholstered chairs, her laptop open and balanced on her legs.

Peggy was on the couch next to her, looking at her phone. She quickly turned off her phone and slipped it into her back jean pocket when Hank entered the room.

"Find a seat, please, fellas," Hank instructed as he pulled a chair from the window area to sit in front of the others. He hollered out for Ryan to join them, and she appeared in the doorway in a few seconds. She leaned on the doorframe, refusing to take a seat without exactly saying those words.

"Ok, good. We're all here. Let's keep this short. We have a million things to do in the next couple days." Hank gestured to Hazel to take the lead on the meeting's agenda.

Hazel started out by mentioning how the rooms at the Amish Inn were already booked out through the first three weeks. She looked up at Hank for feedback. Hank responded to Hazel with a flat tone, "Good. Please continue."

Moving on, she began to address each item on the list of remaining tasks to be completed, asking for each person to acknowledge their responsibilities and give their assurance that everything would be completed on time. Hank responded when necessary, reminding each person to keep in mind that the inn was to represent the Amish lifestyle in every way possible. He expected everyone to do their part selling the Amish goods he had displayed throughout the bed-and-breakfast, the baked goods that Ryan would be preparing, and even the flowers and plants that would be on display out on the front porch.

"I expect all of you to know a lot about the Amish culture by now, so that you can answer any questions our guests may have. Ideally, we want our guests to experience all of it here, not to go looking for it in the shops in town." Hank paused before continuing. "Ok, I think that's everything. Everyone can go back to work," Hank instructed with a wave of his hand. The Amish Inn team members quickly dispersed and went their own separate ways to tackle each one of their tasks leaving Hank sitting alone in the living room. He let out a sigh of relief. *I think this is going to work*, he thought.

Chapter Eight

The afternoon sun was shining bright over Little Valley, the sky a brilliant blue scattered with puffy clouds that looked like cotton. Anna was lounging on her front porch enjoying the beautiful day while patiently waiting for her sister to return from lunch. Her legs stretched out in front of her, her feet resting on the edge of the patio table as she sat leaning back on the soft cushions covering the wooden porch swing. Beth's husband, Noah, had built Anna's porch swing for her and Eli some time ago as a wedding anniversary gift. It was the perfect anniversary gift because sitting on the swing side by side in the warmer evenings quickly became one of the couple's most treasured ways to spend time together. Like Anna and Eli, the swing was older now, its surface covered in fine lines, but it remained sturdy and comfortable. Every few years, Noah would apply a beautiful dark cherry stain on the aging wood.

Moving back and forth in a slow rhythmic motion, the swing creaked quietly as if it were singing a sweet melody and Anna's thoughts drifted as she closed her eyes.

Little Valley was the only home Anna ever knew. She was so grateful for her family, her friends, and the quaint little town. The land that she and Eli shared with Beth and Noah provided a beautiful space to call home and a bounty of wonderful vegetables and fruit. Eli's farming business earned more than enough income needed to raise their children and save for their future. For this, Anna was especially grateful, but despite their seemingly perfect life on the farm, Anna and Eli had recently discussed what it would take to relocate and convince their family to move somewhere safer. They could not ignore the crimes that had taken place over the last year. There were murders before, and now Jacob and Rachel Schwartz's barn was burned down to the ground. They were again terribly concerned for the safety of the community, and for their family.

Anna had shared her thoughts of leaving Little Valley with her sister several weeks back, to which she wasn't the least surprised when Beth reacted with tears. It was almost as if Beth lived in denial, hiding from the truth, and so much so that she was even able to convince Anna recently that her own thoughts were silly and that it would somehow get better. Anna knew she could never leave her twin sister behind, so she needed to convince her and Noah to consider that it might be time. A long deep breath exhaled Anna's lips. She was sure that would take a lot of prayer.

The clip-clop sound of Beth's horse and buggy brought Anna out of her worrisome thoughts. She opened her eyes and greeted her sister with a big smile, raising her hand in the air to wave at her. Before grabbing her purse and the box of cinnamon rolls that she had packed for the Schwartz family, Anna instinctively checked to tuck any stray hairs into her *kapp* and bounded down the porch steps.

"Well, it took you long enough," said Anna, with a grin on her face. She jumped into the buggy and held on tight to the door handle on her right. Ever since the sisters' buggy had turned over and crashed, Anna felt more comfortable holding on tight.

"*Ach du lieva*, you act like we're going to drive full speed to see Rachel," Beth said with a chuckle. She rolled her eyes and signaled the horse with a kissing sound to trot forward. "What have you been thinking about up there on your favorite porch swing?"

Anna responded, "Nothing. I was just enjoying the freshness of Spring." Beth glanced over at Anna, and Anna was sure that Beth knew she wasn't telling the whole truth. It was almost impossible for the sisters to hide anything from each other.

"*Ja*, it is a gorgeous day," Beth answered.

Changing the subject, Anna asked, "How are Jonah and Abigail doing?"

Beth proceeded to catch Anna up on Abigail's funny stories and Jonah's struggles with Noah. Anna was grateful for the distraction. Beth was still talking when their horse and buggy pulled up in front of the Schwartz home. Rachel was sitting on the top step of her porch designing a beautiful planter with yellow daffodils, blue and yellow primroses and purple and pink violas. She looked up and greeted the sisters with a smile and a wave as they stepped out of the buggy.

"*Gut daag*, Rachel!" Anna called out as they approached, Beth chiming in with the same greeting.

"I see you are welcoming Springtime," Anna said, gesturing toward the flowerpot.

Rachel set her gardening tools down and stood. "*Ja,* I got these flowers at the market last weekend and I'm only just now getting around to planting them. I'm glad I waited though, because it is just what I needed today. I was planting the primroses and thinking about the proverb about being grateful for the roses instead of complaining about the thorns." She cast her eyes down and then looked away. Anna could see that she was fighting tears, so she reached out and gently squeezed her arm for reassurance.

"That is one of my favorite proverbs," Beth said. "We are here to help, Rachel. No one should have to face this kind of thing alone, so please let us know how we can lend a hand."

"*Ja*, and we want to talk to you, too, about the best timing for a barn raising, as well," Anna chimed in.

Rachel removed her gardening gloves and wiped her cheek with the back of her hand. "*Denki*. To both of you. Really. It means the world to me that you are here and helping organize that. Jacob has a lot of work ahead of him to rebuild all the orders he had completed and lost. I'm sure that is overwhelming him. He is at Noah's right now, working with his tools and supplies to try to get a head start. He will have to figure out what he has on his plate and where to start. It will be a huge undertaking since all the details of his orders went up in flames with his work. He and Noah spent most of the past few hours rummaging through the destruction seeing if any of the metal tools... or anything at all... survived the fire."

Rachel suddenly slapped her hand on her thigh and gasped, "Where are my manners? Please do come in. I will put on a pot of coffee... or tea? And we can sit down and catch up before we get down to business."

Chapter Nine

J acob pulled his horse and buggy up to the front of the Packers' house.
Before jumping out of the buggy, he bowed his head and said a quick
prayer, hands clasped together in his lap. *Gotte, please give me the strength
and courage I need to face my failures. I will accept whatever you think is
best for my consequences but know that I seek forgiveness with a full heart
of sincerity and so much gratitude for this wonderful life you have given
me. It is because of you that Rachel and I were blessed with Grace and so
much more, and it is my dream to lead a more faithful and honorable life
with you by my side.*

Raising his head, he inhaled a full deep breath and stepped down onto
the ground. Jacob patted his horse on the head lovingly as he reached for
the reins and tied him to the stake set up in front of the porch for visitors
like himself. He silently counted the steps on the way up to the front door,
hoping to settle his racing heart before he came face to face with Bishop
Packer.

When he reached the door, he paused for a moment. The door was
made with a few large pieces of walnut lumber, the knots from the tree

defined among the different dark shades. Jacob remembered when the bishop had requested he craft a "unique front door" made of this very special wood. Wood such as this was typically used for flooring, not necessarily doors, and Jacob was skeptical of how the finished product would look. But he ended up having a wonderful time creating a unique panel pattern that was simple enough, but with just a touch of something extra special. He was proud to see that it still looked flawless almost twelve years later.

Jacob knocked politely. Margaret Packer opened the door and greeted Jacob, "*Gut daag*, Jacob! It is *gut* to see you. Please come in. Joseph is expecting you. Would you like some tea?"

Jacob nodded his head and returned the greeting, "*Denki. Gut daag*, Mrs. Packer. It is nice to see you, too." He couldn't help but notice that Margaret was quite thin, her face looked tired, and Jacob wondered if she was well. He made a mental note to encourage Rachel to pay her a visit soon.

"No, *denki*, Mrs. Packer, no tea for me this afternoon. I just had a tall glass of water before heading this way," he said.

Jacob followed Margaret into the small room beside the living room. It held a simple wooden desk and matching hard chair. A ficus tree sat in the corner on one side of the room's only window. A tall-back upholstered chair sat on the other side with a small round table to the side and a floor lamp positioned behind it. The bishop was sitting at the desk when Jacob entered. He turned around right away, and rose to his feet, his arm outstretched to welcome him with a handshake and a one-armed hug.

"*Hallo*, Jacob Schwartz. *Wie bischt?*" The bishop smiled at Jacob, a warm smile, his kind eyes twinkled.

Jacob responded with the same warmth, "*Denki* for your time today, Bishop. It is a beautiful day, and I don't want to take much of your time."

"Nonsense," the bishop said, waving his arm in the air. "Have a seat, and please, tell me what's on your mind."

Jacob nodded and sat down in the upholstered chair. He welcomed the comfort of the soft cushion, and he wondered how many men before him must have sat in the same chair with worries to share. Surely, none of them could be as severe as his, he thought, and his heart again began to race. He cleared his throat and his voice cracked slightly as he told the bishop everything. The words came rushing out like rain through a broken gutter, spilling on the ground. It was a bit of a relief to finally sit face-to-face with the bishop and to tell him all of his mistakes and fast held secrets. He looked down at the floor through the entire confession, ashamed to look the bishop in the eyes. The bishop sat silently listening and allowing Jacob to speak without interruption.

"...so, that is why I'm here," Jacob concluded. A tear escaped his eye and trickled down his cheek. For this last sentence, he took a quick breath and summoned the courage to look up and meet the bishop's eyes. "I am so sorry, Bishop Packer, and I am not ashamed to beg for forgiveness." The bishop's head moved only slightly, and Jacob couldn't tell if it was a nod. So, he continued, "Rachel and I are forever grateful for this community. It is our home. Our family. What I did was unspeakable, and to think that I have brought danger to everything - and everyone - I care so much for... well, it breaks my heart. I have asked *Gotte* for forgiveness, too, of course. It would be a blessing if you would give me the chance to make things right. I would do anything."

The bishop held up his hand slowly as to gently interrupt Jacob. His eyes narrowed a bit, and he said softly, "*Denki*, Jacob, for coming to see me today and for sharing this with me. I can see that you have regrets. As you know, we have shunned men in the community who have gambled at the Little Valley Pub in the past, but none of them came to me to bare their soul and ask for forgiveness in this way. It was the right thing to do to first ask *Gotte* for forgiveness. The next step will be to forgive yourself."

Jacob nodded and brushed another tear from his cheek, his eyes locked with the bishop's as he listened intently. "*Ja*, that is most difficult, I agree, Bishop. I also have yet to confess to my wife. She has been through so much, and I do not want her to worry."

Joseph interjected, "Oh, you must do that right away, Jacob. Rachel is a kind woman. You must trust that she will provide you comfort and not judgment in the end, but the sooner you have an honest conversation with her, the better."

Jacob nodded again. He waited to hear of his fate with the community. He took another quick breath and was deciding how to ask if he and his family could stay, but as if the bishop was reading his mind, he continued with his answer.

"As for the community, I will speak with the elders, but I am confident that everyone will agree with my thoughts. You and your family have been a big part of our community here in Little Valley. We do not want to see you leave, especially since you are asking for forgiveness. We will grant you forgiveness but be prepared to inform everyone about what we are facing." The bishop tugged on his beard. "I will stand next to you and provide whatever support you need, but it is the right thing to do."

Jacob nodded. He had already expected this would be necessary. He knew it would be difficult, but he trusted it would be the safest thing in the end.

"We were so sorry to hear of the fire - and so relieved to hear that no one was harmed." The bishop paused for a moment and rubbed his eyes. "We still have a problem, though. It's Sam Graber, and possibly Hank Davis, too. We are going to have to figure out what we need to do to protect our community."

Jacob pleaded, "What can I do, Bishop? I will do anything to make this right, but I am so lost. The sheriff told me to stay away from Sam and Hank, but I'm not sure..."

The bishop interrupted, "Absolutely, do not approach Sam. Let me discuss this with the elders and we will decide on the next steps. You just go and take care of your family, Jacob, and talk to your wife. I'm sure there will be a barn build to help with your losses, and it may be just what we need. Barn builds are always such *wunderbaar* quality time with everyone." The bishop smiled and leaned forward to touch Jacob's arm, lifting gently as Jacob stood. "I will be back in touch with you in the next few days to work out the logistics of the announcement and more. Get some rest. This has taken a toll on you, and you need to take care of yourself." He paused before continuing, "And don't forget what I said about the importance of forgiving yourself." He hugged Jacob and walked him to the front door.

Jacob thanked Bishop Packer again before climbing into his buggy and heading home. His shoulders felt so much lighter, and he was eager to tell his wife next. On the road home, Jacob glanced up at the sky, his right hand covering his heart and he said out loud, "*Denki*, my Lord. You are my saving grace."

Chapter Ten

Arriving at the Little Valley Pub just minutes before his shift started, Archer Melgren pulled into the back lot and parked next to Sam's truck. Sam Graber was the owner of the pub and Archer's employer. Archer detested Sam and everything about him. His loud, boisterous voice grated on Archer's nerves. Sam's lack of manners and terrible customer service made Archer question how he was even in business. Even the sight of Sam's large bright yellow truck with black trim evoked an unsettling feeling.

Archer shifted his Toyota Camry into park and wrapped up his phone conversation with his mother. "I'll call you tomorrow, Mom. I just pulled up to work," he said, reaching to grab his phone from the mount on his dashboard. "I love you. Have a great day today!"

He slipped his phone into his pocket and grabbed the keys out of the ignition. A defeated sigh escaped his lips before he opened the back door of the pub and entered the dimly lit storage area. It's only a means to an end, he reminded himself. Archer had big dreams of going to law school, but he had made some poor financial decisions during his first years of college and found himself overwhelmed with debt from a failed business venture he had fallen into with some close friends. The debt would need to be resolved in order to obtain funding to further his education.

Archer's Uncle Jack lived in Little Valley and had invited Archer to move in with him temporarily until he could get caught up with things. Jack Melgren was a regular customer at the Little Valley Pub and had become acquaintances with Sam Graber. Any chance he could, Jack reminded Archer how he pulled some strings to get him the bartender position. Archer was grateful for the income but working for Sam was far from pleasant.

Turning around to lock the back door behind him, the sound of Sam's boisterous voice traveling across the otherwise silent pub greeted Archer like an icy gust of wind on a cold day.

"Archer, is that you?" Sam hollered from his seat at the front bar.

"Yep!" Archer responded, attempting to set a positive mood with his tone. "It's me." He walked into the front area and behind the bar. Sam and Hank Davis were sitting at the bar. Sam had a short glass of what Archer knew to be whiskey, Sam's drink of choice. It looked like Hank was only nursing a glass of iced water.

"Hey there," Archer greeted them. "How's it going this morning?" He began to unload the clean glasses from the dishwasher, placing them carefully on the shelves behind the bar.

"Morning, Archer," Hank responded with only a second of eye contact. Sam grunted as he finished off his drink. He set the glass down, tapping it on the bar and motioned for Archer to pour him another.

Archer could quickly tell that he had interrupted their conversation, so he poured Sam's drink and turned his back, slicing lemons, limes and celery on the counter at the back wall.

"I'm no idiot, Sam. I know you hate them," Hank said.

Sam responded, cool as a cucumber, "You *are* an idiot if you think I am the one that set their barn on fire. Yeah, I'm not a big fan, but if I wanted to hurt them, I wouldn't have set *a barn* on fire. I think maybe you don't know me like you think you do." He chuckled.

Archer felt his shoulders tense.

"Look, all I'm saying is that I want nothin' to do with that foolery," Hank continued. "You know the Amish Inn is opening in just a few days, and I don't want any trouble from them... or from the law."

Sam scoffed, "Yeah, good luck with that. The law is one hundred percent on their side, all the time. If you're a suspect in that fire, then you're gonna have trouble."

"That's my point," Hank responded, running his hand through his hair. "I don't wanna risk everything I've put into this. I know we tried to bully that guy, Schwartz, into lettin' us have their land. I don't want nothin' to do with that now. If anything, I need those people to trust me right now, and burning down their barns ain't gonna help with that. Just leave them alone, Sam. If something happens and I get blamed, I can't promise I'll have your back."

Archer heard the movement of a bar stool pushed across the hard floor. He turned to see Sam standing over Hank, his face leaned in close, his eyebrows drawn together and his finger pointing just an inch from Hank's face. "I said I didn't have nothin' to do with that fire, Hank. You try to turn over on me, and I'll make sure that you regret that you ever knew me. I've done a lot for you and that stupid Amish Inn idea of yours. I can destroy it just as fast."

Hank stood and puffed out his chest. "I'm not scared of you, Sam. And I'm not comin' for you either. I'm just saying, let it go. Messin' with them is a losing battle. It's only going to lead to more trouble for you and the pub. As much as you've done for me, I've done for you." Hank turned to grab his keys off the bar and winked sarcastically at Sam, responding, "Keep your threats in your pocket. They don't work on me."

Sam's face relaxed a bit, and he took a small step back before resting again on the bar stool. "Yeah, yeah. Mr. Tough Guy. Go back to your little Amish hotel. I got nothin' else to say to you."

"Yeah, that's a first," Hank chuckled as he walked towards the front door.

Sam turned his attention to Archer. "What are you looking at?" He asked before tipping his glass back again.

"Just pulling inventory," Archer replied, hoping that his voice didn't give away any discomfort he was feeling.

"Yeah, well make sure you get it right this time. The next time we run out of Jack Daniels, the lost sales will be comin' out of your pay." Sam stood and walked back to his office leaving his empty glass on the bar. A moment later, Archer could hear the door slam.

Chapter Eleven

Beth and Anna headed back to the parking lot where their buggy was parked to retrieve the remaining storage bins of cookies, leaving Eli and Noah to finish setting up their table and banner. The air was crisp, and the sky was overcast, filled with light gray clouds that threatened rain.

"I hope we don't get rained out today," Beth said, pulling her shawl tighter.

"*Ja,* me too. I overheard someone say that the rain is predicted to hold off until this afternoon," Anna responded, tucking away stray strands of hair that had slipped out from under her *kapp.*

"Is Eli sticking around with us this morning?" Beth asked.

"*Ja,*" said Anna, thinking back to her and Eli's conversation over breakfast just hours earlier. Eli confessed he had mentioned their thoughts about moving out of town to Noah. Anna wondered if Noah had said anything to Beth yet. She never kept secrets from Beth, and it felt terribly uncomfortable to do so now. But she justified it in her mind that it was just a conversation between Eli and herself. There were no plans in place. They only spoke about possibly traveling to visit some nearby communities to see if they were safer and a good fit for a future home, but they had not committed to a date or anything of that nature.

"You seem distracted, *Schwester*. Is everything ok?" Beth asked, reaching into the buggy and handing one of the containers to her sister. She grabbed the other bin and the two women headed back.

"Everything is fine," Anna responded, slowing down her pace.

Beth slowed her pace to match her sister's. "Something is on your mind. I can tell," she insisted.

"*Ja*, I have a lot on my mind lately, but everything is fine. We should sit down and have a cup of tea after the market this afternoon. I feel like you and I haven't had a chance to connect in a few days." Anna looked at Beth. She hoped she wasn't causing her stress. She knew that she had a lot going on in her life with Eva's arrival scheduled for the next week and with a bit of friction between Noah and Jonah. Beth was a worrier and Anna had always felt like she needed to protect Beth, not add to her worries.

Beth nodded and smiled. "I would love that. I was just thinking the same thing this morning. Plus, we need to put the plans together for the Schwartz barn raising. That's right around the corner."

Beth and Anna returned to their booth just as Eli and Noah were setting up the chairs and cashbox. Their table looked beautiful as always with a colorful patchwork tablecloth that Beth and Anna had sewn together several years ago. The tablecloth had turned out just as they had imagined, representative of an Amish handmade quilt. Each square displayed a unique handmade pattern, mostly pictures of hearts, lanterns, horses, and flowers.

On top of the tablecloth sat a stainless-steel tiered display of cookies on one side and the clear plastic case of pastries on the other. Three pies with spatulas next to each sat in the center of the table. The apple pie had apple shapes cut-out of the top crust, the sugar cream pie had a golden meringue top layer, and the dark chocolate pie had a contrast of white dots of whipped cream placed uniformly around the outside rounded edge. Boxed orders ready for pickup sat organized and labeled below the table on a small bookshelf that Noah had created when their business began to grow, and pre-orders had come into play.

A simple banner reading Amish Baked Goods stood at the back of the booth. The sisters had not particularly wanted to display a banner, but it was required in the vendor rules for the market. The two women had agreed upon a pale blue background with a white basic font for the design and had ordered the banner and its stand from the Little Valley Print Shop. It was not an inexpensive purchase, so they made sure to take extra care of it, storing it in its original tube each week.

"This looks great, as always, fellas! Thank you so much for your help!" Beth said cheerfully.

Eli nodded, and Noah responded, "Glad to help. Good luck today, ladies. I think you're all set here. I'm going to head over to Jacob's booth to give him a hand. Eli, you're staying though, right? I will be back later to help with the breakdown."

"Sounds *gut,*" Eli responded. "Good luck with Jacob's booth today, too. I know he appreciates your help."

"*Denki, lieb,*" said Beth. "Have a *gut mariye.* I'll see you later today."

Anna was already helping their first customer when Noah headed towards the parking lot. Beth jumped in to help the next customer, an English woman with her young child in a stroller.

"My husband and I just love your cinnamon rolls," she said. "We have made it a tradition to have them every Sunday morning," she laughed and then she leaned in and placed one hand flat next to her mouth as if she was sharing a secret with Beth and Anna. "I'm not gonna lie, your goodies are so much better than what they have at the bakery in town. Everyone knows it, too." The woman winked at Beth.

Beth and Anna looked at each other. Anna knew instantly that Beth was uncomfortable with the customer's comment, so she stepped in and replied, "Thank you so much. I'm glad to hear that you and your husband enjoy our cinnamon rolls! They are a crowd favorite, for sure." She collected the woman's money and responded, "See you next week!"

After the woman packed the box of cinnamon rolls in the netting at the bottom of the stroller, she thanked the sisters and walked on to continue shopping.

Anna checked in with Beth. "Are you ok?" She muttered under her breath, with a smile still set on her face for customers walking by to see.

"*Ja*, I'm fine. You know those sorts of comments make me cringe," Beth said. Her eyes were downcast as she adjusted the displayed goods so that they were all the same distance from each other on the table in front of her. Anna knew that organizing and "making things perfect" was a coping mechanism for Beth's autism, so she took a step back from the table and let Beth continue sorting things on the table and in her mind.

Anna took a moment to survey the crowd. There were so many unfamiliar faces. Anna could remember when the farmers' market customers used to be all the same people. Now, people drove in from neighboring towns and counties to visit Little Valley. Their farmers' market had become well-known, and word had begun to spread. Watching all the people greet each other used to be Anna's favorite part of selling at the market, but the crowd's energy was different now.

I wonder if the person who started the Schwartz barn fire is here today, Anna thought to herself.

"Well, good morning, ladies!" Shannon Graber stood on the other side of the table, a broad smile spread across her face. "And, Mr. Miller," she nodded to Eli who sat in one of the chairs near the back of the booth. "How is everyone doing this fine morning?"

"Hi there, Mrs. Graber!" Anna responded.

Beth chimed in, "Welcome, Mrs. Graber!"

"Oh please, you know you can call me Shannon," Mrs. Graber insisted. "How's business? I feel like I haven't seen you in a while."

"Yes, we were thinking the same thing. You haven't been here in a few weeks, it seems. Is everything ok?" Anna asked. Shannon Graber was a regular customer at the sisters' market booth, and the women were always glad to see each other. She was so kind and always complimentary. For several years, she purchased their baked goods for every event she had, from weekly Bible study nights to an occasional baby shower. Anna and Beth really enjoyed seeing Shannon each week, and it was a shock to find out that she was Sam Graber's mother.

"Oh yes, everything is good. I have been out-of-town visiting my sister the past couple of weeks." Shannon looked to her left and then to her right and said, "Beth and Anna, I am so sorry to hear about the fire. Sam was just telling me about that yesterday when he came over for dinner. I hope no one was hurt."

Beth jumped in and said curtly, "It's a blessing that no one was hurt, but the whole community is pretty shook up about the whole thing."

"Yes, it was indeed terrible," Anna interrupted Beth before she could continue. Word had spread through the community that Sam Graber was behind the fire, but she was sure that Shannon had nothing to do with any of it. And Anna didn't want Beth to come across as rude or accusatory. "We are relieved that no one was hurt, and we are coming together to build another barn for the Schwartz family soon."

"I am so glad to hear that," Shannon continued, her eyes soft. "I have always been so impressed with how your community cooperates to support each other. I know it has been a rough few months for all of you, and I am not alone when I say that Little Valley is here to help if you need anything." She paused briefly and then continued, "And I hope that the horrible person who set the fire is caught and punished very soon. I can't imagine what the motive could've been to do something like that to such nice people like y'all."

"Well, thank you, Shannon," said Anna. Then, wanting to change the subject, she asked, "Have you tried our new dark chocolate pie yet? It's pretty popular."

Beth agreed, "Yes, we worked hard to perfect the recipe, and the feedback we are getting is that it is just wonderful."

Shannon was convinced. "Oh! Well, I must take a piece for myself for tonight then, and is there any chance I can order a batch of your sugar cookies for Wednesday night's Bible study?"

"Absolutely!" Anna said. "We can deliver those to you early next week and you can pop them in your refrigerator until Wednesday."

"Perfect!" Shannon responded. She collected her nicely wrapped piece of pie after handing the payment over to Beth. "Thank you so much. It was great to see you! I'll see you in just a few days then." She wished Anna, Beth and Eli a good day and headed off to continue her shopping.

Just as Shannon walked away, Jessica McLean walked up to the sisters' table. She was cheerful as always. "Good morning!" Jessica said, dragging the words out as if she were singing a song.

The sisters greeted Jessica by returning warm smiles and hellos. Beth bent down and pulled two boxes out from below the table.

"We have your orders right here," Beth said cheerily.

"I knew you would," Jessica responded, grinning. "My customers at the diner are starting to expect weekend butterscotch cinnamon rolls. You two can never stop baking these," she winked.

Anna replied, "Of course not. We also included a new strawberry cream cheese danish for you to try. We haven't started selling them yet, but we will be harvesting fresh strawberries soon enough and we wanted to have something a little different to offer this year."

"Oh, yum!" Jessica clasped her hands together in front of her. "That sounds delicious! Anytime you two need someone to test your recipes, I'm in!"

Olivia Black appeared out of nowhere and stood next to Jessica. "What's this about a strawberry cream cheese danish?" she asked, looking over her glasses at Anna.

Anna saw Beth clench her hand into a fist out of the corner of her eye. Olivia Black owned the only bakery in Little Valley. The shop's catchy name was Something Sweet. The first few times the sisters had met Olivia, they didn't know she owned the bakery. She presented herself as a customer, buying one of everything, before Jessica told Anna and Beth who she was. She had been purchasing their goods to judge her competition. Olivia had even approached Jessica recently and asked her to stop selling Beth and Anna's baked goods in her diner. Olivia offered Jessica a deep discount to purchase and sell the desserts from Something Sweet instead, but Jessica declined. She knew her customers looked forward to Anna and Beth's delicious treats, and she wanted to support their business.

"Hi, Olivia," Jessica said, without the same melodic tone as her earlier greeting to Beth and Anna.

Olivia ignored her and began inspecting what was in the plastic case in front of her.

"Good morning, Mrs. Black. Can I help you find anything today?" Anna asked politely.

Olivia had long gray hair that extended past her shoulders, pulled back away from her temples with small clips. Small metal framed glasses were perched near the end of her small pointy nose, and crow's feet surrounded her dark eyes. "What do you have that's new?" She asked, pushing her chin down to again look over her glasses at Anna.

"Well, our dark chocolate pie is probably our newest item today, but you tried a piece of that last week, if I remember right." Anna responded with a small smile.

Beth interjected, "Yes, how did you like the chocolate pie, Mrs. Black?"

Olivia ignored Beth and continued, "What are the strawberry cream cheese danishes I heard you talking about? When are those coming out?" She asked, sounding annoyed.

Anna didn't like the way Olivia ignored Beth, so she turned to Beth to allow her to answer Olivia's question instead. Beth took the cue and responded, "Oh, we are still just working out the kinks in the recipe for those. We don't have any for sale just yet."

Olivia shifted her attention to Beth. "I see," she said, squinting her eyes as if she were suspicious of Beth's answer. Without another word, she turned on her heel and walked away.

"Wow. I'm sorry she is so rude to you," Jessica said. "You two don't deserve that. It must be hard to be kind to her when she is so disrespectful."

Anna waved her hand as if to brush it off. "No worries, Jessica. *You* certainly don't have to apologize for *her* behavior. It doesn't bother us. "

Beth chimed in, "We have a proverb that says, 'Kindness, when given away, keeps coming back.' It's not always easy to remember that, though, I'll admit."

"Well, if that's true, then your lives should just be overflowing with kindness! I always say that it makes perfect sense that two such sweet women like you would bake the most delicious treats. You are definitely in the right business," Jessica smiled and thanked Anna and Beth one more time before gathering her order and heading off to open the diner for breakfast.

"She is such a nice girl," Anna said, watching Jessica walk away.

"Oh, I agree," said Beth, leaning her hip on the table. "And something tells me Matthew Beiler feels the same way."

"What? What do you mean?" Anna asked, her curiosity piqued.

"I guess I didn't tell you that I saw them at the diner together when I was there with Abigail and Jonah? The two definitely seemed to be happy to see each other." Beth grinned sheepishly.

Anna rolled her eyes. "I really like Jessica, but I can't imagine Matthew wanting to date an *Englisher*."

Beth raised her eyebrows and closed her lips together. "You're probably right," she said, but she didn't believe it. She was confident that there was some chemistry between those two, but Jessica wasn't Amish and Matthew had just been baptized weeks before since returning to the community.

There's no denying that a relationship between those two could become problematic, especially considering the current growing friction in Little Valley between the Amish and the English. The only way it would work is if either Jessica joined the faith or Matthew chose to leave the community. She made a mental note to include Matthew and Jessica in her evening prayers. She was hoping for the first option.

Chapter Twelve

"**M**mmm, mmmm," Sheriff Mark Streen said as he pushed his gear shift into park in front of the home of Amish elders, Solomon Fletcher and his wife, Charity. "I can't believe this happened again," he muttered as he pushed the driver's door open and stepped out of the car. The smell of burnt wet wood hit their noses, an odor too familiar to both the sheriff and the deputy.

The Fletcher home was right next door to the Schwartz's property, separated only by about an acre of trees. The Fletcher family was highly respected in the Amish community. Their family was one of the first families to settle on the land in Little Valley, and this second arson meant that the sheriff and the deputy would have their hands full convincing the rest of the folks that they were safe.

Sheriff Streen mounted the porch steps, skipping every other one, and Deputy Jones was right behind him. Isaac Fletcher, the Fletchers' oldest son, greeted them at the door. Isaac invited the two men into the home, after a brief introduction, to find Solomon sitting on a rocking chair in the living room, his walker parked within his reach next to him. Solomon's wife, Charity, was sitting on the couch. Both Solomon and Charity were frail. Mark guessed that they might be in their late eighties.

"*Maem, Dat*, have you met Sheriff Mark Streen? And this is the new Deputy, Christopher Jones." Isaac gave an introduction as if he knew the two gentlemen; however, they had only just met a minute before at the front door.

Both men removed their hats and nodded a hello to Charity to which she responded with a small smile. The sheriff reached his hand out to Mr. Fletcher, bending over at the waist. Mr. Fletcher reached out and shook the men's hand, one after the other, first shaking Mark's hand and then the deputy's hand right after, remaining seated. "I hope you don't mind if I don't stand," Mr. Fletcher stated. His accent was thick, and he spoke each word slowly and carefully.

"Not at all," Sheriff Streen responded with a wave of his hand. "We won't keep you long," he continued. "We were so sorry to hear about last night's fire, sir. Did any of you see anything?"

"No, nothing. But get him the note, *sohn*," Mr. Fletcher said.

Isaac stepped into the dining area to retrieve a note from the table and handed it to the sheriff. Mark immediately recognized the same type of heavier paper as the note that Jacob handed him just the week before. He unfolded it and found the same neat print with black ink. At first glance, it looked like the same handwriting, and he looked forward to comparing the notes side-by-side. This time, the note read, "Got any more aces up your sleeve?" Mark suppressed a sigh. This brought even more direct suspicion to Sam Graber, considering the gambling reference. He needed more than inferences, though.

Christopher pulled a smaller plastic evidence bag out of his back pocket and held it open for his partner. Mark dropped the note in the bag without a word and turned back to the Fletchers. "Pardon me, ma'am," he nodded to Charity and turned his focus to Solomon and Isaac who was now standing right behind his father. "Do you have any idea who would want to set fire to your barn?"

Isaac rested his hand on his father's shoulder and responded, "We all know who is behind these fires. It's Samuel Graber. Jacob confessed everything to the community on Sunday after service, and the note explains it all. Please, Sheriff, can you arrest him now?" Mark recognized the frustration in his voice.

"Unfortunately, we need more evidence," Mark said, "but we are going to do everything we can to put an end to this. I promise." With these last two words, he held his hat to his heart and looked directly at Solomon. "If it's okay with you, the deputy and I will take a look around the crime scene, er, your barn. And then we'll get out of your hair."

Solomon nodded, and the two men followed Isaac to the back door. Standing on the back porch, they could see what was left of the barn. It looked as if the Mainstay County Fire Department arrived a bit earlier this time, leaving a shell of what used to be the barn instead of just a pile of ashes like at the Schwartz's property. Starting their search, Mark and Christopher were disappointed to find the same dozens of footprints layered on top of each other, the same fire truck tracks mixed with those of horses and buggy wheels. There was nothing left behind in the rubble that they could see. Mark feared that it would be another dead end.

The two men returned to thank the Fletcher's for their time and give more assurances that they would put a stop to the terrible crimes happening against their community. They jumped back in their car and pulled out of the driveway. Instead of heading back toward the highway, Mark turned on his blinker to turn left. He didn't have to explain it to Christopher. The deputy knew where they were headed.

Chapter Thirteen

S am Graber was standing outside, leaning against the wall, smoking a cigarette when the sheriff's car pulled into the parking lot of Little Valley Pub. Sheriff Mark Streen made eye contact with Sam as he stepped out of his vehicle.

"Just the person I was looking for, "the sheriff called out. Sam didn't respond. Instead, he took another drag on his cigarette and paused a minute to size up Deputy Jones with his eyes.

"Well, lookie here, you must be the new deputy dog," Sam said with a sarcastic grin, his words dripping with disrespect.

The deputy planted his feet, straightened his shoulders, puffed his chest out just a bit and stuck his thumbs in his belt. He set his eyes with a cold hard stare directed right back at Sam and slightly cocked his head. He didn't say a word.

Sheriff Streen spoke to Sam again, breaking up the staring match that Sam and Christopher seemed to be having. "Where were you last night around one in the morning, Sam?" The sheriff asked casually.

After a dramatic pause, Sam shifted his eyes to Mark. "Make up yer mind, Sheriff. Are you asking me where I was last night or this morning?"

The sheriff couldn't stand this guy and he certainly wasn't feeling like playing games. He took a deep breath, maintaining eye contact with Sam, and rephrased the question. "Last night, Sam. Tell me about your night."

"Am I being questioned for something?" Sam asked, again belligerent.

"I would say that was a question, yes," said the sheriff. Mark turned to Christopher, "Did that sound like a question to you, Deputy?"

Christopher responded, "Oh most definitely. But maybe what Mr. Graber is saying is that he'd rather come to the station to tell us about where he was last night."

The sheriff turned back to Sam, "Is that true, Sam? You want to come down to the station to chat?"

Sam scoffed. "What is this? You two gonna play good cop, bad cop now?" He chuckled.

The sheriff squinted his eyes and began to speak again, "I just want to know..."

Sam interrupted him. "I know why you're here," he said, flicking his cigarette butt on the ground. "You think I started that fire last week." He stopped and licked his lips and stepped forward. "Well, you're wrong," he hissed. "I ain't got nothin' to do with that. I know they all think I did it, well, because those people are not exactly my friends, if ya get what I mean. And trust me, a few of 'em have definitely given me reasons to seek some revenge on 'em. But," he paused, "it wasn't me. And because of that, you're not gonna be able to prove it."

Mark waited for him to continue. He hoped Sam would put his foot in his mouth.

"Why would I want to burn their stupid barn down, anyway? If I wanted to hurt 'em, I'd do better than that," Sam said. He snorted and sent a ball of spit onto the ground next to him.

"Is that a threat?" The sheriff hoped to provoke some sort of confession.

"Hell no, that ain't a threat. You think I'm stupid enough to threaten somebody in front of two lawmen?" His voice remained calm and casual. "I'll tell ya again, you're wasting your time with me. I ain't the one you're looking for."

The deputy prodded him, "You know who did it, then?"

"Nope," Samuel said, staring hard at Christopher. "I don't have the foggiest idea."

Mark couldn't tell if Sam knew anything or not, but he could tell that they would get nowhere with this. He interjected, "Well, Sam, we sure do thank you for your time." This time, Mark wore the sarcastic grin. "You know where to find us if you ever want to confess or roll over on one of your friends." He winked and tipped his hat before he and Christopher walked back to the car. As Mark turned over the engine, he watched Sam light another cigarette.

"Well, he's an interesting guy," Christopher said. "You'll have to catch me up on his story sometime."

"Yeah, he and I go way back" the sheriff grumbled as he backed up the car and headed back to the station. "Let's send that note out for prints. We've got to sort this out and soon. I think we're going to need to pull out our secret weapon."

"What's the secret weapon?" Christopher asked.

"The sisters," Mark replied as he turned onto the highway.

Chapter Fourteen

"There are few things that compare to a barn raising in Spring," Beth said to Anna as the Schwartz home bustled with women of all ages working together to set a breakfast feast to be ready when the hardworking men outside needed some refreshment. Tables were set up outside close to the house, under the shade of the oak trees. The men had spent the early hours of the day removing the rubble from the fire and prepping the foundation for a new barn. Piles of stacked lumber and supplies were laid neatly off to the side, and the men worked in orderly fashion, combining their talents to complement each other. Noah and Jacob were in charge of the build, and Beth loved how they communicated what they needed from each person with respect, positivity and grace. There was so much love that went into a barn build and so much gratitude from those on the receiving end.

For this particular barn build, Beth couldn't help but think about how perfectly aligned it was with the season. Springtime brought a sense of renewal and the new barn would do the same for the Schwartz family. However, already into mid-morning, there was an energy that was hanging over the community that differed from anything Little Valley had ever experienced, for as long as Beth could remember. It was a sense of unrest.

Jacob had confessed to the community the mistakes he had made with Sam Graber, and although the elders and the bishop had decided that Jacob would be forgiven and the Schwartz family could stay, the community members had become concerned. With the recent second fire, an unsettling fear had spread like wildfire. Discussion of families moving away, finding homes in a safer town where they would feel more accepted and welcome, had moved outside of private homes and was being shared among each other.

Beth knew she was one of the few that wanted to stay. Little Valley was her home. She loved her life there, including her community and her English friends, too. But, in the past week, both her daughter Abigail and her own twin sister had confided in her that they were considering moving. It broke her heart to hear her loved ones talk about leaving, and she was determined to convince them to stay.

Beth and Anna took a seat at one of the picnic tables, sitting across from each other. They each had a cup of hot coffee and shared a danish. "How are you doing this morning?" Anna asked her sister.

"I'm enjoying this beautiful weather we are having," answered Beth. "It has turned out to be a perfect day for the Schwartz barn build, thank *Gotte*."

"*Ja*, it really has. Little Valley does have beautiful spring seasons," Anna said.

"This danish is quite good, *Schwester*. I think we may have perfected the recipe." Beth changed the subject, sensing that her sister was patronizing her. When Anna had mentioned the possibility of moving, Beth had cried and pleaded with her to change her mind. She couldn't stand the thought of living apart, and she informed Anna that she would not be leaving Little Valley. Anna had mentioned this once before and Beth had thought it was resolved, packed away for good. She was upset that Anna had not let it go and was reconsidering such an absurd idea.

Moments later, Rachel Schwartz approached the table and asked, "May I join you two?" She set a cup of tea down on the table next to Beth.

"*Ja,* of course," said Beth, patting the seat next to her on the bench and pushing the remaining danish her way. "You must try this! It is our newest recipe."

Rachel sat down and reached for a fork to grab a bite. "Mmmm... it is SO good! The two of you make the most delicious treats!"

"Please, finish it," encouraged Anna. "I've had more than my share of food this morning," she chuckled.

"Me too," said Beth, patting her stomach. "I can't keep eating like this," she said, chuckling as well.

Rachel finished the danish in two more bites and after taking a sip of her tea and setting her fork down, she said, "I can't thank you two enough for helping plan this day. I haven't been on the receiving end of a barn raising in many years, and it brings back happy memories to replace the sad ones." She paused, blinking away tears, and said, "So, *denki,* Anna and Beth. And Beth, Noah has been so *wunderbaar.* He has helped Jacob so much."

"You don't have to thank us, Rachel," Beth said, reaching out and touching Rachel's arm gently. "We are all part of a family here in Little Valley. We support you and are here for you, Jacob, and of course, Grace."

Rachel smiled and said, "You are so kind." She paused and looked at her hands in her lap. "I know Jacob has brought so much heartache to this community with his actions. If there is anything he or I can do to fix things, I hope you know that we will do it. We will do anything to make it right and to make all this fear go away. We pray to *Gotte* every day for wisdom, but the elders... and the sheriff... they all say to leave well enough alone and leave it up to them. Did you know that the bishop and the elders are talking about handing over some of our beloved land to that awful man? Poor Jacob would feel just terrible if it came to that." A tear trickled down her cheek as she continued, "And we were so guilt-ridden and heartbroken when we learned of the fire at the Fletcher home. Will it ever stop?" Rachel rested her head in her hands, her elbows propped on the table. Her shoulders moved rhythmically as she cried quietly.

"It's ok, Rachel. It's going to be ok," Beth said, gently patting her back.

"Rachel, please do not worry. *Ja*, it's true that Jacob made some mistakes and got mixed up with the wrong people, but if there is anything that Beth and I know, it's that the person behind the crime is not always who you think it is." Anna and Beth locked eyes. "Beth and I are going to do some investigating on our own and see if we can get to the bottom of this before any rash decisions are made or any other fires are started." The sisters continued to look in each other's eyes, as if they were communicating without words. "We've proven to be quite good at getting to the bottom of things like this," she chuckled.

Beth knew Anna was attempting to lighten the mood, but she also knew her sister was dead serious about it being time for them to get involved. Beth felt the all-too-familiar stomach uneasiness that resulted from the perfect mixture of excitement, anxiety and a tinge of fear. She looked across the table at her sister, her mirror image. Anna was right. It *was* time that the two of them, known well as the wise women of the community, stepped up to the plate and stopped this crime, too.

And maybe, just maybe, thought Beth, *we can convince everyone to stay in beautiful Little Valley.*

Chapter Fifteen

T he Amish Inn stood tall, the late morning sun peeking out from behind the arched roof. Anna and Beth pulled up to the front, but they hesitated before stepping out of the buggy.

Looking straight ahead, they simultaneously reached out for each other's hand and squeezed tight. Ever since they were little girls, they would hold hands whenever they were facing something that made them feel uneasy in any way. Joining their hands brought them comfort and strength through connection.

"Alright, let's talk about what we're doing here," said Anna. "Remember, the sheriff thinks we can build trust with Hank and maybe get him to talk. This will be our first time to go undercover - I think that's what they call it."

"Right," Beth said, nodding her head. Her heart was racing. "The main goal is to get Hank to trust us enough to uncover some type of evidence."

"Ok, so we have to walk in here with an open mind, and be friendly," Anna said.

"I'm ready, if you're ready," Beth said, turning to look at Anna and giving her hand one last squeeze.

"I'm ready," said Anna, grabbing the box of cookies they had prepared to present as a gift.

After tying the reins to one of the white picket fence posts, the two women walked up the porch steps and entered the front door. A welcoming scent of cinnamon hung in the air. Beth and Anna were silent as they looked around the room. There were two tall-backed upholstered chairs set on either side of what looked like a very comfortable loveseat on one wall. A matching couch sat against the opposite wall, a coffee table centered in front of the couch. A crocheted blanket was thrown over the back of the couch and a handmade patchwork quilt hung on the wall. There was a wood-burning stove across the room, a perfectly stacked pile of logs sat on the hearth next to it. An oil lamp sat on a round table by the door. Small wooden carved figurines of horses and faceless people dressed in traditional clothing were set on end tables and shelves around the room. The coffee table held a vase of fresh flowers and a hand-carved candle.

The sisters were in awe as they soaked in all the details. They weren't sure exactly how to feel as they surveyed the room. It almost felt like they were in a strange museum full of things that represented their lives, but yet it didn't feel authentic. All the decor was clearly made by people in their community, but it would actually be odd to see a home decorated in this manner in their community.

Hank appeared in one of the internal doorways, surprised to see the sisters standing in the front room. "Well, well, well, isn't this a nice surprise?" Hank said, sounding friendly.

"Hi, Mr. Davis," Anna returned his greeting cheerily. Beth began to fidget, smoothing her apron and checking for any loose strands of hair that may have fallen out of her *kapp*.

"Please call me Hank. And forgive me, but are you Mrs. Miller or Mrs. Troyer?" Hank asked Anna politely.

Beth stepped forward. "I'm Mrs. Troyer, Hank, but you can call me Beth."

"And I'm Anna Miller," said Anna.

"Ah. Well, it's nice to see you both," Hank responded with a smile. Beth couldn't help but take note of how friendly he was. The Hank that everyone knew was never this nice, so she was suspicious. But she was also willing to play along. "What brings you by today?" Hank asked the sisters.

"We wanted to see the new place and bring some of our sugar cookies for you and your guests as a grand opening gift." Anna responded with a warm smile. She handed the box to Hank.

"Oh, thank you!" Hank said as he peeked in the box. "I'm sure these are delicious. You two have quite the reputation around here for your desserts, you know."

The sisters smiled and there was a few seconds of awkward silence before Beth spoke, "So, how is business going? Have you had any new guests yet?"

Hank responded, "Oh yes, we have a couple visiting us now - they are out shopping and sightseeing. But we have had someone every night since we opened and we have bookings a few months out, as well. Our customers are fascinated with the Amish, er, your wonderful way of life." He stumbled over his words. "Can I show you around? The place isn't that big, but me and my team have put a lot of work into it and I would love to know what you think," he said enthusiastically.

"That would be great, thank you," Beth responded. She hoped she didn't sound as eager as she felt. She had become intrigued, she wanted to see more of what the fascination was with the Amish Inn.

Anna and Beth followed Hank to the back part of the inn where he showed them the vacant rooms. There were detailed panels with wainscotting on the walls and elaborately carved wooden bed frames. Beth chuckled to herself. Although the Amish create beautiful pieces like that for *Englishers*, it would actually be very rare to find such decor in a traditional Amish home. The Amish lived simple lives based on their faith, and it would be unusual to find such elegance in the homes of anyone in their community.

After seeing the rooms, Hank led them back through the front room and into the kitchen. "Last but not least," he said, "I would like to introduce you to the chef that makes all the delicious Amish meals for our guests. Ryan Green, this is Anna Miller and Beth Troyer."

Ryan was chopping onions on a large cutting board. She looked up without stopping and said, "Nice to meet you." Her voice was deep and less than enthusiastic. Ground beef was cooking in the skillet on the stove next to her. She set the knife down to stir the beef, breaking it up into smaller pieces.

"Nice to meet you, too," Anna said politely. Beth was uncomfortable with the thick tension that filled the room.

Hank seemed a bit embarrassed by Ryan's lack of welcome and said, "Beth and Anna brought us some of their sugar cookies, Ryan. These ladies sell their wonderful baked goods at the farmers' market each weekend. They are quite popular." He walked over and set the box down on the counter next to the sink.

"I'm excited to try them," Ryan said, barely louder than a mumble. She returned to chopping onions and said, "I'm sure they're great. Hank here will probably expect me to replicate them."

It didn't take a wise woman to see that Ryan was not a big fan of Hank. *This could work in our favor*, she thought to herself. Finding her voice, she asked Ryan, "Are you from around here?"

Ryan added the onions to the ground beef and stirred the mixture, turning the knob on the stove just a fraction to lower the temperature. She grabbed a bulb of garlic off the counter and used the side of her knife to break it into cloves. Without looking up, she responded while dicing the cloves of garlic. "I'm actually from Little Valley originally. I left to go to college years ago. I tried to make it as an artist, but it didn't pay enough to support me, so I went to culinary school instead." She added the diced garlic to the meat and returned to stirring it. She looked up and continued, "I came back because my mother is sick."

Before the sisters could react, Ryan continued. She patted Hank on the back roughly and raised her voice as she spoke. "And that's when I landed this awesome job here at the ol' Amish Inn. Isn't that right, Hank?" A sarcastic smile spread across her face.

Hank appeared to be frustrated and headed toward the back door. "I almost forgot to show you two the back patio. It's not quite done..." his voice trailed off as he headed out the back door, expecting the sisters to follow him.

Anna quickly followed with Beth close behind. Beth stopped before closing the storm door, and said, "It was nice to meet you, Ryan. If you're ever at the farmers' market, make sure you stop by our booth."

Ryan waved her hand in the air in a half-hearted goodbye, her back turned away from Beth. She returned to her cooking, stirring a can of crushed tomatoes into the skillet.

When Beth caught up to Anna and Hank, she could hear Hank's explanation that the back patio was almost ready for guests, but not quite. "I still need to build a fence to block the view of the shop next door." He motioned toward Nichols Garage, situated right next to the Amish Inn.

"Yes," Anna chuckled, "that is certainly not something you would see in an Amish community."

Chapter Sixteen

N oah sat at the table and watched as Beth floated around the kitchen cleaning every single surface. When Beth fell into a cleaning frenzy, it was usually because she was anxious, or she was excited. Today, she was excited, and her energy was contagious.

"It feels like a holiday, doesn't it?" Noah asked Beth, a broad grin spread across his face.

"*Ja,* it does. I can't wait to see everyone today!" Beth squealed with excitement. Her cousin's daughter, Eva Zook, had arrived just yesterday and all the Troyer kids were coming home to welcome her. "I was so surprised that everyone was available to visit on the same day. Peter and Faith both said they could make it around noon. Amos will be a little later, but he said he'll be here. Jonah's definitely coming, and there's no telling when Abigail will arrive. You know how Abigail is always late to everything." Beth chuckled. "I know everyone is so busy, but it feels like it has been forever since we've all been together."

Amos was Beth's second son, Peter was her oldest son, and Faith, her youngest daughter. Amos, Peter and Faith and their families came home for Sunday dinners regularly, but it was rare for everyone's schedules to align with Abigail's and Jonah's, too, like they did today.

"It will be quite the crowd, indeed. It's a good thing the weather is nice. We can gather outside and let the kids play," Noah said, sipping his coffee. "How was Eva's trip, by the way? Is she feeling settled?"

Right at that moment, Eva walked in the door looking fresh as a daisy with her lavender dress and white apron. Her blonde hair was tucked away neatly in her *kapp*. "*Ja,* I slept like a baby," Eva said, laughing. "*Gute mariye*! Can I help with anything?" She asked Beth, walking towards the sink to grab a cloth.

"Oh no," Beth answered quickly with a smile. "Please, sit and eat some breakfast. I know you must still be tired from traveling."

"*Gute mariye,*" Noah said. "It is nice to see you this morning."

"*Denki* to both of you. It is so exciting to finally be here. I have looked forward to this for many months," Eva said. "Little Valley certainly is a beautiful town. I have dreamed of living here ever since I visited as a young girl."

"How are your parents?" Noah asked.

Eva sat and poured herself a cup of coffee from the coffee pot on the table. She scooped a teaspoon of sugar and added a drop of cream, stirring before taking a sip. "They are both well, *denki* for asking. *Maem* is a bit heartbroken that I have left Worthton, but she adores Beth and Anna and hopes to visit soon. *Dat* stays busy with the farm. They send their love."

"I am glad to hear they are well, and I know that Beth and Anna are happy to have you. As you know, they are both very talented bakers, so I am sure you will learn a lot from them." Noah stood and stretched, his arm reached high and his back arched. "Now, if you'll excuse me, I have yard chores for myself this morning. With the beautiful Spring, we have new grass to mow and flowers to tend to."

"Jonah said he is coming by earlier today to speak with you, *lieb*. I'm sure he can help with the yard, too, while he's here," Beth said.

"Oh, that will be *gut. Denki* for breakfast, dear." Noah said. He pulled on his work boots and his straw hat and headed out the back door.

Beth rinsed her rag, wrung it and folded it neatly, setting it down on the counter next to the sink. She sat down next to Eva and poured herself another cup of coffee.

"It smells *wunderbaar* in here, Beth," said Eva. "*Denki* again for having me here. I don't want to be a burden, so please let me help wherever I can."

There was a soft knock at the back door, and Anna entered. "*Hallo?*" Anna called out, her voice cheery.

"*Gute mariye!*" Beth greeted her sister.

"Ah, *gute mariye*, Anna!" Eva said, jumping up to give her a hug.

"Well, I'll say that you have grown quite a bit since I last saw you!" Anna said, laughing. "*Wie bischt?* How is your mother? Tell me about your trip!"

Anna sat down at the table, and the room soon filled with excited chatter. Eva recounted her experiences traveling from Worthton. She shared her excitement to learn everything she can from Anna and Beth. She talked about how she had mastered making fudge but needed help with pastries and pie crusts. "I have big dreams to open a bakery right here in Little Valley one day," Eva said, her eyes lit up as she spoke about it.

Anna and Beth exchanged glances. "Oh, that does sound exciting," said Beth. She and Anna had been asked on numerous occasions when they were going to open a bakery, but they loved the idea of keeping things simple with their booth at the farmers' market. And in their generation, a young woman opening a business of her own would push the boundaries in the community. Eva's generation, however, was quite different. Beth wondered why Eva had not yet married, but she would have plenty of time to dive into Eva's story in the upcoming months.

The sound of a horse and buggy arriving distracted Beth. She jumped up muttering, "Oh, excuse me, please. That must be Jonah." She rushed to the front door, swung it open and squealed, "Jonah!" She was always so excited to see her youngest son, and today was no exception. She greeted her son with a big bear hug. Jonah returned the hug, his strong arms and broad shoulders wrapped tight around his mother, lifting her off her feet for a brief second. Beth laughed and said, "*Gute mariye, sohn!* Please come in and say hello to your cousin, Eva. She just arrived in Little Valley last night."

Jonah followed Beth into the house and greeted Eva. He was a few years younger than her and had no recollection of her visit years ago. "*Gute mariye*, Aunt Anna," he said. Then, with a tip of his hat, he greeted Eva. "It's *gut* to meet you, Eva. I know my *maem* is very excited to have you visiting."

Anna stood and gave Jonah a hug. "*Ja*, it has been very quiet around here since Jonah left. He was the baby and the last to leave the coop."

Eva said, "The last time I saw you, you were just a toddler. I think maybe just learning to walk. You've definitely changed." They all laughed together and spent the next few minutes chatting about the weather and catching up with each other's lives before Jonah excused himself to go find his father and lend a helping hand. Beth followed him out the door, promising Anna and Eva that she would be back in just a few minutes.

Pushing open the back door, Jonah almost ran right into Noah who had seen Jonah's buggy and was headed inside the house to greet him. Noah's face lit up when he saw his son, and the two embraced. "It's so *gut* to see you, *sohn!*" Noah's voice boomed, filled with happiness. Beth stood by to relish the moment of seeing the two reunite again. Her heart was full.

"Same here, *dat*," said Jonah, and then as if he just remembered something, he continued. "Oh! I'm glad I have you both together. I have some news to share, and I wanted to tell you both at the same time."

Beth bounced up and down, her hands clasped in front of her chest, "Oh! I'm so excited! What is it, Jonah?"

"Here, let's sit," said Noah, and the three settled on the seats of the picnic table just a few steps beyond the back porch.

Beth leaned in as Jonah began to speak, his thumb hooked in his suspenders by his chest, his back straight. Even though Jonah was a young man now, at age twenty, sometimes she still saw that toddler Eva was just referring to when she looked at him. Anna said Jonah was the baby, and she was right. He was her baby, and she adored him.

"Well, my big news is that I got a job offer that I am actually really excited about," Jonah said.

Beth threw her arms around her son, exclaiming, "That's great, Jonah! *Gotte* is *gut*!"

Noah smiled, "Congratulations, *sohn*. What is the job?" Beth knew Noah was holding his breath waiting to hear if Jonah would be working with wood as he had dreamed.

"Well, it's a bit of a variety. I'll be a sort of handyman, fixing things." Jonah's face beamed with pride.

"That's *wunderbaar*!" Noah reached over to give his son a loving pat on the back. "I'm very proud of you, and I know you will be very successful."

Jonah smiled from ear to ear. "*Denki, Dat.* Your words mean the world to me."

Beth interjected, "So, where is this *wunderbaar* job?" She asked, excited to hear more.

"It's in town, at the new Amish Inn," Jonah replied. Silence fell over the table. The smiles disappeared from Beth and Noah's faces as they exchanged worried looks.

Chapter Seventeen

"I can't believe it," said Beth, wringing her hands and pacing the kitchen floor. "Thank *Gotte* that Eli was up early enough to extinguish the fire before it blazed high."

"*Ja*," Noah said, his head hung, and his shoulders slouched. "This has to stop. When is enough going to be enough? We can't keep going like this."

"I need to go see Anna," said Beth. "Why don't you go back to bed and get a bit more rest. I'll just be gone a little while, and I can wake you when I return."

Noah agreed and dragged himself back off to bed, his feet shuffling as he walked. Beth watched him walk away and then quickly threw a shawl over her shoulders before heading out the back door. *I wonder if I should lock the door?* That thought had never crossed her mind until now, but she was scared. The fires had hit too close to home this time with Eli's barn being the target. She knew Anna was frantic, and Beth wanted to help console her.

Beth knocked softly on the back door of Anna's home and turned the knob. The door creaked open, and Beth could see a light flickering from a candle in the front living room. She called out to her sister softly, "Anna?"

Anna answered, "*Ja, Schwester*, I'm here."

Beth entered the living room to find Anna rocking back and forth slowly in her rocking chair. Her hands were holding crochet needles, the blanket was laid out in her lap, and her hands moving rhythmically. Her cheeks were wet from tears and her eyes were red.

Beth sat down on the couch close to her sister and leaned forward, reaching out to hold her sister's hand. "It's ok, *Schwester*," Beth said softly. "I know that was so scary."

A new tear slid down Anna's cheek. She set the crochet needles down and held Beth's hand cupped in hers. Her face was still turned down when she said, "*Denki, Schwester*, for coming over. I just don't know how I could do life without you."

Beth wiped away a tear with her free hand and said, "Of course, Anna. I am always going to be here for you." Then, after a brief pause, she asked, "How is Eli? Is he able to rest?"

"*Ja*," Anna nodded. "I gave him some chamomile tea, and he is resting now."

"I'm so sorry this happened, Anna," said Beth, squeezing her sister's hand.

"Me, too," said Anna. "Me, too." She paused and reached with her right hand to blow her nose with her handkerchief. She squeezed Beth's hand back and then released it. Beth leaned back and Anna returned to crocheting. There was a moment of silence as the two women sat there together in the dim light.

"What are you thinking, *Schwester*? Do you know how it started? Did Eli see anything?" Beth asked, her mind racing with questions now that things had finally settled down and she could think.

Anna spoke without looking up, "*Ja*, Eli said he saw Sam Graber's truck leaving the property after the fire was started."

"What?" Beth couldn't believe how calm Anna sounded. "Are you sure?" she asked.

"*Ja*, he is sure. Sam is the only one in town that drives that ugly bright yellow truck. It's so bright that Eli could even see it in the early dawn." Anna spoke with no emotion, as if she were bored. The tone of her voice worried Beth.

Anna continued, "I don't know how we can stay in Little Valley after this. I don't think this is ever going to stop, and I can't live in constant fear."

Beth sat quietly. Anna was upset, and with good reason. She was sure that she would come to her senses after some time and rest. If there was one thing she knew about her twin sister, it's that she didn't give up.

"I know you want to stay, Beth, but I need you. Promise me, *Schwester*, that you'll consider moving with us to a safer community?" Anna's hand rested in her lap, her face turned to her sister, her eyes wet with tears. Beth knew what she needed to hear, but she couldn't lie to her sister, and she had no intention of leaving Little Valley.

"We need to find out who did this, *Schwester*," Beth said, avoiding the question her sister had asked. "Let me think."

Anna sighed. Beth knew she was defeated, and she needed to figure out how to bring her back. It was only hours earlier that Beth's children and their families visited. Anna and Eli were over at the house, too, and everyone was laughing, playing, smiling, and happiness filled the air. Beth would not let someone ruin all of that for them, but she needed her sister to help find the evidence they needed for the sheriff to arrest Sam.

"The sheriff!" said Beth, with a loud whisper. She was careful not to speak too loudly. She didn't want to disturb Eli. "Does Sheriff Streen know about this yet?"

Anna shook her head. "No, of course not. It's still early, and Eli and Noah were able to put the fire out themselves, thank *Gotte*."

"Well, we're going to have to go tell him about all of this right away this morning," Beth said. "Maybe there is another clue left behind this time," Beth was hopeful. "There has to be something we're missing."

Anna nodded, and the women fell silent again. Anna stopped crocheting, gathered the blanket, needles and yarn and set them aside in the wicker basket on the floor next to her. She blew her nose again and grabbed a clean handkerchief off the table next to her, wiping the tears off her face.

Beth sat still, waiting to see what Anna was going to do next.

"The sun is starting to shine now. Shall we have a cup of tea, *Schwester*?" Anna smiled a half-smile at Beth and reached out for her hand again. The two rose to their feet together, straightening their tired backs. Leaning into each other, the sisters threw their arms around each other for a long tight hug before pulling back. Standing face to face, their hands clasped together again, Beth said, "I love you, *Schwester*." A tear slid down her cheek.

Anna wiped Beth's tear away and smiled. "I love you, too, Beth. *Denki* for being here," Anna said. "Now let's stop crying, go have some tea, and talk about what we need to do to put this criminal behind bars."

Chapter Eighteen

“ I am so sorry, Anna,” said Sheriff Streen. “I hate that this happened to you and Eli. And I am so relieved that Eli and Noah were able to catch it before much damage was done.”

Mark sat behind his desk, still drinking his first cup of coffee. Anna and Beth were sitting in the guest chairs placed side by side, facing him. The front door swung open as Deputy Jones entered briskly.

“Oh my gosh, I’m late. My apologies. The kids were troublesome...” he stopped mid-sentence and greeted the women, removing his hat. He nodded at the sheriff and said, “I hope this is just a friendly visit and that everything is ok?” He pulled his desk chair over to the edge of the sheriff’s desk, paper and pen in hand.

“I’m afraid not,” Mark answered, rubbing his forehead as if he were suffering from a headache. “There was another fire started last night, well, early morning, it sounds like. This time it was at Anna’s house. Her husband, Eli, caught it quick enough and was able to extinguish it before any real damage happened. But here’s the kicker: Eli caught a glimpse of Sam Graber’s yellow truck pulling off the property.”

"Ok," said Christopher, taking notes. When he looked up, he said to the group, "Well, I guess it's something that we have the truck ID now."

Mark nodded, but he exhaled. "Unfortunately, I don't think that's going to be enough. We need more than that. We sent the notes off for fingerprints," Mark pulled a plastic bag containing the notes out of the drawer and dropped them on the table in front of Anna and Beth, "but nothing matched criminal records." He stopped abruptly and asked, "You didn't get a note tacked to your door, did you, Anna?"

Anna shook her head. Beth reached out to examine the notes. The paper was thick, a little heavier weight than normal, and the writing was immaculate, almost perfect print. The question mark matched on each note and was unique, with a curly curve at the top that had an elegant style. Beth passed the notes over to Anna to review as well.

The sheriff continued, "We spoke with Archer, the bartender at Sam's pub. He told us about a conversation that Sam and Hank had where Hank was basically asking Sam to leave y'all alone, but Archer says that Sam never actually admitted starting the fires. He told us that Sam did threaten y'all, but said that he would do way worse than set your barns on fire."

"Which is what he told us, too," Christopher said.

The sisters exchanged worried looks. Anna spoke up, "So you don't think Sam Graber is responsible for the fires?"

Beth chimed in, "Well, if he didn't do it, who did? Who else could want to harm us like this?" She paused briefly, "Do you suspect Hank Davis at all?" She braced herself for the answer. She and Noah were so worried about Jonah starting work with Hank, and she hoped Hank was not behind all of this.

Mark shook his head, "No, I don't think it's Hank. I know Sam is behind this. I just have a gut feeling about it, and there's really no other explanation." He ran his hand through his hair. "We just have to get some circumstantial evidence so we can finally lock him up."

Anna interjected, "I agree with the sheriff about Hank. Our son-in-law, Moses, said he came into the hardware store just the other day and bought some supplies. He said he was really friendly and mentioned that things had started off on the wrong foot, that he wanted to make peace with our community." She turned to Beth, "And then you and I had a pleasant experience with him when we went to the inn the other day, too."

Beth nodded. "It's true," she said, "but I'm still not sure if we can fully trust him. He actually just hired my son, Jonah, to work as his handyman. He starts tomorrow, so I think we should pay the inn another visit to check on things."

Anna agreed. "*Gut* idea, Beth. Plus, we could go pay Shannon Graber a visit, too. She has always been so kind to us..."

Beth interrupted, "*Ja*! We actually have to deliver her cookie order, so that's perfect!" Beth was sitting on the edge of her seat, her leg bouncing up and down as if her body was about to explode with excitement.

Mark chimed in, "Excellent!" He smiled at the sisters, a sense of hope hanging in the air. He turned to Christopher, "Ok, so Anna and Beth will visit Sam's mother and the inn. You and I will go pay another visit to Sam and find out why - and how - Eli could've seen his truck this morning. Ladies, please let us know what you find out, if anything. And please," the sheriff stopped and leaned forward with a serious expression, "*please* be safe. We do not want you to put yourselves in danger. Promise us you will stay safe?"

The sisters smiled angelically and nodded in agreement.

Chapter Nineteen

S hannon Graber answered the door just seconds after Anna and Beth knocked. She let out a small squeak of excitement when she saw the two women standing on her doorstep.

"I'm so excited to see you two! Please say you'll come in this time!" She held the door wide open and motioned for Anna and Beth to enter her home. "I simply won't take no for an answer," she said. She smiled and sounded cheery, but Beth immediately felt something wasn't right.

"Thank you, Shannon! We would love to come in and chat for a few minutes. That's very kind," Anna said, returning the warm greeting.

Beth smiled in agreement. "You have such a beautiful house," she said. Complimenting one's home is not traditional of the Amish, but Beth knew it meant a lot to *Englishers* and she wanted Shannon to trust them.

"Aw, thank you so much. Please have a seat, but then remind me who is who. I am so sorry. I know you must get asked that all the time, but I really can't tell the two of you apart!" Shannon asked kindly.

Anna and Beth took a seat at Shannon's large dining room table. It was wooden with a heavy coat of lacquer giving it an unnatural shine. The chairs were almost designed to look regal, with a fancy design carved into the top of the tall back of each, floral upholstered material covering the seats. The sisters sat on one side of the table, with Shannon directly across from them. Behind Shannon was an oversized china cabinet filled with royal blue and white porcelain dishes. Matching blue goblet glasses were on display as well as a variety of small crystal figurines.

When Beth shifted her eyes back to Shannon, she realized that Shannon, sitting perfectly under a ray of sun shining through the large picture windows behind the sisters, looked pale. *That's what is different,* thought Beth. She wondered if maybe Shannon just wasn't wearing as much makeup as she would normally wear when the sisters had seen her at the farmers' market.

On the table between them, sat a beautiful china tea set. "Oh, this is very pretty," said Beth, as Shannon handed her a dainty small cup and a saucer. The cup was filled with an aromatic tea. Beth closed her eyes and held the cup under her nose, trying to distinguish the scent floating above her cup.

As if Anna read her mind, she asked Shannon, "What type of tea is this? It smells absolutely wonderful."

Shannon smiled and responded, "It's actually my favorite. It's a vanilla chai tea. Have you ever had chai tea before?"

"I'm not sure that I have," said Beth, "but it is delicious. I can taste a blend of cinnamon and clove, I think."

Anna agreed, "Yes, it is very good. I think maybe there is cardamom spice, as well? It is very unique."

Shannon chuckled, "That's right! All of that blended together, plus I think there is also nutmeg and a touch of ginger. And of course, the vanilla adds the extra sweetness. It makes me so happy that I can introduce a new tea to you!"

"Well, it certainly makes us happy, too!" Beth said with a wink. She and Anna laughed along with Shannon.

"How is your day going, Shannon?" Anna asked before taking another sip.

"Not too bad," Shannon said. "How about you two?"

"Oh, we're busy, as usual. Our younger cousin is visiting from Worthton and we are spending a lot of time with her getting her settled in and teaching her our recipes. She wants to be a baker, and she dreams of opening a bakery one day." Beth shared with Shannon, hoping to steer the conversation to families.

"That's wonderful!" Shannon exclaimed. "You know, my daughter went to culinary school."

"Oh?" Anna said, "I didn't realize you had a daughter."

"Oh yes. She is actually a better artist than she is a cook, but she is making more money as a cook, that's for sure." Shannon scoffed, her eyebrows raised and then relaxed again.

A feeling of Deja vu swept over Beth. She knew she had recently had a similar conversation with someone else about this same thing, but she couldn't place it.

Shannon continued, "Yeah, my kids never got along very well. My husband passed away years ago when they were young, and I had hoped they would grow up close. But things don't always turn out as you hope. My daughter and son, they're close in age, but they fought so much growing up. I knew that she couldn't wait to move away, so I let her go find her own path. Sammy, though, he stayed home with me. He and I were always very close. He is such a smart businessman, you know." Shannon's face beamed with pride.

Beth wondered how Shannon could see a completely different side of Sam Graber than the rest of the world, and she quickly pushed away doubt that maybe her kids were not who she thought they were.

A timer went off in the kitchen, and Shannon jumped up. "Oh, one minute. That's a reminder for myself that I have to take my medicine. I'll be right back." She left the room.

Beth and Anna exchanged glances but just seconds later, Shannon reappeared. "I'm so sorry about that."

"It's fine, Shannon," said Anna. "Is everything ok with your health?" She asked politely.

"Well, actually, I'm kind of embarrassed to admit it, but I told a tiny fib to you two the other day at the market." Shannon poured herself another cup of tea and topped off Beth and Anna's, as well, while continuing. "I mean, I'm totally fine, but I said that I was away visiting friends when I was actually in Wilsonville at the Wellness Institute there. I was diagnosed with cancer a few months ago, and I had to have some treatment there." Her words sped up, falling off her lips quickly. "But everything went very well, and they suspect I will go right into remission in no time."

"I'm so sorry, Shannon," said Anna. "We didn't know."

"Yes, we will definitely be praying for your body to heal quickly," Beth chimed in. "Please let us know if you need anything."

Shannon smiled at the women and said, "That is very nice of you both, but Sam and Ryan are taking good care of me. Ryan actually moved home, and she has a job now. Ironically, she's working at the new Amish Inn, making Amish cuisine! You just have to meet her! I'm sure she could learn so much from the both of you!"

Anna and Beth sat across from the table, stunned and speechless.

"Oh. We didn't realize.." Anna stuttered.

Beth jumped in, "We just met Ryan the other day, actually, when we visited the new inn. We had a tour of the place, and we had no idea that she was your daughter."

"Yes," said Anna, wanting to help, "that's right. She seemed very..." Her words trailed off as she looked to Beth for help to finish her sentence.

"Confident. She seemed very confident. Let's see, I think she was cooking something with beef that day we were there. It smelled so good."

Beth squeezed Anna's hand under the table.

"Oh good! I'm glad you got to meet her. She hasn't made any friends here yet. Between us and the wall, I will say that she can be a hard person to like. She has held a grudge against me for years now. She always accuses me of favoring her brother over her, and it's just not true. I love my children equally, as I'm sure all parents do, right?" Shannon looked to the women for validation.

"Oh yes, that is true. And I don't think it's uncommon for one child to feel left out at times. I'm sure you are a wonderful mother." Anna responded.

Beth wanted to steer the conversation back to Sam, trying to stay focused on collecting evidence. "How has Sam been holding up since your diagnosis?"

"Oh, Sam is a strong man," Shannon said, a broad smile stretched from ear to ear. "He has really done well with the bar." She set down her cup and looked at both girls with softened eyes. "I know he has said some pretty terrible things about your families in the past, and I wish I could make that right, I honestly do. He blames your community for losing the table games which were bringing in a good chunk of money for him. I'm sure you can understand why he would be so upset about that." She paused half a beat before continuing, "But I promise you ladies that Sammy is a sweetheart. He wouldn't hurt a fly. It's kinda like what they say about small dogs, he's all bark and no bite." Her smile was back, but this time, Beth felt like it was a little forced. Or maybe it was just fake. She couldn't quite tell, but that uneasy feeling in her stomach was back, and she knew it was time to go.

Anna and Beth squeezed each other's hand under the table, pleasant smiles held fast on their faces.

"Thank you, Shannon, we will try to remember that," Anna said half-heartedly.

Beth nodded, "Thank you for such a lovely tea, but we should probably head out. We have a few errands left to run." She and Anna stood to leave.

"Oh, bummer! I feel like I talked about myself and my family the whole time. I didn't even get a chance to learn about you and your wonderful families." Shannon pleaded, "Please do come back again. I would love to get to know you better."

The twins thanked Shannon for inviting them in, and for the wonderful tea. They wished her good health and said they would see her next weekend at the market. They said everything but promises that they would return for more conversation. The sisters jumped into their buggy and headed home, sitting next to each other silently. Beth signaled her horse to pick up the pace. She and Anna needed to get home where they felt safe, so they could process all the information they just received.

Chapter Twenty

Beth and Anna had been lost in their own thoughts ever since they said goodbye to Shannon Graber. They drove straight back to Anna's house and started working silently side-by-side, setting the table for lunch. When the table was ready, the two sat down across from each other, making sandwiches for themselves. After taking a few bites, Beth started the conversation.

"Ok, so what just happened?" Beth said. "Can we take it piece by piece and try to make sense of all of this?"

Anna nodded, "*Ja*, I don't see any other way. That was just much more than I ever expected, honestly, but I don't think we got what we went for. That's the confusing, and frustrating, part."

"Oh, I know. I completely agree with you, *Schwester*, but let's see." Beth set her half-eaten sandwich on her plate. "First of all, let's start with Shannon. I can't believe she was diagnosed with cancer! That poor woman."

"Yes, but is she a nice lady? I think I am confused about that. The end of the conversation started to take a weird turn. I don't think we should start with Shannon." Anna said. She took her last bite.

"Ok, good point. Let's start with Ryan then. I know you were just as shocked as I was to find out that Ryan is Shannon's daughter." Beth said, raising an eyebrow at Anna.

"*Ja*, I was just as shocked as you were. I definitely was not expecting that," Anna said.

"So, what do we know about Ryan?" Beth held out her fist and started counting on her fingers, outstretching one finger at a time. "She and her mother do not get along. That's one."

Anna interrupted, "Maybe that explains why she didn't mention family names when she talked about her family at the inn."

Beth nodded.

Anna continued, "She and her brother do not get along. That's two."

Beth chuckled, "That is probably the least surprising part of this whole thing." Anna laughed out loud.

"Ryan works at the Amish Inn. That's three, but we knew that," Beth continued.

"Wait, back to number one. I don't know if it's important, but she blames her mom for a lot of things. And I didn't realize their father died when they were children, either. What number is that?" Anna said.

"Four. That's number four," Beth said.

"What else?" Anna asked.

"I think that's everything, right?" Beth said, genuinely wondering if they were forgetting something. "Now, let's move on to Sam since he was the whole reason we were there to begin with."

Anna nodded. "What did we learn about Sam? I'm trying to remember now, and I'm not having any luck."

"It feels like the only thing we learned is how much Shannon loves Sam, but did we already know that?" Beth asked, her forehead wrinkled in confusion.

"I think so. It became strange at the end of the conversation, though, right? Or am I imagining things?" Anna asked.

Beth responded quickly, "Oh no, that wasn't your imagination. What I can't figure out is either Shannon truly believes Sam is harmless," she held out another finger, and said slowly, "*or*, she wants *us* to believe that he is harmless."

Anna nodded. "*Ja*, that is the confusing part, but regardless, Eli saw his truck this morning. So, he's *not* harmless."

"*Ja*, I do feel like we're missing something. I think we're going to have to sleep on it." Beth said.

Anna took a deep breath and exhaled slowly, allowing her shoulders to drop and relax. "Let's talk about something else for a few minutes. I need to clear my head of all of this, or I won't sleep at all tonight."

"*Gut* idea, *Schwester*. This all feels very overwhelming. It feels like we are so close to the truth, but it's just out of reach. Maybe Sheriff Streen is arresting Sam right now, since he said he was going to go talk to him again today."

Anna put her hands together as if she were praying and turned her face up towards the ceiling. Beth chuckled.

Beth stood and cleared the table of their dirty dishes. "Let's go sit on the couch and relax. And you've got the right idea. Let's take a few minutes to pray over this and leave it in *Gotte's* hands for the rest of the day."

"*Ja*, that sounds *wunderbaar*," said Anna. She stood and stretched, groaning about feeling old. Beth grinned and said, "Don't forget we're the same age, *Schwester*. Watch what you say about being old." She winked at her sister.

"I said I *feel* old. I didn't say I *was* old," Anna laughed, "but we are definitely not as young as we used to be. My body, and my mind, remind me of that every day."

"Well, come on, old woman, let's go sit down, then," Beth teased her.

The sisters headed into the living room and relaxed next to each other on the couch. They held hands and bowed their heads in prayer. Anna began to pray, her voice level just above a whisper, "Dear Lord, give us the wisdom to help the good sheriff and deputy stop these fires from continuing. Bring peace to our town and our community. Protect us, Lord, from those who want to hurt us, and help us find forgiveness in our hearts as you forgive our sins. Help us to live a life of faith and purity and serve as an example to those around us, spreading your love to all." Anna paused and gave Beth's hand a gentle squeeze.

Beth continued the prayer, "Lord, please be with Shannon Graber as she battles her illness and with Ryan as she settles into Little Valley. Help her find what she is looking for, Lord, and help her to be kind to her mother. And with Sam, please help him find his way to your heart, Lord. And *denki* for my family, *Gotte*, and for this beautiful town we live in. For these things, we are forever grateful." Beth stopped and gave Anna's hand a gentle squeeze.

"Amen," Anna said.

"Amen," said Beth.

The two women opened their eyes and released their hands, leaning back on the soft cushions of the couch.

"I always feel better after praying with you, *Schwester*." Beth said, turning her face toward Anna.

"I do, too, *Schwester*. I do too." Anna said, as she smiled at her identical twin. "Now, you never did tell me about Matthew and Jessica. I'm so eager to hear about that. They are both such *wunderbaar* people."

"Oh, that's right!" Beth said, and she started to tell Anna about that day at the diner when she saw the two of them chatting. Before she could even say much at all, though, Beth looked over to see that Anna had fallen fast asleep. She stopped talking and covered her up with a warm blanket before sneaking quietly out the back door.

Chapter Twenty-One

B eth woke up with mixed feelings. She tossed and turned all night playing the conversation with Shannon over and over again in her head. The visit left her more confused, and she desperately wanted answers. On the flip side, though, she was excited to go visit Jonah on his first day on the job at the Amish Inn. She had decided that she was going to have faith that Hank Davis had made some positive changes and was going to treat Jonah with the respect that he deserved, so today's visit would be less about protecting Jonah and more about celebrating and supporting him.

Noah was spending the day helping Jacob again with his long list of orders, and Eva was spending her day with Abigail. Beth slipped on her shoes and headed over to her sister's house. Anna was watering her container plants outside on her back porch. One of the many things about her home in Little Valley that Beth loved was that her back porch had morning sun and her front porch had evening sun. It allowed for beautiful flowers to bloom in both places, and it worked the same for her sister whose house sat side-by-side with hers.

"*Gute mariye!*" she called out to Anna.

"*Ja, gute mariye* indeed," Anna returned the greeting. "I guess you already watered your plants this morning?"

"*Ja*, I was up early today," said Beth, walking up the porch steps.

"Everything ok?" Anna asked, checking in on her sister.

"*Ja*, I just didn't sleep well. Too much on my mind, I guess," Beth winked at her sister.

"Don't I know it," said Anna. "Well, come in and let's plan our day together."

Beth followed Anna into the house. "How's Eli this morning?" Beth asked. "I seriously can't even believe the fire was yesterday early morning. It feels like several days have passed already."

"I was thinking the same thing," said Anna, "but it still seems very fresh for Eli. He is like you. I'm not sure he slept much last night. He said every little sound had him on edge."

"Oh, that's *baremlich*. I will pray for him tonight," Beth said.

"Well, hopefully the sheriff has good news for us today," said Anna. "When are we headed out to see him?"

"I want to go see Jonah first, and then we'll catch up to the sheriff after that, if that's ok. I know Jonah is expecting me earlier in the day." Beth explained.

"*Ja*, that is fine. After all, he that knows patience, knows peace," Anna said to Beth with a wink. She knew Beth loved proverbs.

"Ooohh, that's one of my favorites! And perfect timing, *Schwester*!" Beth grinned.

Anna chuckled at her sister as she slipped on her shoes and straightened her *kapp*. "Shall we go?"

"*Ja*! I'm ready," Beth answered enthusiastically, heading for the door.

The sisters mounted the buggy, and Beth gave the signal for the horse to trot. On the drive to the Amish Inn, the sisters discussed the baked goods for the weekend's market.

"Has Jessica placed her order yet?" Beth asked Anna.

"Not yet, but I suspect it will be the same as the last two weeks," Anna said.

"We should stop by today and check in. I wanted to hear what she thought about the new strawberry cream cheese danishes, too." Beth said, keeping her eyes on the road in front of her as modern automobiles passed them.

"*Gut* idea," said Anna, "and maybe I'll get a sneak peek into the romance that's happening." The sisters laughed.

"I didn't get a chance to finish telling you about that," Beth said. "You fell asleep right after talking about how old you feel."

Anna knew Beth was teasing her, so she played along, "Well, maybe you need to work on your storytelling skills."

The two continued to banter and laugh the rest of the trip, pulling up in front of the Amish Inn in a light-hearted mood. They jumped down out of the buggy and after tying the reins to the same fencepost as a few days earlier, they walked up the porch steps and entered the front door. This time, there was a man, a woman and a young child sitting in the front room. When Anna and Beth walked in, the room fell silent and all eyes turned to them.

The sisters were not new to gawks and stares from the English, so they smiled and greeted them softly with Good Mornings as they passed by and headed into the back area. They found Jonah there, bent over the bathroom sink.

Beth whispered, "*Hallo*, Jonah."

Jonah spun around and said, "*Maem*! Aunt Anna! *Hallo*! Perfect timing. I need advice on how to get this sink unclogged. I've been working on it ever since I got here and nothing is working."

"*Ach du lieva*," said Anna, leaning in to take a closer look. "Let me see."

Jonah moved out of his aunt's way and smiled at his *maem*. "I'm so glad you came!"

Beth glowed. She loved feeling needed, and Jonah was so special to her. "*Wie bischt*? How's your first day going?" Beth asked.

Jonah leaned in and said, his voice lowered, "I think it's going really well. At least it was until I ran into this drain problem."

"You'll be fine," said Beth. She leaned towards Anna who was looking under the sink. Jonah had disassembled the piping, and the pieces laid on the floor next to the sink. Turning back to Jonah, she said, "... unless someone out there needs to use the restroom." She winked.

Anna stood up. "Ever since we put in the plumbing, I've had this issue off and on. I know just what to do, but Jonah, you'll have to put this back together first. The problem is further in the pipe, in the wall, or maybe even further. All we need is some baking soda and vinegar to flush it out after you put everything back together."

Jonah's expression showed relief. "Ok, I'll put it back together right now. *Denki, denki*, Aunt Anna."

"We'll go get the baking soda and vinegar and we'll be right back," Beth whispered to Jonah. Jonah nodded and sat down on the floor, quickly reinstalling the pipe methodically.

The sisters headed to the kitchen. They wondered if they would run into Ryan, but the kitchen was empty. Even the visitors in the front room were nowhere to be seen. It seemed as if the place was empty except for Anna, Beth and Jonah - *which is ironic since it is the Amish Inn*, Beth thought to herself with a chuckle. Beth and Anna started opening cabinets looking for the ingredients they needed. The women thought surely there would be baking soda and vinegar stored somewhere in the kitchen, and they were on a mission to find it.

Beth opened her third cabinet without luck when she heard Anna ask, "Wait. What is this?"

"Did you find it?" asked Beth, her head was deep into one of the lower cabinets, and she was sorting through the baking ingredients.

Anna didn't respond. Beth pulled her head out of the cabinet and looked up. Anna was standing on a wooden step stool holding what looked like a large pad of paper with binder rings at the top. Anna had flipped over the first page and Beth could see and read the words "Sketch Pad" on the cover, even though it was upside down.

"What is it, Anna?" Beth asked, standing up.

"It looks like a drawing of the Little Valley Pub building and some redesign plans," said Anna, sounding confused.

"Step down," Beth said, "and let me see it."

Anna stepped off the stool and set the pad down flat on the counter. There was a well-drawn image of Little Valley Pub but the word "Pub" was scratched out furiously. Below that drawing was a drawing of what looked like the inside of a fancy restaurant. There were tables covered in tablecloths with candles set in the center of each. The light fixtures looked very modern. The curtains on the windows were drawn to look like lace.

Beth turned the page. A drawing of what looked like the front of a restaurant menu had the words Sous un Arbre spelled across the type, printed immaculately. A tree was expertly drawn around the words. Beth and Anna did not recognize these words, but the beauty in the picture struck them. In the bottom corner of the paper, a question was printed neatly. It read, "Do I like this name?" The question mark had a distinct curly curve to it that Beth and Anna immediately recognized.

"*Ach du lieva*!" Beth whispered to Anna, closing the pad of paper. "Put this back exactly as you found it. We've got to go tell the sheriff. I think we solved the case!" Beth was bouncing up and down on her toes. Anna moved quickly to put the pad back exactly as she had found it. Beth opened the next cabinet below and found the box of baking soda and a bottle of vinegar. The sisters grabbed the food items and ran to find Jonah still assembling the pipe.

"I'm sorry, dear," Beth said, her voice was rushed, and she leaned over Jonah, "but we have to go. Something very important has just come up."

Anna interjected and said, "Listen carefully, Jonah. You need a pot of boiling water. You pour that down the drain first, then follow it with a cup of each of these." She placed the ingredients on the floor just outside the bathroom. "Then, cover the drain with a cloth for about 10 minutes and then pour another pot of water down the drain."

Jonah nodded, "Ok, I got it. *Denki*, Aunt Anna."

The sisters turned to leave, and Jacob said, "Wait!" They stopped and turned around.

Jonah asked, "Is everything ok?" He had a look of sincere concern on his face.

The sisters looked at each other, and then they looked back at Jonah. Beth answered him with an impish smile, "Actually, everything is really, really *gut*, Jonah. We'll see you later, *sohn*." Beth rushed back to give Jonah a kiss on the forehead before following Anna out the front door.

Chapter Twenty-Two

B eth untied the reins from the fencepost outside of the Amish Inn and jumped into the buggy next to Anna. She started to turn the horse when Anna yelled out, "Wait! Look!" Her finger was pointed in the direction of Nichols Garage next door to the inn.

Beth followed the direction of Anna's pointed finger, and a squeal escaped from her lips. "*Ach du lieva, Gotte* is *gut!*" She exclaimed, spotting the sheriff's car parked in the lot. She raised her eyes to the sky and said a silent, quick prayer of thanks. She signaled for her horse to head towards the garage next door instead of turning back the other way down Main Street.

Once in the Nichols Garage parking lot, the women jumped out of the buggy, leaving the horse untied and ran to find the sheriff. They found him in conversation with Wyatt Nichols, the garage owner. The deputy was standing next to the sheriff. Anna and Beth knew Wyatt from years ago when they were younger. They grew up in Little Valley together. Wyatt was always very respectful of the Amish community, and he would often say hello at the market when he was shopping, sometimes stopping to buy a treat.

As they approached the men, Anna and Beth could hear Sheriff Streen asking about Sam's truck. The sheriff say, "So Sam Graber says he left his truck here on Tuesday for an oil change…"

"Sheriff!" Anna called out before Wyatt could answer. The men turned to see Anna and Beth just a few feet away. There was a sense of urgency on both of their faces.

"Excuse me, Wyatt. Deputy, you want to take over here?" The sheriff asked.

"Sure thing," Deputy Jones responded as the sheriff headed towards Anna and Beth to see what all the fuss was about.

"Sheriff, we're so sorry to interrupt," Anna continued, "but we know who did it."

Beth chimed in, "We know who has been starting the fires." She said in a breathy voice.

The sheriff pulled the two women aside. "I've got bad news for you, ladies. Sam didn't even have his truck the day that Eli saw it. It was here in the shop, overnight, waiting for an oil change."

Anna and Beth nodded. "We know it wasn't Sam," Anna whispered, but before they could say anything else, the deputy called out to the sheriff.

"Sheriff, I think you're gonna want to see this," he was waving his arm, motioning him over.

"Ok," the sheriff said, "just hold on and stay right here. Don't go anywhere. I'll be right back."

Anna and Beth nodded. They strained to hear what was being said, but they were too far away.

"Anna!" Beth whispered and pulled her sister close, "Look!"

Out across the empty lot, Anna and Beth could see Ryan standing on the back patio of the Amish Inn. Clearly, Hank had not finished putting up his fence just yet, and the sisters could see Ryan standing there, hands on her hips, watching as Anna and Beth huddled together, just a few feet away from where the sheriff and deputy were questioning Wyatt.

Beth looked back to where the sheriff and deputy were standing with Wyatt and watched as Wyatt handed a folded white piece of paper to the sheriff. Wyatt looked up, and when he saw Ryan standing on the back patio, he lifted his arm and pointed at her. Both the sheriff and the deputy turned their heads in her direction. Beth and Anna looked that way, as well, and they all watched as Ryan took off running, disappearing around the other side of the inn.

The sheriff yelled "Ryan! Stop!" and he and the deputy quickly pursued her on foot, sprinting past Anna and Beth.

The sisters ran to their horse and buggy and Beth jumped in. She looked over at Anna who remained standing on the ground. "Come on, Anna! We can stop her!" Beth said firmly. She knew Anna was scared, but she didn't want Ryan to get away.

"Beth, we are not going to be able to stop her. We are not police officers. And the last time I was riding high-speed with you in a buggy, we almost died." Anna said. "I'm staying out of this and leaving it to the police," she said.

"Anna, please get in," Beth pleaded with her sister. "I promise I'll be careful! We can't let Ryan get away or we'll always worry about the next fire!" She begged Anna, but Anna took a step back. "I'm sorry, Beth, I promised Eli."

"Anna," Beth said more calmly now. "We've come so far. Please come with me. I need you. And Little Valley needs you."

Anna sighed and climbed into the buggy slowly, without saying a word. She grabbed a hold of the handle on her right with both hands.

Beth looked at her and smiled, "*Denki, Schwester.*" She signaled for her horse to gallop, and he ran. The breeching held secure, and the buggy held tight as Beth and Anna caught up to the sheriff and deputy in no time. They could see Ryan still running about half a mile ahead.

Beth yelled, "Whoa!" to her horse and the horse came to a stop. Beth jumped out and yelled for Anna to do the same. Beth didn't have to tell Anna twice. She was eager to get out of the buggy. She moved fast and was by Beth's side in an instant.

Beth gave the reins to the sheriff. The deputy climbed into where Anna was sitting, and Beth gave the signal to her horse to start running. They took off in Ryan's direction as the sisters stood, arm in arm, safe and sound, watching Ryan being handcuffed only minutes later. The sisters remained silent, both overcome by emotion. It was finally over.

Chapter Twenty-Three

Anna and Beth sat outside on Beth's front porch enjoying the cool breeze and warm sunshine that Little Valley weather offered on a Spring afternoon. They had spent the morning baking with Eva, preparing for the farmers' market the next day. The day before, the women rested between visits from their fellow Amish family and friends. Word of Ryan's arrest had spread, and the sisters were showered with wonderful gifts of delicious food, flowers, and kind words and sweet sentiments. The entire community felt a sense of relief knowing that the person responsible for all the recent fires was sitting behind bars, and once again, they had Anna and Beth to thank for their help.

"Those snowdrop bulbs really did turn out nicely this year, didn't they?" Anna asked, admiring their beauty. "I wasn't sure when you planted them if they were going to disappoint you like the tulips the year before."

"Oh, right. Those silly tulips. I think I needed better soil for those. Maybe I'll try those again next year," Beth said. She loved the way the phrase "next year" sounded. She smiled and let out a quiet happy sigh.

The sheriff's car pulled up in front of Beth and Anna's homes. Sherriff Streen and Deputy Jones stepped out of the car, both greeting Anna and Beth with cheerful faces. Anna and Beth stood up and waved hello. They were excited to see the men and couldn't wait to hear more details about the arrest.

"*Gute daag,*" the sheriff said, his accent a little off. He laughed and asked, "Did I say that right?"

"You were close enough," Anna said.

Beth said, "Not bad at all for an *Englisher*!" They all laughed.

"Come on in," said Anna. "Can I get you some tea or anything?"

"No, thank you, and don't get up," Mark said. "It's a beautiful day. Let's just sit outside and chat."

Christopher spoke up, "I agree! This weather is absolutely perfect!"

"That sounds good to me, too," Beth said, nodding and sitting back down on the swing, patting the seat next to her for Anna to join her. Anna sat and the sisters leaned back. They began to move the swing slowly back and forth, relaxing with the movement. The men each took a seat on the cushioned tall Adirondack chairs.

"This is way too comfortable," Christopher joked. "Am I seriously getting paid to sit outside on this beautiful day with you fine folks in these amazing chairs?" He chuckled.

"This is the good life, for sure," Mark agreed. Then, as if it were an afterthought, "Something tells me Noah Troyer made these chairs, by the way, Christopher, if you're looking for some porch furniture for that new house of yours."

"Ah, good to know. Good to know," Christopher nodded.

"So, tell us! We're so eager to hear about the arrest! We want to hear all about it!" Beth had been so patient, waiting to hear more about what happened.

"Oh, right. We're here on police business," Mark teased. "Well, before I get into it, I have to ask how you two knew that Ryan was the criminal starting all the fires. Was it something her mother said?"

"Well, kind of," Anna responded. "We found a sketch pad in the very back of the far left cabinet in the Amish Inn. As you probably know by now, Ryan was an artist well before she was a chef. She only went to culinary school because she couldn't support herself with her art."

Beth interrupted, "Which is actually surprising when you see her drawings. She is quite good."

"It's true," said Anna.

Beth continued the story where Anna left off. "The sketch pad showed her designs to renovate and redesign the Little Valley Pub. She dreamed of making it a five-star restaurant. She had picked out a name, she drew what the interior would look like, that sort of thing."

Beth paused and Anna spoke up, "Ryan's mother, Shannon, had mentioned that there was a wedge in their relationship, that Ryan always thought Shannon favored Sam. Shannon believes Sam is a smart businessman, but we got the impression that she had little of the same faith in her daughter, unfortunately."

As if they were taking turns, Beth spoke up next, "But what really convinced us was the question mark at the bottom of the drawing. It was the same intricate question mark that she had written on the notes."

"And the paper was the same type of paper, too. You know, it was a little bit heavier weight than normal," Anna chimed in. Both sisters were leaning forward now, reliving the exhilaration of finding the sketch pad.

The sheriff said, "That's really incredible that you found the sketch pad. We are going to go confiscate that just as soon as we leave here to make sure that we have enough circumstantial evidence to prosecute Ryan. And, we'll search Ryan's home to see if we can find some more of her writing to compare with the notes." Christopher nodded.

The sheriff spoke again, "So that's what you were trying to tell me in the Nichols Garage. I see now."

"*Ja*, that was what we were trying to tell you before she took off running," Anna said.

"But what did you find out about Sam's truck?" Beth asked. "We still haven't closed that loop in our heads, and can't figure that one out."

Christopher interjected, looking at Mark. "Shall I tell?" He asked, leaning forward, one elbow on his knee.

"Be my guest," said Mark, smiling.

"So, as it turned out, Sam had actually turned his truck into the Nichols Garage for an oil change the day before the fire was set on your barn, Mrs. Miller. Wyatt Nichols had been too busy to get to it before he closed that day, so he parked it around back to take care of first thing in the morning. Coincidentally, there was a baseball game on that afternoon when Ryan came into his shop just after hours. She explained who she was, Sam's sister, that she worked next door, and Sam had asked her to grab something out of his trunk."

"Distracted by the game, Wyatt handed over the keys to Ryan and she never brought them back." Christopher continued, the sisters listening attentively like children being told a story around a bonfire. He continued, "Wyatt didn't even think about it until the next day when he opened shop and he realized he didn't have Sam's keys. He walked around back and Sam's truck was parked where he had left it, so he opened the driver side door, suspicious that Ryan must have just left the keys inside."

"Sure enough," Christopher explained, "Wyatt found the keys, but he also found a strange note on the ground right by the truck, as well. The note was a folded up piece of heavier than normal paper - now we know that to be sketch pad paper," he smiled. "He picked up the note and thought it must've fallen out of the truck and onto the ground, but he shoved it in his pocket and meant to ask Sam about it when he picked up the truck."

"Ah! She was going to leave that note on your door, Anna, before Eli saw her and she had to run," Beth was putting the pieces together in her head.

"Just out of curiosity, what did the note say?" Anna asked, her forehead wrinkled and her head cocked just off center.

Christopher looked at Mark who waved his hand as if to signal that he could continue with the story, "The last note read one simple sentence: All bets are off." Christopher paused.

"Hmmm," Beth thought out loud. "I don't understand the meanings of the notes."

Mark spoke up, "Yeah, we were confused about that, too, until Ryan started saying things like: 'It wasn't me, it was Sam Graber. Read the notes?' Then, we put two and two together and realized that since Sam wasn't successfully framed for the first fire, she had to turn up the heat - no pun intended," he chuckled, "and start to write the notes to put more suspicion on him."

The sisters both nodded. It was all becoming clear now.

"So, the whole thing wasn't even about us. Our community had nothing to do with it," Beth said, looking at Anna.

Anna nodded and said, "Ja, the crimes were driven by jealousy."

Christopher added, "And jealousy of Sam Graber, of all people, too." He shook his head.

Mark said, "In my line of work, I've noted that jealousy hardly ever works on its own. In most cases, jealousy is a cousin of greed, and I think that's what was happening here, too. It sounds to me like we're going to find out that maybe Sam doesn't own the pub... or maybe he doesn't own it yet. It wouldn't surprise me if Shannon Graber holds the deed to that place and only had intentions of leaving it to Sam, not Ryan."

"Wow," said Beth. Anna shook her head.

"And did you two hear about how we went with Jacob Schwartz and Bishop Packer to meet with Sam yesterday afternoon?" Christopher asked.

Beth gasped. "No, we didn't hear about that," she said, instinctively reaching for her sister's hand.

"Well, it's the perfect ending to the story, actually," Mark said. "I guess Jacob was able to raise the money he owed Sam with all the work he has been able to deliver lately, and he paid his debt in full. Sam agreed to put everything behind him and consider it water under the bridge."

Christopher nodded and smiled, "They shook hands and everything."

The sisters looked at each other, broad smiles spread across their faces. They shared the same thoughts without saying a word. They both knew how hard the community had been working to help Jacob's business get back on track.

Beth muttered another favorite Amish proverb, "Many hands make light work."

Mark grinned, "Well, I would say that's gotta be the perfect proverb for all of this."

Chapter Twenty-Four

Tulip Park was buzzing with people of all ages, gathered to attend another wonderful farmers' market weekend in Little Valley. This weekend's farmers' market was organized with a Spring seasonal theme, and the local vendors seemed excited to take the lead on offering goods that represented the season. Booths were set up around the perimeter of the park, offering an array of things like rosewater infused handmade soaps and lotions, strawberry ice cream, cherry blossom scented candles, and of course, Spring inspired Amish baked goods.

Anna, Beth and Eva kept busy welcoming family, friends and new customers as they stopped by to purchase treats or to just say hello. Their table was drawing a lot of attention with a white lace table runner positioned over the center of a bright yellow tablecloth. A silver tray of sugar cookies with strawberry frosting and another tray of stained-glass cookies were on one side of the table, and a tiered display of cupcakes with beautifully piped buttercream frosting made to look like flowers was on the other. A pile of lavender paper napkins sat neatly in the center, a small smooth stone placed on top to keep them from blowing away in the light breeze.

"Wow! This is quite the turnout!" Eva said with excitement as she reached down to grab a box of cookies. The tray of sugar cookies was almost empty, and she took the free second to restock it.

Beth smiled, "*Ja*, it is another beautiful day in Little Valley!" The sisters waved to Jessica McLean as she approached the table.

"Well, hi there! Y'all are sure busy! Ooohh! Your cookies look delicious! I'm not at all surprised!" She said, rubbing her hands together.

"The only surprise here is that you still have cookies left! Look at those beauties!" Matthew Beiler said, appearing out of nowhere.

Jessica's face beamed at the sight of Matthew. "Hi, there, Matthew! Good to see you!"

"Hi, Jessica! I saw you earlier. I was wondering if you were going to come say hello." He teased.

"I just hadn't made it over to see your beautiful flowers yet, but I had definitely planned on it," she smiled and pushed a strand of curly hair out of her face.

He looked almost mesmerized by her movement. Beth watched the scene in front of her and elbowed Anna. Matthew cleared his throat and shook his head lightly as if he were snapping out of a trance. He turned to Anna and Beth and held out a small vase of tulips to Anna. "I brought this to add to your table," he smiled.

"*Denki*, Matthew! They are lovely," Anna said. Beth set the vase on the table, grinning from ear to ear, and arranged the flowers until they formed a perfectly symmetrical arrangement.

"They're perfect!" Beth said, "*Denki*, Matthew! How are things going over there?" She nodded in the direction of his flower booth across the park. Logan Clark was manning the booth.

"Very *gut*!" Matthew said, "And I should probably get back over there and relieve Logan. He has been working very hard helping out at the shop these past few days. I will see you two at dinner tomorrow night." He nodded to the sisters, and then to Jessica, he touched the tip of his hat and said, "I'll see you later this afternoon at the diner?"

"I hope so," Jessica said, smiling with closed lips, her cheeks turning light pink.

Beth hated to do it, but she interrupted. "Before you leave, I want to introduce the both of you to our cousin, Eva Zook," Beth said, gently pulling Eva over to say hello.

"Eva, this is Jessica McLean. She owns Heaven's Diner in town, and this is Matthew Beiler. Matthew owns the flower shop across the street from the diner," Beth said.

She turned to stand next to Eva, facing Jessica and Matthew, "Eva is our second cousin. She traveled here from Worthton. She is a very talented baker and helped us make our selection of cookies today."

"Oh, very nice to meet you, Eva! How are you liking Little Valley?" Jessica asked.

Eva responded, "I like it very much, thank you! I love the name of your diner. I look forward to eating there soon."

Matthew greeted Eva next, welcoming her to town, then politely said, "I should run. I will see you tomorrow night, as well, then!"

"*Ja*, I will be there," Eva responded cheerily.

"Have a *gut* day," Matthew said with a wave before he walked back across the park.

As Eva and Jessica continued to chat about Eva's travels, baking, and life in Little Valley, Deputy Jones approached with two cute little blonde-haired boys in tow. "Good afternoon, Anna and Beth!" He said, holding on to his sons' hands tightly.

"*Hallo*, Christopher!" The sisters welcomed him with a warm smile. "Who do we have here?" Anna asked, sharing a friendly smile with the children.

"Billy and Stephen, say hello to Mrs. Miller and Mrs. Troyer, and you can pick out one cookie each," Christopher said, bent slightly at the waist.

"They look so much like you," Beth said, "Please help yourself. Do we get to meet your wife today?"

"Ah, yes, she is around here somewhere," Christopher said, looking around, just as a woman with short blonde hair and warm brown eyes walked up and slipped her hand into one of the boy's hands.

"Hi! I'm Suzanne. Christopher has told me so much about you two! It's really great to meet you!" She said, smiling.

"It's so nice to meet you, too," Anna said. "We are big fans of your husband."

Sheriff Mark Streen walked up next, "Well, fancy meeting the Jones family here! And hello, Beth and Anna! I'm glad you are getting to meet everyone! Aren't these boys just the cutest?"

"*Hallo*, Sheriff! Great to see you today! Please, help yourself to a cookie," Beth said.

"Oh, I can't. I've been eating too many cookies lately," he laughed, patting his stomach.

"Nonsense. There is no such thing as too many cookies," Anna said, chuckling.

"It's true, Sheriff," Jessica chimed in before extending a handshake and introduction to Suzanne Jones.

Beth said, "Oh, Sheriff Streen, meet Eva Zook. She's our cousin from Worthton. She's here in Little Valley learning some baking techniques from me and Anna, but she's opening a bakery on the corner of First Avenue and Jefferson here in a few weeks." She continued introducing Eva to the deputy and his family, as well.

"Well, congratulations, Eva, and welcome to town!" said the sheriff. "I'll pass the word about your new bakery."

"What?! I didn't know about that," Jessica exclaimed! "That's so exciting! We'll definitely have to talk more. You'll be right around the corner from my diner! Let me know if you need help with anything."

"Thank you so much," Eva said graciously.

The day continued with similar wonderful visits from Anna and Beth's children and grandchildren and from new friends and old. The women's cookie and cupcake supply ran dry just before the market came to a close. Eli and Noah jumped in to help break down the booth, pack up and load the buggy to head home.

After an easy dinner of leftovers, Beth headed over to Anna's house to say goodnight and spend a few minutes recapping the day. She knocked softly on the back door, entering quietly. She knew Eli would already be in bed. He woke early each morning to start his day on the farm which meant he was also typically the first to turn in for the night.

Anna was sitting in her rocking chair, her crochet needles in hand, a blanket draped across her lap. She called softly for Beth to come in.

"*Hallo, Schwester,*" Beth whispered as she tiptoed across the kitchen floor into the living room.

Anna chuckled, "You know you don't have to be that quiet."

Beth grinned and settled onto the couch next to Anna's chair. "I can't believe you haven't finished that blanket yet. It feels like you've been working on it for months," she teased.

"I'm taking my time," Anna said with a small smile. Her hands continued to move the needles methodically.

Beth stretched her arms above her head before relaxing them again, leaning back on the couch. "It was a good day, huh?" She asked.

"*Ja,* it was, indeed," Anna responded. "I was just thinking about how lucky we are to live in such a *wunderbaar* town, surrounded by so many loving friends and family." Anna paused briefly before continuing, "With all that this town has been through, it's the people that truly are the saving grace."

Beth grinned. It made her so happy to hear her sister say those words.

Sneak Peek into Good Intentions

E va Zook turned the key in the lock to open the back door. It was the second week of business for her new bakery, Sugar on Top, but every day felt just as exciting as the first. She turned on the lights and locked the door behind her. It was still dark outside, not dawn just yet, and the glow from the shop's lights lit up her little corner on First Avenue and Jefferson. She set her purse under the counter and filled a teapot with water, placed it on the cold stovetop, and ignited the gas flame under the burner with the knob on the stove. While she waited for the water to boil, she set the oven to preheat and began taking out the ingredients she would need for baking.

Eva could barely hear a soft knock at the back door over the whistle of the teapot. She jumped. *Ugh! Why does that scare me every time?* She thought to herself, as she headed to the door.

"Who is it?" she called out, her hand on the doorknob and her ear to the heavy metal door.

A muffled voice that Eva just barely recognized responded, "It's me, Eva!"

Eva stepped back, unlocked the door and pulled it open, "Good morning, Peggy!" She greeted Peggy Fremont with a smile, holding the door open with one arm and motioning for her to come in with the other.

"Good morning," Peggy said, her voice deep and sleepy. Her hair was swept back into a messy bun, but Eva noticed right away as Peggy walked past her that she had missed a chunk of hair on the right side of the back of her head. It laid against her neck, separated from the rest of her hair.

"You look tired," said Eva. "Did you have a rough night?"

"Yeah," Peggy said, setting her purse next to Eva's. "I couldn't sleep." She grabbed a hair net out of the box on the shelf, and as she was putting it on over her bun, she felt the chunk of hair left out of the hair tie. She sighed and held the hair net in her teeth as she reached back to fix it. Once all of her hair was pulled tight into a bun, she put the hair net on and began to wash her hands.

"Well, how does some coffee sound? Have you had a cup yet this morning?" Eva asked. She had so much compassion and admiration for Peggy. She knew she was working two jobs just to make ends meet and raising her two daughters on her own. It amazed Eva how she kept it up without collapsing. She knew Peggy to be a hard worker. She was dependable, and she paid attention to the details, which was important to Eva.

"That sounds like heaven," said Peggy. "I haven't had a thing yet this morning." Eva used her favorite little pour over funnel to make two cups of coffee, and the women sat in the chairs in the kitchen.

"So, how are the girls?" Eva asked.

"They're doing amazing. My oldest is so smart. She is gonna make straight As again this semester, I think. And my youngest just won a scholarship for a fancy tennis camp this summer. She's a star on that court, I'll tell ya." She smiled, paused and took a sip. "I sure am lucky to have those two. They're really good kids."

"Well, you're a really good mother, Peggy. You work so hard to give them everything they need. I'm sure they see that." Eva said, lifting her cup to her lips and blowing the steam off the top.

"Yeah, well, you know what people say about good intentions," Peggy muttered. Her chin quivered, and she blinked back tears. She sniffled, stood up quickly and said, "Well, it's already past five o'clock. Where do you want me to start?" She walked to the sink, her face turned away from Eva and washed her hands again.

Eva didn't want to pry, but she could tell something was bothering her. And it was clear she didn't want to talk about it, so Eva let it go. She grabbed a hairnet, slipped it over her *kapp*, and the two women started their morning prep in silence.

Find Good Intentions on Amazon at https://tinyurl.com/ALMSBook4.

A Note From the Author

T hank you for reading The Amish Lantern Mystery Series, Volumes 1-3.

Thick as Thieves was my debut novella and will most likely be my forever favorite with a very special place in my heart.

When I started on this journey, I knew I wanted to write a cozy mystery, but I wasn't sure exactly how to make it truly unique until my dear friend Jenny mentioned her love for Amish fiction. I was instantly intrigued, and after many hours of research, I began to embrace everything that the Amish lifestyle represented. It was a true joy to write a story inspired by Amish beliefs and values.

While writing, I fell in love with the community in Little Valley. I cried as I wrote the goodbye between Sarah and Moses after their visit together in the sheriff's front office, and I had a blast working out all the fun details of the mystery. It is music to my ears when readers tell me how they were surprised at the end!

Secrets in Little Valley was a true labor of love, with many more edits than the first. I thoroughly enjoy the process of writing, and this book was certainly no exception.

Right off the bat, I struggled with the idea of "killing off" Ruby. What is a murder mystery without an untimely death, though, right?

If I had to pick a favorite new character, Sheriff Streen would be an easy choice. I fought back tears while writing the heavy conversation he had with the Packers' in Chapter Ten. I hope you felt how he managed that with much needed compassion.

I was so excited to bring Sarah and Moses back into this story and to introduce Moses' childhood friend, Matthew. I was equally excited to introduce a few more villains into the story, as well.

Chase's storyline was written and rewritten a number of times. There was much debate among my beta readers and editors over whether Chase should be attracted to young Ruby or not, but that's how the story unfolded in my mind. Instead of a creepy side of that, I hoped for the takeaway and the focus to be about Ruby – she was certainly a special girl.

Overall, the most treasured parts of this book are definitely the Amish recipes and the pieces that tell a bit more about my favorite twin sisters, Anna and Beth.

And then there's *Saving Grace*. I wrote this book a little bit differently than any other book in the past – I started with the title.

The title of this book actually came to me during the time when I was still writing *Secrets in Little Valley*. I was playing a game of tennis with my mother one early morning, and she was winning. She served a double fault, and I thought to myself, *well, that was my saving grace.* I had this strange reaction to the phrase "saving grace" in my head, like *where did that come from?* It definitely wasn't a phrase I use often, but I immediately knew that was going to be the name of my next book.

Per usual, when I have an idea like that, I can't let it go. So, I wrapped up *Secrets in Little Valley* and found myself super excited to get started on *Saving Grace.* As I started writing, though, I ran into writers' block after writers' block. I think the biggest struggle was due to the coincidence that Grace was Ruby's best friend in *Secrets in Little Valley.* I didn't want her to experience any danger since Ruby was the victim in the previous book. I knew I needed to have another twist.

I had also decided that I wanted to veer away from murder for this book. I know it's fiction, and this is a cozy mystery and all, but I just wasn't sure about there being a murder in the charming, small town of Little Valley every few months or so. I wanted to change things up a bit.

I loved introducing new characters in Saving Grace, and there turned out to be quite a lot of opportunity to do so. And, as always, I enjoyed developing the sisters' characters, as well. And finally, my editor, and friend, insisted that I include recipes again, so cheers to Jenny Raith for pushing that to be a tradition.

If you're on the edge of your seat, wanting to read more Amish mysteries like these, please visit my website at marybbarbee.com to sign up for my new release list.

Thank you again for choosing *The Amish Lantern Mystery Series: Volumes 1-3* to add to your book selection. If you enjoyed it, please consider leaving a review on Amazon or Goodreads or recommending it to a friend!

With so much gratitude,

Mary B. Barbee

Acknowledgments

Gratitude is a big part of the Amish culture, and it's an important part of my life, too. This book simply wouldn't be ready on time, or maybe near as enjoyable, if it weren't for a few very important people. And so, I want/need to take the time to send my love here.

I am dedicating this book to Yoko. She was my rescue pup, and I had the great pleasure of sharing my life with her for over seven wonderful years. She was my little writing buddy, snuggled up next to me while I wrote into the late hours of the night. Life looks different now, but she's forever with me in my heart. I am so grateful for the lessons of love and dedication that she taught me.

Thank you, again, to all my friends, my family, and my readers – I'm not sure there's much difference between those three! Your support is unwavering, and I continue to be overwhelmed with gratitude as I receive your beautiful compliments.

Thank you, thank you, thank you to my mother, Molly Misko, my dear friend, Jenny Raith, and my sweet sister, Julie Rietze. Your unwavering dedication to read, review and suggest edits along the way of each of my books' journey is so amazing. Your insight, your support, and your love shine through in every single comment you leave, and in every conversation we have. I can't thank you enough for everything you do.

As the Amish say beautifully, *Denki.* I am forever grateful.

About the Author

Mary B. Barbee is the author of the *Amish Lantern Mystery Series*. As an avid fan of all mystery and suspense in print, on television and in film, Mary B. believes the best mystery is one where the suspect changes throughout the story, keeping the audience guessing. She enjoys providing an exciting escape for a few hours with stories her readers can't put down - and always with a surprise ending.

When not writing, Mary B. is either playing a couple sets of tennis or a strategy board game with her two witty daughters and her kindly competitive mother. The four of them share a home in the Inland Northwest in the beautiful town of Spokane, Washington with their really cute - but sometimes naughty - chihuahua.

Mary loves to hear from her readers. Connect at:
marybbarbee@gmail.com
www.facebook.com/marybbarbee
www.instagram.com/marybbarbee
www.marybbarbee.com

The Amish Lantern Mystery Series

Find excerpts, purchase links and more at www.marybbarbee.com.

Thick As Thieves – Book 1

Robberies are running rampant in Little Valley, and the quiet small-town lives of the Amish community are suddenly thrown into chaos.

https://tinyurl.com/ALMSBook1

Secrets in Little Valley – Book 2

With the bishop's daughter suddenly missing and a new sheriff in town, Anna and Beth find themselves roped into solving another mystery in their small town.

https://tinyurl.com/ALMSBook2

Saving Grace – Book 3

The Amish community in Little Valley is facing big changes, and big threats, with tourism booming. It becomes clear that some of the new businesses want control of the market, and it looks like they are willing to go to great lengths to get it.

https://tinyurl.com/ALMSBook3

Good Intentions – Book 4

Hazel Thompson is found dead in Little Valley's now-famous Amish Inn, and there's a long list of suspects with plenty of motive.

https://tinyurl.com/ALMSBook4

A Blessing in Disguise – Book 5

Jessica McLean opens shop to find a man has been left for dead on the floor of her diner. Could the crime be related to Jessica's new relationship with their beloved Matthew Beiler?

https://tinyurl.com/ALMSBook5

Christmas Chaos in Little Valley – Book 6

Beth finds out that the Little Valley library is shutting its doors due to a terrible combination of anonymous threats and a lack of funding.

https://tinyurl.com/ALMSBook6

Amish Apple Butter Caklets with Caramel Sauce

Non-stick Cooking Spray

    2 cups all-purpose flour

1 ½ teaspoons baking powder

¾ teaspoon ground cinnamon

½ teaspoon baking soda

¼ teaspoon salt

¾ cup butter, softened

½ cup granulated sugar

½ cup packed brown sugar

2 eggs

1 cup apple butter or pumpkin butter

1 tablespoon vanilla

2 tablespoons vinegar or lemon juice

15 ounce can evaporated milk (2/3 cup)

½ cup chopped walnuts, toasted if you like

Caramel Sauce (recipe follows)

Lightly coat twenty-four 2 ½ inch muffin cups with cooking spray; set aside. In a medium bowl combine the flour, baking powder, cinnamon, baking soda and salt; set aside.

In a large mixing bowl, beat butter with an electric mixer on medium speed for 30 seconds. Add granulated and brown sugars; beat until fluffy. Beat in eggs. Beat in apple butter and vanilla.

Stir vinegar into evaporated milk (mixture will curdle). Add flour mixture and milk mixture alternately to apple butter mixture, beating on low speed after each addition just until combined. Stir in chopped walnuts.

Spoon batter evenly into prepared muffin cups, filling each about ¾ full. Bake in a 350 degree F oven for 18-20 minutes or until a wooden toothpick inserted near the centers comes out clean. Cool in muffin cups on wire racks for 5 minutes. Remove from pans. Cool slightly. Serve warm or cool.

To serve, place each cake on a dessert plate. Spoon about 1 ½ tablespoons of the warm Caramel Sauce over each cake. If you like, garnish with walnut pieces. Makes 24 servings.

This recipe was adopted from https://MidwestLiving.com

Caramel Sauce for Apple Butter Cakelets

3/4 cup granulated sugar

¼ cup packed brown sugar

¼ cup hot water

1 cup whipping cream

2 tablespoons honey or light-colored syrup

¼ cup butter

1 teaspoon vanilla

Place granulated and brown sugars in a 2-quart saucepan, spreading sugar evenly. Heat over medium-high heat (do not stir). Heat until some of the sugar is melted (it should look syrupy). Reduce heat to medium-low. Begin to stir only the melted sugar to keep it from overbrowning, and then gradually stir it in remaining sugar as it melts. Continue to cook until all the sugar is melted (should take about 8 minutes total).

Remove from heat. Carefully stir in hot water (mixture will spatter and sugar will become hard). Heat and stir over medium heat until the sugar melts and no hard lumps remain (should take about 3 minutes). Use a whisk to gradually whisk in whipping cream. Stir in honey. Bring to a boiling over medium heat. Reduce heat to medium-low and boil gently, uncovered for 8 minutes. Remove from heat. Whisk in butter and vanilla. Cool about 1 hour (sauce will thicken as it cools). Serve warm over apple butter cakelets.

Cover and chill any leftovers for up to 3 days. To reheat sauce in your microwave oven, allow 15 to 30 seconds on high power. Makes about 1 ½ cups.

This recipe was adopted from https://MidwestLiving.com

Amish Meadow Tea

2 quarts water (8 cups)

1 cup fresh mint leaves, packed

½ cup sugar

1 tablespoon lemon juice

Lemon slices for garnish

Pick mint from your garden early in the morning if possible. You can cut sections off stalks with pruning shears or just pick off individual leaves. Wash and rinse off your fresh mint carefully to remove any dirt or pests.

Fill a large pot with 2 quarts of water and bring it to a boil over high heat. Add mint leaves. Place a tight-fitting lid over top and remove pot from heat.

Let the water and mint leaves steep for around 2 ½ hours or more, until the water turns a mint green color. After it's done, strain and discard the mint as you transfer the tea into a container of your choice.

Add in the sugar and lemon juice, stirring until it's completely dissolved. Refrigerate until chilled. Serve over ice with lemon slices and extra mint for garnish, as desired.

This recipe was adapted from https://www.MarketsatShrewsbury.com.

Amish Butterscotch Cinnamon Rolls

I package dry yeast

1 ½ cups warm water

½ cup sugar

1 ½ teaspoons salt

cup shortening

2 eggs

1 cup lukewarm mashed potatoes

7 to 7 ½ cups bread flour

Filling Ingredients:

¾ cup brown sugar

1/3 cup butter or margarine

Cinnamon

Milk

Powdered sugar

Dissolve yeast in water. Stir in sugar, salt, shortening, eggs and potatoes. Add 3 cups flour and beat 2 minutes. Add remaining flour and knead until dough is smooth and elastic. Place in greased bowl and cover for about an hour, until dough doubles.

For the frosting, cream together brown sugar, milk and butter, add a small amount of water to the mixture so it spreads on dough easily before rolling up. Reserve remaining frosting mixture.

Divide dough in half. Roll each into a 9"x15" rectangle. Spread with remaining frosting mixture and sprinkle with cinnamon. Roll tightly starting at wide end. Pinch edges to seal. Cut into 1½ slices. Place on greased 9" x 13" pan.

Allow rolls to double for 2 to 2½ hours. Bake 20-25 minutes at 350 degrees F.

This recipe was adapted from https://www.Amish365.com.

Dark Chocolate Pie

P ie dough for a 9-inch pie, either homemade or store-bought

⅔ cup granulated sugar

⅓ cup cornstarch

½ teaspoon salt

4 egg yolks

3 cups whole milk

2 tablespoons butter, softened

2 teaspoons vanilla extract

2 cups dark chocolate chips, divided

Whipped cream for serving

If using homemade pie dough, roll out into a circle and fit into a 9-inch pie pan. If using refrigerated pie dough, unroll and fit into a 9-inch pie pan. Cover with plastic wrap and refrigerate for 30 minutes.

Preheat oven to 400 degrees. Tuck under any excess dough that hangs over the edge or cut it off. Crimp the sides of the dough to form a scalloped edge. Pierce the bottom and sides with a fork. Cover the pie crust with a double layer of aluminum foil and fill with pie weights or dried beans.

Place in oven for 10 to 12 minutes. Remove the beans and foil and return to the oven for another 10 to 12 minutes or until golden brown. Let cool.

In a medium saucepan, stir together the sugar, cornstarch and salt. Whisk together the egg yolks and milk. Gradually pour the milk mixture into the sugar mixture, whisking while you do so.

Place over medium heat. Whisk continuously until mixture comes to a boil. Boil and stir for 1 minute.

Remove from heat and stir in the butter and vanilla. Add 1 3/4 cups of chocolate chips and stir until completely melted. Pour mixture into the pie crust. Cover with plastic wrap, pressing onto the surface of the pie.

Let cool on counter for 30 minutes. Refrigerate until firm and chilled. To serve, cut into slices and top with whipped cream and remaining chocolate chips.

This recipe was adapted from https://SpicySouthernKitchen.com

Strawberry Cream Cheese Danish

I box puff pastry sheets, thawed

1 egg

1 tablespoon water

2 cups fresh strawberries, each cut into 8 pieces

⅓ cup sugar

3 tablespoons water

2 tablespoons cornstarch

8 ounces cream cheese, room temperature

⅓ cup sugar

1 teaspoon lemon juice

1 teaspoon vanilla

1 cup powdered sugar

3-4 tablespoons heavy cream

½ teaspoon vanilla

Preheat oven to 375°. Spray a baking sheet(s) with nonstick spray or line baking sheets with parchment paper. Set aside.

In a small bowl, mix cornstarch and water together.

In a medium saucepan, add strawberries and sugar. Heat over low heat until sugar has melted, and then add cornstarch mixture. Stir until strawberry sauce has thickened. Remove from heat and let cool.

In a medium bowl, beat cream cheese until smooth, about 2 minutes. Add sugar, lemon juice and vanilla, beating for another minute or two.

Gently roll puff pastry a few times until square on a lightly floured surface. Spoon half of the cream cheese mixture down the center of each puff pastry, leaving about 1-½ inches free from filling at each end.

Once strawberry mixture has cooled, add about three heaping tablespoons of mixture on top of the cream cheese filling, gently spreading. Repeat with the other puff pastry.

Cut two slits at each end of the pastry about 1-inch long. Fold over pastry on top of the filling and secure to prevent mixture from leaking out.

Cut off the top and bottom side pieces at an angle and continue to make cuts into the pastry along each side, making sure not to cut too close to the filling. Once the ends have been secured, start folding each piece over each other like a braid and secure.

Brush egg wash over both pastries and bake for 25-30 minutes or until golden brown.

In a small bowl, mix powdered sugar, 3-4 tablespoon of heavy cream and vanilla together until smooth. Add more heavy cream, if needed, for desired consistency.

Cut pastry braid into 1 or 2 inch slices and enjoy.

This recipe was adapted from https://www.GreatGrubDeliciousTreats.com